The Geometry

of Sisters

Also by Luanne Rice
Available from Random House Large Print

The Deep Blue Sea for Beginners
The Edge of Winter
Last Kiss
Light of the Moon
Sandcastles
Summer of Roses
Summer's Child
What Matters Most

The Geometry of Sisters

LUANNE RICE

RANDOM HOUSE
LARGE PRINT

Copyright © 2009 by Luanne Rice
Title page photograph by Robert Aichinger

All Rights Reserved

Published in the United States of America by Random House Large Print in association with Bantam Dell, New York.
Distributed by Random House, Inc., New York.

Cover design by Shasti O'Leary Soudant
Cover photograph by Jethro Soudant

The Library of Congress has established a Cataloging-in-Publication record for this title.

ISBN: 978-0-7393-2828-6

www.randomhouse.com/largeprint

FIRST LARGE PRINT EDITION

10 9 8 7 6 5 4 3 2 1

This Large Print edition published in accord with the standards of the N.A.V.H.

For Susan Robertson

The Geometry of Sisters

Beck & Carrie

PART ONE

1 ON LABOR DAY MY MOTHER and brother piled the station wagon with all our things. Well, except for the ones that had already gone ahead, our furniture and books, on the Whiteflower Van Lines moving truck. So our car is packed with suitcases, duffel bags, Dad's hats, our computer, and our two cats. We stood on Lincoln Street in front of our house—I refuse to say "our **old** house," even though it's been sold and new people are about to move in—and Mom told us to say goodbye.

I felt like an invisible girl observing the scene: Mom, shorter than I am, thin, shoulder-length brownish hair, wearing jeans and one of Dad's old shirts; Travis, a beanpole with shoulders from all that football, dark brown hair in his blue eyes, Dad's blue eyes—the men in our family have dark blue eyes, Carrie's are light blue, and Mom and I have hazel.

Both Mom and Travis were looking at our house, white with green shutters—I painted those shutters with Carrie and Travis just last summer—and the

two maple trees and the dogwoods and big mag-
nolia in the front yard, shady and nice. Carrie
taught me how to climb those trees.

Mom looked up at Carrie's room. Travis stood
there with his hands in his pockets, gaze as blank as
the windows he was staring at. Actually, that's a lie.
He had frown lines between his eyebrows. How
could he not, about to leave the only house our
family had ever known? Me, I refused to say goodbye. If you don't shut the door on something, it
means you can always walk back through, right?

Mom taped a note on the door. Can you believe
that? As if Carrie is just going to walk up the sidewalk and read that we've gone to Newport. Just as
if we've gone to the store, or to the ball field, and
will meet her back here for dinner. It's sad, if you
think about it. Not just that Carrie won't be home
to read any note, but that Mom would even think
of leaving one for her.

Anyway, we turned and got in the car. Travis sits
up front with Mom. I ride in back with the cats.
Neither Travis nor I mention the note, but we do
give each other a look. **Strange,** his eyebrows say to
me. **Whacked,** my grimace says to him.

So that's how we left Columbus: one of us snuf-
fling, one of us frowning, one of us petting cats. At
fourteen, almost fifteen, I'm too young to drive.
But Travis is sixteen, so he helps Mom out, taking
the wheel for hours at a stretch. They keep asking

me if I want to pick the radio station, or if I'm hungry and want to stop, or if I need to use the restroom. But nothing can pry words out of me. I just ride in back, hunched up into a ball, reaching into the cat carriers to pet Desdemona and Grisby. Des is mine. Grisby was my sister's. I'm taking care of her now.

I have what's called "stubborn anger." That's what the shrink said. Because everything is wrong. What happened last summer made me lose my mind. That's different from stubborn anger. That's not being able to stand the feeling of air on your skin because your sister is gone. For months afterward, I couldn't draw a breath without feeling someone had stuck a knife into my heart. My mother thinks it's just normal grief, but it's not. My grades, well, let's just say they have suffered. English, C; Earth Science, B−; Art, D; Geometry, A. I'm okay in math, so even though I haven't applied myself, I get by. I skipped regular math last year, went straight into high school geometry.

The strange thing is, I've been dreaming in math. Figures, equations, notations—as if there was a problem to solve, and it involved numbers instead of words. Words get in the way. Numbers don't lie. We are two sisters; add us up. Carrie + Beck = Us.

My friends have gathered round me . . . kind of, anyway. The ones who haven't deserted me, that is. The ones who still speak to me have held me up,

carried me through. I couldn't have survived without them. I'm holding on to the fact that a few
people still like me.

And now my mother's taking me away from
them. Away from Carrie. Without Carrie, I'm less
than a person. It's like subtracting one from one.
That equals zero. Except, as all mathematicians
know, there's really no such number as zero. So I
live my life in confusion. Logic and emotion are
at war.

That's where the stubborn anger comes in. I refuse to accept my mother's decision to move us
away from Columbus. She says she needs a job to
support us, and I say fine—does it have to be in
Rhode Island? Doesn't she know without my sister
I'll cease to exist? Just try **x** minus **x.** Where does
that leave you?

Exactly.

My mother explains that we don't know that
Carrie is in Columbus anymore, in fact we are
pretty sure she's far, far away. She doesn't have to
tell me that we all have our own special ways of losing our minds, and Carrie's seems to have involved
running away from home and, after a lifetime of
being the perfect older child, turning into a street
person somewhere. Have I mentioned that this is
not a recent development?

My older sister left home, or should I say the
cabin, the very same day our father died. That was

over a year ago. She had a major flip-out, I guess you could say. And that flip-out is the gift that just keeps giving. We get the occasional hang-up and the once-in-a-blue-moon postcard. Even though we haven't received any emails from her, my mother has set our family email to a permanent away message: **Carrie! We love you! We are moving to Newport and want you to be with us! Here is our address and phone number. Call, sweetheart!**

I mean, Jesus Christ!

Here's what I plan to do: ride all the way from Ohio to Rhode Island without saying one word. I'm not going to eat, either. Hunger strike. Eventually we'll get to Newport. Mom will point out the apartment she and her sister lived in when they were young, before whatever happened that drove them apart.

She'll mention that it's a fresh start, that we have our whole lives to look forward to. One thing she will not mention is the water, which will be **everywhere.** Then she'll pull up to the private school where starting next week she will be teaching English and Travis and I will (theoretically) enroll as students. Here be rich snobs!

That enrollment will not happen, trust me. Can you imagine attending a school full of millionaire brats where your mother teaches? Why don't I just put my eyes out instead? It would be more fun.

I will helpfully empty the station wagon. I will carry the cats into the house Newport Academy has given my mother as part of her teaching contract. My sister's photographs, the ones she took and called her "Great Girls" series, will go straight into my mother's room. I will feed the cats, show them their litter box, remind my mother and Travis that they are **not** to go outside—Carrie always wanted Grisby to be an indoor cat, and that is how it will be.

Then, the minute my mother and brother are asleep, I will walk out the door. I've got funds stashed for the trip home. Birthday cash, baby-sitting money, contributions from my best friends Amy and Ellie. Plus a little extra from what the school shrink says is another cry for help—let's not go into it, but I stole a couple of things, including money from my mother's wallet, and got caught. I gave most of it back. But I kept a little, to help me get home.

"So, my little storm cloud," my mother says from the front seat. "Are you comfortable back there?"

I grunt instead of speaking.

"You're not hungry, you don't care what music we listen to, you haven't said one word."

"She'll eat if we stop at Cracker Barrel," Travis says. "She likes the buffet."

"What do you say, Beck? Should I get off the highway?"

I just keep petting Grisby. What is wrong with Travis? Seething doesn't begin to cover what I'm feeling. **Carrie** loved Cracker Barrel, not me. Caroline Anne Shaw. Get it straight!

I'm Rebecca Grace Shaw. I may have been joined at the heart with my sister, but my taste in roadside food is different. I like the Pancake King. The highway flies by in a blur. Cars, trucks, exits, all taking us closer to Rhode Island. I want to jump out before we cross one more state line.

"Let's stop, Mom," Travis says. "We'll eat and then I'll drive for a while."

Easy for him to be sweet, I think. Ally is so in love with my brother she'll fly east constantly just to see him. Her father's a doctor and has the money. He's divorced from her mother and bribes Ally to love him best. Ally wants for nothing, not even Travis. So he's got nothing to lose from this whole move, not like I do.

My mother puts on the signal light. Slouched in the back seat, I hear it, **click-click-click.** Trees along the exit ramp. We merge onto some big ugly road parallel to the highway; it's filled with billboards and stores and restaurants, one after the other, so many to choose from. I shut my eyes tight, because I don't want to think of food and feel hungrier than I already am.

My stomach rumbles. I'm starving.

"Okay, storm cloud," my mother says. "Come

on, now. Let's go in and have something good for dinner. . . ."

I pull the cats closer. I refuse to eat. All I want is to go home. I want my sister, and I want to go home. One hand slides into the thick envelope where her pictures are, and I slip a few out so I can see. This one shows a six-year-old girl jumping rope. Here's one of a woman pinning clothes to a clothesline. And another, two girls talking at their lockers in school.

I don't want to go to a school where my mother teaches. This is her first job since getting her master's. She is nervous and trying not to show it, which gives me a stomachache. If she's worried, how am I supposed to feel? I can't even think about the water. They call Newport "the City by the Sea."

My brother stands outside the car making impatient noises while my mother opens the back door, leans in to put her arms around me, her lips to my ear, and whispers, "Put those away for now, sweetheart."

"I don't want to."

So she does it for me—takes the pictures out of my hand, slides them back into the envelope. Does she do that because she thinks looking at them makes me sad? Or is she afraid I'll damage Carrie's pictures in some way?

"Things will be better when we get to Newport," she says.

"Stop," I say, the ghost of my old lisp coming back, and I hear "shtop."

I hate Newport and we're not even there yet, and besides, I don't believe her. All that water. I want to stay here, make things right. Make everyone like me again. Most of the time I say my **s**'s and **l**'s perfectly. No one makes fun of me for that anymore—I got through it.

Carrie helped me get over my lisp. She coached me through my speech exercises. With my sister, I overcame the obstacle. She can't help me with this, though. C + B = Us. I hold on to that truth. Mathematics and logic don't lie. So I sit in the back seat in perfect silence, just glaring into my mother's eyes. She doesn't know what I know about Carrie's last day. See, when she's ready, Carrie is coming back.

Storm clouds don't speak. And there's no such number as zero.

2 NEWPORT GREETED THEM with bright blue water sparkling everywhere, a fresh September breeze blowing off Narragansett Bay, thick roses tumbling over high stone walls. Maura Shaw's hands were clamped tightly to the steering wheel as she drove along Farewell Street, between the two graveyards at the foot of the bridge. She drew the first deep breath she'd taken since leaving their house in Columbus early yesterday. She'd finally gotten them here.

The trip from Ohio had taken longer than she'd expected. Maura couldn't help it: every car on the highway, every exit off the interstate, all potentially could be where she'd find Carrie. She'd driven carefully, eyes on the road. But one part of her attention, a big part, was spent darting over to the passing Dodge Ram, the young hitchhikers, the broken-down Chevy, the ambulance speeding in the opposite direction.

Carrie's postcards had been from places out West. Santa Fe, New Mexico, had been the first;

Billings, Montana, was the last. But who was to say she might not have changed her mind? A girl who could run away the very same day her father died, having never purposely done one thing to make her parents fret or worry, who had never been anything less than sweet, reliable, and incredibly smart, might in fact be capable of changing direction and heading east instead.

So Maura and the two younger kids had spent one night in a Days Inn near Allentown, Pennsylvania. This was out of the way; obsessing about Carrie, she'd taken a wrong turn, and the kids hadn't realized. Travis had been navigating, doing a great job, but after a while, assuming they were basically on autopilot, he'd turned to text-messaging Ally on his cell phone.

Suddenly Maura had started seeing signs for Gettysburg—they were heading south instead of east. She almost panicked. She couldn't let the kids know they were off course. Not because of pride or a need for infallibility, but because she wanted to give them a sense of safety, reassure them that she had it together, was on top of her game. Especially Beck, who had become a teenage nihilist, who doubted all that was good, who had seemed to retreat into a world of cats and numbers, and expected only disaster of real life.

Maura had quietly adjusted course, off one exit and back on the other way, not telling the kids they had traveled fifty miles out of the way without her realizing, and trying to keep herself from pondering the symbolism of driving straight toward one of the bloodiest battlefields in America while thinking of where her oldest daughter might be.

And here they were: The southern end of Aquidneck Island, Newport jutted into the Atlantic Ocean, and the sea was everywhere: down every alley, across every lawn, surrounding the city. She had come home to her New England roots, and in spite of everything, she felt a sudden surge of joy. She pressed the buttons to open all the car windows, ignoring the kids' protests as their hair blew wildly.

"Smell the salt air," she said.

"It's bothering the cats!" Beck said.

"She speaks," Travis said.

"I don't believe the cats mind the air," Maura said. "I think they love it. They know we're almost home."

"Home is Columbus," Beck said.

"Honey, this is where we live now," Maura said.

"Mom, don't even bother," Travis said. "She's going to give you a hard time no matter what you say."

"You don't know anything," Beck said. "Why don't you text Ally and say you're a bonehead?"

"You're not even making sense," he said.

"Right," Beck said. "She already knows it, so why would you have to tell her?"

"Hey," Maura said. "Stop it."

And they did. They liked each other, in spite of how they were acting right now. For so many years, this had always been one of the great blessings for Maura and Andy: the way their kids had been real friends, not just siblings.

Maura concentrated on driving. The streets were crowded with late summer traffic. She knew Newport like the back of her hand. She and her sister had lived here many years ago, while they were in college, back when they'd still been close.

In recent years, after finishing her master's degree, she'd started receiving emails from educational placement services, private schools, and tutoring services looking for teachers. She'd filed them all away. Andy and she had decided she would wait to start teaching until Beck started high school.

But then everything changed. Andy died, and Maura felt as if she'd been hit by a truck. Everything was broken. Her family was wrecked, in grief, in tatters. Insurance covered some things, but she got slammed by the second mortgage, car payments, shrink bills for Beck, detective bills to look for Carrie, and just when she wanted to crawl under the covers and never come out, her family needed her to provide for them.

Several months after Andy's death last August, just over a year ago, she got a mailing from Newport Academy and jumped on it. Ted Shannon, the headmaster, flew to Ohio for an alumni event, and Maura interviewed and got the job. It had seemed like fate.

Newport: so much had happened here to set the course of her family's history. Maybe by coming back, Maura could find peace. But there were more pressing reasons to leave Columbus. They needed the money, and Newport Academy paid well. Besides, Maura knew she had to get Beck out of there, away from all the talk.

Maura wanted to take her younger daughter away from the reputation she'd gotten in school. Maura knew she would outgrow it, that people would forget, just as no one remembered now that she'd once needed speech therapy, and the kids teasing her about the way she'd talked had long ceased.

But stealing was more serious, and Beck was deeply ashamed and confused, even as she was trying to change her behavior. Her grades had slipped badly except in math—high school level and even beyond, according to her teacher, an accomplishment that both shocked Maura (neither she nor Andy had been particularly good at or interested in mathematics) and made her very proud. So Maura had grabbed the chance to come to Newport, a place she knew her kids would love once they settled in. A bonus: the school offered housing as part of the package.

Salary, insurance, reduced tuition for the kids, and a place to live: all the bases covered, and that was necessary. Without Andy, they were having a hard time. Grief still was fresh, a constant, aching emptiness. Maura had stayed home with the kids; it had always been the plan for her to start teaching once Beck finished middle school. Ironically, they were right on schedule.

Beck would be starting Newport Academy as a freshman, Travis as a junior. And Carrie was who knew where. Maura knew there wasn't a chance in the world that her daughter would find that note she'd left on the door, but she'd left it anyway. Leaving Columbus without Carrie had been something like driving away without her right arm. Only it hurt a lot more.

"Okay, you two," she said, as they drove up Memorial Boulevard, crested Bellevue Avenue, and started down the hill toward Easton's Beach. "Watch for Cliff Avenue on the right."

"There, Mom," Travis said, pointing.

Maura took a right, drove a short way, and then spotted the tall iron gates. A discreet sign, **Newport Academy,** was set into the stone post. Her stomach flipped as she realized that this was it— the start of a new life. She drove through, onto a private drive lined with venerable old trees, branches interlocking overhead.

Breaking into a clearing, they saw the main school building—a limestone mansion with turrets, balconies, pointed-arch windows, and gargoyles—built on the tall cliff's edge, overlooking the crashing Atlantic. Spectacular, and she tried not to think of the pictures Carrie would have taken of this place.

"That's the school?" Beck asked.

"It is," Maura said.

"It looks like a prison!"

"It does not," Travis said. "It looks like a castle."

"I hate it," Beck said.

Maura didn't speak. She just followed the road behind the main school building—the grand mansion—past other smaller but no less elegant houses, around an ancient, sprawling copper beech tree, into a darkly wooded laurel grove. Several small outbuildings were set here, including the small brick carriage house where they would live.

"This is **it?**" Beck asked, sounding incredulous.

"Yes," Maura said. "Home sweet home."

"It's tiny and dark!" Beck said. "It's horrible!"

"It's not tiny," Maura said. "It has three bedrooms, one for each of us."

"We had four bedrooms in our other house!" Beck said. "Three's not enough. You know that. . . ."

"Beck, honey," she began, her throat shutting tight.

"Beck," Travis said, "there aren't five of us anymore. Only three. Come on, you can add."

"You mean subtract!"

"Don't make it worse."

"Shut up, shut up," Beck said. "Why did we have to leave? What if Carrie tries to find us? How will she, Mom? Have you **really** thought about that, aside from leaving that lame note?"

"Beck, Jesus, stop," Travis said.

"Um, yeah, Beck," Maura said. "I've thought about it just a little."

"Don't be sarcastic to me!"

"Well, don't treat me like an idiot. If you don't think I think about Carrie, oh, let's see . . . twenty-four hours a day . . ." Maura took a deep breath. **Be calm, don't lose it, be the mother.** "Beck, I have tried everything and will keep trying every single way to find Carrie. I have a detective on retainer. Police forces from here to California have her description. I left word with Justin and all her friends, and I've left a forwarding message on voicemail—"

"Voicemail!" Beck shrieked. "Carrie's gonna find us through voicemail?"

Maura threw up her hands—literally. This was like traveling with a three-year-old. Beck was overtired, overstimulated, and exhausted from the ride and her own bad temper.

"Why didn't you just leave a trail of **bread crumbs?**" Beck sobbed.

Travis, good boy that he was, climbed out of the car and started unloading it. Maura saw him carry the heaviest suitcases to the front door, then stand there waiting for her to unlock it. Beck clutched Carrie's portfolio.

"I want Dad," Beck said. "I want Carrie."

"I want them too," Maura said, turning to reach into the back seat for her hand. Beck wouldn't take it, so Maura faced front again.

"I don't want to be here," Beck said.

"I know, Beck," Maura said, staring at the house.

Beck was right—it was doll-size. Set far from the cliff, deep in the shade of oaks and maples, tall mountain laurel and rhododendron bushes, it nestled in darkness. She thought of the big, airy house they'd just left. This carriage house came furnished, so the movers would be dropping most of their big furniture at a storage facility outside town—maybe that would make it easier, not having to look at all their things.

She hadn't been able to store Carrie's pictures. She'd kept them here in the car, wrapped in a quilt. Pictures of other girls, strangers as well as Carrie's friends. Her daughter had aimed the camera, snapped the photos, and they had traveled here in the way-back of the car, and now Beck was holding them as if they were Carrie herself.

Maura breathed salt air. Soon school would begin, a fresh start. She glanced at Beck in the rearview mirror, saw her sitting there in a knot, arms tight across her chest and the portfolio.

"Ready?" she asked.

"Ready, Mom," Travis said, back at the car, holding out his hand. Maura handed him the key so he could unlock the front door.

"Come on," Maura said. "Let's get the cats inside. They need water."

"They need to go back to Ohio," Beck said.

Maura grabbed the two cat carriers, and Beck loaded her arms with Carrie's photos, and they followed Travis into their new home.

■

Travis sat with Beck on the cottage steps, wanting to make sure she wasn't going to bolt like Carrie. While his mother waited for the movers and Beck went into the world of tangents, pentangles, quadrangles, triangles, and whatever, plotting her escape—as if he and their mom didn't know her plan—he was checking things out.

Then, continually circling back to see what was happening in the house, to make sure Beck hadn't darted through the bushes for her big return to Ohio, he prowled the walkways of Newport Academy in search of, among other things, a spot where he could get decent cell reception.

He looked for the athletic fields. Down a path and across a gravel road, he found them. The gym looked pretty new. The football field seemed okay. He had tryouts scheduled, but that was a formality. The coach had talked to him on the phone, seemed excited he'd be playing for them.

When he got close to the main school building, he realized he had four bars on his phone. He saw he had five missed calls from Ally, started to call her back, suddenly noticed something odd about the mansion. Approaching the building from the woods, he saw a big portico extending over a circular driveway. There were large doors on either side, words heavily etched into the limestone above: **Girls' Entrance** over one door, **Boys' Entrance** over the other.

Staring up at the words, wondering how lame it was going to be to go to a school with rules like that, separate entrances for boys and girls, he didn't hear the golf cart. A security guard zoomed over, bouncing across the gravel drive. Old, fat, with dark aviator-style glasses and a shaggy mustache snowy with doughnut sugar that also sprinkled down his bulging belly, he slammed on his brakes in front of Travis, blocking his way.

"What are you doing here?" the security guard said.

"Uh, looking around."

"And you are . . . ?"

"Travis Shaw," he said. "My mother's the new English teacher."

"Got some ID to prove that?"

"Relax, Angus!" a voice called from around the building. "He's with us!"

Digging his wallet out of his jeans pocket, Travis handed the guard his license and leaned back to peer around the portico's pillar. There, sunning themselves on the lawn by the cliff, were three girls, all wearing bathing suits. They looked about his age, or maybe Carrie's—a year older.

"Logan, the headmaster catches you out there like that, you'll be in trouble again," the guard yelled.

"I know, Angus, but he's still in Europe and won't be back till school starts Monday, and you're not going to tell him, right?"

Angus tensed his shoulders, handing Travis back his license with a glare. "Don't expect to get away with anything once classes start," he said. "They don't pay me to look the other way. You go over there and tell your friends what I said."

Travis nodded, putting his license away, jamming his wallet into his pocket as he headed across the perfectly manicured grass. The three girls looked up at him, smiling. Their hair was long and straight, their gazes curious, and because he was loyal to Ally he tried not to notice anything else.

"I'm supposed to tell you they don't pay him to look the other way," Travis said.

"Oh, Angus," one of the girls said, laughing. She was small, blonde, very tan, with short cut-offs over a faded green bathing suit. "He's the biggest joke. Truly, he's a softy. He never busts anyone for anything."

"Do you go here?" Travis asked.

"Uh, yeah," the taller of the two brunettes said. She had huge cat eyes—widely spaced, gold-green, and looked very familiar. "Why else would we be sitting on school property on a perfect beach day?"

"Well, why are you?" he asked. "Considering school doesn't start until next week."

"We board here," the smaller brunette said. "Day students don't arrive till the minute classes start, but boarders can move in up to a week earlier. We have delicate spirits and need time to adjust to being away from home." She gave him a big grin that made her bright blue eyes sparkle even more, and managed to make him think she was both funny and wicked.

"Where's home?" he asked.

"Well, my grandmother's house is in town here, but really, I come from Grosse Point, Michigan," she said.

"The Midwest!" he said.

"Are you a boarder too?" she asked. "A fellow Midwesterner?"

"Sort of," he said, watching the Whiteflower Van Lines truck pull into the driveway, heading toward the carriage house. "That is, I'm from Ohio. But now I live here."

"Was that your sister I saw you with before?" the Michigan girl asked.

"You board, you mean," the blonde girl said at the same time.

"No. Well, not exactly. I live over there," he said, pointing into the laurel grove. "As of today. That's our moving truck. And yes, that's my sister." One of them, he thought.

"You're the new English teacher's son!"

"Yeah," he said. "Travis Shaw."

Introductions were made: the tall brunette was Logan Moore, the smaller one was Pell Davis, and the blonde girl was Cordelia St. Onge. Logan was from Los Angeles, Pell from Grosse Pointe but had grown up summering with her grandmother in Newport, and Cordelia came from Boston. Travis tried not to stare at Logan, wondering where he knew her from.

"Want to sit with us?" Pell asked.

"I should go help unload the truck," Travis said. He was glad for its arrival, because he found Pell's invitation, and the smile in her blue eyes, ridiculously unsettling.

"We could help you unpack," Cordelia said.

"Speak for yourself," Logan said, stretching out, face to the sun. "I don't unpack moving vans."

"Spoiled Hollywood child," Cordelia said, and

Logan smirked without opening her eyes, and that's when Travis figured it out. She looked just like Ridley Moore, the actress.

"Is your mother—" he began.

"Yes," Pell said, answering for Logan. "That's her."

"Cool," Travis said, hearing the truck's metal door clang open, starting to inch away from the girls.

"Hey, I'll walk you home," Pell said.

"You don't have to," Travis said. But she ignored him.

"Word to the wise," Pell said, when they were out of hearing of the others, "and I say this with love. Don't be impressed by people's parents. This school will eat you alive if you don't know that."

"Thanks, I guess," he said. "Just because I asked if that was her mother didn't mean I was impressed."

"Well, whatever you say," she said, humor in her eyes. He saw her looking at him that way, and felt his face and neck get scalding hot. His cell phone rang. Looking at the screen, he saw Ally's number.

"Who's that?" Pell asked.

"Hey, Al," Travis said, answering the phone, ignoring Pell's question.

"Hey, you," Ally said. "How is it going there? Why haven't you called me yet today?"

"Really crappy cell reception," Travis said. His

eyes locked with Pell's. "I miss you," he said into the phone, turning away.

Ally told him about what he was missing, how they'd gone to the lake for a midnight swim, how she'd lain on the raft staring up at the stars thinking of him, how football practice was under way and how badly the team was going to do without him. His stomach clenched at that—even more than hearing about the raft and the stars—and missing the team as much as he missed her made him feel guilty.

"When can I visit?" Ally asked.

"As soon as you can get here," Travis said.

When he turned to glance at Pell, she was halfway across the grounds on her way back to Logan and Cordelia. Just as well. She'd figured out he had a girlfriend. That's what he wanted. Put it right out there.

"Trav!" his mother called, waving him over.

He gestured that he'd be right there, spotted Beck still sitting on the front step, elbows on her knees, fists bunched up under her chin, staring down at her math notations. His younger sister looked like the scruffy tomboy she was: freckles, reddish brown hair in braids, an Ohio State T-shirt over baggy shorts. He knew she'd never be impressed by anyone's parents, but he stared at her, thinking that if those three girls were any indication, the school would eat her alive anyway.

For Carrie, it would have been easy. After his father's memorial service, one of her teachers told their mother Carrie had grace. That was true. She could fit in anywhere. Everyone who met her wanted her for a friend. She'd have outclassed all three of those girls, no contest. They'd have been lucky to know her. Travis knew his mother had heard from her over the last year, but nothing the last month or so. He couldn't stand to think it, but he wondered if she was still alive. He could not believe she'd be out of touch with him, with them, for so long if she was.

"Travis?" Ally said. "You still there?"

"Yeah, Al," he said. "I am, but the truck's here. I have to help unload."

"Call me as soon as you can."

"I will," he said, and hung up.

Then he ran toward the carriage house, dropping one shoulder as if blocking a play, dodging, faking left, right, running for a touchdown.

"Dork," Beck said. "This isn't a football game."

"Oh, really?" he asked, tugging one of her braids and flicking her paper. "It's not a math problem either." She protested, pulling her paper back as he turned to grab a carton of books from one of the movers. He happened to look up, across the clearing, and saw Pell watching. Even from here, he caught her grin.

He wheeled away, carrying the box into the small, dark house.

■

J. D. Blackstone knew Maura was back. His friends and her sister had told him, and it made everything about Newport different. Even the air currents and tides seemed to have shifted; he felt restless, and had started swimming more. His dreams were of her, but that wasn't new; they'd always been. The dreams were immediate, here and now, not buried in the past. He could almost believe she'd walk through the door, and they'd be the same as they were. It was happening again.

Days became weeks, weeks months, two years short of two decades. There had been another woman; he might even say there'd been love. The way some would define it, that was true. He'd "found someone." He'd been faithful, stayed with Linda five years; she had wanted him to move into her big house near the bridge in Jamestown. She'd thought he would marry her. He'd tried to want that too. But in the end, he backed away. He'd already given himself to one person.

Maura had been gone a long time. She'd left him to go back to Andy, calling what she had with J.D. a "young mistake," or something like that. The exact words didn't matter, because he knew she'd been lying. What happened that summer made them belong to each other forever.

He held on to certain thoughts. Once they were making love on his bed behind the boxes. The windows were shut so no one would hear. The air in the brick building was stifling, the hottest all summer. Her back stuck to the sheets with sweat. It was after the catwalk, it might have been their fourth or fifth time together.

He'd already needed her. The friction of their bodies melted them into each other. They were starting to figure each other out, and this was going to be their life. Their eyes locked. This is it, he told her. I know, she said. Yet no words came out.

This is it: that was the truth then and still was now.

J.D. couldn't help that. Maura wrote her name on his heart that summer. It was there forever, like it or not. And now she was back in Newport.

3 THE WEEK PASSED QUICKLY AS they unpacked and settled in, trying to get used to everything being new. Maura checked voicemail back home constantly. Nothing. Travis met with the coach, started workouts with the team. Beck refused to leave the house, spending all her time on her bed with Grisby, Desdemona, and her faithful notebook full of proofs and numbers, patterns of shapes. Maura tried to bribe her, offering a picnic out on the lawn, with that sweeping view of the Atlantic.

"No way," Beck said.

"Honey, it's one of the benefits of living here. Do you know how much people would pay to have a house overlooking the water?"

"I'd pay **not** to," Beck said, huddled over her notebook.

As much as she craved the view, Maura served dinner in the small, dark kitchen. She had tried to cheer it up—new curtains, Carrie's pictures on the wall. But the tiny space made her think of who was gone, realize the five of them never could have fit in here. She, Travis, and Beck sat at the small enameled table. They stared at their food, trying to get used to a new house without Andy. They'd left a place for Carrie, wondered if she'd ever fill it.

Each night Maura took a cup of tea out to the cliff. She thought of Katharine. She wanted to call her; it felt strange to be in Newport and not see her. But she was afraid of how her sister would react.

She'd walk past Blackstone Hall, the school's main building, and sit on the grass, listening to the surf roar below. The sound was loud and constant. The harder the waves broke, the better; they'd shatter against the cliff, and the spray would fly up, and she'd know the waves had been doing the same thing forever. The ocean touched every continent, every bit of land; it seemed to pull everyone together.

Maura thought of the word **estranged.** Is that what she and Carrie were? And if so, had Carrie learned the possibility of estrangement, of family members not talking to each other, from Maura and Katharine? Did broken families follow through the generations?

The night before school started, she watched twilight fade and the stars come out. The sight made her eyes sting. Carrie had always loved the night sky; she'd known every constellation. On her

eleventh birthday Andy had surprised her by painting her bedroom ceiling with the stars visible the
night she was born. He'd researched the almanac,
found glow-in-the-dark paint, done the work while
Carrie was at school.

Carrie had been bowled over. She'd gotten out
H. A. Rey's **The Stars,** compared the constellations
in her favorite book with those her father had
painted over her bed. They'd both been delighted,
but then, they so often were.

Maura stared out at the lavender horizon, at a
light blinking in the distance. The beam flashed
once, twice, then a long beat, and then it flashed
again. She pictured the lighthouse on Lake Michigan. Almost an apparition, a ghost lighthouse, it
had appeared out of nowhere three summers ago.

Nights around the campfire, the family had listened to the loons and watched the beam flash
across the water. Travis said no matter where they
were on the lake, or hiking in the woods, they
could use the tower to guide them to their cabin.

Carrie had been mesmerized by the lighthouse,
had taken many photos of it. Maura had loved it too,
felt both comforted and unsettled by it, stared at it
for hours, getting lost in her memories and imagination.

She'd been here in Newport the summer before
Carrie was born. Andy had stayed home in Colum-

bus, painting their apartment, getting it ready. They'd met their first year at Oberlin College, dated ever since. Andy claimed he'd known the first day that he was going to marry her. Maura had known right away, as well.

What was not to love about Andy Shaw? He was the classic, all-American, true-blue good guy. As a kid he'd shoveled the sidewalks of all his elderly neighbors—without being asked, and never taking pay. Andy's mother had told Maura, and Maura had loved that story.

Maura had started Oberlin with a broken heart. Her high school boyfriend had told her they should break up and see other people. She'd met Andy that first week, at orientation. He'd noticed her sadness, right under her skin, and immediately set out to cheer her up. He had a car, and he took her apple-picking out in the countryside. They drank cider, sitting under pines by the reservoir, and she found herself telling him everything, just like a best friend.

They went to the movies, he took her on hikes. She went to his soccer games. Winter came, and he took her snowshoeing. Through it all, they talked and talked. She even told him about her father.

Andy was kind, conscientious, completely honest. He was five-ten, trim and athletic, loved sports. He was too sensitive to be a true jock, and she loved that about him. People relied on him. If someone needed a ride, Andy drove them. When an assistant coach's child was hit by a car, Andy organized a fundraiser. He was always helping, always pitching in. He was warm, wonderful, true, and dear.

Maura remembered being glad they were far away from Katharine. As much as she loved her sister, she'd been afraid of how she would see Andy.

Katharine was an artist. The two sisters had grown up in Connecticut, in a small Cape Cod–style house with a nice yard, across the street from a golf course. Their family had driven first a Ford and then a Volvo station wagon. They looked normal from the outside, but behind their closed doors, there was sadness and worry.

Their father sold public address systems. Amps, tuners, speakers, microphones. He went to all the colleges, theaters, auditoriums, and companies in the area, trying to sell equipment. He wore beautiful suits and expensive ties. His shoes were always shined. He had a slow, crooked smile that made you feel so happy when you said something to bring it out. He met with purchasing agents. He played golf with his clients. He'd have drinks and dinner with administrative assistants, because they could influence their bosses' choices. Frequently he didn't come home.

Their mother held her pain inside. She sipped tea and made pen-and-ink drawings. Sometimes she'd write haiku to go with them, holding herself together with tea, India ink, and Japanese poetry. The person who showed her anguish most was Katharine. Maura would watch her sister every afternoon. She'd seem to grow paler by the minute, until their father walked through the door. Then Katharine would become alive, happy and animated.

On nights when he didn't come home, Katharine would stay in their room after dinner. She wouldn't come out to watch TV, or to do homework, or have snacks. Maura would go looking for her, try to cheer her up. Katharine would usually be sitting on her bed, sketching.

Sometimes, the worst times, she'd be on her knees at the bedroom window, watching down the street for their father's headlights. Maybe she was praying; Maura never asked. Often she had tears in her eyes, and when Maura would start to talk, Katharine would just shake her head hard. And Maura would go away.

Maura had watched both her mother and sister retreat into art. She'd seen her neighbors' lives— people with children, good jobs, summer vacations, a round of golf after work—as being sweet and real. She'd imagined becoming a teacher, having holidays and summers off, falling in love with someone she'd want to have kids with. She didn't want to marry a missing man and turn out like her mother, who hid in line drawings and poems of seventeen syllables and tried not to think of her husband with another woman.

People always said that artists were edgy, but they didn't know Katharine. She was razor-edgy. She fled the suburbs of Connecticut at the very first opportunity, off to art school: the Rhode Island School of Design in Providence.

She was different; not just the way she dressed, a uniform of black T-shirt and pants, a tuxedo jacket for fancy occasions, high-top red Converse sneakers, eyeglasses with heavy tortoiseshell frames, but also in her art. She worked with metal—sheet metal taken from junkyards, iron girders, beams, columns, and cables; a journey-level ironworker, she learned to cut, weld, and rivet them into large sculptures.

The shapes used to be abstract, but after a while she'd started to create animals, extinct animals— for reasons no one but Katharine knew: the quagga, blue pike, Steller's sea cow, saber-toothed tiger, dodo bird, and Caribbean monk seal.

Katharine's material was hard and sharp, and as time went on, she seemed to take on those qualities herself. No one but Maura, and maybe their mother, had ever seen her cry. She'd shed so many tears for her father, it seemed as if she never wanted to do that for anything else. Certainly not for any other man.

Art school and ironworking opened brand-new worlds for her. She met other people like herself, independent contractors and artists who didn't do anything automatically, who questioned their parents' ways, who broke free of anything traditional, who went looking for their own answers, who thought rules were for people who needed to be told what to do. Artists followed their own compulsions and didn't always know why they did what they did.

Katharine didn't understand their Connecticut neighbors. Maybe she never had—perhaps her upbringing, the sorrow of always hoping for more from her father, had demonstrated too vividly the traps of expectations and conventional married, suburban life. It wasn't simply that she judged the neighbors: she didn't even **get** them. She saw the sweetness of their lives as being a snare, the steadiness of their existences to be stultifying.

"Can you imagine coming home to a guy mowing the lawn in madras shorts?" Katharine had asked one early summer night when she was home from RISD, watching Mr. Sisson push his mower back and forth. The two sisters sat on the front steps, drinking lemonade as pollen danced in the golden twilight.

"Kind of," Maura said, embarrassed.

"Not me," Katharine said. "Check out the pink polo shirt."

"He's so nice," Maura said, staring at Mr. Sisson. And she thought, **At least he comes home.** She babysat for the family, and she'd seen how he treated Mrs. Sisson: put his arm around her, danced with her in the kitchen, brought her tea by the fire on cold nights. They never fought. There were no long silences and arguments about money, about where he'd been, not like between Maura and Katharine's parents.

"Nice," Katharine said. "Maybe it's an act."

"It's real. I know."

"That's just in front of you. Maybe they're different when they're home alone. Besides, how boring."

"You don't want a nice man?"

"Look at his hair."

"What's wrong with it?"

"He thinks about it. He goes to a barber, probably has it scheduled into his calendar, gets it cut just so, and combs it neatly. You want that?"

"It doesn't bother me."

Katharine laughed. "Maybe you just haven't met someone who doesn't care about everything being so tidy."

Maura had stared across the street at the big white colonial house on the edge of the golf course. Spreading trees, beautiful old maples and oaks, shaded the lawn and a pool lined with gray-blue stone; a picket fence separated the yard from the golf course. Mrs. Sisson had a rock garden. In the spring, scillas bloomed, filling the yard with tiny bright blue flowers. She glanced at her sister, trying to understand.

"I don't want nice and neat," Katharine said. "I don't want a guy with hair cut in a perfect line just above his collar. I don't want a conventional life in madras shorts. Who knows what hides behind that pink polo shirt? He might be just like Dad, out for himself."

"Just because they live across the street doesn't mean they're the same. . . ."

"I don't care; I don't want it. There's more. You know the expression 'reach for the stars'?"

"Yes."

"It's just a saying. No one really does it. At least no one around here. We're in the suburbs, Maura. To the Sissons, 'reach for the stars' is something they'd write on a graduation card. To them, nature is the green, green grass of the golf course fairway. Give me wild, soaring, indefinite, and unpredictable. That's what's real . . . that's the only way to really get to know someone. When they dare to show you that—that's when you really become close."

"Sounds scary," Maura said.

"I'd only trust someone who showed me his craziness," Katharine said.

Katharine never said she didn't like Andy when

they finally did meet, but Maura knew: he reminded her of Mr. Sisson. After college Andy had gotten a job coaching in his native Columbus. After four years in Ohio, Maura needed a summer by the sea. She and Andy had made plans to be together, but the truth was, Maura was panicking. She had doubts about settling down with Andy—or maybe settling down at all.

Her sister was here in Newport. Before Katharine had bought the saltwater farm about seven miles north in Portsmouth, Rhode Island, she had had an apartment on Spring Street and a welding studio on a back alley near Brown & Howard Wharf, and they planned a sisters' reunion, their last before Maura's "real life" started.

Katharine had talked about the alley. She'd made it sound dark, dangerous, filled with wild energy and creative, exciting people. She'd mentioned a guy, a kindred spirit. Someone who didn't play by the rules, never wore a suit, taught Katharine how to weld. His parents had money, but he wouldn't take it—he worked as an ironsmith in the same seedy back alley as Katharine.

"He works with elements," Katharine had said on the phone, the winter before Maura graduated. "Metal and fire."

"Just like you," Maura had noted, hearing a new tone in her sister's voice.

"He's a madman. Sometimes we stay up all night,

drinking and talking. Sometimes we don't even need to drink—he tells me his ideas, and I tell him mine, no holding back. We go out to Breton Point and watch the sun rise. That's where he told me that when he was little he kept a list of extinct animals, just like me. . . ."

"He did?" Maura had asked.

"Yes," Katharine had said. "And he gave me his list, so I can add them to mine."

"Why extinct animals?"

"You're not crazy enough to understand," Katharine had said. "But J.D. is."

"You're in love with him!"

Katharine had laughed. "It's not like that."

Maura, waiting, had wished it was. Katharine had always seemed so focused on her art, on inspiration and where it took her. She'd had a couple of boyfriends—rebel types their father had hated, boys with long hair and guitars. But they'd never been enough, not even close, for Katharine. But who was? Maura had wanted Katharine to find someone she loved as much as Maura did Andy.

"Why isn't it?" Maura had asked. "It sounds romantic."

"It's not that at all," Katharine had said. "The way we feel about each other is too big."

"I don't mean hearts and flowers," Maura had said, embarrassed. "I mean, you showed him your craziness, right? Didn't you always say that was the test? And don't yell at me for this, but he sounds like your soul mate."

To her shock, Katharine hadn't howled. She'd just listened, letting that clichéd phrase hang between them. "That comes close," she'd said quietly.

"Does he have long hair?" Maura had asked teasingly, knowing that was Katharine's type.

"Not really. When it gets in his eyes, I cut it for him."

"Then why not more?" Maura had asked, stunned at the image of her sister cutting some brooding ironsmith's shaggy hair.

"Because that's all there is, Maura. Don't make more of it, okay?"

"Okay," Maura had said. She'd taken her sister at her word.

Now Maura took her last sip of tea, got ready to stand, when she saw a man sitting in the shadows, on the school's wide marble steps. He was watching her, and the sight shocked her. At first glance she thought it was Angus, the security guard. But no— this man was younger, thinner. She could see the angles of his body, the lines of his cheekbones.

He saw her look over, raised his hand to wave. But Maura just bowed her head and pretended not to see. She hurried home, wondering how long he'd been watching her stare across the water.

The next morning, the first day of school, Maura lost her keys. Eight a.m., with classes scheduled to start at eight-thirty, she stood outside her classroom, balancing an armload of blue notebooks, rummaging through her book bag. Her first day as a teacher, and she was blowing it before the bell rang.

"Can I help you with that?" a man asked. She barely looked up, starting to panic as she realized her keys were really lost, getting a fleeting impression of khaki pants and blue shirt, polished brown wing-tip shoes. Raising her gaze to his face, she realized it was the man she'd seen on the steps last night.

"That was you!" she said.

"Yes," he said. "You looked lost in thought, and I didn't want to disturb you. But right now, it looks as if you could use some help."

"Oh," she said. "I can't find my keys."

"Hang on," he said. "Do you mind?"

He took the book bag from her before she could even think to protest. Reached in, came up with a key ring.

"These?" he asked.

"Yikes," she said. "Yeah."

He fit the right key in the lock, heard the sharp click, and opened the door. She preceded him in, feeling embarrassed. Dumping the notebooks on her desk, she turned to him. He had very dark hair and eyes, a friendly wide smile with a slightly crooked front tooth, and that angular body, sharp cheekbones.

"I'm Stephen Campbell," he said. "I teach math."

"Maura Shaw," she said, shaking his hand. She knew that hers must feel like ice, but he didn't react. "I teach English." She paused, then added, "This is my first day."

"At Newport Academy, I know," he said. "Welcome."

"No, I mean as a teacher," she said. "My first day ever. I've practice-taught, in labs with supervisors, but I've never stood before my own class."

"You'll do great," he said.

"How can you tell?" she asked.

"Because you're nervous. If you didn't care, you'd just be coasting. Here you are, ready to illuminate your students' minds, fill them with poetry and drama and new ideas. . . ."

"For a math teacher, you're very eloquent," she said.

"Ha, that's a typical English teacher's way of looking at mathematics. I don't teach computation—I teach philosophy," he said.

"Hello, Stephen, and hello, Maura!"

Wheeling, Maura saw a big, rumpled man, dressed in tweed, with bushy eyebrows and a neatly trimmed beard, burst into the room. She'd met him once before, when he'd been in Ohio and she'd interviewed.

"Maura," Stephen said, "you know our headmaster, Ted Shannon."

"Good to see you again," she said, feeling grateful to Stephen for getting her out of the jam with her keys, hoping that he would be Beck's math teacher; she had the feeling they'd speak the same language. "Thank you for this opportunity. . . ."

Ted laughed, shaking his head. "Glad to have you with us, Maura—yell if you need anything."

"Thank you," she said. Feeling good, she caught Stephen giving her an odd look.

"He recruited you," he said.

"Well, if you can call it that—he sent out a general mailing, I think."

"I'm sure it was more personal than that," Stephen said, gazing down at her, making the top of her head prickle. Just then the bell rang, long and resonant and echoing down the stately stone hallway, and Maura's heart clutched. She glanced at the clock on the wall: eight-thirty sharp.

"Good luck, Maura," Stephen said, heading out the door, leaving her to pass out the blue notebooks, one on each desk, and wonder about what kind of math teacher taught philosophy, and what he'd been doing alone on the school steps last night.

■

Beck had stood outside the school in the early morning light, sun bouncing off the ocean, practically blinding her, reminding her that water was lapping at the rocks, just waiting to get her. She'd stood with Travis at first, but then some girl with long seal-brown hair, straight as corn silk, very gorgeous, Ally's worst nightmare, had walked over, said she wanted to introduce him to some other juniors. The girl had shined her baby blues at Beck, saying, "I saw you the day the moving van came! Love your braids!"

Beck was too busy plotting her next move to do anything but say, sounding like a complete dork, "Uh, thanks."

"I'm Pell," the girl said.

"This is my sister Rebecca," Travis said.

"Hi, Rebecca," Pell said.

"She likes to be called Beck," Travis said.

"Then why didn't you introduce her that way?" Pell said, laughing, pulling him toward the older kids. "Brothers are idiots."

"Got that right," Beck said under her breath, but she was sorry to see him go. She hung back, major case of dry mouth, what the hell was she doing here in the midst of Lifestyles of the Rich and Stupid? All these dumb girls looking as if they'd stepped straight out of **In Style.** Beck gave less than a rat's ass about anything but getting the eff out of here, away from the water, back to her real home. C + B = U.

The bell rang. Scramble, scramble. The rich kids finished up talking and sending messages from their iPhones, just as if they were a mini-cadre of little businesspeople, all doing more important things than heading into high school. She watched her brother break off from talking to Pell and some other very cute girls and walk through the **Boys' Entrance** door, and her heart broke a little. When had Travis become such a sorry conformer?

Beck stood there at the base of the shallow steps, determined not to walk in. She felt that by entering the school she'd be selling a big piece of her soul. On the other hand, those thick walls would surely block the sound of waves lapping at the shore. The ocean was so much more intense than she had thought, an endless expanse of water waiting like a monster to swallow her.

"Hey," a girl said.

"Hey, what?" Beck asked.

The girl giggled. She gestured Beck over. Small and round, about the size and shape of a muffin, the girl had braces and glasses, and Beck felt a little of the ice around her heart melt. She reminded her a little bit of Amy.

"I'm Camilla," the girl said. "And this is Lucy."

"Beck," Beck said.

"Cool name," Lucy said.

"Thanks," Beck said, checking Lucy out. She had that long, tall, turned-up-nose, ironed-hair **In Style** look that put her straight into Pell's league. So what was she doing hanging with little Camilla?

And talking to Beck? Beck hadn't exactly tried to leave the Buckeye State behind; she wore braids, a faded madras shirt, and a pair of dark green cargo pants with an Ohio State patch on the butt.

"Was that your brother you were standing with?" Lucy asked.

The nickel dropped. So that's why Lucy was giving her the time of day: she wanted a line on Travis.

"Yeah," Beck said, starting to back away. She could fade behind the bushes, run around the building, grab her stuff, hit the road while her mother and brother were in school. The bus station was downtown, and she could hop the next one for New York, head home from there. A bunch of boys lingered under a tree; she saw one, a tall, gawky, awful redhead, look over, catch her eye, and laugh. What's his problem? Beck wondered, scowling at him.

"My sister told me about you two," Lucy said. "That you're from the Midwest."

Beck nodded. "Columbus, Ohio," she said proudly, turning her back on the boys.

"Pell and I are from Michigan."

Beck stood there. Just hearing the word "Michigan" made her shiver with grief, paradoxically making her feel closer to home than she had in days.

"We almost never get to go back," Lucy went on. "We come to our grandmother's for the summer— she lives up on Bellevue Avenue. And then school starts. . . . I went to middle school in Portsmouth, and now here I am at Newport Academy with Pell."

"You live here? You board?" Beck asked.

Lucy and Camilla both nodded.

"We both do," Camilla said. "I'm from New York."

Beck had never met anyone from New York before, but right now she couldn't look away from Lucy. They stared at each other, drinking in the friendliness, openness, and wonder of the great Midwest. The pack of boys moved closer, wanting their attention, but the three ignored them.

"You never get to go back home?" Beck asked.

Lucy shook her head. "Hardly ever. We used to get to go to the Upper Peninsula one week a summer, to visit our other grandparents, but our grandfather died last year, and my grandmother's selling the house. I miss that so much. . . . It was so rustic, and there were loons that came back every year, and there were so many stars!"

"Our family goes to Mackinac Island," Beck said quietly, picturing the sky. "I know what you mean."

"Well, there will be tons of stars when we go to Third Beach at night, if the seniors deign to let us, that is, little freshmen that we are. It's so dark, no streetlights at all," Camilla said.

"Not like Michigan," Lucy and Beck said at once.

An engine sounded, and a golf cart roared up. A

big, gross old guy with a mustache beeped his horn as he drove past, calling, "Inside now! School is starting!"

"Come on, we'd better get in there," Camilla said.

"Well," Lucy said. "Shall we?"

Beck stared from one to the other. It felt disloyal to Amy and Ellie, not to mention Carrie, to even consider walking in with them. She'd spoken to Amy last night, promised she'd be back in Ohio by the weekend. She had plenty of friends who would hide her, let her sleep in their basements and attics. She would spend her days looking for Carrie.

"I have English first," Camilla said.

"Oh, Jesus," Beck said, aware that the boys were coming closer. They'd all find out her mother was the English teacher sooner than later.

"What, you hate English?" Lucy asked. "So do I. Give me math any day!"

"Math?" Beck asked.

Lucy smiled, nodding. "You too?"

Beck nodded.

"Are you in Steve—Mr. Campbell's class?"

"I think so," Beck said.

"Cool—see you there!" Lucy ran after Camilla.

Beck should have followed right behind her, but now she was stuck. Glancing over, she saw the red-head kid standing right there, as if sent to monitor her. Across the grounds, she spotted the security-patrol guy watching the kids straggling by the door.

She'd never be able to sneak past him. Her heart banged in her chest, and she had the feeling that once she walked into the school, her plan would fall to pieces. She'd never get back home.

She watched Camilla and Lucy walk up the wide and stately limestone steps, past the urns spilling over with ivy, white petunias, and perfect pink geraniums. They entered through the **Girls' Entrance,** holding the door open behind them for Beck. She licked her lips, clenched her fists, felt as if she was about to parachute out of a plummeting plane.

The red-haired boy sprang up the steps to the **Boys' Entrance.** He opened the door ceremoniously and stood there waiting for her, daring her with a wild smile.

"You think I'm a boy?" she asked, pointing at the chiseled words.

He grinned even wider. "I think you're a rule-breaker," he said.

"I'm not," Beck said, offended.

But then, and she couldn't even say why, she walked straight through the boys' door as he neatly crisscrossed, a double helix, behind her as he walked through the girls'. They met inside, in a common hall that proved the entrances were just stupid, some dumb tradition invented by the school founder. But Beck found herself grinning back at the kid, and they high-fived as Beck followed Lucy and Camilla up a wide staircase to their first classes.

■

That night, the campus was dark and still. Lights burned in some of the rooms—most boarders lived in the main building, a few others in smaller houses on the cliff and along the side streets.

The Shaws' house was silent. Windows were open to allow the night air in, and the cats lay on the windowsills, listening to the crickets and crashing surf, gazing out into the darkness. Beck and Travis were asleep, so the cats were the only ones to see Maura quietly slip into her shoes, find her keys, and step outside.

The car was parked around back, in a small garage also used to store garden equipment. The structure muffled the sound of the engine starting, but Maura winced as she backed out, gravel crunching under the tires.

She passed academic buildings, faculty houses, and the security cottage. No lights on anywhere; the whole campus seemed to be asleep. Then she happened to glance through the trees, toward the mansion—completely dark now, but what was that on the top floor?

A green light glowed from the tall windows. She stopped the car, gazed upward. She peered through foliage, inching her car forward for a better look.

The glimmer danced, green-blue and cool. And then she realized: it was the ocean reflected on the ceiling. Bouncing through the great seaward windows, refracted upward.

That had to be it, right? She stared another few moments, wondering about the light source. There was no moon to illuminate the waves. Starlight? She thought of Carrie, her love of the night sky. Maura's memories of her had been so magnified since their arrival in Newport. Was it possible her daughter was here, close by?

She stared at the shimmering light, realized it was the reflection of a swimming pool. A pool on the top floor of a boarding school? It seemed so jarring, decadent in a very-Newport way, and she wondered why she hadn't seen anything about it in the school brochures, why no one had mentioned it, why the pool wasn't at the large athletic facility.

In that moment the fourth floor went dark, and she put the questions from her mind. She had a mission.

Maura drove down the tree-lined drive, through the arching iron gates, toward town. On Bellevue Avenue she passed the grocery store where she and her sister had shopped, the Newport Casino with its grass tennis courts hidden behind the dreamy old shingled façade by McKim, Mead, and White, all the big houses. Newport had a great story, full of history not taught in school.

Breathing deeply, Maura tried to clear her head. She'd just taught her first day. She'd worked hard to get to this point, and wished she had someone to celebrate with. Beck had come in after school, hadn't said a word. Travis had been sweet, congratulating her on a good job—two of his new friends had been in her class, told him that they'd liked what she'd written on the blackboard: Chaucer's observation that life is a **"thinne subtil knittinge of thinges."**

And that was true. Last night's emotions and memories had stirred her up—things knitting together here in Newport. Being here brought back that summer, how she'd nearly ruined her relationship with Andy. She ached for him, the father of her children, the feeling dissolving into something else, an old longing she'd kept below the surface all these years. But tonight she couldn't wait any longer.

The city had sections, clearly divided. Thornton Wilder, in **Theophilus North,** had written about them, but Maura made her own distinctions. Leaving the very rich Bellevue Avenue, she headed down the hill, crossed Spring Street—where she had lived with her sister so long ago—and descended toward the wharves.

Time had changed the city. Condos were everywhere. T-shirt shops, ice cream parlors, saltwater taffy stores and bed-and-breakfasts had replaced hardware stores, marine repair shops, and boat sheds, all that was new offering tourists the chance to buy a feeling: the sense of being part of amazing, magical Newport. But the true essence could never be bought. It had to be lived, breathed in like the sea air. Maura had done it that summer.

The wharf area, mostly developed, still had one dark and gritty stretch. Half a block down from Spring Street and up from Thames Street, away from the water, hidden from sight, was a row of warehouses.

She had to turn off the main road, onto Blackstone's Alley—a narrow cobblestone drive from the era of whaling, steamships, and carriages. Her heart beat harder, out of control. What if she saw him? Nothing here had changed since their summer together.

This area still reeked of industry. It was the part of Newport that stayed hidden, that tourists weren't supposed to see. Within sound of the harbor—the happy din of visitors strolling, eating, drinking, taking pictures—this was the Newport no one cared about. There were no views, lawns, gardens; instead, it was a place of ramshackle garages, machine shops, abandoned carriage houses, ancient boat sheds, some with iron rails heading down to the harbor.

Her sister's welding studio had been here before she converted the barn in Portsmouth. Maura passed it slowly, almost seeing Katharine standing there in her fireproof mask, wielding a torch. Shuttered for the night, it and all the buildings were deserted. A stray cat sprang across the road, startling her. She braked, watching the cat chase a rat behind a brick garage.

Inching along, Maura felt every sense alert. This was where she had come to life. She'd discovered the danger in her own heart, found the thrill of it all. If the alley had been torn down, razed, developed into yet another condo complex, she might have gone back to Newport Academy, quit then and there, packed up the kids, and returned to Columbus. For she hadn't realized until right now, this very instant, how badly she needed this. She needed something not to have changed.

She needed the alley and warehouse to be just as it was. There was the other building she knew so well, the square structure just four doors down from Katharine's, up ahead. She stopped a few yards back.

With the car windows open, she heard the faint sound of halyards whipping and clanking in the harbor a block away. Or was it the **ka-chunk** of J.D.'s machine press, working there behind the corrugated steel shutters of the old warehouse? She'd met him here in the alley, one day when she was visiting Katharine's studio. They'd both stepped outside into the sunshine.

Sometimes everything in life crystallizes in one moment, one place. Time doesn't matter; years trickle away. For Maura, all that had happened since was linked to what took place long ago right here. The roar of a motorcycle, the defying of gravity.

Maura thought of Andy. She had loved him with all she had. For seventeen years they'd had the happiest family they could make. But she knew he would have divorced her if he hadn't died, and she understood that this place was why.

Patterns in the old brick: the arch of concreted-up windows, holes where gales had roared off Narragansett Bay, grabbed the mortar and shaken it loose, cast iron reinforcing the corners. J.D.'s great-grandfather had been a shipbuilder, had constructed this warehouse and most of the others on Blackstone's Alley.

Some people said James Desmond Blackstone had run Newport—not as mayor, not in any legal or recognized form of government, but from this grimy, hidden warren where he'd made a fortune, halfway between the waterfront and the world of high society. An uneducated man, he'd been determined that his children have the best, attend school with the children of rich men. He had founded Newport Academy.

J.D. had been proud of his family heritage, of his great-grandfather's vision and might, but he had paid his family rent for this place. He had needed to pay his own way, cared nothing about power. He'd wanted one thing: Maura.

Did he still come here? What would he look like? Would she be able to bear seeing him after all that had happened? She closed her eyes and imagined him still climbing towers, scaling bridges, scaring girls almost to death. The vision was so acute and cruel, she actually moaned.

She had another visit to make, and it wouldn't be easy; she had to see Katharine. Something between the O'Donnell sisters had broken at the end of that summer. The distance between Rhode Island and Ohio wasn't all that kept them apart. How could love do so much damage?

Katharine would know how J.D. was, whether he would even see her. Maybe telling J.D. the truth would finally set Maura free; perhaps it would return her to her sister, give her back Andy, help her find Carrie. Maybe it would give her back herself.

Or none of the above . . .

4 WHILE MOST OF THE GRAND Gilded Age mansions of Newport were built for the summer enjoyment of wealthy New York and Boston families, designed for lavish balls and grand-scale entertaining, Blackstone Hall, the main building at Newport Academy, had always been intended for education.

The founder had come from Ireland and had strict notions of propriety—separate entrances for girls and boys, distinct living quarters, and a chapel on the third floor. There were many hidden passageways, built so the teachers and masters could spy on the students, make sure they were behaving.

Those corridors had been boarded up for years. But rumors of secrets remained. Students claimed they heard the ghost of old James Desmond Blackstone roaming the halls at night, keeping everyone in line. They saw apparitions of a young girl, Mary Langley, who'd died one winter day a hundred years ago—the December anniversary commemorated school-wide each year.

"Who was she?" the new students would whisper.

"The richest girl in America," some upperclass-men would say. "So wealthy her father demanded she have her own private floor, the top floor of Blackstone Hall."

"Her father was a rival and the brother-in-law of the Dark Lord—Percival Vanderbilt—of Newport's second-richest family, and he wanted Percival's envy. He sent Mary to school practically on Percival's home turf, with every luxury imaginable."

"Her own private carriage."

"Her own private swimming pool."

"Her very own elevator."

It was true: a creaky, rarely used elevator existed. Sometimes it would growl to life, frightening students who hadn't heard it before. They lived in large, bright rooms with tall windows overlooking the grounds and ocean, the walnut-paneled walls lined with bookcases.

Upperclass students had rooms with wide fire-places built of Italian marble. At night, with a sea wind rattling the panes, wood fires would crackle on the hearth and the students would gather round to study.

They would hear the elevator climb to the fourth floor, stop, and then descend. Wanting to see the ghost of Mary, the students would dash down to the ground floor, waiting for the elevator to inch downward.

But then the doors would open and Angus

would walk out into the grand hallway, pushing a huge cart full of shattered roof tiles or a cracked gargoyle—things the sea wind had smashed, loosened from their pinnings, that if ignored could fall from the roof and hurt someone on the ground.

Passing Stephen Campbell on campus one early morning, Maura pointed up at the fourth floor and told him about the strange lights she'd seen there a few nights earlier. He'd nodded.

"The reflection of Mary's swimming pool," he said.

"Mary's pool?" she asked.

"You've heard about Mary Langley, right?" he asked.

"The school ghost . . ."

"Right," he said. "Well, when Mary became a student here, her father got the school to build her a pool. Apparently she loved to swim."

"He must have adored her."

Stephen nodded, gazing at her. "Most people react differently—they say he spoiled her. But Newport is Newport—families like the Langleys had unimaginable money. Importing marble from Italy, hiring the best architect, making sure their pool was better than anyone else's . . . that's how it was."

"He loved his daughter," Maura said. She thought of all the ways she'd tried to show Carrie how much she loved her. And now, how she would spend her last penny to find her: she had just authorized another five thousand dollars for the private detective. "Maybe that's all it was. And he realized life is short."

"It is," Stephen said.

"Who uses it now?" she asked. "The pool . . ."

"It really isn't used," he said.

"That green light bouncing off the ceiling," she said. "The pool was illuminated, and someone was swimming."

"Must have been moonlight shining through the windows . . ." he said.

"No, I don't think so," she said, staring up at the building, early morning sunlight glancing off the Atlantic, shimmering across the limestone face. "Someone was there."

"Let's see," he said. "Light from an unknown source, plus speed, plus distance, divided by the legend of Mary and her swimming pool, and there you have it." His smile was crooked and boyish.

Gazing at the second floor, she saw morning light hit the chapel's stained glass window. She thought of how J.D. had described his great-grandfather, a man of Irish faith combined with New England austerity; she knew he must have had a sentimental side to allow a student's father to demand a swimming pool for his child.

"It's really not in use?" she asked.

"Let's just say it's not open to the school community," he said, smiling. "By the way, Beck is your daughter, right?"

"Yes."

"She's very good at math," he said. "She's already standing out in my class."

"Thank you," Maura said. And she hurried across campus, to call the detective before her next class, just in case the latest payment had inspired him to work hard and actually find something out.

■

Travis had worked out with the football team back home all through August, so he was ready for Newport Academy. He made the cut, no problem, and soon found out that the Independent School League was a long way from the Midwest.

Newport Academy was not a football school, not the way Thurber and Savage were. Back home, sports were front and center. Here in Newport, everything was aimed at academics, and football was a second thought. The team had the dumbest name he'd ever heard: the Cuppers, as in the America's Cup, the yacht race that used to be held in Newport. Still, Coach Bishop used a spread offense, a three-step/five-step passing game, and a gap-control defense, eight men in the box, stuff that made Travis feel right at home.

He trained for his position as tight end, falling into step with Jeremy Lathrop, Ty Cooper, and

Chris Pollack as they ran up and down the hills of Newport. The September weather was warm; the sun baked the top of their heads, but a cool breeze blowing off the ocean cooled them off. The temperature made it almost too easy.

Chris was quarterback, and at the first game against Exeter—the first Saturday after school started—Travis blocked for the first touchdown, went out for a last-second third-down pass to confuse the defense for the second, blocked for a long fourth-quarter drive, and finished the winning day as Newport's leading receiver.

"Hey, you're our secret weapon," Chris said, slapping him on the back as they left the field.

"Thanks," Travis said. "You threw some great passes."

"Man, where'd you come from?" Ty Cooper asked.

"The Cuppers might actually have a season this year," Turner Reed said.

Travis didn't reply, but he felt proud. They walked off the field to the cheers of a small crowd nothing like the monster hordes they'd get at his public school back home. He scanned the bleachers and saw his mother standing with a few teachers. She waved both arms, embarrassing him. No sign of Beck, big surprise. But Pell, Logan, and Cordelia had come; he saw them out of the corner of his eye, and after he and the guys walked out of the gym, they were still waiting there in the sun.

The September Saturday was hot, almost like summer. The class load was heavy, but a general feeling of celebration was in the air, and everyone planned to head down to the beach. Travis hung back. He wanted to join in, but he'd promised Ally they could talk. The academy gave all the students brand-new laptops, so he and Ally had started web conferencing—talking online with the camera going so they could see each other. She had said she wanted him to see what he was missing. He worked at controlling his expressions, wondering why seeing her didn't make him miss her more.

"Hey," Pell said, breaking away from the others to run back to where he was standing by the gym.

"What's up?"

"You were great in the game," she said.

"You like football?" he asked.

She laughed and nodded. "Yeah," she said. "My dad played in college at Brown and got us to love it. I was hooked early. I love watching you guys mangle each other! The harder you hit them, the better I like it."

That got his attention, sort of surprising him. She looked so delicate and expensive. He'd come out of a total jock school, where everyone lived and breathed sports, and this place did anything but. There was a politeness about the Independent School League, about Newport Academy's football program, but here was this elegant girl socking her fist into her open hand, hungry for blood.

"I'll remember that," he said. "Next time I'll annihilate someone just for you."

"Yay," she said, shaking her hands as if she was holding pom-poms.

"I thought maybe Michigan had left you," he said. "Considering you spend the whole year in Newport, pretty much."

"It could never leave me," she said. "It's true, I stay with my grandmother. But you only have one home . . . right? And even when you move away, it's where you think of when you think of where you belong."

He nodded. She was right. Maybe that explained the heaviness he felt. This didn't feel like his team—his real team was back in Columbus, in their stadium, with all his friends. His mom had come to the game, but he missed his dad.

"So," he said, checking his watch. "I better get going."

"You're not coming to the beach?"

"No," he said.

"Why?" she asked, surprising him with her directness.

"I have to talk to my girlfriend," he said.

"She's back home?"

He nodded. It was already four; he was late calling. But Pell was gazing at him with those wide blue eyes, and he stood there staring back.

"You'd better go call her," Pell said after a minute. "Tonight we're hitting Truffles, a club downtown. But if you finish up talking to your girlfriend and want to come find us now, we'll be at Third Beach."

"Third Beach?" he asked.

She nodded. "There are three . . . Easton's, right at the bottom of the hill, then past St. George's School to Second Beach, and you just keep going, all the way to the end, to get to Third."

"Is it far?"

"You'll need a ride," she said. "But call, and we'll come get you."

"I have my mom's car," he said. "But I probably won't make it."

"Hope you do," she said.

He nodded, started to walk away. "Hey," he said. "Why go all the way over to Third Beach when Easton's is so close?"

She grinned, giving him that wicked sparkle he'd seen the first time he met her. "Because it's Saturday," she said. "And we want to be far from the prying eyes of school."

He stood there, watching her run to catch up with her friends. Seniors could have cars on campus, so she piled into a Jeep with a bunch of older kids he'd seen in the halls. Hesitating, he felt the pull, wanting to call out and say he'd changed his mind, he was going to the beach. Instead he turned and started to run, across the field, along a stone walkway, through a woodland path that led straight to his front door.

Letting himself in, he saw his mother was already there, correcting papers. He felt churned up, bewildered. She smiled at him, coming across the room to hug him.

"You were amazing," she said. "They won because of you!"

"No," he said. "Chris is really good."

"Yes, he's an excellent quarterback. But you just shined. It was thrilling, it really was. The teachers I was sitting with practically screamed themselves hoarse."

"Thanks, Mom," he said.

"Your dad would have been proud."

He nodded; his eyes stung. The words hung between them, and he hoped she wouldn't say more. He watched her mouth quiver. He always knew when his mom was going to cry.

"It's okay, Mom," he said.

"He should be here to see you," she said.

"I know," Travis said.

"This place," she said, looking around. "It's so new, so different. And you're already doing so beautifully. You're such a fine player, Travis."

"Because of Dad," he said. "He helped me get this far. All through last season, even without him . . ."

"He believed in you," she said.

Her words, the emotion in her eyes, made him feel as if he were upside down, all the blood rushing to his head. At first, any mention of his dad had made him feel he could die himself—the top of his head blow off. He couldn't believe the reality, couldn't stand it—none of them could.

It was unbearable, the idea of never seeing his dad again, never having his dad see him play again. Even more incredible, worse in a way, was the fact that they were all getting used to his absence, Carrie's too. They were missing in separate ways, but neither one was here. A year had passed, and the mention of them no longer made Travis feel as much like exploding, and that upset him.

"You okay?" he asked his mother.

She nodded shakily. Tried to smile. Did smile. "I'm fine," she said.

"Good," he said, even though he didn't believe her.

"Oh, Ally called," she said after a minute, relieving the tension. "She wanted me to remind you . . ."

"I know." He started toward his room.

"Would you like something to eat?" she asked. "Dinner's not for another couple of hours; how about a sandwich? Grilled cheese?"

He shook his head. Usually he was starving after a game, but right now he had no appetite at all. Food was the farthest thing from his mind. Ally had known his father. He just wanted to make the call, to see Ally's face and hear her voice, to be reminded of what he was doing, where he was going, and where he came from. To make a connection back to his past, to Ohio, to his father and sister. To get his mind off Third Beach and who was waiting there.

■

Beck sat on the stone wall, ten yards back from the chain-link fence along the top of the cliff. Far in the distance was a lighthouse. She could just make it out on the horizon, and it made her think of the tower that had suddenly appeared on the island in Lake Michigan. She tried to focus on height, distance, declination, but her usual method of filtering scary things through math wasn't working.

She felt dizzy. But she told herself she was safe here—she couldn't possibly tumble off the wall, over the tall steel fence, and down the steep ledge into the water.

From thirty feet back, she couldn't even see the waves breaking on the rocks sixty feet down. But she saw white spume geysering straight up, and when she licked her lips, tasted salt water sprayed by the wind. Tourists walked along the path between her and the cliff, craning their necks for a sight of the school. She realized they saw her as a real live Newport Academy student, attending one of the most prestigious institutions on the East Coast. The thought made her jump up and run away.

Camilla and Lucy came across campus toward her, walking with Redmond O'Brien.

"Hi, Beck," Lucy said. "You missed a good game. Your brother was the star."

The last game of Travis's she'd gone to, she'd sat between her parents. Carrie had been in the row ahead of them with Ally. Last year, without her father or Carrie there, she'd avoided every game. She'd known it was killing Travis to play at all.

"You couldn't be bothered to go watch?" Redmond asked, his Boston accent making it sound like "bath-ud."

"Like it's any of your business," she said and watched him turn red. God, he was so provokable.

"Yeah, you probably don't want to go to the beach either," he said.

"Got that right," she said.

"Want to head down to Bannister's Wharf?" Camilla asked. "Lucy and I have a major craving for hot chocolate chip cookies."

"There's a cookie place?" Beck asked.

Lucy nodded. "They bake them right there."

"Come on, let's go to the beach," Redmond said.

"It's all upperclassmen at Third," Lucy said. "My sister would not appreciate me showing up. Besides, we don't have a car."

"I mean right down there," Redmond said,

pointing at Easton's Beach. Beck glanced at the long strand glistening in the sun, the hard silver sand left wet under the wash of long, lacy waves. She stared at the water. It spread to the horizon like a blanket, like eternity, and you couldn't see what was underneath, and in spite of the day's heat, Beck felt a long chill slide down her spine.

"Cookies," she said to the girls, turning her back on Redmond. "Let's go get cookies."

So they did. But they couldn't shake Redmond. He walked along with them, all the way down to the wharf. He was tall and lanky, totally gawky, with corkscrew curls of carrot red hair springing off the top of his head. He wore big goofy sneakers, a bright green Celtics T-shirt, and rumpled beige cargo pants. Beck noticed that: she liked cargo pants too.

"Lots of pockets," she said as they walked along.

"Yes," he said.

"Isn't it great that your name gives you the perfect nickname?" she asked.

"What?"

"Red," she said.

"Uh, gee, that's original," he said.

She stared at him, squinting in the afternoon sun. "You know, your freckles form a perfect map of Ohio across your cheeks," she said.

He tightened his lips, and she suddenly felt bad. She wanted to tell him she meant it as a compliment. The thing was, she did tease a lot. It was one of her bad habits. She opened her mouth, started to say she was sorry, then clamped it shut again.

They walked along America's Cup Boulevard, crossed the street to Bannister's Wharf. It was cobblestoned, lined with stores and restaurants. The shops were small, quaint, filled with lovely things, the kind of places Beck had had problems with in the past. Her fingertips tingled, and she shoved her hands into her pockets. Suddenly Lucy pointed out one place whose heavy wooden sign bore a carved mermaid with two curving tails.

"That's the Candy Store," Lucy said. "It's one of the best restaurants, and the Sky Bar's upstairs, where all the sailors go, and the Boom Boom Room's downstairs, and that's where people go to dance."

"The Boom Boom Room?" Beck asked.

"It's very Newport," Lucy said.

"It's where all the older yachties go," Camilla said.

"Kids my sister's age—you know Pell—go to Truffles. It's over there," Lucy said, pointing toward the next wharf.

"But what are 'yachties'?"

"Sailors," Redmond said. "With yachts." But he made it sound like "yawts."

"Does your grandmother have—" Beck started to ask Lucy.

"She does," Lucy said. "It's docked right out there. Want to see?"

Beck hesitated, but no one noticed. They stopped into the bakery and bought huge, warm-from-the-oven chocolate chip cookies, then walked past the red umbrellas of the Black Pearl's outside terrace, past the shingled building at the end of the wharf, through a white gate that said **Private: Yacht Owners Only Past This Point.**

Beck's stomach flipped as they walked through the gate. The harbor lapped beneath the slatted wood under her feet. Lucy and Camilla strode down the dock as if they owned the place. Beck and Redmond hung back slightly. The pier was made of wood, and although Beck was afraid it would wobble, it was solid as a brick wall. Refusing to look down at the water, she focused on enormous boats tied to the dock, some bigger than the carriage house, and saw the owners sitting in the shade on their decks, and knew she didn't belong here.

"You like boats?" Redmond asked.

"Not really," she said.

He didn't reply. For all she knew, he was the biggest boat-lover in the world. She wanted to amend her comment, to say it wasn't that she didn't like boats, it was that she was scared to her bones of water. But then everyone stopped, and they were staring at what even Beck had to admit was a vessel of rare grace; all polished wood and bronze, belonging to another century.

"Grandmother!" Lucy exclaimed.

"Lucille," the old woman said with a smile that somehow didn't touch her eyes. Sitting in the shade of a wide blue awning, she had silver hair pulled back in a French twist, white pearls at her throat, and huge diamond rings on her gnarled fingers. She wore a navy blue silk dress, and appeared to have been deep in conversation with a younger man with wavy blond hair, wearing a starched blue-and-white-striped shirt.

"We were at the wharf, and I wanted to show my friends **Sirocco,**" Lucy said.

"Grandmother is very busy," the woman interjected in a warning singsong.

"I know, we're not going to bother you. We just . . ."

"Well, you can't just drop in and not come aboard," she said, sounding suddenly indulgent. Beck stared at the foot-wide space between the dock and deck and suddenly couldn't breathe, terrified at the narrowness of the pier and the closeness of the water. She prayed that Lucy would decline to go on the boat. "Perhaps you'll be so kind as to introduce your friends," Lucy's grandmother continued. "Say hello to Jonathan Bowles, Lucille."

"Hello, Jonathan," Lucy said.

"Lovely to see you, Lucille . . ."

"Grandmother, you remember Camilla? She visited us this summer?"

The woman regarded Camilla with a mouth like an upside-down horseshoe. Then, recognizing her, or just deciding to make the most of it, she gave a wobbly smile. "Well, yes. Hello. Come now, darling. All of you. Step aboard!"

A white-uniformed crew member set down a small metal ramp that attached to the boat and slanted down to the pier. "Come now, up the gangway," the grandmother urged, gesturing.

Lucy strode up. Her grandmother nodded with approval, then turned her gaze on Beck, Camilla, and Redmond. Beck could almost feel her assessing their unsuitability, and guessed they weren't half as attractive as the old woman would've liked them to be.

Camilla climbed up the gangway; it looked easy, even with her short legs. Redmond followed, glancing behind to see if Beck was coming. But she was rooted like an old oak, feet clamped to the dock, her gaze magnetized to the thin strip between the pier and the boat. Only about a foot wide, and she could see treacherous water moving down below. She felt so dizzy she had to close her eyes.

"Come aboard, dear. Have you not heard me?" Lucy's grandmother asked, and Jonathan Bowles laughed appreciatively in a boyish trill. Beck glared

at him. His horrible wavy hair looked dyed, an un-
natural shade of yellow, and his skin was leathery
and tan, tight as a mask. She hated feeling scared,
so she channeled all her fear into stubborn anger
and despising Jonathan Bowles.

"Come on, Beck," Lucy said, offering her a
hand. "Please, and meet my grandmother, Mrs.
Edith Nicholson."

"I forgot something," Beck said, backing away
from the slit where she'd seen the water moving,
trying to catch her breath. "I have to go. . . ."

"Wait!" Lucy called.

"How very odd!" Mrs. Nicholson said.

Beck went tearing down the dock, her footsteps
pounding in her ears. She tried not to look left or
right, at the drop-off to the harbor's surface. She
slammed through the gate, bending from the waist
with relief, holding her stomach and whooping in
air as she tried to breathe.

"Hey," came a voice from behind her.

Wheeling, she saw Redmond running up to her.

"Are you okay?" he asked.

"I'm very odd, didn't you hear?" she said. "I forgot, I have to get home. My mother . . ."

"Your mother's the English teacher, right?"

"Got to go," Beck said, starting to walk.

"I was sitting in front of her at the game," he said.
"I knew it was her, because she was cheering so
hard for your brother." **Cheerin' so hod for your**

brotha. "But I also heard her say she had papers to correct. She probably wouldn't mind if you hung out for a while."

"Listen," she said. "You don't get it, okay? I have to be home."

He turned fiery red, nodded, and said, "Okay." Beck didn't stick around to hear any more. The crowd on Bannister's Wharf was thick, but they heard her running and parted. The ground was paving stones, solid as could be, but Beck still felt water moving. She hadn't been on a boat since the canoe, and even walking down the dock she'd felt the rocking motion, the tipping back and forth that Carrie and her father must have experienced.

The store sprang up in front of her. She saw the door open, a personal invitation. She made herself slow down so she wouldn't be noticed. The shoppers were from all over. She could tell from their accents and clothes. Hardly anyone in here was dressed like Newport: she might have been in a mall. It felt good.

She walked around the store, looking at everything on the shelves. Little ceramic lighthouses, potholders shaped like lobster claws, a brass door knocker shaped like a scallop shell. She saw boxes of note cards with pictures of boats, photos of Newport's waterfront. So maritime, completely nautical.

But then she spotted a large glass bowl filled with

tiny china pineapples. Pineapples! They were so cute, and had nothing, nothing to do with the sea, with water. What significance could they possibly have to the tourists of Newport?

Without thinking, she reached into the bowl, palmed a baby pineapple no larger than a walnut, and continued her circuit of the store. Her heart rate slowed; her breath came more regularly. She felt the small object, oblong in her hand. Solid and grounding, it seemed to tether her to the earth. The pineapple held her together, a magical yellow orb, a little ceramic sun in the palm of her hand.

Still holding it, she walked past the checkout counter. Every footfall registered in her mind. **I am safe, I am safe, I am safe,** she told herself. The little pineapple was her talisman, and it guided her out the door, and in that instant became the first thing she'd stolen since arriving in Newport. She stepped into the Saturday sunshine of the wharf, and she turned away from the harbor and with the ceramic pineapple in her pocket walked up the big parabolic hill toward school and her mother and the refuge of her math homework.

■

Maura stood in the kitchen, staring into the cupboards, wondering what to make for dinner, when Beck burst through the screen door.

"Hi, honey," Maura said. "Where were you?"

Beck launched herself at Maura, crying so hard she couldn't speak. Maura led Beck to a chair, sat her down, crouched, and held her hand while she sobbed.

"What's wrong, Beck? What happened?"

"I hate it here, Mom. Why did we have to come?"

"Oh, Beck . . . We've talked about this. . . ."

"It's terrible," Beck said. "There's water everywhere. And no one likes me, Mom."

"I thought you were making friends," Maura said.

"I'm just so different from them," Beck said. "I don't know about yachts, and clubs, and stuff like that. I don't care about any of it! I'll never fit in, I wouldn't even want to. Newport is nothing but mansions. Even this school—it's so big and fancy and gross. Some rich person built it for his spoiled kids, I bet. . . ." Her voice caught. "And I miss dad."

"I miss him too," Maura said. She stared at Beck, seeing the shape of Andy's face, the line of his cheek, his ears, his brow. Time made missing him less intense, but didn't take it away.

"He would hate this place," Beck said, swallowing a sob that exploded as she said, "And so would Carrie!"

Maura heard footsteps, turned around, and saw Travis standing in the door. Maura hated how familiar the look on his face was—shock and fear, steeling himself for a new trauma.

"Beck's having a tough day," Maura said. "And I've just decided: we're going out to dinner."

"I thought we were saving money," Travis said.

"I don't care," Maura said. "We need a treat."

They fed the cats, changed into nice clothes, and got into the car. Travis let Beck sit in front; Maura gave him a grateful look in the rearview mirror as she took them on an impromptu tour. They passed the Elms, Chateau-sur-Mer, Rosecliff, where **The Great Gatsby** was filmed, Mrs. Astor's Beechwood, and Rough Point, Doris Duke's mansion, all along Bellevue Avenue.

Ocean Drive hugged the rocky shore, past Bailey's Beach, and Hazard's and Gooseberry beaches, and all the hidden coves and stretches of granite ledge, and big, many-chimneyed houses with sloping lawns. Maura glanced at Beck; safe in the car, she didn't seem to mind the water.

They turned inland, and the landscape gave way to rolling hills and thickets of beach roses, gorse, bayberry, and laurel. The farther they got from the sea, the more the neighborhood started to feel like home.

Maura watched Beck notice the Fifth Ward's smaller houses, the tidy yards, the basketball hoops in the driveways. She drove north on Spring Street, silently glancing down the side street that led toward Blackstone's Alley, then past St. Mary's, the big Catholic Church where Jacqueline Bouvier had married John F. Kennedy.

They crossed Memorial Boulevard, passed the Franklin Spa—the lunch counter where she and Katharine used to meet—then Trinity Church, the white church with the tall steeple and quiet churchyard; she pointed out the two-family red house across the street from the small cemetery where she and Katharine had had their apartment. Ten minutes later, they wound up in the Point section on Narragansett Bay, just south of the Newport Bridge.

The eighteenth-century houses here were lovely, well kept, neatly painted clapboard with center chimneys, much more modest than the marble and limestone palaces of Bellevue Avenue. These colonial-era houses had been built by sea captains, fishermen, merchants, tradespeople, and shipbuilders. She saw Beck relax a little more, feeling not so overwhelmed by size and status.

"See?" Maura said. "Not every house in Newport is a mansion."

"I like this neighborhood," Beck said. "Who lives here?"

"Regular people," Maura said.

"You mean people who don't go to Newport Academy," Beck said.

"You might be surprised," Maura said.

"What do you mean?"

"Newport Academy was founded by a man who lived in this neighborhood," she said, thinking of J.D.'s grandfather. "He came from Ireland with nothing. He worked hard building ships, and made a lot of money. But no matter how much he made, he felt his family could never get ahead enough to be accepted by Newport society."

"I told you, they're horrible!" Beck said.

"He decided his children needed a good education. They couldn't get into the other private schools, so he built one for them."

"Newport Academy?" Travis asked.

"Yes," Maura said.

"A man from this neighborhood built that fancy mansion?" Beck asked.

"He did," Maura said. "He wanted to attract children from all walks of life, and he knew the robber barons wouldn't send their kids unless the school had everything the other schools had."

"What was his name?" Beck asked.

"James Desmond Blackstone."

"How do you know all this?" Travis asked.

Maura hesitated, gazing out at the water. The Newport Bridge was close by, and its white lights were starting to twinkle in the violet twilight. "I knew his great-grandson a long time ago," she said. "He told me."

"What's **that?**" Beck asked suddenly, sounding

shocked as she pointed at the carved pineapple above the doorway of the Georgian colonial Hunter House.

"Fruit, Beck," Travis said. "Try not to freak out."

"The pineapple is a symbol of Newport," Maura said. "It means welcome. . . . When sea captains would return from their voyages, they'd bring pineapples from the South Seas, and their families would place them over the door to invite people to visit."

For some reason that tale made Beck slouch down in her seat and grow quiet again, so Maura kept driving through the narrow streets. She thought of James Desmond Blackstone and the night J.D. had told her about the origins of Newport Academy; they had been sitting on a cement wall by one of the public driftways to the water, within sight of his great-grandfather's house. The bridge lights had sparkled overhead that night too.

"This is where you came from?" Maura had asked him.

"It's where my great-grandfather first lived when he came to America," he'd said. "So yes, because of him, I come from right here."

"Will you show me the house you grew up in?" she'd asked.

"I'll show you everything," he'd said. He'd looked into her eyes as if he couldn't believe she'd appeared in his life, as if he was afraid this wouldn't last. His arm felt tight and strong, and she'd leaned into him, fascinated and swept away by a man she barely knew. Thinking of that now, she pushed the memory down and concentrated on her children.

But once he'd entered her mind, it wasn't easy. Being back in Newport brought so much flooding in, images and feelings she'd spent her life since then trying to escape. Driving along, she scanned every face. It was her habit, watching for Carrie. But here she was looking for J.D. too.

Maura knew the kids were getting hungry. When they got close to Brick Market, she found a parking spot. They walked along the street, stopping to look at menus posted in restaurant entrances. Maura and Travis let Beck choose—the Black Duck, a sandwich and burger place.

Entering the restaurant, Beck seemed calmer, at ease. Travis liked the ship's lanterns and big leather menus. Maura smiled, told them they could order whatever they wanted, listened while Travis read the legend of the **Black Duck,** a rumrunner's boat that used to sneak into hidden coves.

But part of Maura had stayed behind on that seawall, where she'd been young and so had J.D., gazing at the bridge and knowing she wanted him to show her everything, everything.

5 ME AGAIN—BECK HERE.

You're wondering why I haven't gone home to Ohio yet. Well, so am I. My mother's trying hard. I don't want her to fall apart, and that's what might happen if I left. We don't have much money, but she took me and Travis out to dinner last night. He was missing Ally, and I . . . well, I'm back doing what I shouldn't. Fun fact: I'm a thief.

I tell myself to keep walking, stick my hands in my pockets, and it's as if they have minds of their own. They reach, grab, hide. Things disappear in this life, you know? Try not to let it happen to you, try really hard.

This school is a nightmare. Not only is it surrounded by the ocean, the main building has a pool on the fourth floor. That's what all the kids say, although no one is allowed to swim in it. From the girls' wing, you can smell faint chlorine. They're all whispering about it—it's just been filled again this year, after being empty forever. Some kids swear they've seen a man going up to swim—

the joke is that it's the ghost of James Desmond Blackstone. And the truth is, I saw him too—but he's no ghost. I'll tell you in a minute.

Lucy and I were studying in her dorm room two nights ago; we both like math—and working together. Surprise, surprise. Lucy wanted the window open, even though the evening had turned chilly, and I could hear waves rolling in and smashing the rocks on the shore. It started me hyperventilating. Lucy thought I was shivering because I was cold, so we went next door to Pell's room—she has a fireplace—and Pell had the dorm mother light the fire.

But that just made things worse, because I could hear water moving, the sound of someone swimming—upstairs, overhead. Can you imagine sleeping under a pool? All that water sloshing? What if the pipes burst, or the tiles cracked, and the ceiling caved in? You'd drown.

I kept looking up. Pell asked why. I said I didn't like the sound. Pell said she let the watery music lull her to sleep, thinking of the two sisters long ago who loved each other: Mary Langley and her sister, Beatrice, who came here to visit after Mary died.

That was a dagger in my heart, I won't lie to you. I pretended to be tired, and said good night in a friendly way. Inside, I was on fire. My father is dead, and Carrie, my Carrie. Lucy has Pell, this Mary apparently has Beatrice, but where is my sister?

I went downstairs. On the way out I headed for the security desk to ask Angus how dangerous it was. What if the weight of water really **did** crash through the ceiling? I wanted to know that Lucy, Pell, and the other girls would be safe. Angus is gruff, but I like him. He's an outcast too, but you can tell he cares about the school. I got to his desk, and this is so weird: the elevator doors were just closing behind him, and I swear I saw someone in a wheelchair in there.

"Who's that?" I asked.

"Who's what?" he asked. "I didn't see anyone."

"I saw someone in there. In a wheelchair."

"Haven't you heard about the ghost of James Desmond Blackstone?" he asked me, arching his eyebrows. "Everyone knows James Desmond loved a good swim."

"Ghosts don't swim," I said.

"Are you sure about that?" he asked. "You're new to Newport Academy—this is the cool school with the ghost pool."

"That's what I want to ask you about. What if the water damages the ceiling? Could it pour down into the dorm rooms?"

Angus shook his head. "Mary wouldn't allow it."

"You don't really believe that."

"Of course I do. Everyone knows about Mary. You'll hear the stories about Mary Langley and her pool the longer you stay."

"If I stay," I muttered, walking away.

A ghost's pool. Right. Mary Langley, whoever she was. She had a sister too. Beatrice. Lucky ghosts. Even they have each other.

Things to hold on to—that's what you need. Hold tight, stay safe . . . Because you never know what's going to be yanked away from you. I used to say that my sister was like having a permanent best friend. But then I found out nothing is permanent.

You have to hold on to your sister, hold on to your friends.

My friends are back home. Many wrote me off, hating me, calling me **klepto.** But the ones who stuck with me were loyal and true, and I felt so grateful that they still loved me. To think of life in Columbus going on without me is a little like imagining what will happen after you die: people can survive you being gone, and that is an ugly fact. It makes me want to grab what I can, what is here and now. Even china pineapples. And brass mice— I have one of those now too, from the display case in the library.

After dinner last night, Amy called to say Megan has taken my place both on the bus and in home-room. It's not even an alphabetical thing—like her name comes next in line and she'd naturally just slot into my spots. No—it was willful. Megan wanted to sit there, and she took the seats. Megan was one of the people who talked about me most, called me a thief to my face. What kills me most of all is that Amy and Ellie didn't kick her out.

Amy sounded mad, like "that bitch is trying to take over," especially on the bus. But the thing is, the seat Megan took is right next to Amy. And did Amy move or in any other way protest? No. And I asked, believe me. Is this how it goes? Megan's their new friend, they've embraced her as if she never talked badly about me, and here I am making new friends with Lucy and Camilla.

But that's nothing like missing Carrie. We were each other's other half. I don't really exist without her. You love a person, and you can't imagine life without them. But suddenly something happens, and they're gone, and you just keep breathing, eating, sleeping, waking up.

Her photographs are here, and she's not.

■

September's heat lingered into the first week of October, making the kids restless and yearning to be outside. Maura was impressed with their ability to concentrate and read, connect with the material she assigned them. She was teaching four English classes: Composition, English Lit, and for AP students, the Art of Fiction, and Russian Literature. Each required extensive writing on the part of the students.

Maura had bought blue notebooks for everyone,

passed them out the first day, and told her students to write about their lives, just as her favorite professor had done.

The Art of Fiction caught her every time. Fiction existed in life as well as literature: the ways people deceived themselves and those they loved most. Not always out of malice, but out of love and mysterious desperation. Maura understood that to her bones.

Every story she assigned, each time she read about a family and the way it worked, the way people wove fictions into their lives and relationships, the more haunted she felt about her own life.

People pretended. They fell in love inconveniently, tried to escape the consequences. They betrayed the ones they held most dear, struggled to hide the truth, hoping no one found out. They stole each other's loves, tried not to be caught, not to be punished. But what good were lies, when you had to live with them every day?

Carrie, more than anyone, had borne the weight of what Maura had and hadn't been able to admit to herself. It was as if Carrie had always known.

As a baby she'd gaze into Maura's face, as if trying to tell her it was all okay. And Maura had lied to herself, all through Carrie's growing up, that the truth didn't matter, wouldn't change anything. But it had mattered.

Overwhelmed with work, trying to find her

bearings, Maura had put off calling Katharine all through September. But teaching this class had only heightened her feelings, made them almost unbearable. She could lie to everyone else, even herself, but not her sister. She had never been able to: between her and Katharine, their emotions had all been right out in the open.

She had taken another late-night drive, north to Portsmouth, past Katharine's farm. She'd seen the big yellow house, the old barn where Katharine did her work, and the enormous metal sculptures roaming the hayfields, extinct beasts brought back to life.

Slowing down on the country road, she had almost stopped. The house lights were out—was Katharine home? Maura imagined her sister asleep. She could let herself in the rickety back door. That's how it used to be—Katharine had always expected Maura to walk in.

Today at lunch, Maura went to a corner of the teachers' dining room and dialed her sister's phone number. The machine answered: "You've reached Katharine. Leave me a message." And Maura did: "Hi, it's me. Maura. I'd . . . like to speak to you. Please call." She left the number of her cell phone, knowing Katharine already had it, as well as the number at the carriage house; she wondered what her sister would think about the 401 area code.

Something happens to sisters who've stopped

talking to each other for any stretch of time. Once it has happened—once the pattern has been set, and months and years go by, they get used to it. The unthinkable becomes thinkable. They imagine they can live without each other—because that's what they're doing. Even if they make up, get back together, at the first sign of strife, they might revert to not speaking.

The initial break is so wrong, such a crime against nature and love. They might tell themselves it's justified, that she did such-and-such, that she deserves so-and-so. Everyone knows that we're most hurt by the ones we love most. Drastic measures, turned backs, the buttoning of lips, the childish pronouncements—"I'll never speak to you again!"—might feel momentarily satisfying and righteous.

But it burns deep. And if it lasts long, watch out. For every day sisters don't talk to each other, a day is taken from the end of their lives. It's that destructive. Their lives are shorter, because their anguish and bitterness destroys them from the inside out. It eats away at their veins, weakens the walls of their hearts.

Maura felt all that, sitting at the cafeteria table. She reached up, placed her hand on her chest, needing to see if her heart was really beating. How had this happened? How could such a rift have formed between her and Katharine? She felt

trapped by the situation the two of them had created so recklessly. Something else: did it contribute
to Carrie staying away? Had she learned from her
mother and aunt how not to talk to her family?

When Maura looked up, she saw Amy Bramwell,
a biology teacher, standing by the table with her
brown bag.

"Are you finished with your call?" she asked. "I
don't want to disturb you if you're not . . ."

"Please," Maura said, clearing space on the table.

"Lunch hour's when I always catch up on the
million things I have to do," Amy said, unwrap-
ping her sandwich. Maura nodded; her pulse had
spiked at the sound of Katharine's voice, and it still
wasn't back to normal.

Stephen Campbell walked in with Ted Shannon.
Maura's gaze followed them as they headed across
the room. Was it her imagination, or was Stephen
watching her out of the corner of his eye?

"He was asking about you," Amy said.

"Who?"

"Stephen."

"Our paths keep crossing," Maura said. "At very
odd times."

"Really?" Amy asked.

Maura nodded. "We're both night owls, and for
a while I kept seeing him out by the cliff."

"He's a pensive sort," Amy said.

"What's his story?"

"Oh, he grew up in Newport and went here as a kid. He and Ted were in the same class," Amy said. "They were really good friends with Taylor Davis."

"Why does that name sound familiar?"

"He was Pell and Lucy Davis's father."

Maura nodded.

"Anyway, Taylor was a wonderful guy, from everything I've heard," Amy said. "He came from Michigan, went to the academy, met the daughter of a socialite—in fact, the über-socialite, Edie Nicholson—and never quite fit into Newport life. He played football at Brown, and saw Lyra when she was home from Vassar. When he went back to Michigan, he took Lyra with him."

"I did that," Maura said. "Moved from the East Coast to the Midwest . . ."

"Yes, but you weren't debutante of the year, with all that goes with it. Lyra didn't take to the move," Amy said. "She married Taylor, had two daughters before she realized she wasn't cut out for that life. She left him with the kids, came back east, wound up moving to Italy, I think."

"But the girls board here?"

"Yes," Amy said. "They have to. Taylor died a few years ago."

"How awful," Maura said. "Do they ever see their mother?"

"No," Amy said. "And they don't talk about her."

"That's so sad," Maura said, thinking of her own

distant, missing daughter. Did Carrie ever talk about her? Of course, it was the opposite situation. . . . Carrie had left.

"Pell and Lucy live with their grandmother part-time, but that's a fate you wouldn't wish on anyone," Amy continued. "Ted and Stephen do their best to watch out for the Davis sisters."

"Is that why you say Stephen's pensive?"

"Not really. He's conscientious, smart, and he used to be incredibly funny. But he went through a nasty divorce himself, and he hasn't been the same since."

"I'm sorry to hear that," Maura said, glancing across the room at the two men. "Was his wife someone from Newport?"

"Well, she was. Now she's living up the bay. In Bristol, I think."

"But he met her here?"

"Yes," Amy said. "This is such a small town, when you get right down to it. His ex-wife is Patricia Blackstone—great-granddaughter of James Desmond Blackstone. . . ."

"The founder of Newport Academy," Maura said. Stephen had been married to J.D.'s sister. Excusing herself, she left the lunchroom.

6 THE GENIE WAS OUT OF THE bottle, and Beck couldn't get it back in.

Every chance she got, she put something else in her pocket. The school seemed not to believe in locking things up; they made it too easy for her. Silverware from the lunchroom, cello strings and violin rosin from the conservatory.

She stole an emerald earring.

The most expensive object she'd ever taken, almost too beautiful for words. It was delicate, it was old, it dangled. Holding it in her hand, she thought of the emerald as solid water, but not cold like ice. A square green pool. Water that had turned to stone.

They had been in Lucy's room, sprawled on the big blue and amber Oriental rug. She and Lucy were challenging each other, doing proofs for Mr. Campbell's class, making patterns of shapes, of motion and change, geometric diagrams that contained meanings and poetry that only mathematicians could understand.

"Hey," Beck said, pointing at the page. "Check

this out. . . ." She tapped her pencil on the notation $f(x)g'(x) + g(x)f'(x)$.

"Stephen will love that one!"

"Why do you call him Stephen?"

Lucy's pencil made quick and spidery notations that reminded Beck of magic spells. "He was one of my father's closest friends," Lucy said as she worked. "They went to this school together, along with Mr. Shannon and their other best friend, J. D. Blackstone. After my father died, Stephen and the others became our protectors."

"Protectors?"

"Like godfathers. They help us with things our grandmother can't."

Beck put down her pencil. "How did your father die?"

"He had a brain tumor," Lucy said. "One day he looked at Pell and called her 'seahorse.' He tucked me in with a blanket and said 'starfish.' He fell down and shook. We thought he was trying to be funny, so we stood there doubled over laughing."

"He wasn't?"

"He was having a seizure."

"Where was your mother?"

"She'd left," Lucy said. "She was long gone. So we stared at our dad shaking, thinking it wasn't really very funny and wishing he'd get up, and then we saw blood from where he'd bitten through his tongue. So we called 911, and they took him to the hospital. He died less than a year later."

"I'm sorry," Beck said.

Lucy glanced over. "How did your father die?"

"He drowned," Beck said. "He was in a canoe with my sister, and they capsized."

"I'm sorry. Your sister . . ."

"She survived," Beck said. "But she ran away."

"Why?"

"We don't know, exactly."

"Oh my God," Lucy said. "I'm so sorry."

Beck thanked her. Lucy asked a million questions, and Beck didn't even mind. Was Carrie unhappy? Did she have a boyfriend? Did she take drugs? No, she used to, and no. Beck loved having a friend who got it. Both girls had families whose hearts had been ripped out.

"Where did our fathers go?" Beck heard herself ask.

"After they died, you mean?"

Beck nodded.

Lucy looked up at the ceiling as if she could see through it, straight to the pool. "They become ghosts," she said.

Beck stared at her.

"Well, not ghosts like in scary movies, but spirits who are right here, who haven't left this earth. Their energy remains, and if they want to materialize, they do. But they can't unless we meet them partway." She sat up and looked at Beck, waiting for her to help.

Beck blinked hard, the thoughts clicking into place. She forced herself to stay with it, concentrate. Just like someone trying to remember a dream, pulling the strange nonsense together and making it add up. "Wow," Beck said, starting to get it.

"Do you think?" Lucy asked, eyes shining.

"It could be," Beck said, her voice shaking as she reached for her paper. She'd heard the phrase so many times before, but suddenly it made real sense. Not just theory, but something she could count on. " 'Ghosts of departed quantities,' " she whispered.

"Adding up the infinitesimal," Lucy said.

Beck hesitated, staring at the paper, then looked up. "The mathematics of change and loss," she said.

"Because . . ."

"There's no such number as zero," Beck said.

"Exactly!"

"So if we do proofs, work at proving infinity . . ."

"We'll understand where they went. What they are now . . . your dad and my dad. Our ghosts."

"Easier to find ghosts than my sister," Beck said.

Floorboards creaked overhead, then a splash, making Beck jump.

"You must hate hearing that," Beck said.

"I love the sound of water. J.D. swims there. But so does Mary," Lucy said.

"She's real."

Lucy nodded. "And if Mary can walk the earth, so can my father. I'll see him again. You'll see your father too. We can do it together! Work on proofs, add up infinitely tiny pieces, so tiny they're almost not there, and find our way to them."

"Yes," Beck said, but her heart skipped at the idea of what Lucy was saying, what they'd thought up together. Could it be possible?

"We're going to do it," Lucy said, her voice shaking as she clutched Beck's hand, making a pact. "We'll see our fathers again!"

Beck gazed at Lucy's open book and fine notations. She felt weak and light, about to faint. Just then Pell walked in. She lived in the room next door; had she heard her sister's voice rising? Lucy's eyes glistened, and Pell sat down and put her arms around her. Beck knew Lucy had her own problems: Grief kept her awake. She had a hard time sleeping.

Beck watched Pell murmur to Lucy, remembered all the times Carrie had comforted her when she was upset. She ached for her sister. The prospect of being able to see her father again, even for a minute, was too much to bear. She began to gather her books.

The Davis sisters seemed not to notice. Backing away, Beck stood by the mahogany dresser. Lucy's silver brush and comb, an oval hand mirror, a hand-tooled Moroccan leather jewelry case, and several tortoiseshell barrettes lay strewn across the surface. Then Beck spied the emerald earrings.

Cool green jewels. She was like a raven, attracted by the brightness. She didn't think, only reacted. Carrie in the water. Bright lake water sparkling, a million shattered emeralds, that summer day after the storm passed. Carrie's gold-flecked blue eyes. Beck's hand closed around one of the earrings. She glanced over at the sisters, saw Pell staring right at her.

Pell watched her slide the earring into her pocket and walk out of the room. In the hallway, through the open window, Beck heard the endless ocean waves curling, collapsing, hitting the rocky shore.

She ran down the hallways and stairs of the old school and dashed outside, just as Redmond was walking toward the entrance.

"Beck," he said, smiling.

But she tore past him, around the side of the building, into the laurel grove, the woodland path that muffled the sounds of the sea, straight to the little house where she knew she'd find her mother and Travis.

■

Travis saw Beck come charging in, past their mother working on lesson plans in the kitchen, straight into her room. He'd been getting a bad feeling from his sister lately—some of the old secrecy and furtiveness that had gotten her in trouble back home—so he walked in right behind her, just in time to see her pull an earring out of her pocket.

"What's that?" he asked, shocked in spite of the fact he'd been expecting something like this. The old force of her stealing and getting caught back home came crashing in.

"Leave me alone," she said.

"Give it to me," he said, reaching for the earring. She hid it behind her back.

"I found it," Beck said.

"Who'd you take it from?"

"Take it from?" Beck asked, outraged. "No one! Stop accusing me!"

Travis opened his mouth, found he couldn't speak. Didn't Beck know that she was the reason they'd moved east? Hadn't she learned her lesson? But staring into her hot, guilty eyes, he could see that she had not.

"You're lying," he said. "Again."

"Shut up."

"And stealing. When did you start back up?"

"You don't know what you're talking about."

"Stealing doesn't help. You know that," he said. "It's not going to bring them back."

"Stop," she said.

"Look," he said. "I'm not going to tell Mom. Just

tell me where you got it, and we'll leave her out of it. Okay? Do you really want to hurt Mom this way? I know you don't. So just come clean with me and it stops here with us. Try again: where'd you get the earring?"

Beck struggled with herself. Travis focused on staying calm. He stared at her hard, not letting her off the hook.

"I found it," Beck said finally, her lower lip wobbling. She was starting to break.

"Where?"

"On . . . in Lucy's room."

"Fine," Travis said, taking the earring from her. He looked at it, the deep green jewel set in fine gold. A row of tiny diamonds dangled from beneath the large square emerald. "Beck. This isn't like a pack of gum from Jenny Drew's backpack. What's going on?"

"Nothing," she said. "I swear, it won't happen again."

"Where have I heard that before?" he asked.

He slipped out the front door. The October night was brisk, and when he started to jog, he saw his breath. Ally would be coming to Newport this weekend. He wanted to have a great game for her, push away the doubts he'd been having about their relationship. But right now he felt weighted down, as if his sneakers were filled with water.

Halfway across the grounds, between his family's

cottage and the main building, he tried to figure
out what he'd say to Lucy. How could he even get
into the girls' wing of the dorm? Maybe he could
just wrap the earring up in notepaper, leave it by
the dorm master's door asking that it be returned.
Just then, he saw Angus patrolling the cliff path
on his cart. Ducking behind some rhododendron
bushes, Travis saw a shadow. Right there—through
the glossy green leaves. He jumped, scared out of
his wits. Someone else was hiding in the same bush.

"This is very strange," a voice said. "I was just on
my way to your house . . ."

"Pell?" he asked.

"Yeah . . ."

He inched left, branches and leaves rattling,
to get closer to her. When they were side-by-side,
he saw her wide blue eyes glowing, a big smile on
her face.

"What were you coming over for?" he asked.

"It's a delicate matter," she said.

"This?" he asked, reaching into his pocket, holding up the earring.

"So you know?" Pell asked.

"Yes," he said. "How do **you** know?"

"I saw her do it," Pell said. "And she saw me see.
It was almost as if she was sleepwalking. And I
know sleepwalkers—my sister does it. It was as if
Beck couldn't help herself."

"That's what the shrink said," Travis said.

"The shrink?"

So Travis told her. Their mother had taken them to family therapy, and Dr. Mallory had explained that the trauma of being onshore while their father drowned, the inability to stop Carrie running away, had caused such despair in Beck, made her feel so helpless, that she was afraid of losing everything. She started stealing to make herself feel safe, surround herself with "things" because she'd lost what really mattered to her.

Pell listened intently. Once Angus was out of sight, Travis and Pell began to walk. Travis poured out the story. Why was it so easy? Most of his friends hadn't heard a fraction of the details; it was private, and they wouldn't understand. Even Ally had judged Beck. But Pell, who'd actually witnessed her stealing, just walked silently beside him, her arm touching his, listening to the whole thing.

"She stopped, we thought," Travis said. "Back in Columbus, before we left. She got caught. Not just once, but a few times. Taking stuff from a mall, books from school, but also things from her friends' houses. People started turning against her. After she lost one of her best friends, she seemed to get it. And stop . . . or so we thought."

"She steals from her friends?" Pell asked. But the question didn't seem sharp, or accusatory. Travis could tell she cared.

"Yeah," he said. "That's the worst part. She sees

people who have what she wants, and they're the ones she takes from."

"What could she want from Lucy?" Pell murmured as they walked. And her voice sounded so sad, so full of despair, Travis stopped. He gazed down at her, into her thoughtful blue eyes. "Our father died too," she went on. "And our mother is thousands of miles away, wants nothing to do with us. Our grandmother . . . she tries, but she didn't sign on to raise us. Even when my mother was young, she had a full-time nanny. So Lucy and I are here, on our own. . . . Lucy's fragile; she can't sleep. What would Beck see in that?"

"Lucy has you," Travis said. "Her sister."

"What about Carrie?"

"That's the question we all ask. We don't know. She came ashore after the canoe accident—my mother rode with her in the ambulance to the hospital, to get checked out. My mother was filling out papers in the emergency room, and Carrie ran away."

"I'm so sorry," Pell said. "I can only imagine how it is for Beck, worrying and wondering."

"Yeah," Travis said. "They were practically joined at the hip, even though Carrie was older. They talked to each other in a way I couldn't even understand. Only they could."

"Sister language," Pell said.

"You have it with Lucy?"

"All sisters do."

Pell's face was tilted up, her eyes gazing up at him. Travis felt a jolt go through his body; he had to hold himself back from kissing her. The sea air surrounded them, damp and cool. Fog had rolled in, thick as a gray blanket. No one could see. He felt as if they'd gone to their own private world. Bending close, he wanted to put his arms around her, pull her tight.

"What about you?" she whispered.

"Me?"

"Beck lost your father and Carrie, but so did you. Do you steal too?"

He shook his head. Her eyes were glistening— tears or something else? He felt heat pouring off her skin. He couldn't hold back, told her everything. She was right; after the drowning, Travis had had some problems. He stopped talking, or almost. He barely had anything to say to his mother or Beck; all he'd wanted to do was practice and play football, pound the hell out of his body. He'd run around the track at school, tell his father how sorry he was. Talking to a person who wasn't there; luckily no one ever saw him.

"I was standing right there by the lake. If I'd swum out, I might have been able to save him," he said now, to Pell.

"Or you might have drowned too," she said, making it sound as if that would have been the biggest tragedy in the world; he held back from telling her there were times he wanted that, to have died not with, but instead of, his father. Suddenly they were holding hands. He wasn't sure who reached first, but there he was on the cliff in the fog, holding hands with Pell Davis.

"Beck never gives up on Carrie coming back," he said.

"Lucy thinks if she excels at math, studies proofs that deal with infinity, she'll be able to go into the world of the abstract . . . time travel or something, visit the afterlife and find my father's ghost."

"Wow," Travis said, not just because Pell might have been describing Beck, but because the pressure of her fingers felt so good against his. He never wanted to let go. They listened to waves smashing down below; the mist was too thick to see the white surf break. The night itself seemed full of ghosts. He looked at her, wanting again to kiss her, and suddenly remembered Ally. He pulled away.

"Thanks for returning the earring," Pell said. "I'll get it back to Lucy before she notices."

"You mean you'll keep this between us?"

"Of course," Pell said.

"Thanks," Travis said, backing away. He had to turn fast, start running. The huge mansion glowed in the fog, lights shining in all the students' rooms. His hand burned from where he'd held Pell's. The warmth spread from his skin into his bones, to the mended knuckles from where he'd punched out his grief and rage. His hand throbbed, old pain coming back. He ran home, feeling Pell with him.

◼

Okay, I know I'm bad. Terrible, actually. If you think I'm kidding, or trying to get you to say I'm not so awful, you don't know me at all. What I'd rather have you say is: **Beck, now you're stealing jewels? Real emeralds? Nice going, you loser.**

I'm not one to blame my troubles on **oh what a hard life it is,** even though it is. I do these things on my own. But this feeling is driving me crazy right now, and I can't stand it. I can't take being so mad.

The time has come for me to tell you what happened to my sister.

It starts with this: we used to be the happy family everyone wants to be. We were one sweet year-round Christmas card picture, all five of us beaming into the camera. Dad coached baseball at Savage High, Mom stayed home with the kids, Carrie got straight A's and had artistic talent, Travis got awards for being an excellent student-athlete at James Thurber High, and I made honor roll at Putnam Middle School four semesters in a row.

Until that August day last year, just about the only bad thing ever to happen to us was two years ago: Carrie got into a car accident. Justin, her boyfriend, was driving, and they went to play mini-golf, and got broadsided by an old man who went through a stop sign, and Carrie got cuts on her face and head, as well as internal injuries. She had to have her spleen removed. Thurber High School had a candlelight vigil for her. She could have died. Justin walked away with a few scratches.

Carrie started taking lots of photographs after that. She began by taking pictures of the nurses. Then her hospital roommate, a girl who'd been hit by a car. The girl had lost her leg but dreamed she still had it. That got to Carrie, her roommate's phantom leg. I won't even go into the fact that now I feel as if I have a phantom sister.

Anyway, when Carrie got home, she started taking pictures of me, self-portraits of herself, shots of Mom. Girl power.

Soon after Carrie's accident they started fighting. Mom and Dad. They'd do it behind closed doors, like we weren't supposed to know or hear the arguments. But parents don't realize, and if you're a parent, take my word, any time kids hear a stressed-out whisper, their stomachs clench and they know it can't be good.

Carrie used to write to Aunt Katharine, who is definitely the black sheep in our family. Just because my mother and she had a "falling-out" didn't mean Carrie couldn't be in touch. She's an artist and an ironworker, Aunt Katharine, and my father seemed worried that Carrie wanted to be an artist herself. A photographer. My father said she'd never make any money doing that, never be "secure." He was a loving, supportive father, but he believed in doing things a certain way.

"There's a right way and a wrong way to do everything," he used to say. He taught us the right ways. To hammer a nail, to rake leaves, to swing a tennis racket, to throw a football. He liked life to be a straight road: right through the center of town, because everything you needed was right there.

Mom likes side roads, the scenic way. She meanders. If life was a Saturday, Dad would spend it fixing up the house. Mom would go antiquing, getting lost in dusty shops and finding strange, wonderful things. Think about it: could there be a better couple? They complemented each other.

Our mother's classes were all at night, so Dad would sometimes drive her to the university and wait for her to be done. Sometimes I'd go with them. I heard them argue about Aunt Katharine. After the car accident, Mom sent some of Carrie's pictures to my aunt, and she wrote inviting Carrie to visit for a week. Carrie was begging to go. I've already told you that Aunt Katharine was an artist renegade type. Also, there'd been the big breach in the family, a tear in the relationship between her and Mom before I was born.

That bothered me—more than you can imagine, because even though they were in touch sometimes, like distant relatives, my mother and her sister didn't really speak. What could possibly have been so bad to cause that? I'd look at Carrie and try, in my wildest wonderings, to imagine what could make me spend my life without her two seconds away. I tried hating Aunt Katharine. Because I could only dream that it was her fault. But I couldn't despise my aunt. I could only feel sad for her, as I did for my mother. Carrie did too. Now I wonder if Carrie didn't learn from the best—how not to speak to her family. Estrangements R Us.

Anyway, in the car that day, Dad blew up: "It all comes down to Newport, I always knew that, and now I'm supposed to agree to send Carrie there?" And Mom whispered, "Stop now. It doesn't matter anymore; it never did. I love you, Andy. . . ." And Dad just kept shaking his head as he drove along saying, "Of course it matters. No wonder you kept her out of our family all this time. She knew."

"Sshh . . ." Mom said, with a tilt of her head toward me. My thoughts were on fire. What **had** caused the distance between her and her sister? What came down to Newport, and what did Aunt Katharine know? I'd always heard of family secrets; I just never knew we had any.

"Hey, how come Aunt Katharine wants you to

visit her in Rhode Island and not me?" I asked Carrie, just before we went to Mackinac Island.

"She wants you too," Carrie said. "But I'm older, so I'd go first."

"Why haven't we ever met her?" I asked.

"I wish I knew, Beck. But I've gotten to know her through her letters," Carrie said. "She's . . . different, that's for sure. But she likes my pictures, and tells me to express myself. . . ."

I couldn't exactly complain about their correspondence—Carrie wanted to be an artist, a photographer, so it was only right she'd get more attention from our sculpting aunt. But still, I felt a little left out. Newport had sounded cool. I will confess that right now. But it sounded a little like Oz—over a rainbow we weren't meant to cross.

Carrie pointed out that Newport was full of kids from the rich side of town, whose parents belonged to the yacht club and wore cashmere sweaters and drove fancy cars, not people like us, whose dad coached baseball and wore sweatshirts and drove an old station wagon. That weekend before we went on vacation she'd started sounding reluctant, said maybe it would be disloyal to our dad if she insisted on going. So she didn't.

I kept wondering what had changed with our father. Did you know that kids feel happy, as if nothing could ever be wrong, when their parents love each other? My father would bring my mother coffee in bed every morning. He'd come home with her favorite ice cream. Every Mother's Day he'd buy her another lilac bush, plant it along the fence. We had the most beautiful lilacs in Ohio.

One summer night when I was six, the windows were open, and I heard laughing in the backyard. I pushed the white curtain aside and looked out. There, under the moon, my parents were dancing. Barefoot in the grass, my mom standing on my dad's toes, twirling around in the silvery darkness. Her arms were around his neck, and holding on, she arched her back to look up at the moon. She smiled, and for a second I thought she'd seen me.

But then I realized she was looking up at my father. She balanced there a long minute, and then he leaned over to kiss her. It was the kind of kiss kids weren't supposed to watch, and even though I prided myself on spying, I ducked down and tiptoed away from the window. I drifted off to sleep to the sound of my parents laughing and singing softly, and knew I was the happiest kid in the world.

That changed after Carrie's accident. No more laughing, no more singing, no more dancing under the moon. No more lilac bushes.

So. The day it happened. Last summer, a year and two months ago, we'd gone to Mackinac Island, this beautiful paradise way up north in Lake

Michigan. The sun was bright, hitting the lake as if it were a mirror. We rented the same cabin as far back as I can remember. This was our summer place. There was one canoe. We had to take turns. Travis took me out first, early our second morning there.

The air was heavy, muggy with August heat. The sky was soft blue, veiled by haze. Easterners obviously think the ocean is the only thing, but they should see the Great Lakes. They are magnificent, endless, too wide to see the far shore. But there were little islands nearby. Sweet little islands that we sometimes saw deer swimming to. And the magic lighthouse.

That's what Carrie called it.

It had appeared the year before that last vacation. After all our summers on Mackinac Island, years of looking out at the tiny islands, suddenly one had a lighthouse on it. It had grown just like a tree in a fairy tale—tall, powerful, graceful—sprung from the island soil during the spring, after the dark winter months. I remember driving down the dirt road, hearing Carrie gasp with joy.

"A lighthouse!" she said. "Where did it come from?"

"The state must have built it," my father said. "Or the Coast Guard."

"It's so beautiful," my mother said, sounding stunned.

"Maybe it's magic," Carrie said. "And only we can see it. It's a lighthouse just for us."

Our last two summers there, we watched the lighthouse at night. The beam would sweep twice, then go dark, then flash twice again. The light traced the bare wood ceiling in the room Carrie and I shared, bisecting all the angles. I'd look over at her, see her waiting for the beam to come again, a soft smile on her face as if someone was looking over us. We always wanted to paddle out to it, but our parents said it was too far for us to go alone, and we only had the one canoe.

So Travis and I hugged the banks, paddling west. I kept looking at the magic lighthouse, wondering how far away it was, imagining that **this** year Carrie and I would go out there. She was sixteen, old enough to take me on our own. My brother and I could smell the bacon frying on shore, Mom cooking breakfast for everyone. But paddling along, Travis and I got distracted by this cool thing: a stream heading into the woods just around the bend, a beaver dam across the stream, and a big fallen tree that made a bridge we could walk on.

We missed breakfast.

We beached the canoe around that bend, crossed the tree bridge, watched the beavers nibble logs into pencil points. It was so cool, we just couldn't stop watching. Finally, when we got home, we ran to tell everyone what we'd seen.

But something was wrong. Carrie was quiet, and our parents weren't speaking. The bacon and eggs were just sitting there on the picnic table, flies landing, as gross as you can imagine. Mom and Dad fighting had gotten to be kind of common, and each time it felt like a knife in my heart.

What bothered me most this time was Carrie. She looked pale. She was clutching her stomach, as if she'd eaten something that was making her sick. And tears were rolling down her cheeks—not in a sobbing, gulping way, but in a scary, silent way. I almost cried just to see her face.

"What's wrong?" I asked, scared.

"They fight because of me," she said. "I just figured it out."

"No way," I said.

"Yes," she said, gesturing toward the cabin. "Dad looks as if he can't stand me."

"He loves you. And they **don't** fight because of you," I insisted, positive. Kids always think it's their fault when parents argue. And maybe it sometimes is—if you fail a test, or punch your brother, or stuff your face with the last piece of chocolate cake. But Carrie was perfect. That was the truth, and we all knew it and loved her for it. "It's not because of you. You're the most wonderful girl in the world, and they know it. We all do."

"What if I'm not?" she asked.

The question sort of shocked me. It was like

being asked "What if two wasn't a prime number?" She looked so disturbed, for a minute I thought she was going to throw up.

I stood beside her, waited to see if she was okay. I wanted to put my hand on the back of her head, the way our mother always did when we got sick, and I wanted her to reassure me, tell me she was exaggerating everything. She gave me a look, letting me know she was all right.

"Come on, Beck. Let's go out on the lake," she said.

"In the canoe? Do you feel well enough?"

"Yes. Let's go to the lighthouse!"

We ran down to the lake's bank, grabbed the canoe from under the bushes, and started to push it out. Overhead the sky was gauzy blue, covering us like a summer-weight blanket.

Our father walked over. He passed me as if I weren't there.

"Carrie?" he said.

Instantly tears filled her eyes.

"Sweetheart, let's go out on the lake," he said. Then, looking at me, he smiled, gave me a big hug. "Be a sport, Beck? Let me take your sister for a spin in the canoe?"

I shrugged, disappointed.

"Carrie, okay?" he asked.

She nodded, a little hesitantly. Why would she

be reluctant about going in the canoe with our father?

"I love you, honey," he said to her, as if he'd never meant anything more. He said that to all of us, all the time. But something in his voice and eyes, and the way he said it right then, and in the way Carrie whispered back to him "I heard you fighting," scared me.

Sitting on the bank, I watched them paddle out. And I watched until they were just tiny specks getting smaller and smaller. They headed toward the lighthouse. Then the air grew still, and I heard low rumbling in the west. And I heard their voices rising, my father's and Carrie's—were they arguing? No, they never fought; that was thunder, it had to be. I couldn't let myself think otherwise, but now, honestly, I doubt myself. Still, clouds came in all of a sudden. The lighthouse was gone. It disappeared, and so did they.

Mom and Travis called me to the cabin, made me take shelter. We stood by the window, the three of us, waiting. I was stiff, frozen. I wanted to ask my mother if she'd heard them, had that been them yelling?

The storm blew up so fast—driving rain, leaves flipping over so their silvery undersides showed. A flock of geese flew in a V, right out of the clouds from the far side of the lake, over the water, landed right in front of us, and the waves were so big, the birds were hidden by their crests. The sky turned muddy, a terrible brown. The wind roared, blowing rain sideways.

Suddenly the rain tapered off; the wind died down, and as the last breeze pushed the clouds away, the sky turned bright blue. Now it was the clearest day you've ever seen. No yelling, no fighting, no voices drifting across the water. The only sounds were rain dripping from the leaves, birds singing in the trees, the gentle lap, lap, lap of small rippling lake waves.

We waited for them to come back, but they didn't. Cops came by in a patrol boat, to make sure we were okay, and my mother told them about my father and Carrie. They went straight out.

They found the canoe floating overturned, in the middle of the lake, on the other side of the island from where the lighthouse stood, out of sight from where we were waiting and watching. Carrie had made it to the island, crawled up toward the lighthouse, half-frozen, in such shock she couldn't talk. My father wasn't with her.

Things happened fast after that. They wrapped Carrie in blankets, radioed for the ambulance. My mother went nuts. She was crying for my father, all over Carrie the minute she hit dry land, hugging her, asking her about Dad, trying to figure out what happened. Carrie couldn't speak. The ambulance guy said she was in shock, and my mother climbed in to take her to the hospital. Carrie's skin was blue. I'm not even kidding.

My father's body was recovered later that day, over by the beaver dam that Travis and I had found. His T-shirt got snagged on the fallen-tree bridge my brother and I had crossed. That's where the searchers found him. Travis and I stood on shore, watching them bring him back. We stayed, to be there when they brought him onto land. We did that for him.

We thought Carrie was being cared for at the hospital. It gave us some comfort, thinking that she would be okay. We would all be together later that night, mourning Dad. Carrie could tell us what happened. We could know his last moments, help Carrie deal with it. That's how our family did things.

Carrie ran away. My mother saw them take her into an exam room, right there in the ER. How much safer can you get than an ER? My mother was showing the receptionist her insurance card, looking at paperwork, trying to get someone to call the cops and find out what was going on at the lake, and in those ten minutes, Carrie disappeared. Off the gurney, back into her wet clothes, out the door.

No one knows why. Of course I have my theories.

One, the most obvious, is that she was pregnant. All that holding her stomach, feeling sick, crying. Justin, that loser, had gotten her pregnant. And Carrie, our perfect girl (and what an idiot I feel like for actually saying it to her, that very day) couldn't take the shame.

Still, that doesn't completely ring true to me. Because how bad, in this day and age, is getting pregnant, even at sixteen? I'm not saying everyone does it, but it's not exactly unheard of. My mother would have been fine about it. And I know Travis and I would have too. So it must be something else.

That's why it's wrong to be here in Newport. Because once Carrie is on her own with her baby for a while, and gets tired of hiding, how will she find us? I know my mother left all these messages, and has the detective guy looking, but why hasn't any of it worked yet? I left a note at home. Not in the house, because the new owners would be there, and Carrie wouldn't be welcome. But out back, in the potting shed behind the garage, where we used to play. That was our place, and we'd put big flower-pots upside down and use them for seats.

I left Carrie a note there, under one of the flowerpots. She'd look, if ever she returned to our house in Columbus. And she will, I know.

We are sisters forever. Nothing can ever take that away. It's what we are, as certain as any prime number. We are each other's blood, we are each other's life.

Carrie is coming back to me. She has to.

■

Maura noticed the tension between Travis and Beck, and she instantly knew: Beck was stealing again. She felt it in the way Travis watched her, with cool, worried eyes. And she saw it now in Beck's defensiveness, the way her shoulders hunched up to her ears, the scowl on her face as she bent over her schoolbook at the kitchen table.

"Hi, honey," she said, coming in one afternoon after classes.

"Hi," Beck said without looking up.

"Is everything okay?"

"Fine," Beck said.

"Where's your brother?"

"I don't know. Football practice."

Good. Maura sat down across from Beck. Travis was attentive and involved, but Maura didn't want to bring this up in front of him.

"Is there anything you want to talk about?"

"Mom, I'm studying."

"I know. But stop for a minute, okay?"

Beck lowered her pencil. She took her time looking up, the tops of her ears fiery red.

"Have you been having trouble?" Maura asked.

Beck shook her head. Then she twirled her hair. Then she bit her lip.

"I think it's time to call Dr. Mallory. She said you could have phone sessions if you want. Or she'd refer us to a therapist here in Newport."

"No!" Beck said. "I'm doing fine here, making friends. I don't want anyone to know about me!"

"No one will know."

"They found out back home. 'She's crazy, she steals, she goes to a shrink.' They'll see me going to the office, those little one-hour disappearing acts I made all last year, and everyone wondered where I was, and then they found out, and it's not like I had something other kids have, like ADD or ADHD or whatever. It's bad enough being how I am, but I don't want to be known for it, and teased for it."

"I love how you are," Maura said.

"You love that I steal?"

"Are you doing that again?" Maura asked.

Beck's eyes flooded. "Behaviors," they were called: stealing, lying, acting out. They stemmed from grief, depression, stubborn anger. Maura reached for her hand, and Beck grabbed it. They sat there together, not speaking.

Maura imagined a wise mother. Someone who would cock her head, smile sadly, say **I want to be able to trust you again; you have to earn people's trust.** Outside, the breeze blew, and golden leaves floated from the trees down to the ground. The wise mother would gesture, say something about seasons changing, the passage of time. **We don't steal. People die, people run away, but still we don't steal.**

"It sucks," Beck said.

"It does," Maura said.

They kept holding hands, even though there wasn't anything more to say.

■

Providence was made up of worlds. College Hill, home of Brown University and the Rhode Island School of Design, campuses and gracious old houses; Federal Hill, the heart of Rhode Island's Little Italy; Fox Point, where the Portuguese fishermen lived.

Carrie lived on Fox Point, in a pink rooming house filled with Azoreans and Cape Verdeans. She'd moved there from Hawthorne House, a haven for girls like her. She had come east over a year ago, traveled far away from her family in Ohio; in a strange way, she'd traveled to Rhode Island to get closer to them.

Sometimes she thought of things she could have done differently. She could have swum stronger, tried harder to stay with her father. She could have lied when he'd asked her about being pregnant, avoided the fight. Or she could have not gotten pregnant in the first place. She'd loved Justin, but getting pregnant was an accident. And somehow she hadn't realized how that fact would destroy her family.

She loved Gracie, more than anything. She was overwhelmed with huge questions—if she hadn't gotten pregnant, hadn't had that fight with her father, maybe he would still be alive. But then she wouldn't have Gracie, right? Was everything in this world so confusing?

The storm had killed her father. Sometimes she wished she had died too. But if she had, Gracie would have as well. Carrie worked all day at the diner, sometimes the dinner shift, counting the minutes before she could get home to her daughter. But the hard, mindless work gave her plenty of time to miss her mother, sister, and brother. Her only comfort came from knowing they had no idea of what had happened between her and her father out on the water.

Her family was in Newport now. Carrie kept track. She'd called home in Columbus a few times over the last year, hung up when her mother answered. The sound of her mother's voice was like a dream from another world. Carrie both wanted it so badly and felt so ashamed to imagine the words she'd have to say, she'd hung up fast, as if the receiver burned her fingers. Then one day in August she called, and got a recording with a new phone number.

A Rhode Island number. Carrie could hardly believe it. She went to the Providence Public Library, used the Internet for reverse look-up. The phone number had a Newport exchange. She Googled everyone's names, found out that Travis would be playing football for Newport Academy. Carrie hardly knew what to think about that: her mother relocating the family near Aunt Katharine and also near J.D. Carrie had been pulled by the same gravity.

Death changed everything. Every single thing. Carrie was young to know that fact, but she did. Her father had died, and her family had fallen apart. She wiped tables, served coffee, felt as if she was in a nightmare.

She had made her way to Providence after the accident. She had had Gracie, and then Dell had helped her get this job at the diner closest to Rhode Island Hospital. J.D. was being treated there.

His sister Patricia had come into the diner one day when she was working. Carrie had seen her around J.D.'s room, so she kept her coffee cup filled and listened to what she and her friend were saying. She learned more in that single hour than she had haunting the waiting rooms, trying to befriend J.D.'s nurses, even sneaking into his room, standing at the foot of his bed.

For one thing, she found out that medically induced comas were not as dangerous as she might have thought. She learned that dreams went on, deeply and darkly, just as they did during sleep.

She had found out on her own that his doctor at Rhode Island Hospital was a renowned leader in research and healing in traumatic spinal cord injuries. He had isolated a protein that encouraged cells to "communicate" with each other, trying to heal. That's what J.D. was there for.

When it came time to pay the check, the friend tried to grab it, but Patricia pulled out her credit card and beat her to it. The friend argued, saying, "I want to treat you." But Patricia held tight to the check. Taking the credit card, Carrie ran it. When she returned to the table, she met Patricia's eyes.

"Do you have someone in the hospital?" Carrie asked.

"My brother," Patricia said.

"I hope he's okay."

"That's very kind of you," Patricia said, warmth filling her eyes. She had dark hair with a gray streak, wore a navy blue suit and tall boots of soft black leather. A few minutes later, she went to the restroom, and Carrie spoke to her friend.

"Will her brother get better?" she asked.

"He had a bad injury," the friend said.

"What happened?"

"He was paralyzed in a fall a long time ago. They're trying some new things," she said.

"Is it . . . helping at all?"

"It doesn't seem so."

"I'm sorry."

The friend nodded. Then she smiled a little. "Being so close to the hospital, you must serve lots of people who need comfort."

"Yes," she said. "Everyone does."

And then Patricia returned and the two women left.

That was six months ago. Carrie still worked at the diner. J.D. had long been discharged, but Carrie often thought of that lunch, of serving Patricia Blackstone. And for some reason the phrase she had used floated back to her now.

Everyone does.

Everyone needs comfort.

Carrie knew she did. Why was she still here? J.D. had gone back to Newport. She had done her best, looked over him the best she could, did for him what she couldn't for her father. She would **never** stop thinking of Andy Shaw as her father. Now she sat in the rocking chair of her small room, holding Gracie. These quiet times were when she missed her mother the most.

What if Carrie took the bus to Newport? She could show up at Travis's game on Saturday. Her family would be so shocked. And happy, right? To meet Gracie? Wouldn't her family be thrilled to know Carrie had a daughter, that they'd come home?

But how could Carrie explain why she'd left in the first place? Why her only option, pregnant and in shock after seeing her father die, had been to leave her mother waiting in the ER? Blackout trauma, it was something she wouldn't wish on her worst enemy. Dream, nightmare, dream, nightmare. Shock, the flashback of seeing her father's white face, seeing him drowning in the storm. And later, trying to make sense of what he'd said about her mother, about her.

Gracie stretched. She clutched Carrie's finger, her tiny daughter who needed her. Carrie stared into her big eyes. She wondered if her mother had loved her this much. Somehow, she knew she had.

Carrie had been raised in a house full of so much love. The story of her parents' proposal was so cool. Carrie had made them tell her over and over when she was little, just because she loved it so much.

Maura O'Donnell and Andy Shaw had seen each other throughout college. The spring of senior year, they'd gone to the Lost Glen bluegrass festival. Lilacs were in bloom, sweet banjo music played, and they strolled the grounds past the antique car show, the quilt exhibit, and the draft horse pull. They picnicked by the river, by a covered bridge, in the shade of old maple trees.

Lying on the blanket, they'd stared up at the rustic bridge. Dark red, ramshackle, about eighty feet long, it crossed the river on private property owned by a family who'd leased their land for the festival, a tradition in Knox County for the past twenty years. Swallows nested inside and flew out through splintered boards.

"How old do you think it is?" Maura asked.

"It was built in 1893," Andy said.

Maura smiled, surprised and impressed. "How do you know?"

"I came here when I was a kid," he said. "Sixth grade on a field trip. My teacher, Mrs. Heller, told us about the old bridge, then told us her husband proposed to her right here on the riverbank, during the festival."

"I love that your teacher told you that! Did she tell you what song the band was playing? Did he get down on one knee?"

"She didn't tell us the song," Andy said, sitting up, brushing himself off as he raised himself on one knee. Maura laughed, thinking he was imitating his teacher's husband.

"Will you marry me?" he asked.

She stared at him. Everything stopped. Her thoughts, her feelings, the birds, the music, the river. And they both even admitted this, even when they told the story years later to their kids: she wasn't ready to say yes, but she did anyway. Because Andy was such a good man, and after the way her father had been, Maura needed someone like that.

Maura said yes. And at the end of the summer,

pregnant with Carrie, she'd married Andy. But their marriage had been based on a lie. Carrie knew that now, and she tried not to blame her mother. But she couldn't help thinking that none of the bad things would have happened if her mother had told him the truth right from the beginning.

Carrie reached for the newspaper and opened to the sports page. She read about the big rivalry between Newport Academy and St. George's. She knew her mother and sister would be in the stands. She wondered if J.D. might too.

If she and Gracie showed up, they could all be one big happy family. Or at least she could catch a glimpse of the people she loved and missed so much . . . maybe she could take a picture of them.

7 THE DAY OF THE ST. GEORGE'S game dawned bright and clear, the sun blasting out of the ocean, throwing down the gauntlet on one of the great prep school football rivalries. St. George's was located on a hill just a few miles from Newport Academy, its square bell tower dominating the inland landscape across the bay from Cliff Walk. Each year the Newport Cuppers built a replica of the tower, stormed it, and tore it down, symbolic of what they hoped to do to the St. George Dragons on the playing field later.

Travis and the team had game-day obligations and traditions, so Maura and Beck went to the airport to get Ally. They headed north to T. F. Green Airport, just south of Providence. They got there early, and waited in the restaurant with the big windows overlooking the runways.

"Thank you for coming with me," Maura said.

"Mmm," Beck said, her head in her book.

"More math?"

"Mmm," Beck said.

"Are we okay on what we talked about the other day?"

"We're fine."

"Dr. Mallory . . ."

"No, Mom. I know what I have to do."

"You're quiet."

"I don't really want to see Ally," Beck said, finally looking up.

"I know, honey," Maura said. "But I wanted us to be together. I've been working too hard, and I know you've been stressed. I don't want us to get off track. You've been doing so well, and—"

"I just don't feel like picking up Ally," Beck said. "She hates me."

"Oh, Beck. She doesn't," Maura said.

"She looks down on me," Beck said.

Maura sipped her coffee, staying calm. She knew that Ally had said some things when Beck had first gotten caught stealing. Maura leaned across the table, closer to her daughter. "I love you," she said. "And I'll send Ally away in ten seconds if she even starts to do that."

"Thanks, Mom," Beck said, holding her math book.

Just then Ally's plane arrived, and they went down to security to wait. People jostled through the gate, heading toward baggage claim. Five five, blonde, blue-eyed, pink-cheeked, Ally wore jeans and a red jacket over a raspberry top and could barely hide her disappointment when she spotted Maura and Beck. Maura's back went up on Beck's behalf.

"Hi, Mrs. Shaw," Ally said. "I know Travis said he had to stay with the team, but I thought maybe that was just so he could surprise me. . . ."

"He would if he could have," Maura said. "Beck came, though!"

"Hi, Beck," Ally said.

"How's Columbus?" Beck asked.

"It's just not the same without you," Ally said, giving Beck a hug. As Maura watched, Beck broke into a surprised smile and hugged back. Maura led them to the garage, listening to Ally chatter about school, some of Beck's friends. Out to the main road, heading south, the conversation continued with Ally including Beck and Beck actually engaging.

"How do you like it here?" Ally asked from the back seat.

"We're adjusting," Maura said.

"How about you, Beck?"

"I miss Ohio and all my friends," she said. "I guess people still think I'm kind of a jerk, though, right?" Maura watched in the rearview mirror for Ally's reaction.

"People know everyone makes mistakes," Ally said, sounding understanding and kind. Maura tried to catch Beck's eye, but she had turned to look back at Ally.

By the time they got to Newport, Beck was completely warmed up and relaxed. Maura loved her daughter's quirky way of seeing places, and smiled as Beck pointed out the graveyards on Farewell Street, the Point section where Newport Academy's founder had come from, the bus station where Beck admitted that she had intended to catch the next Greyhound to Ohio.

"I'm sure your mother and brother are really glad you decided to stay here," Ally said, after the briefest pause.

Maura glanced across the front seat at Beck; it pricked her heart to realize how little it took to make her daughter glow, and she realized with a small jolt how long it had been since she'd seen that happen.

They pulled in through the gates of Newport Academy, and Maura checked the mirror just in time to see Ally's eyes widen as she looked around. The limestone mansion gleamed in the clear autumn light, and sun trickled silver onto the bay. Leaves had been raked, but more fell slowly and constantly, drifts of orange and gold on the wide, perfect lawn. Imposing hedges, impeccably trimmed, ringed the property. Students hurried past, on their way to the game.

Maura parked, and Beck and Ally ran ahead to the field. The bleachers were packed. Energy crackled, electric and wild. Maura heard cheers from both sides, boisterous and getting louder as kickoff time approached. She scanned the stands—Beck and Ally had found a place six rows up and right behind the team. Travis had spotted them, and climbed straight up to hug Ally before the coach yelled at him to get back on the bench.

"Maura!"

Hearing her name, Maura squinted into the sun. Several teachers were sitting off to the side, at the very end of the bleachers. Amy was waving, and Stephen had jumped up to make sure she saw. Waving, she walked over.

"We saved you a seat," he said.

"Thanks," she said, squeezing in between him and Lonnie Delisle, a history teacher she didn't know well yet.

"Travis looks happy," Stephen said, nodding at Travis and Ally.

"He is," Maura said. "He's been waiting for this ever since we got here. His girlfriend is visiting. . . ."

"She flew in from Ohio?"

"Yes," Maura said.

"There seems to be a pipeline between Newport and the Midwest," he said.

"A pipeline?"

"Of people falling in love."

Maura snapped her head around to look at him, but just then Newport won the toss and elected to receive. The crowd went wild even before the kick, and Maura pushed Stephen's words from her mind and was on her feet cheering for her son and the team. Ty Cooper received just out of the end zone; Travis blocked for the first down. The Dragons were fierce, pushing them back on the next play, but then Chris Pollack threw to Travis, and he ran straight down the middle for a touchdown.

Maura cheered—all the teachers did, leaning over to slap her back and congratulate her on Travis's play. Beck and Ally were a few rows away. Turning to see them, she felt a sharp stab. Carrie had always gone to see Travis play. And when Carrie was a baby, Maura and Andy had taken her to see the high school games.

Perfect football weather today—bright, crisp, blue sky. Everyone needed a jacket, but the game was so exciting, layers were peeled off as the touchdowns were scored. Travis was having a great game, moving the ball twenty yards, receiving twice on the same drive, blocking so Chris could score again. At the end of the first half, Newport was up 21–14.

Everyone went to the parking lot to tailgate, and the congratulations on Travis's performance continued to flow. Ted Shannon actually bowed to her, saying her son was going to take them to the championship. The sun was bright, and glinted in Maura's eyes. She shielded her face, thanking him, and as she did glimpsed a young woman at the far end of the parking lot.

Small, dressed in a bulky jacket, holding a child,

the woman stood alone, off to the side, away from the tailgaters. Maura's heart clenched and she felt herself moving through the crowd. Cars, trucks, people between them, charcoal grills, music playing, tall trees, a baby squawking, and Maura started to run. Light flashed, as if someone standing in the shadows had just snapped a picture.

She reached the place where she'd seen the young woman, but no one was there. Standing still, she looked around, her heart pounding. Had she imagined it? A girl with a young child at a football game; Maura could almost feel Carrie in her arms. Time had flown—it was just yesterday that she'd carried her daughter to Thurber Field, snuggled her in the autumn air. The sharp memory brought tears to her eyes. Where was Carrie now? How could she stay away?

Glancing down, Maura spotted a pacifier. She picked it up, brushed away dirt and bits of grass, felt it all come back. So there had been a mother and baby—at least Maura wasn't losing her mind. She saw Stephen approaching with two Styrofoam cups, smoothed away tears, and stuck the pacifier in her pocket.

"Everyone's right," he said handing her a cup of hot cider. "What a game Travis is having."

"He's pretty amazing."

"Is it my imagination, or have you been avoiding me?"

She stared at him, hesitating. Memories were swirling around; she felt the pacifier in her pocket, thought of Carrie's father. "You're married to Patricia Blackstone?" she asked.

"I was," he said. "We're divorced. She remarried, lives in Bristol now."

"I never met Patricia, but I knew her brother one summer," she said, watching for his reaction to that.

"J.D.," he said.

"Is that what you meant by 'the pipeline'?" she asked. "The connection between Newport and the Midwest?"

He sipped his cider, and she saw redness spreading up his neck into his face as he stared into her eyes. The direct gaze made her squirm, but she couldn't look away.

"Yes," he said finally. "Well, partly. Tay Davis—Pell and Lucy's dad—was from Michigan. He married a girl from Newport."

"You know about me and J.D.?" she asked, unable to hold back any longer.

Stephen just nodded. After a pause he said, "He's a good friend of mine. We've known each other since we came to the academy. He talked about you that autumn—after you left to go to Ohio. After."

Stephen didn't have to say it: after J.D.'s fall.

"I was engaged to someone else," Maura said.

"Yeah, I heard," Stephen said, an edge in his voice.

"What did J.D. say?"

"It was a really long time ago."

"Yes," she said. Did he blame her for the rest? She felt her shoulders hunching, closing in, protecting herself.

"We were sorry not to meet you back then," Stephen said, his tone softening. "Ted, Taylor, and I were in Europe that summer. The classic bumming-around-after-college. J.D. was supposed to meet us in Rome. We couldn't get him to break away from his job for the whole two months. . . ."

"He worked hard," she said.

"Yeah," Stephen said. "He never rested on his family's name, that's for sure. But we convinced him to connect up with us for at least part of our trip. He never did, though. He wanted to stay here with you."

"How is he now?" Maura asked.

"He keeps to himself."

Maura waited for Stephen to say more, and he stared at her for a few long seconds, as if trying to decide how much to tell her.

"He went to Providence for more surgery a year ago," he said. "They kept him completely immobile for months. It was a serious procedure, but the complications were worse."

"What do you mean?"

"He developed an infection right after the surgery. It started in his spinal cord, went to his brain. He nearly died."

"After all this time?" she asked.

"Yes. They had to put him into a coma, to get the swelling down. He couldn't move. They kept him that way until he was out of the woods. When he woke up, he realized he wasn't any better than before the operation."

"That's devastating."

"Don't say it to J.D."

"Why?"

Stephen looked down. "He can't stand anyone pitying him. I think he's afraid of giving up. I'm not sure he really believes he'll get better, but he never stops looking into new doctors, treatments, programs."

"Nothing's worked?" she asked.

"No," he said. "At least not that I can see. But J.D. doesn't talk about it. He doesn't want us worrying about him."

"I want to see him," she said.

Stephen glanced away, toward the sea beyond the stately school building. When he looked at her again, she saw a warning behind his eyes, dark and fierce—protecting his friend or, she thought with a shock, protecting her?

Ally came running over as the crowd began flowing back toward the stands. They walked together. Maura waited for Stephen to say more, but he didn't and, swept away with the other teachers, they separated. Maura found herself scanning the crowd for the young mother; she wanted to give her baby back the pacifier.

The second half started. St. George's received. The game went on. Travis scored a touchdown, and Beck waved at her from the stands with Ally. The Newport lead mounted, but Maura was thinking of J. D. Blackstone, of a summer eighteen years ago. . . .

The heat rose from the cobblestones, hardly a breeze in the old alleyway. Katharine was welding in the studio, an ironworker's inferno. Maura stood on the granite step outside, trying to cool off. It had been only a little over a week since she had joined her sister in Newport, but already she felt more at home in New England than she had during her four years of college in Ohio. Hard to admit, but she was glad for the break from Andy, a chance to think about his proposal.

She spied a spigot on a building down the alley. Eight at night, sky still light, stones and metal glinting as if someone had spilled butterscotch; no one was around. Walking over, she glanced up at a small blue metal medallion attached to the old stone building: **Local 23.**

Turning the faucet, she heard water rush through

copper pipes. She wore cutoff jean shorts and a blue shirt, a scarf holding back her long hair. Cupping her hands, she splashed water; untied the scarf, soaked it, and cooled her arms, her throat, backs of her legs. She rinsed out a small tin pail and filled it to drink.

Just then the heavy door swung open, and she felt a blast of heat. A tall man stood there, streaked with soot and sweat. He tilted his welding mask back, staring at her with bright blue eyes. They were alone in the deserted alley with the sun setting behind the old warehouses.

"Want a drink?" she asked.

"Sure, thanks," he said.

She filled the pail, handed it to him, suddenly hyperaware of his eyes, and the feeling of cool water evaporating off her skin in the twilight heat. He drank, watching her. The sense that she had stepped out of time, into the nineteenth century, this hidden byway, these whaling-era buildings and cobblestones, seemed overwhelming.

She crouched by the faucet, wet her scarf again, and handed it to him.

"Thank you," he said, wiping his face.

"You're welcome. It's your water."

"True," he said. "Although everyone on the alley uses my faucet."

"I'm not the first?"

"No," he said. He didn't smile, didn't joke, didn't

flirt. But he stared at her so deeply she felt everything shift.

"Would you like more water?" she asked.

He nodded, and took the heavy mask off the
back of his head, laid it down on the step. He was
wearing Nomex flameproof overalls, and unhooked
the buttons at the top, swung the straps over his
shoulders, let the bib fall down. He had a ripped
gray T-shirt underneath, and sweat made it stick to
him. He washed his hands. She watched him fill
the pail, take another long drink.

"What do you do in there?" she asked.

"I'm welding the railing for a balcony," he said.

"Heavy industry on this alleyway," she said,
thinking of her sister working in her own studio.

"Yeah," he said, wiping his face. "Newport's still
a city."

"Not just docks with big boats," she said. "And
candle shops on the waterfront."

"No, but that's where the bars are," he said. "Do
you want to get a drink?"

She glanced at Katharine's door. Would her sister
mind her going off to hang out with her neighbor?
She knew how obsessed Katharine got with her
sculpting, how often she worked past midnight.
But Maura's own feelings stopped her. This guy was
making her heart pound like crazy, and she kept
thinking of Andy.

The welder waited for her answer, and the streetlights crackled on overhead. She heard the electricity humming through the transformer; it might as easily have been coming from him, or from her. She felt the charge sparking between them, saw it flash in his blue eyes.

"What's Local 23?" she asked, pointing up at the medallion, trying to slow it all down.

"You should know," he said.

"Why?" she asked, laughing nervously.

"Well, because your sister's in it too."

"My sister."

"Katharine," he said.

The alley was small, very few occupied warehouses. Of course everyone would know each other; hadn't he just said they used his water faucet? But the truth began to dawn. She stared at his hair, brown and short, and she knew that her sister had cut it for him.

"Ironworkers Local," she said.

"Yeah," he said. "We're in the same union."

"You're J.D.," she said.

"You didn't know that?" he asked. "I knew you were Maura."

They shook hands, and the feeling of his skin sent another jolt through her.

Katharine had always said they were just friends, and Maura had always hoped she was wrong about that. She had always wanted there to be something between Katharine and J. D. Blackstone.

And now she didn't. She wanted to go to the wharf with him, forget about everything, have that drink.

"Let me clean up," he said.

"Should we ask Katharine to come with us?"

He laughed, a look of warmth filling his eyes as he glanced over at the studio door. It was closed, but through it came the high-pitched sound of metal sparking metal. Arcs of fire welding Katharine's sculptures together.

"She won't come," he said. "She's always so focused when she's in the middle of a piece."

"In other words, you're doing her a favor," Maura said. "Taking me off her hands."

"If that's the way you want to see it," he said, his eyes glinting.

And in that moment that hot summer night eighteen years ago, Maura O'Donnell forgot all about Andy Shaw. And about her sister too.

■

Newport beat St. George's 28–21, their first victory over the Dragons in seven years. Everyone was saying Travis had won the game for the Cuppers— even Chris, the quarterback, said Travis was the hero, he didn't care who got credit as long as they had a winning season.

The students celebrated by taking over Truffles that night. The evening was chilly, but it didn't matter. Ally had worked on her tan, and she was showing it off no matter what. She wore a strapless blue silk dress, high-heeled sandals, the necklace he'd given her for her birthday. Travis would have rather gone somewhere private with her—stayed away from all the others, but Ally wanted the school to see them together.

Everyone jammed into the bar area, where it was too loud to really talk. Truffles served drinks and fancy food. Travis saw kids handing over Platinum AmEx cards; all he had was twenty bucks. That was enough for two virgin frozen daiquiris. Some kids had fake IDs or knew the bartender and were drinking champagne.

Ally pressed against his body, his arms around her. Her skin felt so soft and smooth, and she put her hand behind his neck to pull his mouth down to hers. They kissed, long and hot, in a way he'd been dreaming of since leaving Columbus. At the same time, he was embarrassed, and he hated himself for it.

When he looked up, instead of gazing into Ally's eyes, he found himself scanning the crowd. Pell was by the door, standing with Logan, Cordelia, Chris, and Ty. They talked, leaning together, but Travis saw Pell watching him. Caught, she looked away.

"You were amazing," Ally said, stroking his hair. "Really . . . you showed these preps how we do it back home. Football done right!"

"Yeah," he said.

"So, who are your friends? I want to meet them. Come on, introduce me to all these people buying us drinks!"

And Travis did. He made his way through the group, introducing Ally to all the team members near the bar, their girlfriends, kids from his classes. By the time he got to the door, his friends saw him coming and stepped toward him grinning. Except Pell. She hung back a little.

"Hey, man," Travis said to Chris. "Great game."

"You did it for us," Chris said.

"We've got a good team," Travis said. "So, everyone . . . this is Ally."

"Nice to meet you, Ally," Chris said.

"Hey, Ally . . . " "Good to have you here . . ." Everyone was chiming in.

"Hi," Ally said, her arm locked around Travis. She looked each person in the eye; he felt her taking everyone's measure. He thought he saw Logan flick a glance at her dress. Travis didn't know anything about fashion, but he knew that Ally's shiny blue silk had come from the mall and Logan's matte black satin had come from some fancy Beverly Hills boutique. He tightened his grip around Ally's shoulder.

Two waitresses came over, one serving drinks and the other with a tray of miniature hot lobster rolls. Travis felt his stomach growl. He was starving, but he'd blown all his money on those two drinks.

"Mmm, perfect," Cordelia said, taking a plate.

"What are they?" Ally said, reaching for one.

Travis stopped her, his hand on her wrist. "We can't," he said softly.

"Lobster rolls, and of course you can," Chris said.

"Are those black things what I think they are?" Ally asked as she bent toward the fine china plate to examine the rolls' contents.

"Truffles," Logan said, deadpan. "As in the name of the restaurant."

"Yum," Ally said. "My father's a doctor, and one of his patients gives him truffles every fall."

Travis reddened. He didn't want to have to explain his finances, not to all his friends. How much did truffles cost? If Ally took a lobster roll, the bill would come and he wouldn't be able to pay. "Hey, Al," he said sharply, just as Ally reached again.

"What, I want to try it!" she said.

"Better not, okay?"

"This is on my grandmother," Pell said quickly, stepping forward.

"Excuse me?" Ally asked.

"Please have one, Ally. My grandmother would like to treat us all in honor of Newport winning the game."

"Really?" Logan asked. "When did your grandmother start to care about football? Yachting, yes. Polo, **bien sûr.** But football . . . that doesn't sound like the Mrs. Nicholson we all know and—"

"She insists," Pell said to the group at large. But her cornflower blue eyes were looking straight at Travis. He hesitated, tried to smile. Her gaze was strong and steady. He couldn't look away.

And Ally saw. Travis felt her stare, sweeping between him and Pell, as her hand gripped his.

"Thank your grandmother," Ally said, locking eyes with Pell. "That's so lovely of her."

"Thank you, Pell," Travis said, taking two lobster rolls from the tray, one for him and one for Ally. And he watched Ally bite into hers, melted butter glistening on her lips. He took a bite, tasted the crispy, toasted, buttered roll outside, the briny sea and rich earth of lobster and truffles inside. He looked over at Pell, to nod his appreciation, but she was whispering something to the waitress.

"How are you enjoying Newport so far?" Cordelia asked Ally.

"I love it," she said. "Of course, seeing Travis win the game didn't hurt, but I wasn't surprised. He was always the greatest, even back home. Ohio breeds the best players!"

Travis glanced over at Chris and Ty, but they seemed not to get the slight, or to care. Ally asked Cordelia about her purple purse shaped like a bow, and Cordelia handed Ally another glass of champagne and was saying something about Prada, and Travis drifted toward Pell.

"Your grandmother didn't treat us, did she?" Travis asked.

Pell didn't speak. She just stared up at him with warmth in her eyes.

"You did," he said. "You took care of it."

"I wanted you and Ally to have lobster rolls," she said.

"We didn't need them," he said.

"Nobody needs them," she said, smiling. "But I wanted you to have them anyway."

Suddenly Ally was right there, leaning into him. She was still nibbling the lobster roll. "These are good," she said. "An East Coast specialty, I guess, right?"

"Well, a Newport specialty," Pell said.

"Newport," Ally said. "Back home we have specialties too. Right, Trav?"

"Right," he said, but he couldn't think of any. Then, feeling inane, he said, "Pell's from the Midwest too."

"Where?" Ally asked.

"Grosse Pointe, Michigan," she said.

"My aunt's from Detroit," Ally said. "She said that Grosse Pointe isn't the Midwest. She said it's just like Connecticut. . . ."

Pell tilted her head. "It felt Midwestern to me," she said. "I think of it as home, and I miss it."

Ally frowned; he hugged her, but she pulled away, eyes on Pell. She emptied her champagne glass. Travis's pulse was racing. He felt confused and in between, and he knew he had to get out of there. Putting his arm around Ally, he said he wanted to take her somewhere special, just the two of them. When they got outside, Ally wheeled toward him.

"Was I embarrassing you?" she asked.

"No," he said. "I'm just all pumped up from the game, and it was getting too hot in there."

"Hot because of Pell!"

"Al, no," he said.

She stalked ahead of him, arms wrapped around herself to stay warm. Wind blew off the harbor, damp and cold. While other students had spent twelve dollars to park in a lot, Travis had driven around and around until he'd found a free spot way down Thames Street. The walk to Truffles had seemed romantic, the way Ally had leaned into him, taking in the waterfront. But now she was mad, and he could tell her high heels hurt, and he was reeling with emotions he wanted to push away.

They finally got into the car—the station wagon they'd spent so much time in back home. They had known each other since eighth grade, when Carrie had introduced them; Travis had seen Ally and her older sister Jill hanging out in their backyard, and he'd felt the bottom fall out.

The way Ally looked, her streaked blonde hair and soft skin, the way she smiled, and later, the way she touched him. He'd lie awake at night thinking of her, wanting to be with her so badly he couldn't stand it. He'd sweat so hard, and his head would throb, and sometimes he'd sneak out when his parents were asleep and drive to her house just to look at her window.

He'd sat in this car, alone in the dark, parked on her street. He'd thought he was the only person alive ever to feel this way. Once he'd returned home, found his father waiting up. Travis's blood pounded as he waited for his father to go ballistic.

But his father hadn't. He'd stood in the driveway, leaning against the garage. At the sight of Travis's face, his father had ducked his head slightly—a strange look in his eyes. Travis had seen it, wondered what he was thinking. All his father had said was, "I know."

"You know what?" Travis had asked.

"How it feels."

"I was just taking a ride," Travis said. "That's all."

"Remind me to tell you about the time I once took a ride in the middle of the night from here to Rhode Island," his father said. "Look. Just take care. Of yourself, and Ally too. Okay?"

"Okay," Travis said, not really knowing what his father had meant.

But he remembered the words now, driving

down Thames Street along the wharves, Ally sitting stiff in the passenger seat, not talking. Travis's mind raced. His dad had liked Ally. He'd given them his blessing, in a way. At least that's how Travis had always felt—his father would never know any woman in his life but Ally.

And Ally had been Carrie's friend. Some of Carrie's best shots were of Ally—pictures she took at school, and at the field during one of Travis's games. Ally was bonded to their family, forever immortalized in Carrie's photography.

Even before leaving Columbus, when he'd had doubts about her—about the way she'd come down on Beck, and other things, the way she always wanted to be with lots of people and he usually liked to be alone with her, and the way she always managed to tell people her father was a doctor—Travis had known he'd never break up with her, because she had known his father and Carrie. And because Carrie had taken such loving pictures of her.

"What's wrong?" Travis asked now.

"What do you **think** is wrong?"

"I don't know, Al."

"You were all over her," Ally said.

"Who?"

"Pell!"

"I wasn't all over her! I was with you. . . . I want to be with you."

"You couldn't stop looking at each other. All through the game, even! Every time you scored, you'd smile at her. Don't say you didn't, because I was sitting right there, waiting for you to wave to me."

"I did wave to you," he said.

"Second, Travis. You looked at her first, then you waved at me. I followed your eyes, saw you staring straight at her. In fact, I even asked Beck who she was. She lied and said she had no idea what I was talking about."

Travis drove in silence. He wanted to take Ally somewhere dark and private, where he could hold her and soothe her, and make everything okay. She looked beautiful in her blue dress, her bare arms glistening in the streetlight, and he wanted to remind them both of how they'd felt about each other. He wanted to push Pell out of his mind, and he was grateful to Beck for covering for him, so things with Ally weren't worse than they already were.

"I'm sorry," he said, not wanting to lie and deny what he knew was true. He reached for her hand, tugging her closer to him.

"I've been missing you every minute," Ally said, her throat thick with tears.

"Same for me," he said. "I can't stand being away from you."

"But what about Pell?" she asked.

"We're friends—that's all."

"She doesn't look at you like you're her friend," Ally said.

"I promise, that's all it is. She knows all about you," Travis said. "She knows I couldn't wait for you to get here."

That seemed to relax Ally; she slipped over the console, wedged herself right next to Travis on the driver's seat. His arm was finally around her, and he felt her warm body snuggle into his chest. As he drove, she tilted her head up, kissed his neck, sending shivers all through his body.

They headed toward Ocean Drive. Huge mansions lined the inland hills, their silver slate rooftops gleaming in the light of the moon. Travis rolled down the windows so Ally could hear the sea, feel its mystery. Pulling down a dirt road to a state fishing area, he parked the car in a patch of weeds.

Their mouths were hot, and they fumbled with each other's clothes; he wanted to feel his skin against hers, to remember how they had been, how much he had always wanted her. He needed to convince himself he was wrong, that they were still good, that they weren't ending. He put up the windows to block out the cold air. She kissed him, whispering how well she knew him, saying no one knew him like her, no one could ever touch him the way she did.

And he tried to be with her, right here in the car

where they'd spent so many hours talking and holding each other. He fought the other thoughts pressing on him, making him feel he was doing the wrong thing now, being unfair to her, making out with her while he was so confused about them. His shirt was unbuttoned, and she was stroking his chest, and he'd slid the straps down off her shoulders, and he stopped.

"What?" she asked.

"I don't know," he said, trying to breathe.

"I don't like it here. It's the stupid sound," she said. "Even with the windows closed it's like we're in the middle of a storm, or a wind tunnel."

"That's the ocean," he said.

"Can we move, go somewhere else?" she asked, her hand on his chest, tickling him with her long nails. Why did he feel as if all the air had been sucked out of the car, as if he might pass out?

"Sure," he said, starting the car again. "We can go back to the house, get warmer jackets, maybe walk over to the playing fields."

Travis put his arm around Ally as he drove and knew he had never felt so far from her, from Columbus, in his life.

"Why don't you come back home?" she said, as if she could feel him pulling away. "The coach would let you stay with his family. Or you could stay with Robbie or Jack. My mom would probably even let you stay with us! You could go back and forth between there and my dad's with me."

He tried to smile. "Your father would love that."

"He wouldn't mind," she said, kissing him again. "He just wants me to be happy."

Travis held the wheel. "I'm not sure how my mother and Beck would take it."

"Beck," she said, shaking her head.

"Thanks for sitting with her at the game," Travis said. "She looked as if she was having a blast."

"Everyone has to do their duty sometime," Ally said.

He gave her a look, but she didn't elaborate. Beck came to the door as he pulled into their narrow drive. "Where were you?" she asked.

"Down at Truffles," Travis said.

"Oh, cool," Beck said.

"I'll go get our coats," Travis said. He ran inside, and he started to grab some warm jackets and a blanket. Beck's voice drifted in from the back step.

"Ally, did you have fun today? I liked sitting with you."

Ally's reply was too quiet for him to hear. He paused, listening. And then he realized she wasn't saying anything at all. His sister's statement hung in the cold air.

Travis leaned against the wall, trying to push down feelings he didn't want to be having.

8 THE NEXT MORNING MAURA looked into the kids' rooms, saw Travis burrowed under the covers, Ally sleeping in the extra bed in Beck's room, and Beck wide awake and doing homework. Desdemona and Grisby lay sprawled across Beck's desk as she tried to write on the paper between their two backs.

"What are you studying this early?" Maura whispered, not wanting to wake Ally.

"Just something," Beck whispered back.

"Do you have a test tomorrow?"

"No," Beck said.

"Everything okay?" Maura asked, holding Beck's gaze a few seconds.

"Mom . . ."

"Okay," Maura said. She smiled. "I have a few errands. See you when I get back. Bye, honey."

"Bye, Mom . . ."

Maura pulled on her jacket, the lost pacifier still in her pocket. She drove out the school gates and headed toward Portsmouth. The October morning was bright and cold. Driving past Easton's Beach, she saw long rollers rumbling in over the tidal flats, the wave edges laced white, hard sand steel-gray. Turning left, she passed the salt pond, took a right on East Main Road, and looked for her sister's farm.

The dirt road ran through a field. Her earlier drive here had been at night; she hadn't seen the haystacks, pumpkins on the vine. Katharine's sculptures dotted the hill sloping down to the Sakonnet River. Arcs of bright metal welded together, a menagerie of lost creatures.

Maura saw Katharine's old green truck under an overhang by the yellow farmhouse. Parking under a scarlet maple tree, she saw a hand part the white curtains in the front parlor. She walked up the wide front steps, across the big porch, and knocked on the door. Hearing footsteps inside, she stood straighter.

A young woman answered. Tall, slender, with dark hair pulled into a loose ponytail, paint streaking her hands and oversized blue work shirt, she wiped her hand on a rag and smiled.

"Oh my God," she said. "You must be Kate's sister."

Kate? Maura wondered when she'd started using the nickname. "Yes," she said.

"You look exactly like her. It's unbelievable!"

Maura tried to reply, but normal words, conversation, wouldn't come. She had always wanted to look like her older sister: tall, strong, capable, brave enough to let her eccentricities show. But right now she couldn't handle the small talk. "Is she here?" she managed.

"No," the woman said. "I'm sorry, she's not."

Maura must have groaned—or at least looked so bereft, the woman took pity on her.

"Come on in," she said. "I'd shake your hand, but I'm covered with paint and linseed oil. I'm Darcy, her assistant."

"Nice to meet you."

Darcy led Maura through her sister's house. Looking around, Maura felt pangs of longing and nostalgia. Bookcases were filled to overflowing, volumes two and three deep in the shelves, piled on the floor and under tables.

Her sister's mysterious drawings of extinct birds and fish—studies for her sculpture—were everywhere, along with framed photos of Maura, Andy, Carrie, Travis, and Beck. Maura stared at the pictures she'd sent through the years—with a birth announcement, a birthday card, communicating with her sister just like all the others on her Christmas card list.

They went into the kitchen, a rambling room with a huge stove and refrigerator—big enough to feed a restaurant—long oak table, chairs, two loveseats flanking a fieldstone fireplace, a deep red Murano glass chandelier, more drawings, paintings, and photos. There were bouquets of dried herbs hanging from rafters, pots of plants, bunches of fall flowers and dried grass, autumn leaves strewn across the table, glass bowls full of seashells and pinecones, several pumpkins of varying sizes.

Darcy poured two mugs of coffee, showed Maura the milk and sugar. Maura numbly accepted the mug and drank it black.

"Just like Kate! Your sister is hardcore with her coffee too."

"Where is Katharine . . . Kate?"

"You call her Katharine! I'll have to tease her about that."

Maura remembered how her sister had never allowed anyone to call her by a nickname. Until one person: J.D. had always called Katharine "Tiger." Standing there, quietly waiting, Maura found herself shaking.

"Are you okay?" Darcy asked, reaching for her arm.

"I need to see my sister."

"She's not here right now."

"Is she sick?" Maura asked, her insides turning to ice. With so much distance between them, she'd been afraid of this—having her sister become seriously ill without her knowing, having something terrible happen and not being there. And that made her think of Carrie, of the silence between them, and Maura had to brace herself against the door.

"No," Darcy said quickly. "Kate's in Providence."

"But that's not far—didn't she get my message?"

"I'm not sure. She's teaching a seminar at RISD, staying at an apartment on Benefit Street. . . . I'd try her again."

Maura barely heard, looking around the kitchen as if she might find a clue to why Katharine hadn't returned her call, how since coming to Rhode Island she hadn't seen her sister once. The refrigerator was covered with pictures held on by magnets. She stared, realizing that most of them were of her kids.

Her gaze shifted to the wall, where Katharine had framed finger paintings by Beck, a collage by Travis, a drawing by Carrie. As she gazed at her children's pictures, she realized that she'd sent more than she remembered. And Katharine had preserved them with love. She was a true aunt, even though she'd stayed away from her sister.

Maura focused on the photographs. They were unmistakably Carrie's, and Maura herself had sent them, back when Carrie was still home: a self-portrait of Carrie holding Grisby, Beck climbing the tree by their back door, Maura studying for a final, a close-up of Beck's eyes, sleepy and dreamy. Shaken by the immediacy of Carrie's pictures, the horror of not knowing where she was came flooding in.

"Maura, are you okay?" Darcy asked.

"Tell my sister I miss her," Maura said. "When she gets back from Providence. Will you ask her to call me?"

"I will," Darcy said, and Maura walked out of the kitchen.

The autumn air smelled fresh—Katharine's land sloped down to the Sakonnet River, brackish as it mixed with the Atlantic. Maura stared at her sister's house, so full of love and reminders of her own children. The long silence between them had started because of J.D. Maura still remembered the panic in her sister's voice when she'd called her in Ohio to tell her what happened.

"Why did he do that?" Katharine had cried. He was in surgery, with a broken back. "What did you say to him? Why would he jump off the bridge?"

"He would never jump," Maura had said, filled with shock and grief. "It must have been an accident."

"But what was he doing up there? What did you say, Maura?"

Maura didn't tell her, and never would. The sound of Katharine's muffled sobs: in them, without words, disbelief and despair that Maura could have done so much damage.

Still, they'd spoken all through the fall; Maura would call to ask about J.D., and Katharine would tell her about his progress. For a long time Katharine had expected Maura to change her mind and return to Newport. His recovery was rocky, going slowly, and she knew seeing Maura would make it better.

But leaving J.D., as much as she'd known it was the only way, had broken Maura's heart. Now she had the baby to consider. She was pregnant; she had to make everything right with Andy. Seeing J.D. would make her doubt her decision more than she already did. It would tear her to pieces, seeing him paralyzed. She didn't think she could survive it.

Maura called to invite Katharine to Columbus for Christmas. She asked, as she always did, about J.D.; by then Katharine had stopped telling her details. She'd become quiet, polite; she'd said he was the same. And as she always did, Maura said she was sorry. She felt Katharine judging her, as if she was cold and callous; how was it possible her sister didn't seem to know how devastated she was?

Before they hung up, Maura asked if Katharine could bring some of the family ornaments. She meant it as a peace offering, a way of reminding her sister of their love and childhood, their forever connection. But Katharine seemed shocked, as if wondering how Maura could be thinking of something so dumb and superficial while J.D. lay injured. Maura hated that, but she didn't know how to smooth it out.

The next week a box had arrived. Neatly packed, all the family Christmas decorations. No note. And no Katharine. Maura knew she'd done something terrible, but still, how could her sister turn so completely against her?

"I can't have holidays without you," Maura had said. "I need you, Katharine."

No answer, just hot silence pouring through the phone.

"What about after the baby is born?" Maura asked. "Will you come then? To see your niece or nephew?"

"Don't even go there," Katharine said.

"Katharine. Andy and I are trying to make a family," Maura began.

"What about J.D.?" Katharine screamed. "What about a family with **him?** You don't want him, you don't even care about him!"

"I do care," Maura said, shocked by the passion in her sister's voice.

"His life is over, Maura. I'd give anything to make him better, make him stop thinking of you." Katharine sobbed.

"Katharine, I'm sorry," Maura said, but her sister had already hung up.

A glimmer: Were Katharine's feelings for J.D. more than the deep friendship she had always claimed? Maura couldn't let herself believe that; Katharine had vehemently denied it. Maura told herself her sister was reacting to J.D.'s suffering, to what Maura had done.

They never talked about it again, and they never spent another holiday together. And last Christmas Carrie hadn't come home. Maura had taught her daughter to swim, knit, whistle, garden, do cartwheels. But she'd also taught her how to put time and distance between herself and the people she loved most.

Turning her car around in the driveway, Maura headed out of the pumpkin patch onto the main road. Long, ragged white clouds scudded across the bright blue sky. Yellow leaves blew off the trees, dancing along the asphalt. Maura drove home, oblivious to the October beauty.

■

Travis woke up with Ally in his bed. At first he panicked—his mother was in the next room. But Ally whispered she'd heard her drive away, the only person home was Beck, and she wasn't paying attention. She slid under the covers, still in her nightgown. It was silky, pink, and the slippery feel of it made Travis crazy.

They kissed, his hands sliding down her body, over her curvy hips. She felt blazing, a heater against his skin.

"I've missed you so much," she said.

Travis couldn't answer. He'd barely kissed her last

night, even after getting so worked up in the car. Not because of their fight, but because of what he felt inside. As he came fully awake, his thoughts raced. His body wanted her, but his mind knew it was wrong to be with a girl he didn't love. Building for a while, the feeling's force had hit him last night, and he knew what he had to do. Ally stroked his back with a light touch, her fingernails making him tingle. Her kiss was hot and searching.

She reached down into his pajama bottoms; he pushed her hand away.

"What's the matter?" she asked.

"We can't," he said.

"Why not?" When he didn't reply, she peered at him. "You've been acting strange ever since I got here!"

His arms were around her; he gazed into her eyes. This was the girl he'd loved and cared about all through high school. She'd been Carrie's friend; he'd never imagined not loving her, and he couldn't stand the idea of hurting her. But this had been coming for a while.

"Ally," he said.

"What?"

"We're so far apart now," he said softly. "I thought it would be okay, but it's really hard."

"You think I haven't noticed that? That's why I'm here, Travis, why I flew out to be with you."

"I know," he said, reaching over to stroke her hair.

"Aren't you glad I came? Or do you wish I hadn't?"

He swallowed hard, knowing he had to lie. "No, I'm glad you came."

"You don't seem it."

"This isn't a good idea. Us being together, when you're in Ohio and I'm here."

"I told you last night," she said. "You should come home."

This is home, he wanted to say. But he weighed every word, trying as hard as he could to hurt her as little as possible. "I can't," he said. "I have to be with my mother and Beck."

"And someone else?" she asked, her eyes filling.

"Stop," he said. "This has nothing to do with anyone but us. It's not fair to you, us trying to stay together when we can't even see each other."

"Just say her name," Ally said, shoving him away, sitting up in bed. "Pell—it's about her."

Travis didn't want that to be true—he knew the honorable thing would be to finish things with Ally before letting himself have feelings for someone else. But every time he closed his eyes Pell was there—her sad, gentle eyes, the way they'd talked that night, the way her dark hair angled across her porcelain skin. Shaking his head, he tried to push those thoughts away. "No," he said. "It's because of us."

"Why did your mother make you move away?" she asked, her voice rising. "It ruined everything."

Ally climbed out of bed, walked to the door. She looked vulnerable in her thin pink nightgown. Then she turned away, walked out of his room. Travis hesitated. He wished it could just be over. But he knew he couldn't leave things this way, so he climbed out of bed. Halfway down the hallway, he heard Ally enter Beck's room.

"I have a question, Beck," he heard her say.

"Sure," Beck said. One of the cats meowed, and Travis watched Grisby scoot out of Beck's room toward the kitchen.

"Why did you lie?" Ally asked.

Beck didn't reply, and Travis froze, listening.

"Yesterday you said you didn't know who Travis was looking at—when we were at the game, re-member?"

"I remember," Beck said.

"I asked you a question, and thought you'd be decent enough to tell me the truth about Pell," Ally said quietly.

"He wasn't . . ."

"You haven't changed at all. Lying and stealing. You're a little thief. You stole out in Columbus, and everyone knew it. How long do you think it will be before you drive everyone here away? Carrie prob-ably ran away because she can't stand you. Why do you think your family had to move here? Because of you. They're ashamed of you, just like Carrie would be."

Ally's words and Beck's total silence scalded Travis. He stepped into Beck's room, saw Ally glaring at her with rage. Beck pulled her legs up and sat huddled on her desk chair, head down on the tops of her knees. Travis walked past Ally, put his hand on his sister's shoulders.

"Carrie wouldn't be ashamed of you," he said. "And neither am I. I never could be, Beck."

"I was trying to get her to see that lying and stealing never works," Ally said.

"Neither does being a bitch to my sister," he said.

"It's incredible," she said, backing away. "I don't even know you anymore. You can't see the truth when it's right in front of you. Thanks for having me fly all the way out here just so you could break up with me. I'm calling my father. I want to go home today."

"Ally," Travis began, still gripping Beck's shoulder.

"You think your family is so perfect? One sister's a liar, the other was pregnant. That's what everyone's saying, you know? Carrie was pregnant. And she never even had the decency to ask what Justin wanted to do about it."

"There's no proof any of that is true," Travis said, shocked that Ally would say it. He knew what Beck thought, but he'd never repeated it to anyone. He stared down at his sister.

"You're right—it came from her," Ally said. "Carrie told her a secret, and Beck blabbed it all over town."

"Beck?" he asked.

"I don't know what she's talking about," Beck mumbled.

"Lying again," Ally said.

Travis stood by his sister, staring at Ally. She was striking out at Beck to get at him. Maybe she even thought that if he turned against Beck he'd turn back to her. But what she didn't understand was that Travis never could. What was left of Travis's family meant everything to him. Ally kept talking but Travis blocked out her voice and thought of his two sisters, of how close they had been.

And of how no one knew Carrie's secrets better than Beck.

9 AND I HATE ALLY, BUT SHE'S right, and it's true: the rumors about Carrie being pregnant started with me. I couldn't keep my mouth shut. I told my two best friends. No one but me saw the way she kept holding her stomach that last day on the lake, gripping her belly and rocking back and forth as if she had a baby inside.

I had to tell someone.

I held my worries in as long as I could, but they leaked out sideways. That day at the lake, when they were searching for Carrie and my father, I remember asking my mother, "Is Carrie pregnant?" She said no, and a whole bunch of reasons why not, but nothing she said chased away what I'd seen in my sister.

I couldn't stop thinking about it, but I never asked my mother again. Because after Carrie ran away from the hospital, we all fell apart. But she knew something was wrong with me, because I couldn't hide it. I wore Carrie's secret on my face. It was like being haunted, but not by a ghost: by an idea. By the idea that my older sister was going to have a baby.

Telling your best friends is so much easier. Because you're all teenage girls and you think about sex, it's everywhere right in front of you, but your mother's your mother and your brother is a boy and there you go. They love your sister as much as you do. They don't even have to idealize her because she's already ideal. It just killed me to think of her keeping a secret like that. So I told my so-called best friends. I thought I could trust them.

Maybe ghosts are easier. Lucy is right, our fathers are nearby, and all we have to do is find the right formula to see them again. I want my father. I want him to be here with us, to talk to Travis and let him know I didn't mean to ruin things with Ally. It's true, I saw him looking at Pell. Ally was letting me sit with her at the game, and I didn't want to hurt her feelings. And I wanted to protect my brother. Travis says he isn't mad at me. I guess I'm just mad at myself.

My father would understand. If he were here, he'd put his arm around my shoulder and say, "Hey, take a ride with me." He'd invent some errand—go to the hardware store, or to stock up on weekly specials at the grocery store, or check out the sporting goods department at the Wal-Mart out on Connell Highway.

I want my father for Travis, and I want him for me. I'd ask him about Carrie. About what they talked about in the canoe that day. I hope that wasn't them yelling; I hope it was just the wind that I heard.

My father was the sweetest, nicest father. He was easy, he was calm. Back when things were perfect, I'd see him staring at my mother as if she made him so happy he thought he was dreaming. I almost expected to see him pinch himself. And late at night, after homework when we were all watching TV, she'd look at him with that sleepy, it's-been-a-long-day-but-I-love-my-life way. She was a housewife, but she liked it.

Dad would be lying on the couch, very often with Desdemona curled up right on his chest. She only did that with gentle people, trust me. We had a good family.

Once I asked my mom if her dad was like ours; if he was good, nice, kind, easy. I'd expected her to say yes—because, honestly, I couldn't imagine any other way. But she'd shaken her head. "He was different," she said. "He never seemed to want to be home."

A dad not wanting to be home? What did that even mean?

It made me sad for her and my aunt. I never met my grandparents; they died before I was born. But I felt sorry for them, that they hadn't had the kind of family we did. I know Carrie felt that way too. We were lucky.

Our dad cared about everyone and everything, especially all of us. So I imagine him taking Carrie out for that paddle, trying to soothe whatever was bothering her. It had to be the storm I heard. I tell myself that even though I know it's not true. They were fighting, and it sounded violent. I heard Carrie crying.

I don't feel like myself. Or at least, I don't feel like the Beck I used to be. The one out in Columbus before my family disappeared. We used to have fun. I used to wake up in the morning without a stomachache. I never used to steal.

Lucy says people only see the obvious. The things right in front of them, in front of their faces. But what about the small, dissolving, invisible traces of people we love? When someone dies or goes away, do we feel differently about them? No. If anything, we love them more.

Lucy says that Einstein had it almost right with $E = mc^2$. Except it's not matter, it's love. Lucy says, "Love is neither created nor destroyed." And she hears Mary's ghost, and I've heard it too, so that must mean something. To us it means we have to find a way to break through to our dads.

We need their help.

■

The game had nearly killed Carrie.

She had never felt anything like it, not even on

the lake with her father. Being so close to the people she loved, watching them from a distance. No one knew her, so she could hide, and there was so much excitement and activity, she just stayed on the edges, keeping her family in sight.

Watching Travis play made her feel thrilled, so happy, to see what a great player he had become. She knew how good that must make him feel; football had always been her brother's passion. And seeing Beck in the stands with prissy Ally—it made her laugh. She wished she could have heard what Beck had to say about that. She had to fight the impulse to make her way under the bleachers, grab her sister's ankle, get her to meet her down below.

But the hardest part was seeing her mother. Standing behind the parking lot, hiding in a grove of pine trees, Carrie had thought she was invisible. Her stomach growled from the smell of food grilling, cider mulling. She hadn't eaten since breakfast, and the bus ride had been longer than she'd expected. Every penny counted, so she couldn't even buy popcorn or a hot dog.

She saw a group with a big box overflowing with sandwiches. They ate and drank, and when they were done, they just left the box in the parking lot and made their way back toward the field. Carrie was so hungry. She was starving for her family. She'd fed Gracie her bottle, feeling almost weak in the knees. Spotting those sandwiches, she knew if she ate one she'd feel better; it would make the longing for her family seem more bearable. So she inched out of the pine trees, just in time to see her mother.

She was talking to a man across the parking lot, staring straight at her. Carrie's eyes locked with hers. She nearly yelled "Mom!" She was sure her mother had recognized her. But the sun was behind her; it must have been in her mother's eyes, the way she put her hand up to her forehead, seeming to squint into the bright light. Carrie ducked back into the shadows and took the moment to zoom her camera, snap a picture. That's when Gracie must have dropped her pacifier; but at least Carrie had a photo.

She stared at it now, on the screen of her digital camera: a close-up of her mother's face. Her hazel eyes, so full of stress and worried exhaustion, fine lines in her skin, but still that pretty, warm, loving face Carrie knew so well. Carrie traced the picture with her finger, the way she used to touch her mother's cheeks when she was little. Had Carrie put those lines on her mother's face? Had she caused the stress?

She knew she had. Being so close but so far away was like purgatory. Why couldn't she have taken a few steps into the light instead of shrinking back into the shade, walked toward her mother, placed Gracie right into her arms? The possibility had been right there. Carrie closed her eyes and could almost feel her mother hugging her now.

It seemed like a strange miracle, that they would all end up in Rhode Island. Carrie had come to help J.D. She'd thought that if she could keep him from dying, she might be able to forgive what she'd let happen at the lake. She'd never heard of J. D. Blackstone until the day the man she'd always thought of as her father died.

It felt crazy, but she knew it was an act of love— standing by a stranger's bed, watching over the nurses, and doctors, and people coming and going. She had no practical help to offer, just a need to be there, to lend strength with her presence. He was asleep, didn't even know she was there. Except that one time, when she stood in the shadows, and she saw him open his eyes and stare at her. Was he really awake? He didn't speak, and neither did she.

One day a nurse noticed her and asked why she was there. She wished she could take back that answer. Another time a different nurse noticed her, asked her when she was due, whether she was having a boy or a girl, if it was her first. They talked about babies for a while; that actually comforted Carrie. It was how she'd have liked to talk to her mother and Beck.

At the same time, she couldn't imagine that. It was as if she was living a second life—her first life had been as a daughter and sister. Her family had been Andy and Maura, Travis and Beck Shaw. She'd been an honors student. She'd never imagined breaking any serious rules, hurting anyone she loved.

Her second life was as a pregnant runaway. She had killed—not really, but for all practical purposes—the man she'd always thought was her father. They'd fought, and told each other the truth. The canoe had tipped in the storm, during their fight—and Carrie knew it had been her fault. She'd been so upset, she'd made it capsize.

It hurt to remember. She had loved her father—Andy—so much. She could hardly stand life without him; what must it be like for her mother, Travis, and Beck? How could she have left her brother and sister without their father?

He'd never watch Travis play football again. He'd never see Beck bring home A's on her math tests.

Beck. Carrie had held her little sister's hand, walking to school. They'd stayed on the sidewalk for part of the walk, cut through backyards on another. Beck had talked the whole time, nonstop, just going on and on as the sisters clasped hands and walked along.

The feeling of her sister's hand in hers filled her now, rocked her back and forth. Dell was coming to pick up Grace and take her to childcare. Carrie lifted her baby and kissed her tiny fingers. She whispered a story about Beck, her incredible aunt, and wondered if they would ever meet.

She showed Gracie the picture of her mother. Gracie gurgled and laughed, and Carrie saw her mother in her daughter's face, but nothing of Andy Shaw. Carrie closed her eyes, thinking of how she'd let him slip beneath the surface of the lake, of how he'd loved her her whole life, and she'd just let him die.

Her mother had gotten pregnant before she was married, pregnant with Carrie. Carrie had such love and compassion for her mother. But she had kept the secret all this time, Carrie's lifetime plus nine months. **Like mother, like daughter,** Andy Shaw had said, and it was true. Some things couldn't be fixed or even talked about, not even in a family where everyone used to love each other.

■

The ability to sleep had left Maura. She rested her head on the pillow, and felt as if she'd been through a hurricane. Everything in her life was broken, pieces all around. But outside, the night was calm and still. She climbed out of bed, pulled on her jacket, walked outside.

The sound of the waves began to soothe her. She walked the path, listening to their constant motion, rolling in from far out at sea. She reassured herself that Travis and Beck were safe in their beds, that they were going to be okay. They were together—they'd get through this. The air was cold; she jammed her hands into her jacket pocket, found the pacifier.

It shocked her fingers, tactile memories of her first daughter's earliest days. She thought of that young mother and baby at the football field; she had been thinking of them as herself and Carrie eighteen years ago, but in that instant everything changed. She'd been wrong—the girl in the parking lot had been Carrie, holding her baby, the one Beck had been so sure about.

"Carrie!" she said out loud.

The white waning moon spread a thin net across the ocean. Salt spray misted her face. The sound of honking filled the air: a flock of geese flying south, right over her head, so close she could almost feel their wing beats.

Turning to watch them pass, Maura looked at the mansion. There was that strange light again: the top floor glowed, a green, watery jewel. She saw a silhouette in the window: a person facing the sea, watching her. She shivered, took a step toward the house, and suddenly the lights went out.

She ran toward the building. As a teacher, she had a passkey—heavy, ridged, magnetized metal, and she dug it out of her bag. She climbed the wide marble steps, whisked the passkey in the electronic lock, and let herself into the front door.

Nightlights burned in bronze sconces all along the quiet hallways. She climbed flight after flight of graceful, curving limestone stairs. It was late, but she saw several students in the halls. They looked curious, obviously wondering why she was there. One nodded, and Maura waved as she tore up the steps.

As she passed the third-floor landing and approached what should have been the fourth floor, she came to a brick wall. How bizarre, she thought. Compared with the rest of the mansion's gracious French architecture, this seemed clunky, hastily installed, not at all in keeping with James Desmond Blackstone's vision. The top floor was literally bricked off, but nothing could have kept her out.

In the center of the wall was a wide door with a conventional lock. Maura rattled the knob, but it didn't budge. But somehow the latch hadn't caught; she pushed the door open easily. This walled-off part of the stairwell was pitch-dark and smelled musty, but beneath the dust and dampness was the unmistakable scent of chlorine. Winded from her climb and the triumph of getting through the steel door, she headed up the last few steps.

At the top, she stood in total blackness. Her heart was pounding as she felt her way around. It seemed to be a landing just like those on the floors she'd passed, about forty feet square, with balustrades to prevent a fall to the landing below. Running her hands along the cool limestone walls, she felt what was unmistakably a thick wooden door.

So this had been Mary Langley's room, she thought. She'd heard Beck and Lucy talking about the girl's ghost, about how she haunted Newport Academy. There were intimations of a family tragedy, of a lost sister. . . . Maura had heard some of it, but blocked it out. What significance did Mary have to her? Maura had her own lost girl. "Carrie," she said. Placing her hands on the doorway, she rested her ear against the carved wood, trying to hear inside.

Yes, that was the sound of water. Gentle movement, as if someone was swimming. Maura's spine tingled in spite of herself.

She reached for her passkey. Hands trembling, she felt to see if the door had an electronic lock like the one at the building's entrance. Amazingly, it did. Maura swiped her card, waiting for the click. But it didn't happen. Crouching down, she peered under the door.

There it was, luminous, cool, and green: ghost light. She pressed her eye as close as she could to the space between the floor and the door, and tried to see. There were shadows.

Movement: perhaps it was the flicker of water in

the pool, or maybe it was Mary and her lost sister, wandering the top floor of their old school.

Why did this make her feel so close to Carrie? She'd been thinking about her daughter so hard, it felt almost as if she'd conjured her. Stretched out on the floor, her cheek on the cold stone, Maura stared at the celadon spirit light and felt her eyes flood. She placed her hand against the door; it was warm to the touch. Heat from the pool, from steam . . .

She felt as if Carrie was inside the room. Crazy, she knew. But even so, she lay on the hard floor by the narrow stripe of green light and let the feeling stay in her heart, a gentle glow that took her back to Columbus, to her home, to those beautiful times when nothing was perfect but everything was okay, those days over a year ago when her family was all together, before her husband died and her darling girl ran away.

10 THE NEXT DAY KIDS WERE talking about Mrs. Shaw getting spooked by Mary Langley's ghost. One girl had spotted the teacher heading to the fourth floor at night, when she wasn't usually in the dorm. Someone else had seen her running—flying—back down. Rumors began, and spread fast: she'd climbed the stairs to contact the spirit world, she'd gone to battle dark forces, she'd attempted to investigate the story of Mary's death, she'd wanted to commune with Mary herself.

The streak of brilliant October sunshine ended, and heavy fog rolled in. Gray and cold, it hovered over the coastline, darkened the day. The temperature staggered downward, and the boiler kicked on, making strange creaking noises in the old pipes. The upperclassmen called it "Mary weather." Whenever Mary's ghost was disturbed, she summoned the fog from far out at sea.

It was almost Halloween, and eerie tales of Newport Academy were too delicious not to spread throughout the school. The Pumpkin Carve and

Blackstone Blaze were coming up fast—no one would know exactly when until the stack of firewood for the bonfire appeared by the football field.

"Hello, Ghost Hunter," Stephen Campbell said, stepping into Maura's classroom between periods.

"I'm glad you think it's funny," Maura said.

"Seriously, you're the school's superhero," he said. "My second-period geometry class was in awe of you. They practically had you in a sword battle with the Dark Lord on the fourth-floor landing."

"The Dark Lord?"

"You haven't been here long enough," Stephen said. "Cities have urban myths. Newport Academy has school myths, and that's one of the biggest ones."

"Who is he?"

"Percival Vanderbilt. The White Knight's archenemy."

"And who is the White Knight?"

"None other than James Desmond Blackstone himself. Vanderbilt tried to keep this school from being built—he saw Blackstone's fortunes rising, encroaching on his own. He said that Blackstone was shanty Irish, and as such didn't know a thing about education. He had a lot of influence here in Newport, but Blackstone was a fighter, and he wasn't going to give up. The kids like to say the battle rages on, the Dark Lord and the White Knight."

"What's James Desmond doing haunting his own school?"

"Protecting Mary Langley, cracking the whip to make the kids study, reminding everyone of his power the way he did in life. Pick one. . . ." He gave her a grin, and Maura smiled back in spite of herself.

"Why would he have to protect Mary?"

"She was Vanderbilt's niece," Stephen said. "Her father didn't measure up in Vanderbilt's eyes, and he objected when Langley married his sister. Langley was a friend of Blackstone, and Vanderbilt took his sending Mary here as the worst kind of affront. But as time went on, he wanted to know his niece—his sister had died, and Mary connected him to her. The story goes that Percival picked Mary up at school on a foggy December night, the tail end of a big snowy nor'easter, and his carriage crashed right off the cliff, into the water. Langley never saw Mary again."

Maura couldn't speak: she could feel Langley missing his daughter. She touched her desk. There were paperclips in a tray. A blue notebook. She raised her gaze to the window, to the impenetrable fog, wondered where Carrie could be.

"Have I upset you?" Stephen asked.

"Did she drown?" Maura asked.

"Excuse me?"

"You said that the carriage went off the cliff. Did Mary drown?"

"Yes," Stephen said. "J.D. and Patricia grew up with the story. People ran to the edge, saw the carriage floating in the sea, just like a boat. Mary was inside, hands on the windows. They tried to get down to rescue her, but a big wave swamped the carriage, and it sank."

Maura stared at her blue notebook. She thought of Carrie in the water. She hadn't drowned, but the experience had taken her away.

"Would you take a walk with me?" Stephen asked.

She hesitated only for a minute, then nodded and stood. Her classes were finished for the day and Stephen's must be too. Grabbing her coat, she followed him down the corridor, and went outside to wait while he got his. The air was cold and damp, the mist so thick it blocked any view of the sea. She sat on a bench, and when she looked up, she saw Blackstone Hall disappearing in the fog.

It looked so very like another Newport mansion she knew, that stood a mile south along the cliff. She remembered the day J.D. had shown it to her, the house he'd grown up in. It had been a foggy afternoon, just like this. He hadn't driven her through the front gates; he'd said his parents would insist they stay for dinner.

"What would be so bad about that?" she'd asked. "Don't you like to eat with your parents?"

"That's not it," he said, shaking his head. He

parked his motorcycle in the driveway to the service entrance.

"Service entrance?" she'd asked.

"For deliveries," he'd said.

"You make it sound like a hotel," she'd said. "What kind of house needs 'deliveries'?"

He hadn't answered. Just led her down a path, through a cut in the hedge, onto the public Cliff Walk. They'd walked a hundred yards, waves crashing on the left. The tall hedge on their right prevented them from seeing into the property. Soon the gravel path slanted downhill slightly, and they walked into a stone tunnel under the lawn.

They were quiet. She thought about Andy, his proposal by the covered bridge, knew that she was supposed to leave Newport at the end of the summer. She'd thought, "supposed to." Because by then her feelings had her on such a roller coaster, she wasn't sure she could.

It was dark in the tunnel, except for the opening at the other end, fifty yards away. Halfway there, they stopped. J.D. turned to his right, dug in his pocket for his keys. Maura heard the rasp of a lock. He gave her his hand, pulled her through an iron gate. Inside the gate, they found themselves on stone stairs that led upward, into the private property behind the hedge—J.D.'s yard.

"I made that gate," he said. "When I was seventeen."

She heard him, but was struck speechless by what she saw. There, a football field away, looming out of the thick fog, was the biggest house she'd ever seen. It looked like a French château, something she'd studied in eighteenth-century history. Two wings jutted out toward the sea on either side of a classical garden.

They walked toward it, and as they got closer, she saw more details: columns and a portico, stone lions on the terrace, marble urns planted with cascading flowers. Windows faced the sea, and through them she saw tapestries and large paintings and carved marble fireplaces and a curved staircase.

"Now I know why you need deliveries here," she said. "It's like a museum. You live here?" she asked.

"You know where I live," he said.

"The warehouse," she said.

He nodded.

"Why? You don't get along with your family?"

"I get along with them fine. I just don't like living here. I want . . . more."

"More?" she laughed. "How could there be more?"

He laughed too. "All this gets in the way," he said. "Of what I want."

"What do you want?"

He stared at the house, then turned to her. "Real life," he said.

"Is that why you made the iron gate?" she asked. "Instead of letting your parents hire someone to do it?"

"Yeah," he said. "That's exactly why."

"That's why you didn't want to drive into the front driveway," she said. "With me . . . I'm too 'real life' for this place."

"That's not the reason," he said. He stared at her, blue eyes burning through the fog.

"Then what is?"

"You're going back to Ohio," he said. "You haven't told me why, or who's waiting for you there. Is it that guy?"

"Stop, J.D."

"Look, I know you had a boyfriend," he said. "Katharine told me even before you got here. But that's changed."

She'd clamped her mouth shut, unable or unwilling to talk about it. She couldn't think about Andy or talk about him to J.D.

J.D. held her, pulled her close.

"You know you can't go back," he said.

"We can't talk about that," she said.

"Maybe not now," he said. "But we will. Because I'm not letting you go."

"Shhh," she'd said, letting him kiss her.

"And then," he said, stopping, "we'll find a place—not the warehouse, and not here. A house. We'll live together, and I'll bring you here to meet my parents. You'll be the first girl I've done that with."

"Shhh," she'd said again, and he'd kissed her again as the fog swirled around them.

Eighteen years later she strode with Stephen through the mist; he took her along a bluestone path to the cliff. They passed trimmed hedges, overgrown vines, wind-twisted cedars. They took the path down to the beach, and Maura hugged herself to stay warm as they walked along the hard-packed sand. Off the cliff, away from memories of J.D., she began to breathe easily again.

"It feels good to get away from school," she said.

"I know what you mean," he said. "The walls can really close in. The academy is its own lit-tle world. . . . Besides, I've been wanting to talk to you."

"About what?" she asked.

"Well, why you're here. In Newport."

"Sometimes I wonder why we left Columbus," she said.

"Why did you?" he asked slowly.

"A lot of reasons." She thought of Beck's stealing. "It was too hard to stay in our house. We missed them—my husband and daughter—all the time. I . . . thought it would be easier on the kids to have a fresh start. Easier on me too."

"I'm sorry for what you've been through," he said.

"Did the Davis girls tell you?" she asked, assuming. He didn't reply, and she went on. "Beck's been getting close to Lucy. They always seem to be doing math homework. . . ." She pushed windblown hair from her eyes and glanced at him. "Beck gets lost in it."

"She's very good. I'm trying to test her, to see exactly **how** good. I want the kids, especially the girls, to get past the idea that math is just calculating numbers. When Lucy was younger, after her mother left and her father got sick, I happened to mention something about counting the number of angels who could fit on the head of a pin, and she jumped on it. I realized I was onto something."

"Like what?" Maura asked, head down as they walked through the fog.

He paused; his eyes tightened, and she had the feeling he was weighing what she could handle. The fog surrounded them, made her feel they were in a private capsule. She could see only ten feet in each direction. The sand at her feet was strewn with broken clamshells. She bent down, picked up the perfectly curved outer edge of a quahog.

"Infinity," he said. "Math helps us describe nature in a precise, universal language. Physical nature. Forces of gravity. Architecture is all about math. The angles, how a certain column supports weight. The speed of light is math. Death is math. What happens to the soul after it departs the body.

And love. The rate at which you can get it back after it departs the marriage."

"Seriously?" she asked.

"Why not?" he asked, giving her a wry grin.

"Is it working for you?" she asked.

"No," he said. "Not the last part, anyway. Patricia's with someone else now. We were only married five years when she said she needed time apart. The divorce happened fast, just two years ago—she went to the Dominican Republic. Met someone at the resort, and is married to him now. Her third."

"I'm sorry," she said, and they walked in silence for a minute, the only sound their feet crunching shells on the packed sand. "You never had kids together?"

"Nope," he said. "I wanted to, but it didn't happen. I have Pell and Lucy to care for, though. They're the closest I have to children of my own."

"You must have been really close to their father," she said.

"I was," he said, nodding. "All four of us were like brothers. Truly, we'd do anything for each other. Me, Taylor, Ted, and J.D."

"You're very lucky," she said, J.D.'s name giving her a jolt as intense as her memories of their walk in the fog.

"Earlier," he said. "You said you wonder why you came from Ohio."

"Yes," she said.

"You know the real reason, don't you?" he asked.

She glanced over at him, and through the gloom she saw color rising in his face.

"It's because you were recruited," he said. "Ted sent you a letter asking you to apply."

"Along with how many other new teachers?" she asked.

"Your letter was special," he said.

She gave him a look, but he just kept walking. Hands deep in his jacket pockets, he frowned at his feet. Waves advanced up the hard pewter sand, the tide coming in, starting to cover the shattered shells.

"It was a form letter," she said.

"That's what you were supposed to think," he said.

"What are you talking about?" she asked.

Stephen took a few more steps, realized Maura wasn't moving. He paused, facing away from her. Even just a few feet away, the lines of his body were blurred by fog. Then he turned and came toward her, staring into her eyes. His face looked pale and tense.

"I just told you my friends and I are as close as brothers. We'd do anything to help each other. See, I know everything about you," he said. "And so does Ted. That's why he recruited you to teach here. . . . Last night, when you climbed to the fourth floor . . . what made you do that, Maura? It's almost as if you were drawn there."

"I was," she said, her voice trembling.

"Do you know why?"

"I had to know who was up there, watching me out on the cliff. Someone in the window . . ."

"You know who it was, don't you?"

Maura suddenly felt afraid. She took a few steps backward, then turned to run. Stephen caught her arm, stopped her. Yanking away, she started to fight. But then she caught sight of his eyes—there was nothing frightening about them: just sadness and compassion.

"Carrie," she whispered. "For a minute . . . I thought I saw her at the game. It made me a little crazy; last night I felt her there, watching me."

"No," Stephen said.

"Tell me," she said, unable to stand the look in his eyes.

"It was your daughter's father in there last night. It was J.D."

She stared at him.

"He lives close by, on Shepard Avenue. He was swimming here that night. We filled the pool for him. We thought . . . if you were close to him, if you came to Newport, it might help him. That's why Ted sent you that recruitment letter."

"I have to see him," she said.

"It's just . . . I have to warn you," Stephen said.

Maura felt her heart thudding as she waited for him to go on.

"You know how badly he was injured, right? He's not the same as you remember him, Maura. You have to be prepared."

"Take me to him," she said.

◼

News alert: something's going on between my mother and Mr. Campbell.

Here's what happened. I was just getting out of History when I looked out a window on the second-floor corridor and saw my mom bundled up in her coat, sitting on a stone bench out on the lawn.

I stared out at her. I had this strange feeling I was at the movies—the window glass and thirty yards separated me from her, and she didn't know I was watching. But I saw the way she pulled her coat tight, crossed her arms across her chest, tilted her head back to stare up at the sky.

Or maybe not the sky—possibly the fourth floor. I've heard what everyone is saying, that my mother went up there to see Mary. I asked her about it when I saw her at lunch, and it went like this.

"Did you find her?"

"Find whom?"

"You know. Mary Langley. The girl who died."

"Honey, no. It didn't have anything to do with ghosts. This school is new to me, just as it is to you.

I felt like exploring a little, that's all. Just because a person grows up doesn't mean she stops being curious."

I liked that. It's true that my mother has always seemed young because she never stops looking around. She's not one of those mothers who points her car toward the grocery store and just buys the family's food. No. My mother wanders. She'll head toward the market, and get sidetracked by a rainbow. Next thing you know, we're stopped by a field, and she's staring at the arc in the sky, quoting some haiku her mother wrote:

Light splits the dark cloud
Silver pours down from the sky.
Rain stops for today.

And then we just drive on, maybe to the market or perhaps she gets inspired to go to the library or art museum first. That's just how she is. Look how we came to Newport! She got sidetracked from our life in Columbus, decided to come see the sea, teach at a fancy private school. So it's not at all surprising she'd climb up to the fourth floor just to see what was what.

And maybe that explained why, standing in the second-floor corridor today I saw my mother sitting there in the fog, eyes trained on the top windows. She barely noticed as the school door opened and Mr. Campbell walked out. I saw him head straight for her. He didn't look left or right, just made a beeline for my mom.

And the minute she saw him, she jumped up. He'd startled her. That's what I thought at first. But then I saw how glad she was to see him. They talked like old friends. Through the glass I couldn't hear her words, but I saw her mouth moving—fast. Plenty to say.

Mr. Campbell looked up at the fourth floor too. As if he could see someone up there. Mary? Who else would it be? It seemed he was checking to see if they were being watched, him and my mother.

Knowing my mother was occupied, I felt like walking home to go through her things. Don't ask me why, because I can't explain it. We live together, she's right there under the same roof, but looking at everything she owns makes me feel more secure. As if she's not going anywhere. I learn strange things too. Like yesterday, I rummaged through the pockets of her jacket and found a baby's pacifier. Can you imagine that? It didn't weird me out, though. In fact, I found it kind of comforting.

Considering how she's been acting lately, the fourth floor and all, a pacifier is nothing to worry about. Anyway, I didn't walk home. The bell rang, time for math lab, independent study, a quiet hour by ourselves, to roam the plains of geometry. We were explorers in a wild world. Lucy came running down the hall, linked her arm with me, spun me around.

"Well, you're a happy little thing," I said.

"I just got an A on my history project," she said.

"Take it handy," I said. I've been on a slight Irish kick, because it turns out Redmond's father is from Ireland, and sometimes his Boston accent goes all schizo and he uses these weird Irish expressions.

"I have to ask Stephen if I can miss lab," she said. "Because Mrs. Merrill is free right now and she says she wants to enter my project in the New England Schools Comp . . ."

"You can't miss math," I said. "And besides, Stephen's not around." **Because he's with my mother . . .**

"Even better! He won't miss me. It's just lab," she said. "I can do my homework later. You can help me!"

"No," I said, feeling panicked. Didn't she realize that time was of the essence? She's the one who got me started thinking about the possibilities of infinity, of seeing beyond what's obvious, of finding what they tell us is no longer here. I had to see my father, I had to find Carrie. My chest ached. If a fourteen-year-old could have a heart attack, I was having one.

"What do you mean, 'no'?" she asked, and she laughed a little.

"I mean we have to work together now! Now!"

She backed off as if I'd scared her. Maybe my
voice was a little loud, because other kids in the
corridor turned to look. She calmed down. Stepped
close to me, gave me a little hug. I felt her breath
on my ear.

"You're right," she said. "I'm sorry."

"I'm happy about your history project," I said,
trying to sound normal.

"I know. You're my best friend," she said, and I
saw her gather herself, smile, wanting to reassure
me. I saw that and even as I loved her for it, I worried that I would drive her away, that my stealing
heart would take more of her fatherless self than
she could spare.

"You're mine too," I said.

Best friends. Yes. We were that. But even as I
gave her a hug, I felt dominoes tumble inside me,
click-click-click, a whole long line of them falling
and demolishing the order.

No friendship could be enough. Lucy had Pell.
And I didn't have Carrie. A friend was wonderful,
but my broken heart ached for my sister. My
mother was acting odd; it scared me. The world
was going crazy, and I wasn't sure how much of it I
could take.

11 MAURA AND STEPHEN CROSSED the fog-shrouded campus and hurried along the trail that led into the woods behind the athletic fields, skirting the football field in mist that drifted through the long row of poplars. Leaving the school grounds on a path between two granite pillars, they walked a few blocks from the ocean into a neighborhood of still-large but not palatial houses.

When they got to a stone house with formal landscaping, Stephen steered her up the driveway. She saw by the sign on the lawn that this was the headmaster's house: the Shannon family lived here. But instead of going up the front steps, Stephen led her around back to a separate building, to an old ivy-covered fieldstone carriage house or garage.

She spotted Angus coming out; he hadn't seen them yet. His van was backed in to the massive barn-style doors; Maura saw that it had a wheelchair lift, and that it had obviously just been used. Angus pushed the button to raise the lift into the van and close the door.

"Hey," Stephen said.

"What the hell are you doing here?" Angus asked, his glare shifting from Stephen to Maura as he blocked their way.

"They need to see each other," Stephen said.

"That's not what he says. . . ."

"And you think he knows what he's doing?" Stephen said.

"I've got my orders," Angus said, squinting at Maura. "I'm in enough trouble because she broke through the fourth-floor door last night."

"You can blame this on me," Stephen said. "But we're going in to see J.D."

Angus was puffed up, ready for battle, but something in Stephen's face wore him down, and he shrugged with frustration. "You'll do what you want to do. The four of you always have. This time, it'll probably get me fired."

"As if that would ever happen," Stephen said. "This is for J.D., Angus. I'm doing this for him, okay? You know that."

Angus's eyes burned, and his mouth was tight with disapproval. But turning away, he let them pass. Maura watched him climb into the van, start it up, and pull down the long driveway.

"Angus is loyal to the Blackstone family," Stephen said. "He worked for J.D.'s father and grandfather on the docks. His great-grandfather worked for James Desmond. Their families go way back. . . ."

But Maura wasn't listening. She knew that
Stephen was just making conversation, wanting to
distract her. She stared at the barn doors, at the
wrought-iron latch. Stephen lifted his hand and
knocked.

"Who is it?" came the voice.

"Me," Stephen said.

Maura heard rustling behind the heavy door.
The iron hinges creaked as the door opened. And
her heart turned over.

He was strong, powerfully built. Anyone could see
that he worked out—he wore a thin gray T-shirt,
just as he always had, and his upper body was
lean and muscular. His graying brown hair was
very short, almost a buzz cut. His blue eyes were
as bright as ever, full of humor as they looked
at Stephen. That changed when they swept over
Maura.

She felt every minute, every year disappear. His
eyes were the same, and when he looked at her she
felt loved in a way that didn't come with words or
sense. He knew her then, and he knew her now.

"Maura," he said.

"J.D.," she said, crouching down to look him
straight in the eyes. He touched her cheek. The
contact was light but so intense she couldn't
breathe. If she focused on his face, she wouldn't see
the chair. Metal glinting, surrounding him. But she

had to look, forced herself to see the wheels, the armrests. She fumbled to take his hand.

"You came to see me," he said.

"It took me a long time," she said. "I'm so sorry."

"I didn't want you here."

She heard Stephen slip out the door, the latch close behind him. J.D. and Maura held hands. He had workman's hands, even now. They felt strong, lean. She stared at them.

"I'm so sorry about what happened to you," she said.

"It was a long time ago," he said.

"I should have . . ." she began.

"Maura, don't start that, okay?"

A lifetime had passed; their lives had unfolded without each other. From the minute they'd met, something had been set in motion. Passion, the inability to regulate anything at all. Feelings, behavior, kisses, despair. The realization disturbed her, and she pulled away. Withdrew her hands, stood up, and looked around.

The garage had been transformed into an apartment: paintings on the wall, books on shelves, a bed, an old sofa, and a desk. Curtains were pulled across the windows, and a burgundy drapery blocked off the far end of the room.

"You always lived in unusual places," she said.

"The warehouse," he said.

"Yes. I went down there as soon as I got to New-port. But you weren't there. . . ."

"No," he said.

"You're not at your parents' house," she said.

He gave her a smile that asked if she knew him at all. Wheeling himself to the window, he opened the curtains to a glint of mist. He gestured toward the sofa, and she sat down. He moved closer. His face was angular, almost gaunt; he hadn't shaved in a couple of days. He had high cheekbones, widely spaced eyes, a gentle mouth.

"It's good to see you," she said.

"You really went looking for me at the ware-house?"

"Of course," she said. "It's where I've been pic-turing you all these years."

"It's where I've lived most of them. Just, right now, I'm recovering from an operation."

She nodded, holding back, the questions ready to pour out. She looked at his legs, and he saw. "I don't want you to see me," he said. "I never did."

"I feel as if I did this to you."

"You didn't."

"J.D.," she said.

He stared at her for a very long time. Was it too painful to talk about? Was he afraid of reliving it? She had the strangest feeling he was weighing what details she could handle.

"I did something stupid. I guess you've heard the

details, but I'll tell you myself. I climbed the bridge again, but this time I fell. I was over the redline—forty feet off the ground, I should have died. I fractured my spine. The vertebrae were compressed, the spinal cord nearly severed."

She listened to the clinical description, the lack of emotion. But she saw the strained weariness in his eyes.

"Katharine called me when it happened."

"I know she told you. I told her to keep you away."

Maura stared at him. "She didn't agree," she said.

"There was only one reason I wanted you to come," he said. "And it wasn't to feel sorry for me. There's been improvement, the nerves are regenerating." He paused, looked at her. "Ted told me what he did, getting you to apply to teach here."

"Your friends love you," she said. "That's obvious."

He stared at her, so close and present it felt as if there was no space between them at all. His eyes were ice blue. "I know about what happened last summer," he said. "To your husband. I'm sorry."

"Thank you," she said.

"And Carrie was on the lake with him," he said.

Just hearing him use her name filled Maura's eyes with tears. "She was," she said.

"Tell me," he said, staring hard into her eyes. "I

want you to tell me what you wouldn't admit the night I drove to see you. Tell me I was right."

"You were right."

"We had . . ."

"We had a daughter," she whispered.

His hands rested easily on the handles of his chair, but she saw tears pool in his eyes, his jaw muscles twitch.

"Why didn't you tell me then?"

"When I decided to go back to him," she said, "I shut everything else out. I had to. If I told you she was yours, you'd have wanted to be part of her life. Andy and I couldn't have withstood that."

He didn't respond. She could hardly sit there, knowing what a terrible thing she'd done. She wanted to tell him she was sorry, but the words seemed so inadequate. With one lie, she'd ruined his life—and Carrie's and Andy's.

"Did he ever find out she wasn't his?"

"Two and half years ago she was in a car accident. She was badly injured, and Andy and I went to give blood. Neither of us was a match. So he knew. . . ."

"What did he do?"

"He was going to leave me. He told me the day he died, just before he and Carrie went out in the canoe. We'd made it through the shock of him finding out, and we tried counseling for a few sessions—the kids had no idea. I know they'd sensed trouble between us, the first time ever. But they didn't know why."

He took her hand. "I let you go. I had to because you wanted me to, but I never stopped thinking of you. I knew the minute I heard you were pregnant. I should have . . ." The words tore out of him, and he shut down hard to keep from saying what would hurt them both even more.

"I wish you could have known her," Maura said. But was that true? She had built a fortress around herself and her family. J.D. was right; once she'd decided to cut him out of her life, she had done it completely.

"I feel as if I do know her," he said.

"Really?"

He nodded. "I think she knew about me," he said.

Maura felt startled. Why would he say that? "I never told her. It's killing me, to wonder if she somehow found out. See, she hasn't come home, J.D. She ran away that same day. I haven't seen her since."

"Do you have any idea where she'd go?"

Maura shook her head. "It's all I think about. She sent a couple of postcards, it seemed she was heading out west. I keep thinking maybe she learned what I did, and hates me for it."

"I don't believe that. Tell me about her, what she's like," he said.

"Beautiful in all ways," Maura said. "Sweet, kind, funny, the smartest girl in her class. A good girl. Wonderful to her sister and brother. The best daughter anyone could have."

"Were you close?"

"Very."

"Do you have a picture of her?"

Maura took out her cell phone. She scrolled through, found a shot she'd taken of Carrie the morning of the accident. The lake was in the background, shimmering and blue. She handed J.D. the phone.

He stared at the small screen without saying a word. This was the closest she could come to introducing him to their daughter.

"When I first got to Newport," she said, "this September, I used to drive down the alley looking for you."

"Why?" he asked. "Why now?"

"Because I had to tell you about Carrie. I wanted to make up, somehow, for what I've put you through. And because . . ." she said, tears flooding. "She came from us. I kept you out of her life and I'll pay for that for the rest of mine. What I did was cruel, unforgivable. But she was yours. After she disappeared, I'd think of you. It all came crashing down. I was crazy, obsessed, thinking that you were my only connection to her."

He nodded, and she saw that he was still staring

at the picture. Carrie, Lake Michigan behind her, pine-studded islands dotting the horizon, the light-house rising up over her shoulder. She thought of the night J.D. had taken her up to the top of the Jamestown Bridge. They'd gazed down the dark, sparkling bay, toward Beavertail Light. That had been their beacon, their promise.

After a moment, he snapped the phone shut, handed it back. He turned his wheelchair away as if dismissing her, as if he'd had enough. She stared at the back of his head; her fingertips tingled, wanting to touch him. She had jeopardized every-thing she'd thought she ever wanted for that one summer with him.

"J.D.," she said.

"Look," he said. "I get tired. You'd better go."

"Can we see each other again?"

"I don't think that's a good idea."

"You're obviously strong," she said. "You get around. You swim—I know, because Stephen told me they filled the pool at school for you. I've seen the lights at night. If you don't want me to come here, I'll meet you there."

"No."

J.D. and Maura stared at each other.

"J.D.?" she said.

"Go, Maura," he said.

He backed his chair away, turning around, dis-missing her. Everything seemed to have changed the minute he looked at Carrie's picture—Carrie with the lighthouse in the background.

She remembered the moment she lied. She'd been guilty and confused after returning to Columbus from Newport. She and Andy had just eloped—he believed the baby was his, couldn't wait to get married. Maura had called Katharine to tell her about the baby and the wedding, and the very next day J.D. showed up on her doorstep, completely wild.

"Maura, I love you," he'd said. "Come with me."

"What are you doing here?"

"Come with me," he'd said again.

"J.D.," she'd said, feeling panicked. She'd stood there, staring at him, sweaty and windblown after riding his motorcycle all the way from Rhode Island to Ohio. He'd reached toward her, touched her face. She'd leaned into it, shaking.

"Maura," he'd said. "I brought an extra helmet. Come on."

"Are you kidding?" she'd asked.

He'd grabbed her hand. Their eyes had locked, and she'd felt electricity up and down her spine. All she had to do was grab her bag; there was nothing she needed, nothing she had to take. She could do this.

"Come with me."

"I . . . I'm married."

"Why'd you do that?"

"Because I love him."

"No, Maura."

She'd tried to nod, to tell him yes, she did, but she couldn't.

"Let's go," J.D. had said, pulling her toward him. "Just leave. You can call him, write him, do whatever it takes. But come with me."

"I can't," she'd said. "He's my husband."

"I don't care."

And in that second, neither did Maura. She'd wanted him from their first night together. She was carrying their child. Her hand strayed to her belly, and she'd pulled it away before he saw. But he did see.

"Maura?" he'd asked, his eyes burning.

"The baby's Andy's," she'd said. "Now you know why I can't—can't talk to you, can't see you ever again."

"The baby's mine," he'd said. "I know it—"

"No! It's not!" she'd yelled. "You have no idea!"

"Don't do this," he'd said. "You know what we have, Maura. There's no one else for either of us. You care about Andy, don't want to hurt him. But staying will destroy him, because it's a lie. We're having a baby."

"We're not," she'd said, making her voice hard.

"You're lying," he'd said. "Because you told me the truth all summer. When we were together . . . we love each other. Maura, I know you're having my child."

Maura had stared at him. She saw his excitement and wildness, his bridge-climbing craziness. He'd shown her her own passion, taken her right to the edge and terrified her.

Maura knew Andy so well. They'd been together so long, all through college. She'd been drawn to him because he was so good and steady, nothing like her father. He was the Mr. Sisson she'd always dreamed of. Always wanted. She had stared up at J.D., saw those sharp blue eyes, his lean face.

"I feel safe with Andy," she'd said, breathless.

She'd told him to leave her alone, never contact her again, closed the door right in his face. She'd leaned against the door, feeling him standing there just on the other side, willing herself not to turn the doorknob. And then she'd heard his motorcycle start up.

He'd driven straight back to Rhode Island. He went to the Jamestown Bridge, started to climb up to the catwalk where they'd gazed out at the lighthouse and the dark sea beyond. Maybe he was exhausted from the ride. Maybe he felt rage or sorrow or both. But he'd lost his footing, fallen backward onto the ground.

Maura let herself out of J.D.'s garage apartment and hurried past Stephen Campbell without a word.

■

"That was nice," Stephen said, walking into J.D.'s apartment. "You made her run away."

"You are an asshole," J.D. said.

"You're the asshole, my friend."

"I told both you and Ted I had to do this in my own time."

"Yeah, well, she moved up the timetable."

"Yeah, well, you didn't have to bring her here till I told you. Look how it turned out."

Stephen stared at J.D. He had him on that one. Maura had bolted about as fast as she could. Stephen had seen the devastation in her eyes. He'd felt guilty for bringing her here with so little warning, especially while J.D. and Katharine were keeping to their plan, whatever it was.

"Any word from Katharine?" Stephen asked.

"You're a great guy, and a good friend, but will you mind your own business and teach math?" J.D. asked.

"She was going to see you going to the pool eventually," Stephen said. "If you really wanted to keep your being here a secret, why do you swim at night, when she'll see the lights?"

"Look, I don't have to swim there."

"It's good for you. You need the exercise."

"I can work out fine right here," J.D. said.

"It makes Angus happy to pick you up and drive you to the pool," Stephen said. "Hydrotherapy's supposed to be good. So why not let him do that for you?"

"Well, if it makes Angus happy," J.D. said. He reached over to the desk, picked up a magazine. "He gave me the latest **National Fisherman.** He's got me up in arms about size limits on stripers. You can keep the big ones, have to let the small ones go. But the big ones have the good survival genes, and they're full of mercury anyway. Some guy in the story caught a four-footer. He released him, though."

"Any four-foot bass gets near the **Patty C,** it's coming aboard," Stephen said.

"When are you going to change the name?" J.D. asked.

"Never," Stephen said.

"She's not Patty C anymore," J.D. said.

"Bad luck to change a boat's name," Stephen said. "Your sister divorced me, but I still love her boat. You want to come out with me? We'll go after some stripers. There're still a few stragglers, and I heard there was big action on Sunday in the bay, right by the War College. You, Ted, me, a case of beer? What the hell—Angus can come too."

J.D. shook his head. "Thanks," he said. "But no."

"I hear they're still hooking fifty-pounders," Stephen said. "We catch one of those, we'll see how much you feel like letting it go."

"I'm done with the water," J.D. said, glaring at his knees. "Unless it's in a fucking swimming pool."

"That's ludicrous. Your father and grandfathers would turn in their graves. You have salt water in your veins, J.D. Come on out with me, before the season ends."

"The season already ended. And if I find out you've told Maura what's going on, I'll be even more pissed."

"Katharine will tell her."

"She won't yet. She loves Maura."

"I know."

"Just do me a favor," J.D. said. "Keep Maura away from me. Don't bring her over here again till I work everything out. I'm serious, Steve."

"Yeah, I know."

Lines intersected, bisected, divided. Shapes existed in the latticework of three dimensions. Nothing could be added up because quantities were infinite and went on forever. Seeing the way J.D. loved Maura, was trying with everything he had to bring their daughter back to her, was the closest Stephen could come to understanding the riddle of love.

He started to say something more about fishing, but he found that he couldn't. J.D. was one of his best friends. The accident had taken so much from him. He didn't do the things they used to love anymore. But searching with Katharine and Angus seemed to give him more of a reason to live than he'd had in a long time.

■

Travis was worried about Beck. He knew she felt bad about Ally leaving, and he'd tried to tell his little sister it wasn't her fault. She had listened, nodded, but not said a word—he'd known she hadn't believed him at all. He'd told his mother about it and she said she'd talk to her. But he still felt uneasy.

Leaving History class, he had a free period before football practice, and decided to head over early, to clear his head. The air was cold and wet, but when he got to the field, he saw someone sitting on the bleachers. Walking closer, he saw it was Pell.

"Hi," she said.

"Hi. What are you doing here?"

"I don't know," she said. "I just felt like coming."

"It's kind of lousy out," he said.

"I like the fog."

"Really?"

She nodded. "It makes me feel enclosed. As if I'm being held or something."

"Held by a big wet blanket?"

She laughed. He climbed the bleachers and sat next to her. This was the same seat she'd occupied during the St. George's game. He'd played so well that day. Everyone thought it was because Ally was here, and he'd never tell anyone it was because every time he looked into the stands he saw Pell on her feet, cheering for him, smiling at him.

"I haven't seen you much lately," she said. "Since your girlfriend was here."

"Yeah," he said. "I've been kind of busy."

"Schoolwork and football," she said.

"Yeah."

"How's Beck?"

He shrugged and looked at his feet. "You probably see her more than I do. She's never around. I think she's hanging out with your sister a lot. Did you give Lucy back her earring?"

Pell nodded. "She hadn't even missed it."

"I hope she doesn't find out. What I really hope is that Beck gets it all under control. She lost a lot of friends back home, taking their stuff."

"They didn't understand that she'd lost so much," Pell said. "She was just borrowing their things."

"You're right, they didn't get that," he said, thinking of Ally, of the scorn and rage he'd heard in her voice, attacking Beck.

"They will someday," Pell said in a low voice. "When someone they love dies. Or goes away."

"I wouldn't wish that on anyone," Travis said.

"Everyone goes through loss," Pell said. "Sooner or later. It just happened to us when we were young."

Travis nodded. He glanced over at Pell. Her straight black hair fell across one blue eye. He wanted to push it back, see her gazing straight at him. She cared about her sister as much as he did about Beck, as much as he did about Carrie. He wanted to tell her what it was like to fall out of love with a girl who connected him with his missing sister, but he had a huge lump in his throat.

"So," she said. "Ally's back in Ohio?"

He nodded.

"When is she coming back?"

"I'm not sure she is," he said.

"I'm sorry," Pell said.

"She knew Carrie," he said. "They were friends. My sister wants to be a photographer. She has this theory about herself, about high school girls being really powerful but not believing it. So she tries to show it in her pictures. She took a lot of Ally."

"So Ally's a connection to Carrie," she said. "I know how good it is to have that. Stephen, Ted, and J.D.—Mr. Campbell, Mr. Shannon, and J. D. Blackstone—were my dad's best friends. I couldn't live without them. I see them every day. Well, except for J.D."

"Why, where is he?"

"In Newport. I visit, but he doesn't let Lucy see him much. He thinks it will upset her."

"Why would it?"

"Because she—we—got our hopes up, that he would be better, and he's not."

"What do you mean?"

"He's paralyzed. Lucy and I love him no matter what. But he had surgery that was supposed to connect some very tiny nerve endings, an operation that had never been done before."

She paused, as if picturing J.D.

"He's completely dauntless," she continued. "He could have died. As it was, he got a staph infection, and they put him into a coma. He had to stay completely immobile for weeks. That whole time, we were worried he wouldn't come out of it."

"But he did?"

"Yes, but the surgery didn't work. He believes there's still a chance, that the cells could regenerate, that connections could have been made that haven't quite taken yet. The doctors don't say it, but he does. That's why he doesn't want us to see him. He worries because we went through so many ups and downs with our father's illness. He wants to spare us that. And I think he feels he let us down."

"But you don't . . ."

"Of course not!" she said.

"How did he get paralyzed?"

"Oh," she said. "He was in love. A long time ago. He tried to climb up to a place he'd gone with her, that had been important to them; a bridge, where they'd been together. And he fell. . . ." She closed her eyes.

"I'm sorry," Travis said.

"Thank you," she said. "My grandmother said people thought he'd tried to kill himself. The woman had broken up with him, so he tried to commit suicide. But I know that wasn't true; it was an accident."

"Did he ever talk to you about it?"

She shook her head. "Not about the accident. But he'd talk some about the woman. He never stopped loving her. He told me that one night they'd stood on the bridge, looking out over Narragansett Bay, and they'd seen a lighthouse, and it always reminded him of their time together. So he built one for her. A beacon."

"A lighthouse? Wow—he built it himself?"

"No, he couldn't. But he still owns an ironworking company, and he had his guys build it for her, near a place she would go."

"She must have loved that."

Pell smiled sadly. "She doesn't even know."

"He sounds badass."

"He is. My father always said he never did anything small, and he never held back. He loved him for it and believed he, and we, could do anything. J.D. went out to that lake with the workers, oversaw the project himself for an entire year."

Travis stared at Pell. Now he had to push her hair

back, just brush it behind her ears, so he could see both eyes. Their bright blueness was so startling, especially in the fog.

"He was in love," he said, and the words coming out of his own lips made his skin tingle.

Pell nodded. "Why isn't Ally coming back?" she asked after a minute.

"She said some things," he said. "To Beck. I . . . couldn't let her do that. I took Beck's side."

"You had to," Pell said. "Beck is your sister."

"But Ally was Carrie's friend."

"You could let Ally know," Pell said, staring at him. "That you forgive her. Tell her to come back."

But Travis wasn't thinking of Ally; he didn't want her back. Sitting so close to Pell, he felt the warmth of her body through their coats, through the cold fog. He felt as if he had a fever. He'd always been loyal. Even now, having these thoughts, he felt as if he was letting someone down. Ally, Carrie? He wasn't even sure.

The class bell rang in Blackstone Hall, and the rest of the team headed toward the field. Their shapes were hulking and blurry in the fog. Travis hoped they wouldn't see him sitting there. He wished they'd just pass by on their way to the field house, leave him sitting with Pell, thinking about the kind of beacon a person could use to tell someone he was thinking of her, only her.

12 FOG BROUGHT COZINESS TO Newport Academy. Heat rumbled through the ancient pipes, making them rattle and hiss. The windows were shut tight against the cold, damp air, and everyone wore thick wool sweaters. Beck stayed close to Lucy, and one late afternoon they went to Pell's room to work on their math formulas by the fireplace.

Seeing Pell at her desk, Lucy sprawled nearby on the floor by the fire, made Beck's throat ache. She watched Lucy absently kicking the rungs beneath Pell's chair, saw Pell reach down and gently stop the kicks with a hand around Lucy's ankle.

"Okay," Lucy was saying to Beck, pushing her paper closer. Beck glanced down, saw a series of six thick, fat columns about a half-inch wide. "Limits and infinity, right? That's what we're dealing with. These big, ugly, clunky columns are limits."

"And these," Beck said as beside them she drew six elegant, thin lines, "are infinity."

Everything clicked together in her mind. Mr. Campbell had shown them new formulas that

seemed almost magical to Beck. He'd spoken of infinite divisibility, a theory that went beyond classical geometry. He had them read George Berkeley's
**The Analyst: A Discourse Addressed to an Infi-
del Mathematician,** told them that Berkeley had
lived and worked in Middletown, right near Third
Beach.

She'd read the book with the cats on her bed. The
text was wild, strange, about math but somehow
not. It seemed to be all about small, smaller, invisible. Beck worked as she read, examining how a
tangent drawn to a parabola was performed by
"evanescent increments." How could you not love
that?

She read: "When **x** by flowing becomes **x + o,**
then **xx + 2 xo + oo**: and the area **ABC** becomes
ADH, and the increment of **xx** will be equal to
BDHC, the increment of the area to **BCFD +
CFH.**"

The concepts and equations boggled her
thoughts, but the odd and amazing part was, her
pencil understood it right away—she wrote the
notations, and her mind saw the puzzle and began
moving the parts around. As long as she didn't
worry, didn't tell herself it was too complicated, her
hand moved swiftly over the page, working out the
formula. It was like hearing a new language for the
first time and being able to speak it fluently—as if
she'd known it in another life. The language was

geometry, and it brought her closer to Lucy and, somehow, to Carrie.

"So," Lucy was saying. "We're trying to move from the mass of those columns to the skinniness of the lines. With our proofs we just shrink and shrink and shrink them down to almost nothing, and then we'll . . ."

Pell was listening too, holding Lucy's ankle. The sight of it was a sharp thorn poking Beck's eyes, making them water. Tears bubbled up, the bottomless longing to have her older sister here to do something so simple as grab her ankle. She saw where Lucy was going with the proof, but suddenly she didn't care.

"They're just numbers on a page," Beck choked the words out. "They can't bring anyone back."

Pell met Beck's gaze, and that was even worse. There were good older sisters and bad older sisters. The bad ones made fun of you. They would never let you borrow their sweaters. If they saw you doing something wrong, they told your parents. They laughed at you for being stupid. Carrie was one of the good ones, and obviously Pell was too.

"Beck, I am in awe of your math skill—Lucy's too," Pell said carefully. "If only you could just let it be that—learning everything you can, and excelling. But I know what you two are trying to do. You're on a mission to . . ."

"We're going to see Dad again," Lucy said bluntly. "And Beck's going to see her father."

"I know you want that," Pell said. "So do I. But darling, it's not going to happen . . . not the way you hope it will."

"You don't know," Lucy said. She shook her head with resolution. Beck had seen her stubborn streak and admired it. But right now, watching her draw those spidery lines on the page, saying they were a way of finding infinity, a way to bring back their beloveds, she felt both she and Lucy were a little crazy.

"You have your sister right here," Beck said. "You're so lucky."

"But I want my father too," Lucy said.

"Of course you do," Pell said. "I do too. The closest I ever come to feeling his presence is when I talk to Stephen and Ted. They and J.D. were like his brothers; they loved him so much, and they bring him back for me. Don't you feel that with Travis, Beck? When you talk to him, you feel Carrie?"

Beck didn't reply. She sat by the fire, knees drawn up, staring into the flames. The mention of Stephen, Mr. Campbell, made her feel confused. Her thoughts raced with troubling images. Her mother had gone on that walk with him and she had been quiet and distant ever since. A knock sounded at the door, and Pell jumped to answer. Angus stood there with a big cart filled with logs.

"Need more firewood?" he asked.

"Yes, Angus, thanks," Pell said, letting him in.

He hefted two armloads of wood, carried them in, dumped them into the wicker basket by the hearth. Then he went back, returned with a bundle of kindling. As he bent over in front of Beck, she saw a bunch of keys dangling from his belt. Her spine started to tingle; she felt the bad feeling begin to glow in her bones, and she tried to clench her hands into fists to stop them from doing what they wanted to do.

The fire crackled, sparks spitting up the chimney then twinkling down, little orange stars of fire, back into the flames. Angus crouched, trying to fit more kindling into the iron pot beside the fireplace tools. Pell asked how J.D. was, and Angus grunted that he was fine, just fine.

Beck was in a bubble. It shimmered and wobbled, and she thought of her mother, that day they'd sat at the kitchen table talking about Dr. Mallory, about trust. Then, with the picture of her mother crystal clear in her head, the worry in her eyes so visible, Beck hated herself even more as she reached forward, gently unclipping Angus's keys.

Before anyone noticed, she'd shoved them under the pillow she was sitting on. Pretending to be focused on her math work, she was actually hypersensitive to every detail going on around her. She felt as if she was watching her life on-screen. Girls studying by the fire, friends being nice to the gruff but kindly old school worker, school worker sweeping up bark and twigs before getting to his feet. Bitch of a loser Beck Shaw stealing, stealing.

"When is the Pumpkin Carve this year?" Pell asked.

"Same as every October . . . you'll find out at the Blackstone Blaze," Angus said.

He brushed his hands off, said good night, and continued on down the hall delivering firewood. With Pell and Lucy still distracted, Beck transferred the keys to her backpack.

"Okay, you have to tell us about Pumpkin Carve and the Blackstone Blaze," Beck said, blackout mode coming on. Wipe the slate clean, feel the lovely numbness of post-thievery. "Being as you're an older sister and upperclassman and all."

"I'm not allowed," Pell said, smiling. "They're secret school traditions."

Traditions. Beck had heard about them, had yet to experience one. Private schools like Newport Academy handed lore and rituals down through the ages. To Beck, they sounded so far-off and unattainable, more for the blue bloods like Lucy, Pell, Logan, Camilla, and Redmond than her and Travis . . . but at least her brother was a football star. They reminded her of when she used to lisp. Everyone had belonged but her, and maybe it was still that way.

She felt a jab of loneliness for home. She'd been

thinking of Columbus that way—her friends, school, routines. But what she really missed was her family the way it used to be—her parents, brother, and sister, all together.

Beck turned her attention back to their math. She felt horrible to have swiped the keys, but at the same time, having them made her feel calm. Safe.

She almost relaxed in front of the fire and concentrated on velocities of the evanescent, working to find the magic formula to bring her family together again.

■

Providence wasn't a huge city, but there were plenty of places to hide if you didn't want to be found, especially when you had someone like Dell helping. Carrie knew how lucky she was to have found her. Dell Harwood was like a guardian angel, or the best housemother possible. After leaving Hawthorne House, Carrie had needed a place to live. Dell had helped her get this room with good light, a sliver of a water view, and peace and quiet.

"Well, she came around again," Dell said, showing up at Carrie's door with a paper bag full of hand-me-down baby clothes for Gracie. The baby was asleep, so Carrie put her finger to her lips.

"What did she say?" Carrie whispered, and the two women walked to the far side of the studio, away from Gracie's crib.

"Same as before. Showed your picture, wanted to know if you'd been at Hawthorne House."

"And you told her no?"

"I told her 'no comment.' Confidentiality! We're a home for unwed mothers, we don't give out any information. Nice picture of you, though."

"Which one?"

"Looked like a school portrait. You were wearing a blue sweater, matched your eyes. Very pretty."

Carrie's mother had always helped her get ready on school picture days. She'd brush her hair, help her pick out earrings, tell her how beautiful she looked. Then, when the photos were ready, her mother would always frame one and hang it on the kitchen wall with years' worth of other school pictures—hers, Trav's, and Beck's. She sent copies to Aunt Katharine.

"What else did she ask?" Carrie asked. "Or say about me?"

"Just that your family loves and misses you, and hopes you'll come home. They're in Rhode Island," Dell said with a sideways look. Carrie nodded. "You know that, then?" Dell asked.

"I figured it out for myself," Carrie said.

"Hmmm," Dell said, starting to unpack the bag of baby things. "Most runaways don't keep such careful track of the family they've left behind."

Left behind. The words stabbed her. Carrie could never do that.

"Did my aunt say my mother sent her? Are they in touch?"

"What do you think, I had lunch with her? My job is to protect your privacy. If you want to know that, why wouldn't you just ask her yourself? She did leave this card for you." Dell handed it over, and Carrie saw it was from the Rhode Island School of Design. "She's teaching a seminar at RISD, staying in a house on Benefit Street through the end of this week. After that, you can call her at home in Portsmouth."

Carrie stuck the card in a book, slid it onto the shelf. She felt Dell watching her as she started to sort Gracie's new clothes. Carrie reached for a pair of little red corduroys.

"Why wouldn't your mother and aunt be in touch?"

"Something happened between them," Carrie said. "A long time ago. And they stopped speaking."

"That's very sad," Dell said. "Life is so short. Well, maybe your mother and aunt will get together again someday. People do forgive each other, you know."

"Sometimes," Carrie said.

"Maybe things are already better," Dell said. "Considering your aunt is wearing out her shoe leather looking for you. How do you think she knows you're in Providence?"

Carrie shrugged, although she knew. She'd been

spotted at the hospital, watching over J.D. Either he'd really been awake that time and called Aunt Katharine, or one of the nurses had described her to him, and he'd put it all together. She'd been more careless than she should have been.

"I guess you came to Rhode Island for a reason," Dell said. She stood by the small dresser, folding Gracie's new clothes and placing them into the open drawer. Propped up on it, in a cheap frame Carrie had bought on Wickenden Street, was a print of the photo she'd snapped of her mother at Travis's game. Carrie saw Dell notice, but she took care not to stare.

"Hawthorne House was a good place to stay while I waited to have Gracie," Carrie said, drifting over to the crib.

"You could have had your baby anywhere, but you came here."

"Rhode Island is pretty."

"I don't think you came for the scenery. Family ties are deep. Just the way a root system sustains the biggest oak, family roots spread out and keep a person going when she's far from home. Your aunt has lived here a long time, hasn't she?"

"Yes. And my mother lived here before I was born," Carrie said. "I was conceived here."

"Well," Dell said, as if her point had been made. Carrie stared at her, wondering how it could all be so painful and mysterious, how she could have come to this place, so filled with roots and personal history, yet be hiding from her family. And she knew: she'd had to replace death with life.

"I came to visit someone in the hospital," Carrie said.

"Yes," Dell said. "And he's long since been discharged. I wonder how long it will take your aunt to bump into you at the diner. She's been there twice, but not your shift. The Half Moon diner doesn't have the same confidentiality that Hawthorne House does."

"You own the Half Moon diner," Carrie reminded her.

"I do," Dell agreed, folding the last tiny sweater. "I guess you're lucky I know how to keep a secret."

"I'm very lucky," Carrie said, and she watched Dell pick up the framed photo of her mother, stare at the image as if looking for a resemblance between her and Carrie, and Gracie, and maybe even Katharine, the aunt who had been looking for her all this time.

■

J.D. had tea with Taylor Davis's daughter Pell. They sat in his garage apartment, eating chocolate chip cookies she'd brought from school. He poured them cups of Earl Grey, her favorite. Cold air swirled around, under the garage doors. He handed Pell a spare sweater, to make sure she was warm enough.

"Thanks, J.D.," she said.

"I don't want you freezing," he said. "Catching a cold or something."

"Don't worry about me," she said. "You're the one I'm concerned about. Do you really plan to spend the whole winter in here?"

"Sure," he said. "It's the best of all worlds. Ted and Stephen know where to find me, and if we grab Angus we've got a built-in poker game. I'm within shouting distance of you and Lucy, if you ever need me. Plus, it's pretty handy for you to bring me these excellent cookies."

"I'm glad you like them," she said. "We have the best cook at school."

"Mrs. McFadden, the same as when your dad and I went there."

She nodded and sipped her tea. For a long time he'd avoided mentioning Taylor to her or Lucy, but he'd realized they liked it. Everyone wanted to know the people they loved most mattered.

"So tell me," he said, refilling her cup. "What's new at school?"

"There's a new family there," she said. "From the Midwest."

He put down the teapot.

"Mrs. Shaw teaches English. She's really great, all the kids like her. Her daughter Beck is Lucy's best friend. And her son Travis plays football. . . . He's awfully nice."

J.D. wondered how bad it would be to wrangle details about Maura, to ask his goddaughter about English class and hope she'd say something about her teacher's life, state of mind. But he wanted to do right by Pell, and from the way she blushed just saying Travis's name, he figured that's what she wanted to talk about.

"He's a friend of yours?" he asked.

"Yes," she said. "We're becoming friends."

"Maybe more?" he asked. "Considering you have so much in common . . ."

"Like what?"

"Well, you said he's from the Midwest."

Her cheeks turned pinker. "He has a girlfriend back home," she said.

"Are you sure?" he asked. "Maybe it's not serious."

"I'm sure," she said. "I met her. He . . . well, he said they're not together anymore. She said something about his sister, and they broke up. But I don't know. It's all so new to him, moving out here. He's been through a lot. His dad died, and his sister ran away."

"That's a lot," J.D. said, thinking of Carrie.

"It is. And I don't want to get in the way, between him and his girlfriend if they decide to get back together."

J.D. stirred his tea. He wanted to look this young woman he loved so much square in the eye; he wanted to tell her that she should tell Travis how she felt, forget about the girlfriend in Ohio, take whatever chance she had to follow her feelings.

"I made a mistake once," he said slowly. "I let someone get away."

"The woman with the lighthouse," she said, smiling.

"Yeah," he said. "I've told you about her. . . ."

"She's like a myth," Pell said. "To me and Lucy. The woman our dear J.D. will always love."

"A myth," he said, laughing, wondering how she'd feel to know this mythic woman was the school's new English teacher, the mother of her football player. "You can't help who you love."

J.D.'s hands were cold. He let the cup of tea warm his fingers. His own words echoed; he thought of seeing Maura after all this time. She'd spent eighteen years away from him, and now she was less than a mile away. He swore he felt the air move every time she took a step. But he had so little to give her. He was locked in his body, trapped in a wheelchair.

"She's lucky, whoever she is," Pell said, as if she could read his mind. "To have you love her so much."

"I don't know about that," J.D. said. He smiled at his goddaughter, compassionate and wise. Taylor would have been so proud of her. He was about to say it, but he couldn't speak. Life had given him wonderful people, then taken them away—Maura,

Taylor. Carrie. He shivered. One of the effects of his injury and infections was that he got cold so easily. Pell saw, slipped the extra sweater off and tucked it over his shoulders.

"Hey," he said. "That's for you."

"No," she said. "Besides, I've got to go. I have homework, and I want to check on Lucy."

"How's she sleeping?" he asked.

"Same," she said.

"Have you heard from your mother?"

"Birthday cards," Pell said, and smiled sadly.

"Give Lucy my love, okay?"

"Okay," Pell said, kissing his cheek. J.D. stared at her, this strong, wonderful girl. He had to fight the urge to tell her to go back to school and grab Travis Shaw by the collar. Shake some sense into him. He wanted to tell her about Carrie. Tell her that if he and Katharine had their way, she'd be home soon. That a runaway sister would be one less reason for her to keep her distance from the boy she obviously cared about.

But Katharine had called, said there was no news. J.D. wasn't going to let any hint about Carrie out, nothing that Maura could possibly hear. He wasn't going to risk hurting her that way. He knew how deadly a broken heart could be.

Maura &
& Katharine

PART TWO

13 KATHARINE O'DONNELL HAD been in love. It seemed so sad to blame everything on that, on unrequited love, but the truth was the truth. As much as she'd have liked to change things around, come out seeming less ridiculous, she couldn't escape the real story. She loved someone who didn't have the same feelings. He'd loved her sister instead.

She drove through the gates of Newport Academy. She was an artist, an accomplished sculptor, taught at one of the finest art colleges, she was well traveled and ridiculously independent, but knowing she was about to see her sister after all this time, she felt like a child on her first day of school.

Her hands were shaking and she couldn't get a good breath. Her pickup truck bounced over a speed bump and she glanced in the rearview mirror to make sure none of the pumpkins had bounced out from under the tarp that covered the truck bed. Every year she donated pumpkins from her field, but this year her reason for coming to the academy had nothing to do with Halloween.

Cruising around back, she stopped at the maintenance shed. Angus was there with his grounds crew. They'd just finished raking leaves, and had huge piles ready for the mulcher.

"Thought you'd never get here," Angus said as she climbed out of the truck, and his crew came around to unload it.

"Well, I've been in Providence."

"On a mission, from what I hear."

"Enough of that," she said. "I brought you the rest of the pumpkins. I trust Darcy delivered the first bunch just fine?"

"Yeah, enough to whet the appetite for the fire. Kids are starting to ask. Including your niece."

"Beck," Katharine said, trying to smile. "I'm heading over to their house right now. Where are you going to hide the pumpkins?"

Angus smiled. "That's right, got to get them undercover so the kids don't figure out the timing."

"Should we put them inside?" Katharine asked.

"Damn keys," Angus said. "I lost them somewhere. Ted's making me copies of his, but until then I can't get into the shed. Let me borrow your tarp, Katharine."

"Sure thing," she said, reaching back into the truck bed. "When's the blaze?"

"Just before sunset tonight."

"Let me help you," Katharine said, shaking out the big rectangular tarpaulin as the men stacked the pumpkins next to the shed. "No one will see. Pile some of those leaves over the canvas!"

"Always ordering me around," Angus grumbled. But she saw the smile under his big mustache. After they'd finished, Katharine punched his arm, climbed into the truck, and headed along the sweeping drive toward the carriage house.

She parked under a hawthorne tree. When she climbed out of the truck, she saw her sister.

Maura had stepped outside. Katharine's eyes took her in. But she didn't see the age, or the lines around her eyes, or the wisps of gray in her hair. She saw her little sister. Straight past the years and hurts, an arrow went through her heart and she saw the little girl she'd always loved, from the minute of Maura's birth.

"Oh, Katharine!" Maura said.

"Maura . . ." Katharine said, losing her breath.

Maura walked over. They stared into each other's eyes for a long minute. Laughter started inside Katharine's chest: a sudden explosion of happiness. Maura clearly felt it too. She smiled and couldn't stop. Was it this easy? Suddenly nothing but this mattered. The pain was erased, chalk on a blackboard swept away.

They kissed, and Maura grabbed her sister's hand as they walked into the house. Katharine glanced around the kitchen. The cottage was small, nothing like the big, airy house they'd grown up in. Set in a

glade of mountain laurel, holly, and rhododen-
drons, the leaded-glass windows small and thick,
the atmosphere was dark, slightly grim. The kitchen
walls were hung with Carrie's beautiful photographs. Katharine watched Maura putting the kettle on just as their mother and grandmother would
have done.

"Tea," Katharine said, smiling hesitantly.

"Of course . . ."

Katharine looked at the box: Red Rose, the kind
their grandmother had used. Maura took teacups
from the cupboard.

"Where have you been?" Maura asked. "In Providence all this time?"

"Yes," Katharine said, wanting to tell her sister
everything, show her what she had accumulated in
the black notebook. It wasn't time, she knew. She
needed to tread carefully. "RISD sculpture students
are brilliant, and they know it. They remind me of
how invincible I used to feel. How is it being in
Newport?"

"Where do I even start?" Maura asked.

"Wherever you want," Katharine said, and
smiled.

"I met Darcy when I went looking for you. She
seems nice."

"She's great. Like a little—" She stopped herself.

"Like a little sister?" Maura asked, giving a curious, guarded glance.

"You've been gone a long time," Katharine reminded her.

"You haven't wanted much to do with me," Maura replied.

The kettle whistled. Maura busied herself making the tea, putting milk and sugar on the table. Katharine heard the words hanging in the air. They had been true at one time. Back when they were in their twenties, when life had seemed so long and expendable, she had cut her sister out of her life. It was the worst, most terrible mistake she'd ever made.

"I saw J.D. last week," Maura said.

Katharine kept her face neutral. She had prepared herself to hear about it from Maura; she already had from J.D. They were all so much older now, had been through so much. Maura and J.D. had a child together; Katharine would give anything to find Carrie for them. But her feelings were as deep as they'd always been, and to hear her sister say his name still cut to the bone.

"Seeing him in a wheelchair was so hard," Maura said.

"I know," Katharine said.

"All I could think of was how physical he used to be. I can't imagine how it must be for him now."

Katharine watched Maura wrap her arms around her chest, as if to hold herself together. She remembered the first time she'd seen him lying still, knowing he couldn't walk. She'd promised herself she'd be strong, not cry, stay positive, but she'd broken down anyway.

"It's been so long," Katharine said. "I think he's made peace with it."

But Maura looked haunted by how J.D. used to be: in motion, running, riding his motorcycle, swimming. His efficient, purposeful movements in his workshop.

That summer, Katharine and Maura had gone to Cat Island in the middle of Narragansett Bay, under the Newport Bridge. Katharine had borrowed a boat and wanted to salvage metal off a wreck that had washed up in a storm. They had waited for low tide, and were climbing down the rocks when Katharine saw J.D. swimming out from shore.

His head looked like a seal in the harbor. He was moving fast, swimming against a strong current. She'd watched as he reached the island's far end, where it sloped gradually and made it easy to climb out of the waves. He hauled himself up and ran straight toward them. It was a sprint, it might have been speed trials. His eyes were on Maura the whole way.

And Katharine had understood, and in that moment let something go. It had always been so hard to think about it, or examine too far: some hidden hope, buried wish, that that look in J.D.'s eyes could have been for her.

"He can't walk," Maura said. "Because of me."

Yes, Katharine wanted to say. **Yes.** There had been so many times she'd wanted to scream at her sister, shove her face into the reality of what she'd done. She'd taken something precious and then thrown it away, ruined it. But now, seeing Maura sit there so pale and drawn, seeing tears pooling in her eyes, and realizing all she'd lost, Katharine felt only compassion.

"You took care of him?" Maura asked.

"Only as much as he'd let me," Katharine said. "Which wasn't much."

"But you went to Providence," Maura said. "You were with him for the surgery?"

Katharine heard the question with a start. Was that what Maura thought about her time there? Teaching at RISD, staying at J.D.'s bedside. She nodded, a white lie, realizing it was better than having to explain the reality just yet.

"Just afterward," she said. "He went into a coma, and we didn't think he was going to make it." Even saying those words, remembering how afraid she'd been, Katharine choked up.

"I'm glad he did," Maura said, seeing the tears in Katharine's eyes.

Just then the kitchen door opened, and Beck burst in. "Mom," she said, before she even registered Katharine's presence. "Angus piled up firewood near the football field. It's the Blackstone Blaze!"

"Beck, we have a visitor. Aunt Katharine came to see us," Maura said, and Beck stopped in her tracks and stared.

Katharine wiped away her tears, smiled at her niece. Beck was small with strong shoulders, freckles everywhere, hazel eyes, a tumble of reddish brown hair. She wore a hunter green fleece jacket, a red plaid skirt, and navy blue knee socks, one inching down her calf. She looked like her mother at the same age.

"Oh my God. Beck," Katharine said.

"Hi, Aunt Katharine," she answered.

"It's so wonderful to see you," Katharine said.

"Thank you. You too." Beck smiled.

Katharine tried to smile. This was only her second time meeting her niece; the first had been at Andy's funeral. During the years Katharine and Maura had stayed apart, the kids' childhoods had disappeared.

Two cats stalked into the kitchen, went straight to Beck's ankles. She crouched down to pet them.

"You're in high school," Katharine said.

"Yep."

"Do you like Newport Academy?"

"I miss home," Beck replied.

"I can understand that," Katharine said.

The conversation seemed to make Maura uncomfortable. She fidgeted, went to the window.

"Travis should be along soon. He has football practice, but . . ."

"No, Mom," Beck said. "Practice was canceled. I told you—the Blackstone Blaze is starting! We have to go. . . ."

And just like that, Katharine was swept up into family life. Grabbing coats and mittens, checking to make sure the stove was off—Katharine smiled, felt a pang to see Maura run back; it was just what their mother, and before her their grandmother, used to do—locked the doors, made sure the cats didn't escape outdoors.

The three of them hurried across campus, joining a wave of students and teachers. Katharine spotted Ted Shannon, who gave her a big wave. "Good to see you!" he called as she waved back. Katharine's neck burned, feeling Maura's eyes on her.

"You gave him my address, didn't you?" Maura asked as they strode along. "In Columbus? That's how he knew where to find me?"

"Yes," Katharine said.

They kept walking without another word. She thought back to when they were children, when Maura was feeling insecure about schoolwork, or a sport, or a boy. Katharine had understood her older-sister role right down to her bones. She was there to encourage, lead, guide. She'd loved praising her little sister. And she'd grown up wanting to be there for her all through life. It was a huge blessing to be having that chance right now.

There was no wind. Katharine knew Angus always waited for a calm evening, when no breeze stirred the nearly bare branches, no danger of spreading the fire. Students ran over. Beck's friends gathered around her. The football team came out of the field house.

Katharine saw Stephen Campbell staring at her and Maura, and they exchanged nods. She recognized teachers, staff, kids who lived in town. There was Edith Nicholson, the old bat who dominated Newport society: regal, dressed in fur and pearls, and the huge Nicholson diamond, a blonde blue blood who belonged to the school of thought that said rich women could and should stay looking young forever.

She had purchased two of Katharine's pieces and donated them to museums. Katharine had learned through the years that when Edith possessed art, she believed she also owned the artist. She gestured for Katharine to come over, but Katharine didn't move.

She stood right by her sister. Ted Shannon made a speech, thanking Mrs. Nicholson for her generosity in sponsoring the Blackstone Blaze, reminding everyone of the school's long history, the weaving of traditions and academic excellence. He mentioned the winning football season, the upcoming Middlebridge away game on Saturday.

"That's because of Travis," Maura said proudly. Then, "He's right over there." She gestured at a tall, handsome boy, standing with his friends.

"I'd love to see him play," Katharine said.

Maura nodded. "You will."

An invitation. Katharine felt a lump in her throat. She watched Ted light the torch and present it to Edith, who handed it with a flourish to a beautiful young woman with glossy dark hair. Katharine's gaze was drawn again to Travis, staring at the girl as she ignited the pile of wood.

The sticks began to crackle. A thin plume of smoke wafted into the heavy gray sky. The flames spread, and the smoke thickened. Ted and his wife called everyone over to a long table, to help themselves to hot cider and cinnamon doughnuts. Stephen called to Maura; she shook her head.

Katharine and Maura just stood there staring into the fire, arms touching. Katharine didn't want to move, or even breathe. She'd made peace with her feelings about J.D.; he wasn't between them anymore. She didn't want to take one step away from her sister. And it seemed that Maura felt the same way.

∎

Travis waved to his mother. She was standing with his aunt, a woman he'd met only once in his life, at the funeral. Still, he'd have known her anywhere. She looked just like his mom, only a little older and bigger, with a long braid down her back. He started toward them, but Pell was suddenly there, her hand on his elbow.

She wore a navy blue pea coat and black watch cap. Her lips were pink, smiling, and her breath wisped out into the frosty air.

"Travis, my grandmother wants to meet you," she said.

"Oh," he said, flattered, not sure how to act in front of such an obviously rich and important lady, who stood nearby with Mr. Shannon. Pell pulled him into the small circle. He wanted to make a good impression for Pell, so he stood tall and faced her grandmother. Pell stood by his side, leaning into him slightly, the pressure of her body electric. He felt himself turning red, thrilled that she would want to introduce him to her only family here in Newport.

"Edith, may I present Travis Shaw," Mr. Shannon said. "Travis, this is our wonderful benefactor, Mrs. Nicholson." Pell's smile faltered slightly.

"Pleased to meet you," Travis said, shaking the old woman's hand.

"Where is the other one?" she asked, craning her neck and looking around.

"The other one?" Travis asked. "Ma'am?"

"The other student, Mr. Shannon. Didn't you say he had a sister?"

"Yes, of course," the headmaster said, smiling at Travis. "Where is Rebecca?"

"Beck?" Travis asked, confused. "She's over there, behind my mother."

"Well, call her over," Mrs. Nicholson said, smiling. "I want to meet her too!"

Travis started to go, but Pell pulled his coat to keep him where he was. Mr. Shannon went instead, returning an instant later with Beck, who gave Travis a look as she joined them and Mr. Shannon introduced her too. Travis glanced at Pell; she'd been radiant a moment ago, but now her eyes were downcast, as if she wanted to disappear. Smoke billowed up from the fire, swirling into the darkening sky.

"You're the child, the friend of Lucille's," Mrs. Nicholson said thoughtfully. "Who didn't want to come aboard **Sirocco.**"

"I don't like water," Beck said.

"My dear," Mrs. Nicholson said, fixing Beck with a steely smile, "you've made an odd choice in secondary school . . . considering that Newport Academy is essentially surrounded by **la mer.**"

"La-Mare?" Beck asked, frowning.

"The sea, dear," Mrs. Nicholson said, bemused. "Ted, aren't these children being taught proper

French? Perhaps I should fund scholarships at St. George's instead!"

"Scholarships?" Beck asked.

"Grandmother . . ." Pell said warningly.

"Mrs. Nicholson wished to meet the student beneficiaries of her most generous scholarship gift," Mr. Shannon said.

"We're not on scholarship," Beck said. "Our mother teaches here."

Mrs. Nicholson laughed lightly. "Dear, who do you think pays for the children of faculty to attend Newport Academy? Education costs money. Do you think the funds simply fall out of the sky?"

"Grandmother!"

"Pell," she said, her eyes brightening and an indulgent tone entering her voice. "Learning manners is part of an excellent education. Throughout life, these children will need to know whom to thank and how to express gratitude. Manners are crucial. Now. As you are well aware, I fund these scholarships in memory of your father, a Newport Academy alumnus. I am certain that these commendable students would want to know that, and to remember him."

"Travis, Rebecca," Mr. Shannon said nervously, his hand on each of their shoulders. "Please thank Mrs. Nicholson for her generosity."

"Thank you, Mrs. Nicholson," Travis said, nudging Beck. She stood perfectly still, cheeks bright red the way they always got when she was humiliated.

"The scholarships are in memory of Pell and Lucy's father?" Beck asked finally.

"Yes," Mrs. Nicholson said. "Taylor Davis."

"Beck," Travis said, watching his sister stare at the old woman. **"Thank her."**

"Thank you, Mrs. Nicholson," Beck said, standing tall. "I'll think of Taylor Davis as I study."

Now it was Mrs. Nicholson's turn to be silent. She stared at Beck for a long moment, then cleared her throat. "That would please me," she said. She glanced very quickly at Pell. Then she linked arms with Mr. Shannon and walked away. Travis stared at her back, disappearing into the smoky dusk of a cold evening. When he glanced down at Beck to tell her she'd done a good job, she had already run away. He stood alone with Pell.

"That was embarrassing," she said. "I'm so sorry. I thought she wanted to meet you because you're my friend, and because you've made the team win so many games this year."

"That's okay," he said.

"Sometimes I can't believe the way she acts. She doesn't mean to be so awful. She's just not used to regular people."

"It didn't turn out so bad," he said.

"She has no idea how she comes across. She surrounds herself with people who only tell her what she wants to hear."

The fire roared. Everyone stood back, but still close enough to feel the strong heat. He wanted to tell Pell that people weren't responsible for what their families did. Everyone made their own choices. His father had taught him that, to stand up for himself.

"I'm sorry, Travis," Pell said again. "I didn't know her wanting to meet you had anything to do with scholarships. . . ."

"You don't have to be sorry," he said. "She's right. Beck and I are here because she's paying our tuition. We're grateful, and I won't forget. I'll pay her back, every penny."

"She doesn't need the money."

"I'll pay her back," Travis repeated slowly, more sharply, his eyes burning into Pell's. "Every penny."

"I believe you mean that," Pell whispered.

He couldn't help himself; he touched her face with his bare hand, traced the line of cheekbone down to her chin. She reached up, took his hand in hers. They leaned close together, feeling the fire's warmth surround them. He wanted to tell her the blaze was nothing compared to what he felt for her.

"Pell!" The voice wafted through the air, and they turned to see her grandmother gesturing. "You are coming to dinner with me and the Shannons!"

"Oh, great," Pell said to Travis, waving back at her grandmother.

"You're not staying for the rest of the bonfire?" Travis asked.

"There were no dinner plans until just now. I shouldn't have let her see us together," Pell said.

"She has nothing to say about it," Travis said, standing an inch away from her, staring into her eyes and having to hold himself back from pulling her tight.

"You don't know my grandmother," Pell said.

"And she doesn't know me," Travis said as Pell turned to join Mrs. Nicholson and the Shannons.

14 MAURA HAD A FREE PERIOD, spent it on the phone with Tim Marcus, the private detective she'd hired to find Carrie. He'd traced a postcard she'd sent from Minneapolis, learned she'd bought it on eBay.

"She left the lot number right there on the back," Tim said. "I called the seller out in Phoenix, and it seems she bought ten postcards, various cities west of the Mississippi. That's what the lot was called— 'Western Cities'—and . . ."

"Why would she do that?"

"Well, to throw you off her trail," Tim said. "She bought the cards, then used a postmark service— you send your correspondence, they'll make sure it's postmarked from wherever you say. Child-support scofflaws use it to send birthday cards and stuff, so their exes won't be able to send the sheriff after them."

"Carrie wasn't really in Minneapolis?"

"No, or Santa Fe or Billings, from what I can see."

"She tried that hard to keep me from finding her?" Maura asked, feeling despair.

"Well, that's what runaways do," he said. "But I have to tell you, I think she wants to be found. She's a smart girl, and if she went to all the trouble of using a postmark service, I'd expect her to erase the eBay lot number. It's pretty unmistakable, and contains the seller's ID."

"Does the seller keep records?" Maura asked, hope starting to build.

"Yes, he does," Tim said, sounding pleased. "He's checking to see where he sent the lot containing those three cards. He sells everything from postcards to old cell phones and all kinds of things in between, so he's got a lot of invoices to go through."

"Did you tell him it's about a missing girl?" Maura asked, her eyes filling with tears. To think that some stranger had records that might lead her to Carrie made her want to jump in her car and drive to Arizona.

"I did," Tim said. "He was sympathetic, and what's more, he doesn't want the law to come looking into his business, what he's shipped where."

"Maybe they should," Maura said.

"I'm working on him," Tim said. "Hang in there, Maura. This is the best lead we've had. Once we find out where he shipped those postcards, we're going to find her."

"Thanks, Tim," she said. She hung up the phone and wondered if that place would be Columbus,

Ohio. She'd always wondered if after Carrie had run away from the hospital up north, she had returned to Columbus. Carrie had always been such a loving daughter and sister; Maura used to dream she'd stayed close by, staying silent for her own reasons, but within sight of her family.

A knock interrupted her, and she glanced up to see Stephen.

"Take a walk with me?" he asked.

She hesitated, then agreed. They pulled on coats, headed outside into the chilly air. A west wind had blown all the clouds away; the sky was blue, tinged with the gold light of autumn. Pumpkins were everywhere on campus, balanced on boulders, lining the marble steps, wedged into the crook of branches on maple trees. Some were already carved into grimacing jack-o'-lanterns.

"J.D.'s great-grandfather started that tradition a hundred years ago," Stephen said. "The school buys pumpkins from local farmers, and the kids carve them. The idea is to make them look even scarier than the gargoyles." He gestured up to the roofline of Blackstone Hall. Maura glanced up, looking for J.D. in the window, but he wasn't there today.

"What's the purpose?" she asked.

"For a shipbuilder, he was a pretty sensitive guy. He thought it would give the kids power over their fear."

"Fear of what?"

"The ghosts," he said. "Mary and Beatrice."

"Beatrice . . ."

"Mary's sister," Stephen said. "She was four years older. They say she never got over Mary's death. . . ."

Maura walked along, thinking of one sister losing another, tugged by thoughts of her daughters missing each other, of Carrie sending postcards from places she'd never been. And of Katharine, missing her own sister all this time. How could sisters do without each other? She mulled over Tim's news, thinking again and again of the possibility of Carrie in Columbus.

"I wonder if we've made a mistake coming here," Maura said, stopping at the top of the ledge. "I uprooted Travis and Beck. She's having such a hard time. Last night Lucy and Pell's grandmother embarrassed her. . . ."

"Ted was furious at her," he said. "Everyone knows tuition for teachers' children is included in the compensation package."

"As Mrs. Nicholson said, 'Someone has to pay for it.' "

"She's a dragon," he said. "Don't take her seriously."

"Beck ran home in the middle of the bonfire," Maura said. "Today she woke up with a stomachache. I had a hard time getting her to eat some breakfast, get dressed. . . . I had to walk her to school, to her first class. I want to take my kids out of here, back home."

"Maura, we'd miss you," he said. "You and your kids have already become an important part of Newport Academy."

"My other daughter," Maura said, the words spilling out. "I just heard something about her that makes me wonder if she could still be back home, somewhere in Columbus. I want to go there, be near her."

"What if," Stephen said quietly, "she was here instead?"

"Here, you mean Newport?"

"Why not?" he asked. "If you don't know her exact location, couldn't it as easily be Rhode Island as Ohio?"

Maura's mind raced with images of that young mother at the football game. She had **known** it was Carrie: her posture, the way she'd leaned toward Maura, then run away. Maura's body ached, remembering.

"Her father is here, after all," Stephen continued.

"But she doesn't know about J.D.," Maura said. "And even if she did, I'm not sure she'd want anything to do with him—or with me, once she figured out the truth."

"She's your daughter, Beck's sister," Stephen said. "That means she's smart. You don't know what she's learned, where it's leading her. I haven't known you long, but I've been friends with J.D. our whole lives. He's a good man. I'll bet anything that his daughter, whether she grew up with him or not, has his best qualities. I know she's smart and good, and I bet you anything she knows more than you think she does."

"Why is she staying away? She was always so close to us."

"People have their own mysteries to solve. Think of yourself at Carrie's age. Maybe her case is more extreme, but did you tell your family, the people you loved, everything you were doing? Were you always careful, did you always do the right, predictable thing?"

Maura turned silent. No, she hadn't—far from it. She'd kept one secret after another. She thought of one night with J.D., the night Carrie was conceived, she was sure of it. Carrie's life began out of love and recklessness, wild magic and luminous beauty, her mother stepping far off her normal path of life.

That night, J.D. had pulled up to Katharine's studio on his motorcycle. The air was still and muggy; barely any breeze came up from the harbor. Maura wore shorts and a sleeveless shirt, but she was sweltering.

He didn't even have to ask her. She walked across the cobblestone alley and climbed on the back of his bike. J.D. grabbed her hands, pulled her arms around him. Only one word was spoken.

"Tighter," he said.

She grabbed on as hard as she could, her hands laced across his hard, flat stomach, her breasts pressing into his hot back.

He drove her through town, across the Newport Bridge. The bridge's lamplight had glimmered on the surface of Narragansett Bay a hundred feet below. High above the water, hair blowing out behind her, she'd never felt like this before. Precarious, dangerous, her body welded to J.D.'s.

Lights of ships at sea glinted all the way out to Block Island, a dark wedge on the horizon. Newport and Jamestown sparkled to the east and west. They cruised around Jamestown, and J.D. found a deserted lane bordered by a field and woods.

Maura had shivered with excitement, ready to lie down with him right there, in the field's soft green grass. But no: J.D. had taken her hand, led her through the woods. Bats darted overhead; the sound of traffic seemed to come from the sky. She realized they were just beneath a second suspension bridge—the Jamestown Bridge. He showed her a narrow iron ladder. Arm tight around her waist, lips to her ear, he said, "Climb up. I'll be right behind you. You won't fall."

"I don't like heights."

"You're afraid of them?"

"Yes," she said.

"Don't be. You want to do this—you know you do."

What she wanted was dangerous, and had nothing to do with the bridge. She felt his arms around her, leaned back into his body.

"You want to experience everything, don't you?" he asked.

"Everything?" she asked.

He nodded, his blue eyes bright, teasing, seducing her past the point of any return. She had blocked Andy from her mind, but she thought of him now, waiting for her at home. Their home. He was always so careful, protective. He would never ride a motorcycle; he'd never break the rules and climb a bridge. He'd never ask her to do something reckless. She thought of Andy's bridge, the covered bridge, as safe and pretty as a Currier and Ives print.

"Dare to be great," J.D. said.

And Maura put her foot on the first rung and climbed. She barely noticed the thin metal, the fact there was nothing to break a fall—one misstep and she'd tumble a hundred feet down to the ground.

Studying history, she'd used her imagination to travel back in time to every exploration, each siege, the bloodiest battle. Reading literature, she'd wanted to fall in love like Anna Karenina, like Madame Bovary. She'd wanted to want to die for love. No one could have this with Mr. Sisson.

She felt wild; pressure in her throat, racing heart, not caring what happened next, as long as she got to feel this way, feel J.D.'s fingers brush her ankles, reminding her he was right behind her, close enough to touch.

And they got to the top of the ladder—not to the road surface where all the cars and trucks whizzed past, but the catwalk just below. Narrow and rickety, made of the same metal as the ladder, it ran the length of the Jamestown Bridge. She hauled herself up and turned to give him a hand.

What she saw took her breath away—he had looped one leg through the ladder rungs, was leaning back without holding on—just arching into the wide-open as if he wished he could fly, his wavy brown hair ruffling in the summer wind. It was a moment of sheer joy, pure abandon.

And it was wonderful. J.D. loved life, was afraid of nothing. She felt the smallest ripple of fear, but it was too late: she was in love with him.

Their eyes met and it seemed that he vaulted up to her. He came straight at her, smiling and with the happiest eyes she'd ever seen; she'd thought his joy came from the panorama all around them, Narragansett Bay's west passage extending out past Beavertail Light all the way to the black Atlantic Ocean, but no. It focused in on her, and he put his arms around her, and his mouth hot on hers, he kissed her hard and deep.

He took off his shirt, laid it down on the hard grate, eased her gently down. They lay side by side, stroking each other's faces, gazing into each other's eyes. Words, endless conversation, always such an important part of every date with Andy, played no role. The only sounds came from the traffic speeding overhead—so close it sounded like the trucks might crash through the roadbed and crush them—and warm wind whistling, slicing through the bridge's suspension cables.

He eased her shirt over her head; she wriggled, helping him push her shorts down. They fumbled over his belt buckle, the snap and zipper of his jeans. They never stopped kissing, they didn't close their eyes. Was this what he'd meant by "everything"? Because how could there be anything else?

His mouth scalding hers, their naked bodies pressing together, the feeling of hanging in midair. The catwalk was a cradle; they had left the world. There was no such thing as time. The earth was orbiting the sun, and they were somewhere above the planet, lost to schedules, obligations, promises, plans. This was the moment they conceived their daughter.

"What's that?" she asked when they broke apart at last, pointing at the distant white beacon that swept the water.

"The lighthouse at Beavertail."

"Can we go there next?"

He laughed, holding her tight. "I'd love that," he said. "You want to climb it with me?"

"Yes," she said, stroking his face. "I want to do everything with you."

Maura would never let him go, and she'd never belong to Andy again. That was the new truth, and it nearly swept her over the side—as if a great tidal wave had reared out of the sea, come charging into the bay, to the tall bridge, to claim her. She felt the catwalk give way. And suddenly vertigo kicked in. The world and bridge were tilting.

"I'm scared," she said, clutching J.D.

"You're okay," he said, stroking her hair back from her eyes, understanding instantly. "I have you."

"How will we get down?" she asked, breathless.

"The same way we got up."

But it didn't work that way. Maura was paralyzed. She couldn't let go of him—she was like a tree monkey clinging to its parent. The wind picked up; it was going to blow them off the catwalk like dry leaves. Was the bridge shaking? Yes, it was rocking slightly.

The world below whirled as Maura swayed. She thought of Andy proposing on one knee, on the riverbank by the covered bridge. She felt a sob in her throat—but not of guilt, more of sorrow.

"Okay, Maura." J.D. said her name so gently as he dressed her, helped her into her clothes one leg at a time, even as she clenched her arms around his neck, unable to let go even for a second. "That's it," he said. "There, now your arms, put on your shirt . . . okay, one arm at a time. I have you."

"No," she kept saying, her eyes squeezed shut. "No . . ."

But "Yes," he said. "Yes. We're going to climb down now. You have to do it yourself, I can't carry you. But I'm with you, Maura. I'll be right with you, nothing will make me leave you."

An eighteen-wheeler rumbled overhead, and she started to cry. She felt stupid, humiliated, terrified. She'd never let anyone see her like this before. She'd always been so competent, brave in the things she tried. In high school, she and a bunch of friends had gone kayaking in Vermont, down Mad River. They'd hit white-water rapids, a terrifying run.

Her heart had been smashing through her rib cage, but she hadn't shown her fear—she hadn't made a sound, just concentrated on staying in the boat, upright and alive, and when she stepped out onto dry land, knees buckling, she said she'd had the time of her life.

And here she was on the Jamestown Bridge, all her bravery gone. She might have expected a daredevil like J.D. to laugh or tease her, but he did the opposite. He became even gentler, softer, stroking her arms, reminding her of how strong she was, how she'd hauled herself all the way to the top.

"Going down will be so much easier," he said.

"We'll get closer to solid ground with every step. Don't look down . . . just look out across the water. See how beautiful it all is. It's there for you, Maura. I wanted to show you. . . ."

She forced herself to try. Her hands were glued to the ladder. He went first and kept talking to her, saying, "Move one hand, there you go. Now the other. Your left foot, down one step. Now your right. That's it, Maura . . . you're doing great."

"I can't," she said, frozen about twenty-five feet down from the top.

"You can," he said. "And you are. We're a quarter of the way there. Just keep going, and we'll be on the ground in five minutes."

She grabbed onto that—five minutes, a quarter of the way there. One step at a time, then two, then three. She suddenly knew she wouldn't be climbing the lighthouse, ever. This had been it, their moment above the earth. J.D. was right below her.

She had never been so attracted, and she'd never been so scared. She would return to this moment over and over, the rest of her life. Balanced on a rusty ladder, the earth tilting below. She and J.D. had just become part of each other, and that would never change.

Andy was peace and the river; J.D. was danger and the sea. But love isn't one thing or the other. Love is all of it. Weights and measures: too much of this, not enough of that. Maura's heart kept track. No matter how hard she tried to live in Andy's world, the gentle life he'd made for her and their children, she'd never been able to give up J.D. He'd been with her all along.

Stephen had walked over to a stone bench overlooking the half-moon bay that reached from Newport across to Middletown, the mouth of the Sakonnet River. Follow that river up, and there was Katharine's saltwater farm.

"You can't go back to Ohio. There's another reason you have to stay," Stephen said.

"What?" she asked.

"Look," he said, reaching into his book bag. She stared at a sheet of paper covered with Beck's handwriting.

"It's her homework for my class," he said.

She stared at the "A" in red at the top, along with the words **Congratulations, Beck. You are a natural mathematician.**

The surface was covered with tiny, spidery notations, formulas, and diagrams of triangles, rectangles, rhomboids, and, finally, a circle.

"This was a simple geometry assignment," he said. "She's taken it almost to the realm of calculus. . . ."

"Did you teach her?"

"I've been working with Lucy for a long time. She really wants to do proofs working toward infinity, 'telling a story' behind the numbers and equations. Lucy brought Beck into it—I never expected her to pick it up so quickly." He paused, glancing down at the page. "Her work is amazing. She's got a tremendous aptitude. I'd like her to enter a math competition."

"What sort of competition?"

"The Math Society. She'll go to Providence, compete with kids from private schools all over New England. Whoever wins that round goes to Boston for the nationals. Ten problems each. The students are judged on speed, precision, and style."

"Math, style?"

He laughed. "You'd be surprised. It's like writing . . . you encourage the students to go as deep as they can, say as much as they can, in as few words as possible. It's the same in math. Occam's razor—cut away what isn't needed and get to the heart of the problem. Beck has natural instinct." He paused. "She's a prodigy, if not a genius."

"I knew she was good, but . . ." Maura said.

"She has a rare talent," he said. "She's fearless—doesn't let her thoughts get in the way. It's as if there's a dialogue between her conscious and unconscious, and it gets expressed in math."

She closed her eyes. Beck was Andy's child. If she had stayed here with J.D., she wouldn't have had Travis and Beck. She remembered the evening Andy had shown up in Newport at Katharine's apartment. And she hadn't been there.

Katharine had called her at the warehouse, told her to get home right away. J.D. had had to drive her on his motorcycle. At first he'd refused, said he'd never take her to him. She'd run out to the street, started on her own. Heard the motorcycle start, and J.D. picked her up without a word. She'd had him drop her at the corner.

Andy was sitting in an armchair, staring at her as she walked through the door.

"Where were you?" he asked.

"Down by the wharf," she said. Her heart was pounding and she felt flushed with guilt. "I'm surprised to see you."

"Yeah, I thought you would be," he said.

"What do you mean?" she asked.

"Are you seeing someone else?"

Maura just looked at him. Even now she didn't know what she would have said. Sometimes she believed she'd been ready to tell him the truth. But other times she wasn't so sure.

"Don't answer," Andy said. "I want you to listen to me instead."

"Okay," she said. She glanced around for her sister—Katharine would give her moral support, help her ease Andy through what she had to say when he finished.

"Katharine left," he said. "I asked her to."

She felt stunned—it was very unlike Andy to ask someone to leave her own house. And not like

Katharine to oblige. Slowly she sat down on the sofa, across from him.

"I know you had to come east," he said. "For the summer. You wanted to spend it with your sister, and I tried to understand. Even though it was our graduation summer, and we're engaged, and we have to start real life soon . . ."

Hearing "real life," thinking of J.D. and what he'd said about his parents' life, Maura looked down.

"I told myself that's all it would be," Andy said. "A summer with your sister."

"That's why I came," she said.

"Listen to me!" he said, his voice and eyes so sharp she could hardly believe it was Andy. "Don't lie, Maura. You don't have to, okay? I've heard it in your voice these last few weeks. Every night you sound a little farther away. It's a summer romance—I can live with that. . . ."

"Andy . . ."

He held up his hand. "Please, Maura. Whatever it is, let it stay here in Newport. I want you to come home with me right now."

"Right now?" she asked. Panic rose in her chest. Her mouth felt dry. She looked at Andy, cleared her throat to tell him about J.D.

"I thought," he said, "we were going to be married."

And then he started to cry. He sat in the armchair, buried his face in his hands, sobbing. She saw his shoulders shake, heard him try to hold the sounds inside, but he couldn't. And in that moment, the summer ended.

"I know you, Maura," he said when he could speak. "I know how to take care of you, make you happy. This is for the long term. It's the real thing, real life."

"Andy . . ."

"Maybe you think you're in love. But what we have is real. I'm talking about the rest of our lives. Can you look at me and tell me you can have that with someone else?"

Maura stared at him. If she opened her mouth, she would say "Yes." She wanted J.D., she wanted the summer to last forever. But deep inside, she had the wounds of being her father's daughter. She'd always dreamed of a safe life, her own Mr. Sisson. She knew that no matter how much she loved J.D., she'd always be slightly scared with him.

She wrote Katharine a note, and she left with Andy.

Without saying goodbye to J.D. She'd written him a letter on the way—from the motel where she and Andy stopped, somewhere in Pennsylvania, just across the Delaware River. The first draft tore her apart; she'd said, **I love you.** The second draft had been shorter, measured, logical. **This is better for everyone. I am sorry for everything. Please**

know what everything meant to me, but I have to leave.

"Beck is very gifted," Stephen said now, breaking into her thoughts.

"She's made incredible leaps this year," Maura said.

"She has a friend," Stephen said. "Lucy. They encourage and drive each other to new heights, to discover their limits and then push beyond. With Beck, 'beyond' is exciting indeed."

"It is. Thank you. Her father would be proud."

"It's all her. All Beck. So, Providence for the competition?"

"Yes," Maura said.

"And you'll stay in Rhode Island and not move back to Ohio?"

"We'll stay," Maura said quietly.

■

J.D. finished his swim, and got dressed to meet Angus for their road trip. He gazed out the pool room's tall windows, watched Maura talking to Stephen. The reality of having her at the school, just down the street: she might as well be in Siberia. He couldn't go to her, and she wouldn't come to him.

His bike sat under a cover, somewhere in the back of the garage. BMW R90S, a seriously beautiful and classic motorcycle. He'd kept it perfectly maintained and garaged; the only time he'd ever beat it was the time he drove from Newport to Columbus and back, and the bike was fine, it was J.D. who got wrecked.

Not being able to ride, it still got to him sometimes. Now was one of those times. He wished he could run downstairs, take the stairs, not the elevator, jump on the bike, and go searching the streets himself for Carrie.

There had been too many dramatic moments in their lives—their love, their breakup, his accident. Up the ladder to the bridge, that was one. And the end of it all, when she left and he followed, that was another. The yelling, the crying, speeding close to one hundred miles per hour all the way back home.

But what he remembered most about that summer was how quiet it was. Little things. The morning he gave her a peach. He rode out to the farm stand in Middletown, picked out the best one he could find, brought it back for her. Juice dripped down her chin as she ate it. He wiped it off with a napkin. She just looked at him. Then she handed it to him, but he wanted her to have it all.

On the motorcycle, riding along Ocean Drive. The sun down. No traffic at all. Sea breeze blowing. Swinging around Breton Point, leaning into the road, he felt her cheek on his back against his shoulder blade. She'd turned her head to gaze out at the Atlantic Ocean, where only the waves' white edges were visible, one after the other. But she stared anyway, as if she could see more than waves.

He had never stopped missing the way he and Maura had been, their small moments. Not the big ones. Climbing the bridge, that had been dumb. She could have gotten hurt—look what had happened to him. He'd been young, but old enough to have outgrown wanting to show off for her. So why had he made such a grand gesture?

The lighthouse. Desperate and stupid.

Just such a ridiculous thing to do. And what if it had somehow contributed to what happened to Andy and Carrie? What if it had? The fact that Andy had drowned practically at its foot, certainly within sight—it seemed like an omen, a punishment.

He had hated Andy for taking her away. And, yes, there'd been times, many times, he'd hated Maura for letting him. She hadn't even said goodbye. She'd just left. And taken their daughter with her.

He'd gotten the letter three days later, postmarked East Stroudsburg, Pennsylvania. He hadn't even had to read it: she was gone. That's all the message he needed.

But it never really sank in. He never stopped hoping she'd change her mind and return to him. Seeing her in Ohio, knowing she was having a baby, seeing the love and fear in her eyes. That's why he'd built the lighthouse.

That's all he could think of now, up on the fourth floor, looking out at Maura and Stephen as they stood up, said goodbye, went their separate ways. He'd wanted to tell her. He'd wanted Maura to know that he'd never stopped thinking of her.

He never could. And the best way he knew to show it was to keep looking for Carrie. Angus was waiting downstairs, ready to drive him to Providence in the van.

■

My mom seems proud. The math stuff.

She's been sad and disconnected lately. She's been here, but not here. And I've been the same way. Here but not here. One of the things I love about geometry is how easy it is to disappear. I pick up my pencil, and I'm gone into the world of ghosts—ghost effects in the problems I'm trying to solve, spirits all around me.

Mom came in, walked straight into my room to hug me. I was sitting on my bed with Grisby and Desdemona, working on infinities, and she leaned across the cats and my paper, wrapped me in her arms. My mother smells like my mother. It's hard to explain, a combination of tea, pencils, and shampoo that smells like the color blue. The scent always makes me feel that life is beautiful, that we're all together: Mom, Travis, and I, and, yes, Dad and Carrie.

She sat on the bed beside me, asked to see my work. I handed her the paper. Lots of notations. My handwriting has become very neat. That was the first thing she commented on. We laughed; I used to scribble. She asked what I was doing.

Well, hard to explain, to put into words. I'm not Mr. Campbell, who makes math seem like poetry. His notations are beautiful; I feel as if I could climb aboard them and fly. But all I could do was show my mother my finite quantities, my use of an infinitesimal. In a way it's more like an art project than homework: you have to see it and feel it. At least I do. That's how I make myself understand.

So Mom stared at the parabola I'd drawn, and how the straight line cut the curve. I tried to show her the tangent, and the abscissa, and the ordinates, but I had to remember she isn't speaking this language. I explained as much as I could, and she sighed in the way she used to when Carrie would show her a new picture. So I knew she was content, because she knew I was doing what made me happy.

"You're going to Providence," she said.

"Yeah," I said.

"I'm so thrilled," she said. "You can't imagine."

"Well, it's only regionals. I don't know if I'll win and go on to Boston," I said.

"That doesn't matter," she said. "It's just that I know how hard it's been, moving here. And everything else . . ."

By "everything else," I knew she meant Dad and Carrie. I nodded. I didn't really want to talk about it.

"I know that in the past you've tried other ways to manage stress and sadness," she said. "Even here, a few weeks ago."

"I know."

"I haven't wanted to push you. But I've seen you working so hard, pouring so much of your energy into math. Does it help with the impulses? Is it easier not to take things?"

I nodded. If I didn't speak, was it still a lie?

"I just want you to know how proud I am that you've found this new, better way—working hard and building your math skills. Making friends with Lucy. Focusing on the positive."

"Thanks, Mom," I said. I tried to smile, but my mouth wouldn't turn up. My eyes darted to the hiding place—under the pillow of Desdemona's cat bed—where I kept Angus's keys. I was sorry I had taken them almost the moment I slipped them off his belt. But I couldn't seem to give them back either.

She hugged me again, a little harder than before. My face pressed into her shoulder; I didn't want her to let go. But she had to make dinner. I tried to get back to my proofs. Instead I went over to Desdemona's little bed—plush, covered with a zippered green cushion with her name embroidered in pink thread. She almost never actually slept on it. I unzipped the cover, reached my hand inside.

Angus's keys were there, thirty or so on a big brass ring. Some of them were old-fashioned, and obviously worked in the school's ancient keyholes. Others were modern, common, and a few more were magnetized. I carried them over to my bed, careful to keep them from clanking. Then I was able to work again. I don't know why, but having all the keys to the school helped.

I bent over my paper and got lost in infinity.

15 "HEY," REDMOND SAID. "I HEAR you're going to Boston."

Beck looked up from carving a tall, narrow pumpkin. She held a sharp knife in her hand and thought it brave of Redmond to come so close.

"Dude, let's not jump the gun. Providence first."

"You're gonna ace those regionals," he said.

She grunted as if he'd just said the most ridiculous thing in the world, went back to gouging triangles for eyes.

"You mind if I carve with you?" he asked.

"Sure," Beck said as he picked up a blade. "Just keep that knife away from me."

"Ha, ha," he said.

They sat on the back steps of the dining room, beside the loading dock. Concentrating on their pumpkins, they didn't speak. A food service truck pulled in, offloaded boxes of lettuce, carrots, parsnips, and beans. Then the dairy came by, wheeling in crates of milk and cream.

After thirty minutes, Redmond had carved the

jaunty face of an old sailor—unmistakable with lines, jowls, and a squinty eye; he'd hollowed a spot on his lip for a corncob pipe. Beck watched as he ran out to the lawn, found a twig and an acorn, and made the pipe.

"That looks pretty good," she said.

"My dad taught me how to do it," he said.

"Carve pumpkins?" she asked.

"Make things. Acorn pipes, reed whistles, clamshell daggers."

"Wow," she said, sounding as sarcastic as possible. "If I'm ever marooned on a desert island, you're the man."

"You'd want to be stuck on a desert island with me?" he asked, beaming and turning as red as a maple leaf.

"Uh, no one would ever want that," she said. Then, getting flustered, "I mean, it wouldn't be a good thing, the desert island part. . . ."

"When you go to Providence, I could show you around."

She dropped her knife; it fell to the step below with a metallic clang. Bending over, she retrieved it, her face down so he wouldn't see the blush. It sounded as if he was asking her for a date.

"I thought you were from Boston."

"I am. But my mother's from Providence. We visit her family for holidays."

"I don't know. . . . I probably won't have time."

"You mean you'll be solving math problems every minute, 24/7?"

"Probably."

"Have you ever been to Providence before?"

"Nope," she said.

"Well, you'll need a tour guide so you know where you're going. I'll show you India Point, where my mother's family first got off the boat from Ireland. And I can show you the Van Wickle Gates at Brown University, and the Green, and this cool pizza place." He sounded so excited, nodding his head, his bright red hair bobbing.

She went back to carving her pumpkin. Her heart seemed to be crashing around her chest, banging into her bones. It made it hard to breathe. Why did he seem to care so much? She felt him looking at her with sweet golden-retriever eyes. She actually had to hold herself back from patting him on the head.

"Stop watching me," she said.

"I can't help it," he said.

"Why?" She looked up.

He grinned. "I don't know. Watching your face is like watching a movie. Something big's gonna happen."

She scowled, but she wondered how it would feel to see the sights with Redmond. She worked on the pumpkin's mouth. "Say you did decide to go to Providence when I was there. How would you even

get there, anyway? It's not as if the whole school is going."

"Kids go to away football games, haven't you noticed? The school gets a bus for them. I'm gonna ask Mr. Campbell for transportation. You're the Newport Academy Math Team. The least they can do is let you have a cheering squad."

Beck grunted, and turned back to her jack-o'-lantern. Redmond wanted to root for her. He sat right there on the step beside her, the pile of scooped-out sticky pumpkin seeds between them. Out of the corner of her eye, she watched him clean a smooth oval seed off, put it in his pocket. He was taking a souvenir of this moment—she knew exactly how that felt, and suddenly her heart tumbled over and over, a somersault of strange happiness.

She gave her jack-o'-lantern a great big toothy smile.

"Your pumpkin looks like me," Redmond said, his smile huge and his brown eyes alight.

"Yeah?" she asked, hiding a smile of her own.

■

Newport Academy had won the second-to-last regular season football game on the road against Middlebridge, with Travis scoring the winning touchdown, making a championship berth almost definite. Maura had invited her sister to come watch that game, and this one at home, the last of the regular season, versus Lytton Hall.

They sat in the stands, bundled up, cheering for Travis. As girls they'd never been wild about sports. They'd never really followed their school's teams, except for a brief period when Maura had had a crush on a basketball player in her junior class. Katharine, in art school by that time, had teased her then—and even more when she'd fallen in love with Andy, who wanted to coach.

Arms touching as they watched the game, they were knitting their relationship back together. It wasn't easy, and that was a shock. The girls who had grown up finishing each other's sentences now found it hard to even start them. Katharine knew they were walking on their own private minefield; Katharine's hurt over J.D. was still so deep, ridiculous, embarrassing. She couldn't believe she'd lost nearly twenty years with her sister over a man who'd never even known she was in love with him.

Huddled in the bleachers after halftime, they stared at the field instead of each other. Katharine felt Maura lean into her. She wanted to put her arm around her, tell her how badly she wanted to make up for lost time. Her satchel practically glowed, as if the black book was radioactive. Katharine would show Maura after the game ended, and she could barely wait.

"Wow, it's cold," Katharine said. Then, hearing

herself, "I mean, I don't mind. I'm not saying it's **too** cold."

"Well, it is pretty freezing. Would you like to go inside?"

"And miss the end half? No, no . . . this is great," Katharine said. "Mom would have been proud of Travis. Both of them . . . Beck too."

"Thank you," Maura said.

Mentioning their mother melted some of the ice. In spite of her haiku/watercolor distance, their mother had adored her daughters, called them "my girls." She'd died of lymphoma just one year after their father had died of the same disease, Maura's junior year of college. Such a coincidence, everyone said. Cancer's not catching. Painful love was no less real than easy love—if there was any such thing.

"I miss Mom," Maura heard herself say.

"So do I," Katharine said. "Every day . . . it was hard when we were in our twenties, but I think I miss her even more now, as I get older. I want to share everything with her, ask what she thinks about . . ."

"Carrie," Maura said. "I miss Carrie."

Katharine didn't even think; she reached for Maura's hand. They laced fingers through their thick gloves.

"Take a walk with me?"

Maura nodded. They climbed down from the stands past people they knew. Katharine led the way, along the path to the school's back gates, onto a side street. The row of poplars threw long shadows, and the brightly painted maples scattered falling leaves at their feet.

They headed to Bellevue Avenue. The Newport Casino and Tennis Hall of Fame stood at the top of Memorial Boulevard. The Victorian shingle-style building had always been one of Maura's favorite Newport sights, but Katharine steered her past. She felt pulled to a certain address, the one place in Newport she knew Maura would hear her out.

Walking down Spring Street, they came to Trinity Church, the lovely old wooden Georgian church with the tall white steeple. To the right was the churchyard, filled with graves.

"Our old apartment," Maura said, gazing at the three-story house across the street; they'd lived on the third floor the summer Maura had met J.D.

Katharine led her to the front steps. Someone else lived there now. But this was where she knew they had to be for this conversation. This was the house Maura had come home to through all those tumultuous weeks. Katharine remembered walking up the hill one afternoon in a torrential downpour, and seeing Maura and J.D. kissing on these steps, not noticing the rain. She'd felt insane, needing to watch, to torture herself by imagining J.D. holding her instead.

Gesturing for Maura to sit, Katharine lowered

herself beside her. They stared at the busy one-way street for a few moments, watching cars head toward the Newport Bridge and out of town. Through the graveyard, down the hill, they saw the wharves, the dark gray water in the harbor.

"I sat here with J.D.," Maura said. "So many times."

"Sometimes he'd come upstairs with you," Katharine said. "Other nights you spent at the warehouse. From the time you met, you were barely apart."

"I know," she said. "I never wanted an inch of space between us."

"Neither did he," Katharine said.

Maura nodded. "He gave me a welder's mask so I could sit next to him and watch him work. It was ninety degrees outside, probably a hundred and twenty in the warehouse, but I didn't care. I just wanted to be with him."

"He couldn't let you out of his sight," Katharine said. She glanced at Maura now. "I used to be so jealous of both of you. He was my best friend. But to have that kind of love . . . I wanted to feel it too."

"You could have had it with someone," Maura said.

"Maybe so," Katharine said, controlling her emotions; she wanted the words to come out right.

"But it wouldn't have been the way you and J.D. were. Nothing was."

"I know," Maura said, staring across Spring Street into the churchyard.

"And it never ended," Katharine said.

"Well, it did," Maura said. "When I married Andy."

"Not for J.D. it didn't."

Maura gave her a look. This was the moment: the door was open, all Katharine had to do was step through. The truth of all this had crushed her for so long, but she was ready.

"He never lost sight of you," she said. "Ever."

"But he was here, and I was there. . . ."

"He kept track of you," Katharine said. "He knew when Carrie was born, and when the other kids came along. He knew when you started graduate school, and when you finished. He was waiting all that time."

"For what?" Maura asked, looking shocked.

"I don't think he knew. For you to come to your senses, for you to leave Andy. I don't know. Don't forget, the world pretty much stopped for him after the accident. It wasn't completely sane."

"Stephen said there was someone. . . ."

Katharine nodded. "He saw a woman in Jamestown. She lived right on the bay, not far from the bridge. It lasted a few years . . . but he wouldn't marry her."

"He talked to you?" Maura asked.

"We stayed close," Katharine said. "He couldn't really do his work anymore, not the way he wanted to anyway, but he always wanted to know about mine. And sometimes he'd ask me if I'd heard from you, or tell me something he'd found out. He thought about you and Carrie all the time; that's what really drove Linda, his girlfriend, away."

"Why?" Maura asked. "He knew I wasn't coming back."

"He didn't believe that."

"I never gave him any sign there could be . . ."

"The only 'sign' he needed was the way you felt about each other when you were together. He didn't need anything else."

"He should have," Maura said. "That's crazy."

"Maybe so," Katharine said, her heart pounding. "Love is crazy, after all."

"Doesn't have to be," Maura said.

Katharine took a deep breath, hiding her own feelings, pushing them down. "I think he was living through you all these years, wanting to be a part of your lives, even from a distance. He built something for you. And for Carrie."

"What are you talking about?" Maura asked.

"The lighthouse," Katharine said.

"What lighthouse?"

"On Lake Michigan, where you took your vacations."

Maura's eyes widened. A cold wind was blowing off the harbor, and her cheeks had been bright pink, but Katharine watched the color draining out of her face.

"On the island, across from our cabin?" Maura asked, disbelieving.

"He bought the land, and designed the lighthouse," Katharine said. "He had it built for you, to remind you of what could be, if you reached for it. And for Carrie. He wanted her to see the beam of light, to feel someone watching over her."

"But he didn't know her! And she didn't even know he was her father. She thought Andy was." She closed her eyes, and Katharine knew she was seeing the lake, Andy and Carrie paddling out toward the lighthouse, the violent storm rolling in.

Katharine took a deep breath. "I love you, Maura," she said. "From the minute I heard that Andy had died, that Carrie had run away, all I've been able to think about is you, what you must be going through."

"I can't believe any of this. He built her a **lighthouse?**"

"He did," Katharine said. "And somehow, I'm not sure how, it has guided Carrie right here."

"Right here? What are you talking about?"

"To Rhode Island," Katharine said. She reached

into her satchel, pulled out the large black notebook filled with pictures, drawings, clippings—images she'd accumulated on her days in Providence, unfolding like a dream sequence—and handed it gently to her sister.

"That's where I was when you first arrived in Newport," Katharine said.

"I know, teaching at RISD," Maura said, pure white. "But what does that have to do with Carrie?"

"Maura," Katharine said. "J.D. thinks Carrie went to see him in the hospital last year. And I went to Providence to find her."

Maura jumped up from the step, clutching the scrapbook. Her eyes burned into Katharine's. "She's there? She's **still** there?"

"We think so," Katharine said, standing up beside her.

"Oh my God—I knew there was something. Where is she? Why hasn't she called me? You're in touch with her, and you weren't going to **tell** me?"

"No, sweetheart," Katharine said, trying to grab her sister. "I would never do that to you. I haven't been in touch with her, haven't found her . . . we're not even sure it's her. . . ."

"I had a crazy feeling—like a dream—I saw her at a football game," Maura said. "Across the parking lot, watching me. A girl with a baby. Did Carrie have a child?"

"J.D. said the girl who visited him was pregnant."

"It was Carrie?"

"We're working backward, but we think so. J.D. was in a coma, had an impression of a girl watching over him. He thought it was a dream, but when he went in for a checkup recently, a nurse asked him about her. There were lots of calls to the nurses' station last year, someone asking about his condition. Eventually she showed up at the hospital; I showed the nurses Carrie's picture—J.D. too. They think it was her."

"How far along was she?"

"The nurse said she looked about to deliver. I checked with family services, found a place called Hawthorne House. They wouldn't tell me anything about the girls who live there, but people in the neighborhood said they used to see a girl who looked like her."

"We have to go there," Maura said. "Now."

"Okay," Katharine said. "Let's go."

■

And they did. Katharine drove. They headed north, up Narragansett Bay, across the Mount Hope Bridge into Bristol. Maura could hardly breathe. They pulled into Providence just as the light was dying, the granite buildings soft gray and the brick houses of College Hill faded rose-brown.

Katharine drove straight to Hawthorne House, a rambling blue Victorian at the head of Wickenden Street. In spite of the cold, three girls sat on the top step, each in a different stage of pregnancy. Katharine parked in the lot beside the house, and Maura fumbled in her purse for pictures of Carrie.

"I've been here before," Katharine said, gentle warning in her voice. "Nothing has come of it. . . ."

"We have to try again," Maura said, climbing out of the car. She practically ran to the house, gave the girls her pictures, explained that she was looking for her daughter Carrie.

"We're not supposed to say who's here," one girl said.

"I'm sure Carrie's moved on," Katharine said. "She would have had her baby seven or eight months ago."

"We weren't here then," another girl said.

"Well, I was," the first girl said. "But we have a code. Privacy first."

"Does that mean you've seen her?" Katharine asked.

"Please," Maura said. "I love her so much—I have to find her. She needs me and her brother and sister, and we need her."

The three girls stared at Carrie's pictures. Something about their silence felt sweet and sad, as if they knew that Maura's words were true. Maybe they were apart from their families for reasons of their own, but they knew real love when they saw it. Still, their code was too important to break, or maybe they'd never seen Carrie before. In any case, no one said a word. After a few moments, an older woman stepped out onto the porch.

"Can I help you?" she asked.

"We're looking . . ." Maura began, then saw the woman's gaze settle on Katharine.

"Oh, hello," the woman said.

"Maura, this is Dell Harwood," Katharine said. "I left my card with her before, in case she ran across Carrie."

"Yep, that's true," Dell said.

"I'm her mother," Maura said, walking toward her. "Was she here? Can you please tell me? I miss her more than you can ever imagine. Please, are you a mother? You take care of all these girls, you look after them, help them while they have their babies . . . she was my baby. Please, Dell . . ."

Was it Maura's imagination, or did Dell's eyes flood with tears? The light was dying, the air shimmering with October clarity. Maura's own eyes were streaming as she stared at the woman standing over her three charges, so protective, like a mother herself.

Dell blinked, folded her arms, hardened her stance. Maura stared at her, knew that Dell wouldn't give anything away. She felt her spirit break in half, just snap like a twig, and she heard herself sob.

"I'm very sorry," Dell said. "Many young women come through here. We have to provide a safe haven for them. Not everyone who arrives looking for them has good intentions."

"I want my daughter," Maura wept.

"Come on, Maura," Katharine said, putting her arm around her. Maura leaned into her sister, feeling her legs might give out. Those girls on the steps . . . if she and Katharine had arrived eight months ago, might they have found Carrie? She remembered being young, pregnant, confused about who she loved, and she cried harder.

Katharine eased her into the car. Started it up, began to drive. Instead of heading for the highway south, they cruised the local streets. Maura tried to look at people passing by, walking on the sidewalk, but her eyes kept blurring.

She thought of Carrie. Could she really be in this city? Had she lived at Hawthorne House? What made her come looking for her Rhode Island roots? She glanced down at Katharine's big black book, wondered if the answers were in there. "You met that woman, Dell, before?" she asked finally.

"I did," Katharine said. "I've made a pest of myself there."

"Don't you think she'd tell you, give you some kind of sign, if Carrie had really been there?"

"I think it's her job not to."

"How, why, do you think Carrie was here? What if J.D.'s wrong, and it wasn't her at the hospital? How would she have found him, anyway? How would she even know he exists?"

"J.D. had the strongest feeling she wanted to make sure he had survived the surgery and was recovering. The only way I can imagine she even knew of his existence, since you never told her, was that Andy must have."

"How would she—did she—trace him to Providence?"

"He's listed in the phone book," Katharine said. "And he always left detailed messages on his answering machine when he was away. He left the hospital information on there."

Maura just stared. She thought of the times she'd opened the Newport directory, stared at his name.

"In case you or Carrie ever called him," Katharine went on. "And she must have—it was right after the lake that she was first spotted here."

"But she's out there, alone with a baby . . . why won't she come home?" Maura whispered. "My daughter, and a grandchild. Why won't she come home to me? Does she hate me so much?"

"Maura, she's been through a trauma . . ." Katharine began.

"She has," Maura said. "And I just want to help her."

"I know you do," Katharine said, taking Maura's hand. Maura laced fingers with her older sister and let her drive her around, up and down the streets, knowing she'd been here before, knowing she'd done what sisters were supposed to do: look after, take care, be with, love. . . .

16 MAURA COULDN'T BEAR TO leave Providence. She'd wanted to drive the streets, knock on the doors, never leave until she found Carrie. The East Side was filled with college kids. Maura had had Katharine park the car, and she'd walked down Thayer Street, gazing into every young face. That night, instead of going straight home, Maura asked Katharine to drop her off at J.D.'s apartment.

"Thank you for today," Maura said before she got out of the car.

"You're welcome." Katharine tried to smile, but neither one of them could. They leaned across the seat to kiss, and Katharine made sure Maura took the black book with her. Maura had felt Katharine's gaze, charged and full of emotion, seeing her go to J.D.

Now, walking up the driveway, Maura tried to catch her breath. She knocked on the heavy garage door, heard him call "Come in." So she clicked the wrought-iron latch, let herself in.

"You have to explain things to me," she said. "Right now."

He'd been working out with weights, and he low-
ered them to the ground and wheeled closer to her.
His arms and blue T-shirt were soaked with sweat.
The room felt stifling, and she weaved in place.

"Here," he said, grabbing her hand. He held her
firmly while she caught her balance.

"I'm fine," she said. She stared into his wide blue
eyes, so light and clear. Carrie's eyes.

"What's wrong?" he asked.

"I need to know everything," she said. "Every
single thing that makes you think Carrie visited
you." She watched his gaze flicker, his eyes cast
down at his knees. He took a deep breath.

"You talked to Katharine?"

"Yes. We just got back from Providence."

"Maura, I don't know what to say. I was so out of
it, I might have been dreaming. I didn't want to
start something that would only hurt you more. I
wanted to protect you by being sure."

"But the nurses saw her too, right?"

"They saw a girl who looked like Carrie," he
said. "That's true. She visited me, even when I
wasn't awake. At first I thought she might have
been a volunteer, a high school kid. They sometimes read to the patients, deliver mail, things like
that. But I don't think that anymore."

"What do you think now?"

"One nurse asked what she was doing there, and

she said she had to make sure 'at least one of them survived.' "

" 'One of them'?" Maura asked.

"Her fathers," J.D. said. "That's what she said when the nurse asked."

"She was talking about Andy . . . she saw him die," Maura said, tears flooding.

"I think so." He held her hand. "Once I came out of it, and heard about the girl, put it together and realized Carrie had been there, I called Katharine."

"Carrie found you. . . ."

"All those years," he said, "I left messages on my answering machine, hoping you or she would call. And finally she did."

"She's really here," Maura said. She bowed her head and started to weep. "Why won't she come home?"

"Maybe she has to figure some things out first," he said.

"If Andy told her about you . . . or she heard us arguing . . ." she said, going over the fight she and Andy had had just before he and Carrie had gone out on the lake. "He was so angry, so hurt. He was going to leave me." She stared at J.D. for his reaction, saw only sadness.

"I'm sorry," he said.

Maura thought of the storm. She saw the dark

green canoe out on the lake. She heard Andy's and
Carrie's voices floating across the water, then the
low rumble of thunder in the distance. When she
turned to look west, she saw the dark wall of low
pressure coming fast across the water. The wind
had just picked up hard—trees were shaking, leaves
flying everywhere, and the smooth blue lake turning dark gray and whipped into whitecaps. The
canoe was heading toward the lighthouse. Were
they trying to make it there before the storm hit?
She had never had the chance to ask Carrie.

"You built her the lighthouse?"

"Yes," he said.

"Why?"

"It's not going to come out right," he said.

"I don't care. Just tell me."

"I wanted to be near you, do things for you, be
part of your life, and hers," he said. "I always have.
I never gave up. A couple of years back, I had this
idea. I don't write songs, or paint pictures. But I
fabricate metal."

"You didn't have to do anything."

"Maybe not for you. But for myself. And for her."

"For Carrie?"

"Yes, Maura. For Carrie. My daughter. I built her
a lighthouse." He looked straight at her. "That
night when we saw Beavertail Light from the
bridge—that bridge, that light, that was us, Maura.
I never forgot that. And I wanted whatever I did

for Carrie to be part of that too, part of us. Her parents. So I bought the island across from where you went every summer, and I had it built."

"How did you even know where we went?" Her stomach churned, her emotions ricocheting wildly.

"From Katharine."

Maura took that in. How must it have been for Katharine?

"I never stopped thinking of you," he said. "Either of you. She found me, and Maura, I swear I'll find her for you."

"Oh, J.D.," Maura said, reaching for him. She held him tight, the man who had given her her beautiful girl, and put her head on his shoulder and wept.

■

"Hello?" Katharine said, grabbing the phone when it rang late that night. There was silence on the line, and she wondered if she'd get another hang-up.

"It's me," J.D. said.

"Hey, you," she said. Her heart turned over.

"Maura came to see me," he said.

"She had a big day; we went to Providence."

"I promised her I'd find Carrie," J.D. said. "I hate just staying here. Sitting by the phone waiting, even heading up there with Angus. I feel so fucking useless. Especially after seeing Maura . . ."

"I know," Katharine said. "So do I."

J.D. was silent on the line. Katharine held the phone to her ear, listening to him breathe. They'd been there for each other all this time, both missing the same person. She thought of him in his wheelchair, working so hard, never losing the dream that he could walk again. She knew he'd walk straight to Maura if he could.

"She's not shutting you out anymore," Katharine said. "She came to see you, right?"

"Yes," he said.

"Good," Katharine said. Part of her felt so happy, and part of her broke. She'd had J.D. to herself all this time. She'd never been able to pretend he loved her the way he loved her sister, but she'd had him as her best friend.

"I promised her I'd find Carrie," he said again.

"We'll keep looking until we do," Katharine said.

"Tiger," he said, piercing her heart with the nickname he'd given her so long ago, inspired by the extinct and beautiful saber-toothed tiger. "I've always been able to count on you."

"That's what friends are for," Katharine said. She held the receiver gently, as if it were J.D.'s hand. She'd always loved the impossible, extinct animals, creatures that were never meant to exist in this world. Just like her love for J.D.

17

I FOUND A SCRAPBOOK IN MY mother's room.

It's funny, because she taught me and Carrie to make them when we were young. She said she and Aunt Katharine had kept them when they were girls, and she showed us the fun of documenting our lives in such a visual way. Carrie and I went to the mall and picked out identical cream-colored scrapbooks, except hers had a butterfly on the cover and mine had a cat.

We filled them with class pictures, our report cards, movie tickets, bead necklaces from the fair, brochures and pictures from our field trips to Thurber House. Even though our scrapbooks had certain things in common, you could tell that two different girls had made them. Mine had lots of math in it: quizzes, worksheets, tests where I'd gotten an A. And Carrie's was full of photographs, pictures of our family, the cats, our yard, her school, our town. We were sisters, but I saw the world through math, and she saw it through photography.

That's how I knew this scrapbook wasn't Mom's. How can I say this? It just wasn't her. Let me think about that, and I'll get back to you on how I knew. It showed up in her room the day Travis's team beat Lytton Hall. They're going to play Mooreland for the championship, the weekend before Thanksgiving.

Mom said we've both made her proud this fall— me going to the math tournament, and Travis leading the team to the ISL championship. In spite of all that, our family mood is not one of happiness. I'd say the atmosphere in our small, dark house is filled with a sense of waiting. If I didn't believe the worst that could befall a family had already happened to us, I'd say it's a feeling of impending doom.

When no one's home but me and the cats, I drift through the house. I don't really snoop, but I see what's there. Travis's room: all his football stuff, his computer, Ally's letters, his Matchbox cars, the watch Dad gave him—it used to be our grandfather's, and it's made of gold and way too expensive for everyday—and a bunch of hats Dad used to wear.

You'd think, to a girl with my problem, the watch would be calling my name. You might imagine I'd reach for it almost by instinct, slip it into my pocket just to feel its weight, decide to keep it so I could have a valuable family heirloom. I'd hide it well, in my secret kleptomaniacal stash with the ceramic pineapple, the brass mouse, cello strings, a silver bracelet Logan left in the gym, a glass paperweight from Stephen's office, a button from Lucy's black cashmere jacket, and Angus's keys. But no—I didn't want the watch.

My father's hats—they're another story. He liked hats a lot, had a collection of them. Most were baseball caps, from his team and other schools around Ohio. He had baseball caps from all the stadiums he'd ever visited—he and Travis used to go to games together and come home with souvenirs.

But Dad had other hats as well. See, he was going a little bald. Well, more than a little. He tried to hide it. He wore a baseball cap almost all the time, and he had these cotton hats with bands and little brims to wear fishing and when he mowed the lawn, and he even had a cool safari hat his college roommate had brought back from Africa.

Here's something I don't want most people to know: it upset me, that my father was going bald. We all teased him about it, and everyone laughed, and that used to hurt me. Because if he thought baldness was so great, why would he have to hide it under a hat? I know he didn't like it, and that made me feel embarrassed for him.

My father's hair was a reddish, sandy color—like mine, but lighter, not so brown. From the front, he looked as if he had plenty of it, except for parabolic inlets going back from his temples. Then, in the back, he had lost a circle of hair about the circumference of a coffee mug. And it was increasing in diameter.

So when I go into Travis's room, I always look at my father's hats. Travis has them hanging on a rack behind his closet door. I look inside them, and sometimes find a hair or two—those I take. I keep my father's stray hairs with my other necessary treasures. Travis won't miss those.

Then into my mother's room, where there's a true mother lode. That's a pun, but it's the reality. My mother has so many good things to pick up, look at, think about. Even the anonymous pacifier. I don't have to take anything, because her room is always overflowing with mementos and I can always find them there.

You can't imagine what my mother saves: our baby shoes, our baby teeth, locks of our hair, every drawing we ever made, the first shoelace Travis ever learned to tie, the pink-checked bib Carrie was wearing when she said her first word ("Da!"), finger paintings I made in nursery school.

So discovering a black notebook that was really a scrapbook was both a shock and to be expected. Because my mother is definitely the scrapbook type; but if this was hers, where has it been all along? I would have found it before now. And why is it filled with items about Rhode Island, Providence to be precise?

Open the black cover. Inside, a parking ticket issued on Wickenden Street. Turn the page: a drawing of the waterfront. Precise, almost architectural renderings of buildings and houses: a Victorian house, some two-family dwellings, all under the words **Fox Point.** On another page, Rhode Island Hospital, zooming in on it. A bed. A man sleeping in the bed, and a pregnant girl standing at the foot.

Then a nursery filled with cribs. Inside one crib, a sleeping baby. A watercolor of pink booties, another of a pacifier. The menu from a family restaurant: the Half Moon. Then a sketch of the Half Moon Diner, again the words **Fox Point.**

The book was filled with things like that. I could have spent all day at it. To most people, it would have been a mystery. But not me. I've been at this too long. I pick up belongings and feel a complete connection to the person who owns them. Maybe that's why I like "things" so much: they all come with a story. Unfortunately, no matter who they belong to, the story is usually mine.

But this black scrapbook was different. I knew it was Aunt Katharine's. She's a sculptor, but her work begins on the page. There's a mathematical elegance to her large constructions; she has to spend time with a paper and pencil to get the dimensions, angles, mass, and stability right.

As I looked through the pages, I saw my aunt's future sculptures coming to life. It was like having a mystical vision: someday we'd drive to her house, and in the field, instead of dodo birds and mastodons, there would be an installation of a man sleeping in a hospital bed. We'd go to an art opening, and she'd have a show full of cribs filled with pink-bootied baby dolls.

That's what I told myself. I could see this notebook being the basis for Aunt Katharine's sculpture. Art and math aren't so different. They come from ideas, from a way logic and magic combust. My working with Lucy on formulas to bring us close to our fathers was not so different from Aunt Katharine starting with ideas of Providence and turning them into art.

But the more I stared at the pages, the stranger my feelings got. My gut churned as I saw things that made no sense. And why would my mother have this book? Wouldn't Aunt Katharine need it to complete her projects? Paging slowly through, I heard wind in the laurel leaves outside our cottage. The wind was saying my sister's name: **Carrie, Carrie, Carrie.**

Never have I taken an object from my mother. Money in the past, but not lately. Because she is such a part of me and I of her, I haven't needed any mementos. But this book burned in my hands. It made my skin scream: I felt blisters forming on my heart. My throat closed so tightly, I couldn't breathe. I felt as if the black cover was melting into me, or I was draining into it. Either way, I couldn't put the book down.

I carried it into my bedroom. Because it was too big to fit into my special hiding place, I slid it under my mattress—all the way to the center of the bed, where no one changing the sheets could reach without really trying. The instant I let it out of my hands, the burning stopped.

I kissed the cats; they seemed skittish, as if they could hear the wind talking too. It was time for math lab with Lucy. I grabbed my backpack and ran out of the house, letting the cold and salty November air drench my scorched self.

■

Practice intensified in the week before the championship game, with Travis pouring everything he had into the workouts. He hadn't let himself want this, or even acknowledge what he was doing. But every game, every yard gained, every touchdown scored—he was doing it for his dad.

He couldn't explain it, didn't even want to try. For him, football had always been fun, discipline, playing the best game, doing it for his team. He'd never given the sport a cosmic purpose, never thought it had much meaning beyond a drive to win.

But this season, that had changed. Coming to a new school, losing his old girlfriend, trying to put together an accumulation of time without his father and older sister, had all seemed like challenge enough. He'd never expected to arrive in Newport and ignite their football program. He'd always played hard, to win. His father had taught him rigor, but had reminded him not to lose sight of the fun. That had made Travis a really good player. But nothing before this season had led him or anyone to believe he could be a football star.

The only difference he could think of was his father. He'd started talking to him, on the way to practice, and out on the field. Between plays, after the huddle, he'd face his opponent and hear his father's words: **Truer than true, faster than fast.** He'd hear his dad's voice: **Do it with grace.** His father had coached many winning baseball teams with that spirit; Travis was only now discovering how lucky he'd been to have those words coming at him from his dad, any time of the day or night, no matter what the game, no matter what the obstacle.

Walking over to the field, Travis would tell his father he was going to play true, hit hard, run fast, and he'd do it with grace. He'd promise his dad that no matter what happened he'd hold his head high, shake the other team's hands, thank his coach. And Travis did all those things: every game of Newport Academy's season, he'd remember his promises to his father.

At first Chris Pollack, the quarterback and team captain, had seemed glad of the help. He'd praised Travis, given him the ball whenever possible. The wins started stacking up. Ty Cooper, a junior star and considered to be a sure bet for captain of next year's squad, had started saying darkly, joking at first but then with a kind of glum reserve, that he'd have some stiff competition against Travis.

Travis tried to follow his dad's rule, never compete with your teammates. When interviewed by the **Newport Daily News,** he always gave credit to Chris. And when Coach told him there was a groundswell of support for him as next season's captain, Travis said, "No, that's Ty."

Travis knew that's what his father would have wanted him to say. And the more games that passed, winning every single one, the more Travis felt that his father was with him. He started to understand the players who pointed at the sky after scoring a touchdown, winning a game.

The strange thing was, he really needed his father more than ever. Beck was lost in geometry, his mother had been strangely distant lately, and Ally was long gone. He'd heard from Greg Wainwright that she'd started seeing Cal Steiger, a freshman at

Ohio State. It had been his idea to split up, so he was surprised by how deep it cut to hear she'd found someone else. The knowledge made him run and hit harder, made him catch passes out of thin air, but he knew the main reason for his season was his father.

His mother had left just before the end of the last regular season game, disappeared somewhere with Aunt Katharine. But she was there on Saturday, as she always was, for the championship game. There was no sign of Aunt Katharine. His mother sat in the stands with a bunch of other teachers. Travis located her, just so he'd know. He did the same with Pell. She hadn't missed a game.

And then he let loose on Mooreland Hill. The Newport Academy Cuppers' defense did well in the first half, allowing fifty-two yards of rushing, forcing two turnovers, on twenty-two plays. With thirty seconds left, Chris completed a twenty-five-yard pass for a balletic catch by Travis, who scored. Still, the teams were tied 14–14 at halftime.

When they came back for the second half, it was snowing. Not hard, but steady. The field turned white, then muddy. Travis heard the crowd cheering. He glanced at the stands. Beck had gone to sit with their mother; they were both staring up at the sky, and seeing that, he felt his heart somersault. He wasn't sure why. Maybe they were looking for the same thing he was: a sign that his father was near. Then he scanned the bleachers for Pell again and found her, bundled up in her dark green down parka, looking anywhere but at the sky.

Her eyes were fixed on him. He'd been doing this for his father, and the snow felt like a sign from him. But there was Pell, two rows up, watching him as if her life depended on it. He felt her gaze, felt it fill him up. The huddle broke, and he took his position.

He intercepted the first pass thrown by Mooreland, ran seventy yards into the end zone to score. And that was just the start. The snow tapered off to a few light flurries, but he was on fire. His father had died in summer; somehow winter set him free. He broke through a shell. He scrambled for a late-third-period first down, even passed laterally to Ty for the score. The fourth quarter was explosive, with Chris and Travis trading places, passing then receiving, gaining ground, with Travis punching it, ten seconds to go, to blast over the line and score for the win.

It was Newport's first championship in decades, and the school went wild. Interviews, photographs, college scouts. Party in the ballroom, in Blackstone Hall, with roast beef and Yorkshire pudding, sparkling pear punch, and homemade pies. Most of the kids were heading down to Truffles for Saturday night, but Travis hung back.

"Honey, aren't you going out tonight?" his

mother asked afterward at home, when he'd usually be showered and ready to join his friends downtown. She must have noticed that instead of getting dressed up, he'd put on his old jeans and patched sweater.

"Yeah, maybe," he said. "But I thought I'd take a walk first."

"You want company?" she asked.

He shook his head. "Nah," he said. "I think I'll go alone."

His mother put her arms around him, looked up at him with pride in her hazel eyes. She seemed so small; he'd grown this year. "Your father would have been so proud of you," she said.

He smiled; did she wonder why he wasn't saying anything? He couldn't get the words out past the ridiculous lump in his throat.

"You're the reason Newport won," she said. "For the first time in over fifty years. Ted Shannon is ecstatic. They all are—you've brought glory to the school. But the main reason your dad would be proud is that you're such a gentleman. You're so thoughtful of Chris and Ty's feelings. I heard what you said to the interviewer. That the team was full of champions before you got here . . ."

"It was," he said.

She touched his cheek. "You made it better," she said. "You made it great."

"Thanks, Mom," he managed to say. Then he

grabbed his jacket and hurried out of the kitchen before she could say anything more.

Running across the campus, he felt a little like Beck. He had something he didn't want anyone to see hidden in his back pocket: the red baseball cap—the one his dad had worn to so many Buck-eyes games, the one with a big white "O" on the front. He jammed it on his head as he jogged.

The grounds were white with a light frosting. Snow had started up again, the flakes drifting down. An east wind gusted, blowing snow into his eyes. He wiped his face, slowing down as he reached the far end of the school lawn, just before he got to Cliff Walk.

Now he stood still, looking out to sea. Black waves crashed at the foot of the rocks, sending towers of foam upward to meet the falling snow. Behind him Blackstone Hall was brightly illumi-nated, still celebrating the team's victory. The crys-tal chandeliers sparkled through tall windows, bathing the white ground in brilliant paths of gold and silver light.

"You're not going to the wharf?"

He turned, saw Pell. She looked dazzling, dressed for Saturday night: glossy hair and makeup, a mid-night blue cashmere cape that matched her eyes, something slight and silver and strapless under-neath, tall black boots that seemed to go on forever.

"No," he said. "I don't think so."

"But it's your moment," she said. There was distance between them, a few yards. She closed it, stepping slowly forward as if reluctant to disturb him.

"I have something I have to do," he said.

"So do I," she said.

"Yeah, what?" he asked.

She took another step forward, slid her hand into his. "Stand here with you," she said.

They turned back to the water. This was the Atlantic Ocean, not Lake Michigan, but Travis thought of that stretch of water where he'd last seen his father. He thought of the season he'd just had, of every inch and drive that had belonged to Andy Shaw.

"You're thinking of your dad," Pell whispered.

"How do you know?" he asked, looking down at her with surprise.

"Of course you would be. On this great day . . . when he should have been here with you. I'm thinking of mine too. He went to Newport, loved this school. I think I told you, he played football for Michigan. He'd be so thrilled to know we won the championship!"

"I'm glad," Travis said, nodding.

"You think they're here?" Pell asked. "I know Beck and Lucy think they are. . . ."

"I know they're close," Travis said. He wouldn't have been able to say it to anyone else.

"Did you win for him?" Pell asked.

Travis nodded. Then he looked more deeply into her eyes. "I did it for him," he said. "And then, when I saw you in the stands, watching me, for you . . ."

They kissed then. Their hands found each other; her fingers felt so cold, the wind was whipping off the sea, blowing her fine dark hair into their eyes. She was shivering, so he opened his jacket, brought her inside against his body to keep her warm. His hand traced the smooth, white line of her cheek. He lost himself in the kiss for a long, sweet time.

But he had something he had to do. They stopped, and it seemed a little awkward. She stayed pressed against him, but looked up and asked, "Is it okay that I'm here? Do you have to be alone for something?"

"No," he said. "I'm glad you're here."

Reaching up, he took off his father's baseball cap. Of all his father's hats, this had been his favorite. It had once been bright fire-engine red, but had faded to warm brick. The flannel "O" had lost some of its glue, so one side flapped loose. Travis stared at the cap. He thought of the games he and his father had gone to, the teams they'd seen play. He remembered his father there every time he had played, game after game, calling to him from the bleachers. He thought of the words his father had said to him: **Truer than true, faster than fast.**

"You do it with grace, Andy Shaw," Travis said

out loud. Then he drew his arm back and let the cap fly.

Pell stepped away from him. She let him have the moment alone—him and his dad, and all the games, and all the bright days, and all the words they'd said to each other. The faded red cap caught the wind, then tumbled over and fell into the sea. It floated for a minute on the white fringe of a broken wave; a new roller crashed in, pushing the cap under, taking it away, out of their sight.

And then Pell came back to put her arm around him again. Together they stared at the spot where the cap had disappeared into the sea, and the snow swirled, and they felt their fathers standing with them.

18 ON THANKSGIVING, THE CAM-
pus was quiet. The boarders had gone
home, except for a few students who
lived too far away, or whose families were unavail-
able, and who were invited to dinner at the Shannons' house.

Maura was roasting a turkey, waiting for
Katharine to arrive. She felt on edge. Where was
Carrie? Who was she spending the day with? If she
really was in Rhode Island, might she have figured
out her family was nearby? Could she just walk
through the door, come home? Maura had been in
touch with Tim Marcus, told him about the girl
she'd seen at Travis's game and everything Katharine
and J.D. had discovered. But there'd been nothing
since.

Cooking smells filled the small house. Beck and
Travis were in the living room, watching the Macy's
Thanksgiving Day parade on TV. Maura said she
was going for a walk, and pulled on her parka. The
snow that had fallen the day of the big game had
now melted; the trees were bare, and the grass was

dry and brown. The water was calm, slate gray. Light shined through a break in low clouds, throwing silver on a patch of sea.

She heard a motor, turned around, saw Angus's van backed up to the side door of Blackstone Hall. He had activated the wheelchair lift, and the school door was opening; she saw Stephen pushing J.D. onto the lift, saw it being raised, J.D. being loaded into the back of the van. Maura ran over.

"Where are you going?" she asked.

"To look for her," J.D. said. "Do you want to come?"

Maura hesitated. She did, but the other kids were waiting at home. Stephen got it instantly.

"I'm sure Beck and Travis are expecting dinner," he said.

"They are," she said.

"Stay with them," J.D. said. "I'll call you if I find out anything at all."

"Katharine made up a book," Maura said. "Filled with all kinds of ideas she had about where Carrie could be. I thought she gave it to me, but I can't find it. Otherwise, I'd send it along with you. It might help. . . ."

"Katharine told me pretty much everything," J.D. said. "But if you do find it, or think of anything else, I'll be waiting for your call."

She nodded, watching Angus silently close the doors. She stood there beside Stephen, hugging herself as the van pulled away. The air was cold, smelled of wet leaves and distant tidal flats. Katharine would be arriving soon. Maura could ask her about the scrapbook, if she'd left it in her car. Telling Stephen she hoped he'd have a good Thanksgiving, she turned to go home.

The Half Moon Diner was busy. Lots of doctors, nurses, and patients' families stopped in for their Thanksgiving meals. Owned by the Harwood family, it had been serving Providence since 1938, the year of the big hurricane. Located right off the highway, it attracted all sorts of people.

Truckers off I-95, Portuguese fishermen home from Georges Bank, sailors off ships in the port of Providence, hospital personnel, kids from Brown, RISD, Providence College, Johnson & Wales, rock bands who'd played Lupo's Heartbreak Hotel or the Palace Theater. Everyone came to the Half Moon.

The waitresses Dell Harwood hired were invariably kind, sensitive, and most of all, vulnerable. They could easily be seen by male clientele as lonely-hearted marks. But Dell would have none of that. She had appointed herself the waitresses' guardian angel, plain and simple.

Many of the girls came to her from Hawthorne House. Dell herself had resided there thirty years earlier. Made a mistake with a boy in town on a freighter from Singapore, a sweet young sailor named Lin who'd met her one hot summer night and to whom she'd given her heart and everything else during his time in port. Lin had steamed off to destinations unknown without even realizing he'd left her expecting their baby. Ella Rose was twenty-nine now, and managed the Half Moon.

Wanting to give back—to help other young women as in trouble and afraid as she'd once been—she'd joined the board of Hawthorne House, worked there two days a week, tried to employ as many new mothers at the diner as possible.

Over the years, she'd gotten good at reading her young waitresses' minds. No one wound up at Hawthorne House because their lives were peachy. Girls who got pregnant had plenty of choices these days. When they wound up on the steps of that blue Victorian house, you could be pretty sure that all other possibilities had been considered.

Some girls had been thrown out by their families. Others had been beaten by their babies' fathers. Some were overwhelmed with shame. Certain girls had an exit strategy—have the baby, give it right up, get back to real life. Other girls weren't so sure of their plans. The pregnancy might have caught them so off guard, they had to wait the full nine months and sometimes longer to know what they wanted to do next. Yet other girls were in such complete shock, they seemed paralyzed.

Carrie had been one of those last. She'd shown up on the streets of Providence over a year ago, wandering like a sleepwalker. Bedraggled, emotionally fragile, obviously traumatized, she'd walked into the Half Moon and ordered a bowl of oatmeal. She ate three bites and promptly threw up. Fortunately, Ella Rose had been working that day. She'd called Dell, who'd gone straight over.

Not your classic "on the run" teenager, Carrie was a mystery to all who met her. The mere mention of the word "sister" brought tears to her eyes. Say "mother" or "father," however, and she grew distant and distracted. She seemed to be immersed in a bottomless reservoir of grief. She haunted the hospital; the other girls whispered about the fact that her father was paralyzed, that Carrie couldn't leave Providence until she made sure he would be okay.

Later, after Grace was born and Carrie had started working at the Half Moon, Dell had noticed her studying a photographer taking shots of the scenery. Carrie told Dell she used to love doing that. So Dell got her a camera. What was she in this for, if not to encourage a young person?

Turned out Carrie had a talent. She'd hung around Hawthorne House, doing pictures of all the girls. Later, after the babies were born, she'd take birth portraits and give them to the girls for free. Some hung on the walls of the house.

Then, this last September, a woman had shown up at the Half Moon, then Hawthorne House, asking about a girl named Carrie Shaw. Katharine O'Donnell, the sculptor. She had shown pictures around.

"Your aunt is looking for you," Dell said to Carrie.

"What did she say?" Carrie asked, eyes welling. "Did she mention my mother?"

Dell had narrowed her eyes. This didn't sound like a girl who didn't want her family to find her. The expression in her blue eyes was pure hope. That simple.

"She said your family misses you."

Carrie nodded, wiped away tears.

"Your father is in the hospital?"

"I can't talk about it," Carrie said. She'd asked Dell to keep hiding her, to not tell her aunt where she was. Dell had promised. No questions asked. But she'd seen the look in her eyes, and known it was just a matter of time.

Hawthorne House girls had a lot to work out. That was a given. They had to get their stories straight. Not in the sense of lies, but of meaning— they had to figure out what everything in life meant to them, what mattered, what led them to carrying their babies and giving birth far from their families, in the arms of strangers.

"Two turkey dinners with everything," Carrie called now, standing at the stainless steel counter.

Dell, sitting at the register, looked over at her. What a pretty girl she was, delicate and sweet. She'd thrived as a mother. She was one of Dell's best workers. One wall of Dell's living room at home was filled with the lovely photographs Carrie had taken of women and babies. Dell felt lucky to have such a good person working for her. She smiled at Carrie, ready to give her a proud, encouraging nod, when Carrie ran past her, leaving the turkey dinners behind.

Turning toward the door, Dell saw a husky man with a drooping mustache pushing a younger man in a wheelchair. They were both bundled up; they didn't remove their jackets, just looked around the room as if searching for someone.

"May I help you?" Dell asked, walking over with menus.

"I was wondering if you know this girl," the man in the wheelchair said, handing Dell a photo of Carrie.

"Doesn't look familiar," Dell said. "Why?"

"Katharine O'Donnell told me Carrie might be working here," the man said.

"Lot of people work here, and lots of them quit," Dell said. She stared at the man's handsome face, bright blue eyes; her gaze fell on his legs. She remembered what the girls had said, about Carrie's father being paralyzed.

"Mind if we take a seat?" the other man asked. "Maybe she'll come by."

"Sure," Dell said. "I've got a nice table by the window."

She led the men to the table, watched as the man in the wheelchair positioned himself to face the door. She handed them menus, knew Carrie wouldn't be back as long as they were here. It was a holiday, and Dell couldn't stand to lose the help. Maybe she should give Carrie a push. Tell her to get back to her station or forfeit her job. As a plus, she could connect with her father.

Thanksgiving, a time of togetherness. Dell sighed, knowing she'd have to wait tables herself now. She couldn't fire Carrie, anyway. She just didn't have it in her heart to do that. But she hoped Carrie would figure this out soon. Glancing across the restaurant, she saw a curtain move. Someone was standing in the office.

Hiding behind the curtain, watching the diner's customers eat their Thanksgiving meals, perfectly positioned to stare at the two men who had just come in, one of them with such love and purpose in his clear blue eyes.

19 MAURA ANSWERED THE DOOR. Katharine stood there in jeans and a maroon chamois shirt. She handed Maura a pumpkin pie; she was smiling, but her face was pale; she had dark circles under her eyes. Her cheeks looked more sharply lined than Maura had noticed before.

"Happy Thanksgiving," Maura said, placing the pie on the counter.

"And to you too," Katharine said.

The sisters faced each other. Maura felt as wildly emotional as Katharine looked. Her chin was wobbling; she had to force it not to shake just so she could get the words out.

"What is it?" Katharine asked.

"I've been feeling there's nothing to be thankful for," Maura said. "With Andy and Carrie gone. But seeing you here . . ."

"That's how I feel," Katharine said.

"Our first Thanksgiving in so long," Maura said, reaching for her.

"Oh, Maura," Katharine said, her eyes filling with tears. "I'm so sorry. . . ."

"So am I. I don't know how I've done without you all this time. I really don't."

The sisters hugged a long time. Holidays had always reminded them of each other, even when they hadn't been together. Their mother had taught them wonderful traditions, expected they'd share them forever.

"It smells good," Katharine said.

"I made Mom's stuffing."

"Creamed onions too?"

"Of course!"

"I brought this," Katharine said, digging into her satchel, taking out a sealed container. "Cranberry-orange relish."

"We'll have lots of it," Maura said, opening the refrigerator and showing Katharine the bowl she and Beck had made. It was an O'Donnell sister favorite, taught to Maura by Mrs. Sisson, her beacon of domestic happiness.

The sisters laughed. They stood still, staring at each other. Their first holiday together in eighteen years. The reality was both huge and small, just like all the time that had passed.

"What can I do to help?" Katharine asked.

"Mash the potatoes?"

"Do you use a hand masher or an electric mixer?" Maura gave her a look. "Hand masher, of course!"

"How could I have thought otherwise?"

Maura handed her an apron, led her over to the stove, gave her another hug. "I do have a question, though," Maura said. "You know that scrapbook you showed me . . ."

■

"Have you seen a black notebook?" Beck's mother asked after they had finished dinner, after the turkey was eaten and the dishes cleared, and a second piece of pie offered. Beck, standing in the kitchen, spooned whipped cream out of a metal mixing bowl and tried to keep a neutral expression.

"What notebook?" Travis asked.

"It's really more of a scrapbook," Aunt Katharine said. "It's filled with clippings and receipts, things like that."

"Is it from a trip you took?" Travis asked.

"Sort of," Aunt Katharine said. "But a very short trip—to Providence."

Beck raised her eyes just slightly, enough to see her mother and aunt exchange a look. The way their eyes connected gave her goose bumps. But Travis didn't notice. He said he hadn't seen the notebook and asked if anyone minded if he watched the football game.

"Beck?" her mother asked as Travis headed for the living room.

"Mmm?" Beck said, working studiously on the remnants in the bowl.

"Have you seen it? The scrapbook?"

"No," she said. But she must have said it too quickly, because suddenly the house got quiet in the exact same way it had last spring, after the principal called to say she'd gotten caught stealing.

"Beck?" her mother said, walking straight over, hand on the stainless steel bowl, taking it firmly away. The look in her mother's eyes: pure betrayal.

Beck felt herself blushing as red as she would ever get. She was either going to have to lie or admit she'd taken the book.

The worst thing was hurting her mother in the trust department; the second-worst thing, she wasn't ready to give the scrapbook back. Looking through it last night, she'd gotten lost in a story: the Half Moon Diner, the Hawthorne House, babies in cribs.

"I have math to do," Beck said.

"No," her mother said. "You have to tell me the truth. Did you take the book?"

"The competition is in a week!" Beck said, as if she hadn't heard. "I have to get ready. Lucy told me to call her right after dinner, and I can't keep her waiting!"

Tearing out of the room, she left her mother standing there. Beck hated seeing her like that. They'd had that talk about trust just before Ally came. Her mother had asked about therapy, about setting up calls to Dr. Mallory. Beck could have asked for help, but had she? Of course not.

At least she hadn't lied. Lying felt worse than anything, and the only reason she ever did it was to protect her necessary thefts. That's how she thought of them: survival behaviors much like breathing, eating, drinking water. Without stealing, the pressure of loss would have built up in Beck, and she would have exploded like an over-filled helium balloon. She'd known that way before the doctor said it.

What a sad truth. She despised the reality. Fortunately, math pushed it all away. She grabbed her pencil and tablet, began her work, and wrote: **AB+aB+bA+ab.**

With math, she was able to think about other things. The thoughts drifted like clouds in a blue sky. What had Aunt Katharine been doing in Providence that needed documenting? What did it have to do with Carrie? She knew, somehow, that it was all related. If she wasn't afraid of being further interrogated, she would try to eavesdrop on her mother and aunt right now. But they wouldn't say much anyway; Travis was there in the next room, watching some game. Beck could hear the cheering and commentary from here.

She tried to concentrate, found that she couldn't push the notebook from her mind. Why had she taken it? She wanted to reach under her mattress, pull it out, march into the living room, and hand it to her mother. But wouldn't that be proving to everyone that she was a thief, a bad person?

Grisby, Carrie's cat, stretched out beside her on the bed. Beck absently stroked her fur. She tried to breathe calmly, focus on $(A + a) \times (B + b)$.

But the notebook was just like the pea under the mile-high stack of mattresses: she felt it there beneath her and couldn't concentrate.

Out in the kitchen were her mother and aunt. It was their first holiday together since long before Beck's birth. The sisters were back together. Something had made them remember their love. They were thankful for each other. They had love that went back as far as it could go.

All these years there'd been a jagged rift in their family, between her mother and aunt. Beck remembered geography class, fourth grade. The teacher, Mrs. Newton, had said, "Canyons start with a crack. A very fine fault in the rock. Remember this, class: if you're ever camping, lost in the wilderness, and you come upon a tiny fissure in the rock, follow it. Within ten minutes, you will be standing in a canyon. And water flows into canyons."

Her mother and Aunt Katharine's break had started as a crack. Little things. Long silences, then longer. A day had turned into a year, and into a lifetime. That's how Beck put it together. She knew neither of them had started out wanting that. She was positive.

She thought of Carrie. Her mother and aunt's estrangement had made it possible for Carrie to cut herself off. She had learned from them that silence was possible, that a person could leave her family.

Beck tapped her pencil, thought of how hard she and Lucy were working to find the formula to bring their fathers back. That was math, it was magic, it was just two lonely teenage girls desperately longing for their dead fathers. She thought of the notebook: what if it contained something real? Something that could help find Carrie?

Carrie had run away from the ER after the storm. Beck thought she knew why: her sister was pregnant, and if she stayed, the doctors would find out and tell her mother. Was she afraid now? Of coming home? Was she worried that no one would welcome her back? Did she think the damage was too great? She knew, from watching her mother and aunt, that disaffection had become part of their family.

But what Carrie didn't know, because she wasn't here right now, was that the estrangement was finished. It was **ended.**

Rolling over, Beck startled Grisby. The cat scooted off the bed, into the closet to hide behind a pile of laundry. Beck arched over the side of the bed, wriggled her hand under the quilt and sheets, wedged it as deeply between the mattresses as she could. Her fingers closed around the book's hard covers.

She eased it out and opened it. She gazed at the walking map of Providence's East Side, a receipt for a cup of coffee and a corn muffin at the Half Moon Diner. She studied her aunt's sketch of the porch steps and railings of a big blue house, letters painted delicately above a rose-pink door: **Hawthorne House.**

When she had looked through the whole scrapbook, she tucked it under her arm, stood up straight, and left her bedroom.

This was the hardest walk she'd ever taken: down the small hallway, to the kitchen. Her mother and aunt were at the sink, washing dishes. The football game blared from the TV in the living room, and music played on the kitchen CD player: Carly Simon.

"Mom?" Beck said, her lips parched.

"Remember the concert at Foxwoods?" her aunt was saying.

But her mother wasn't hearing Carly now, she had turned to look at Beck and was waiting for the truth, the disaster.

"Mom," Beck said again, her mouth drier than before. She could barely get the word out.

"Beck?" she asked.

Beck could have said she just found it. She'd gone looking in her mother's room, come upon the notebook in her drawer, or on the bookshelf, or under the night table. But she didn't say any of those things. Her whole body was trembling. She felt as if she had an evil force inside her, a terrible spirit, and she had to get it out.

"I took it, Mom," she said.

"Oh, Beck . . ."

Beck screwed up her face with shame; she had disappointed her mother again. But when she brought the notebook out from behind her back, her mother didn't even take it. She just wrapped Beck in the biggest hug possible, rocked her back and forth.

"Why are you hugging me?" Beck asked. "I stole it."

"I'm so proud that you've brought it to me, on your own."

Beck realized: it was true. This was the first time she had done that. She buried her head in her mother's chest, eyes closed, feeling that she had finally done the right thing. And that made her think of the other objects she'd stolen, and how she suddenly had a burning desire to return them all to their rightful owners.

"Thank you, Beck," Aunt Katharine said.

"Will it help you find Carrie?" Beck asked.

Aunt Katharine didn't waste time in platitudes,

in maybes or "we'll see's." Beck saw in her eyes a woman who worked with numbers, formulas, math, and logic.

"Yes," Aunt Katharine said. "I think it will."

"Honey," her mother said, "get your brother."

Beck tore into the living room. "Hurry," she said, and he did. They hustled back to the kitchen, stood staring at their mother and aunt. Beck could hardly breathe.

"What?" she said, shaking her mother's arm. "You have to tell us."

"We don't know this for sure," her mother said. "But it seems possible that Carrie is in Rhode Island. In Providence . . ."

"Mom!" Travis said.

"How do you know?" Beck asked.

"Someone saw her," her mother said.

"Who?"

"Never mind . . . that part's not important," her mother said, turning bright red. What was that about? Beck wondered, but she was too blown away by the thought of Carrie so close by. She'd felt her sister all this time, sensed her presence almost as if she was watching over her.

"We've been looking for her," Aunt Katharine said. "Carrie and her . . ." She glanced at their mother.

"Her baby," their mother said.

"Carrie did have a baby?" Travis asked.

"Yes," their mother said. "We're pretty sure she did."

"Is that why she's stayed away?" Travis asked, his voice breaking. "Does she think we wouldn't love her?"

"She knows we love her!" Beck said, scoffing. "No matter what."

"I think she has other reasons for staying away," their mother said. "That have nothing to do with you two. They're between me and Carrie."

"I don't believe that," Travis said. "What could you have done?"

"Who cares who did what, or anything like that?" Beck asked. "Carrie is here! In Providence! And guess where I'm going for the math competition? That's right! I'm going to find my sister!"

■

In the days after Thanksgiving, I began to go straight. It was like waking up after a long, strange dream. Carrie was in Providence! I wouldn't have to miss her anymore. We'd run into each other's arms and be whole again. I wouldn't be missing half of myself. All the things I'd stolen arrayed before me, images that added up to a dark, nonsensical subconscious blur. Why had I taken such dumb things, as if they could fill the void left by my sister? A ceramic pineapple? **Really?**

Between History and English, I returned the

little brass mouse to its home, a glass-front book-case in the second-floor reading room of Black-stone Hall. I had to wait for Logan Moore and Ty Cooper to finish snuggling on the chintz loveseat before making my move. They looked at me as if I was a perv, spying on their makeout session. I didn't care.

My months of stealing had given me practice in casing various joints. Only this time, I did it in reverse. Instead of waiting for the right moment to grab the goods, I bided my time for the precise opportunity to return them.

"There's a library, you know," Logan said as I browsed through the books.

"I know," I said, my back to her.

"What's your name, Becca?" Ty asked.

"Beck," I said.

"You're Travis's sister."

"Yeah," I said, still not turning around. But I knew that made me okay in Ty's eyes. Being my brother's sister had gotten me accepted by a lot of older boys and football players over the years. I was the squirt sister. There was a place for me in their universe. Deal with it, Logan.

"I just think, if you're looking for a book, there are more choices in the library," Logan said.

"Thanks," I said as I continued to peruse the shelves.

"This room is more for reading," she said. "The library is for research."

The thing is, in spite of the fact she was chewing face and not reading at all, she was right. Newport Academy had a great library. It was on the front of the building and faced east, over the sea. The tall windows had been specially tinted, to protect the thousands of volumes arranged over two levels, and the whole library was modeled after the Long Room in the Old Library at Trinity College, Dublin. Apparently old James Desmond Blackstone had worked there as a porter when he was a boy, shelving books and doing general janitorial duties for the librarians, and to him a grand library like that was the sine qua non of a fine school. He wanted it to happen, and it did.

But I avoided our school library for the exact reason that others loved it: it faced the water. Water is still my downfall. I avoid it, even the sight of it, whenever possible. That's how I'd come to discover the reading room, this little star sapphire of a chamber. Blue shantung silk on the walls, three tall mahogany bookcases, one with a glass front, a seating area with loveseat and two armchairs, all covered in faded old chintz patterned with blue flowers—thistles and forget-me-nots.

Set in the middle of the second floor, between the boys' and girls' wings, it has no windows at all.

There is a cozy fireplace for warmth, with a white Italian marble mantel carved with lilies; it was one of my favorite places to hide out and commune with trigonometric functions. I waited for Logan and Ty to leave, to get tired of enacting their mad passion with me five feet away.

Just as an aside: it's kind of weird watching super-attractive people make out. It's like watching a movie, everyone's features so chiseled, and their bodies nothing like yours or mine. Even the spit in the corner of Ty's mouth as he shoved his tongue into Logan's was kind of mesmerizing. I turned away, stared through the glass-paneled doors on the one bookcase.

There were six shelves. Five were filled with books—obviously the oldest volumes, bound in red or green leather, the titles in delicate gold. The sixth shelf was filled with small objects: a crystal globe, a pressed shamrock, dry and brown, in a small frame, silver-framed photos of distinguished-looking men and women, a framed clipping from the local paper about the swimming pool on the fourth floor, the first of its kind in the whole United States. And two brass mice—I had the third in my pocket.

A title caught my eye: **Rose Hawthorne: A Life.**

I knew nothing of her, whoever she was, and biographies are far from my favorite reading material. I prefer anything on mathematics, books by

Bertrand Russell, or even Bishop George Berkeley. But the name shimmered: **Hawthorne.** Hawthorne House. Carrie, my aunt's scrapbook. So I took the old red leather-bound book down from the center of the shelf.

Sitting in a chair kitty-corner to Logan and Ty, feeling the fire's warmth on my legs, I read a page. Rose was the second daughter of Nathaniel Hawthorne. Her father had called her "Rosebud." She had lived from 1851 to 1926. The family had spent time in Italy; she'd had a spiritual conversion, become a Catholic, founded a religious order, and opened a hospital for the poor. She was saintly.

I was lost in thought. Could there be some connection with the Hawthorne House Aunt Katharine had discovered in Providence? With Carrie? When I looked up, Logan and Ty were gone; they had slipped out without my noticing. But Redmond had come looking for me. He stood in the doorway, his corkscrew red hair zinging all over the place. He looked at me with a goofy grin.

"Guess what?" he asked.

"Uh, you have a new freckle?"

"I got the word from Mr. Campbell. I can go to Providence with the math team."

"Yeah?" I asked.

"Yeah. I can carry your books for you."

"I have to tell you something," I heard myself say. "My sister is in Providence. She ran away a year ago. I haven't seen her since then. I don't even care about math anymore. I just want to find my sister."

"Thanks for telling me that," Redmond said. "It . . ."

He turned so red, he matched the fire. I waited for him to finish.

"It makes me feel close to you," he said.

"Me too," I said. "Close to you."

I smiled at him and put the Rose Hawthorne biography back on the shelf. Next to it was another book, a smaller one I hadn't noticed before. Its cover was tattered and the words **Love** and **Sorrow** were written on it in ink, in a delicate script. The words might have been written just for me, to describe the way I felt.

That's when Redmond held my hand. Just held it, standing there by the fire, thinking of going to Providence.

20 MAURA AND KATHARINE GOT together every night after work. The first few nights after Thanksgiving they huddled at the kitchen table, talking about Carrie and what they could do. Together they went through the details, Katharine using the notebook to remind her of everything she'd learned.

They talked to Tim Marcus, who said he'd finally gotten the eBay guy to tell him what they already knew: that he had sent the lot of western postcards to a postbox in Providence, Rhode Island.

They cooked dinner together. Chopping vegetables, seasoning the sauce, setting the table. Travis and Beck pulled up chairs to the kitchen table, asked everything about Carrie. Maura filled them in the best she could, leaving out the parts about J.D. Katharine told them about her drives through Fox Point, the people she'd talked to and given Carrie's picture to.

Maura loved watching her kids interact with her sister. It seemed both so simple and so extraordinary. Why had this seemed so hard? How could they have messed up so many years? It was difficult for Maura to not blame herself, think of ways she might have made things better, reached out, invited Katharine to more family events—holidays, graduations, spring concerts. She'd catch herself feeling the old bitterness, regretting her own actions, wishing Katharine hadn't shut her out for so long, wishing she herself hadn't made so many mistakes.

And then she figured it out. The morning of Beck's math competition, when they were all getting in the van to go to Providence, Maura caught sight of J.D. He had wheeled himself out onto the sidewalk to watch them go. Maura raised her hand to wave, turned to Katharine to make sure she saw him, and caught sight of the look in her sister's eyes.

Katharine was gazing at J.D., not with the warmth of friendship, but with the longing of a woman in love. That glimmer came back, the one Maura had felt on the phone eighteen years ago, when she'd wondered if both she and Katharine were in love with the same man. Everything clicked into place. The truth was right there in her sister's face; Maura stared for a few seconds, and then she had to look away.

■

Okay, this is how being completely distracted by my sister helped me to win the competition. The first thing is, I didn't care. I really didn't give anything close to a crap about winning. All I wanted to do was drive north, enter the city, and find Carrie. I know that sounds naive, but that's how we're connected. I felt as if I were within a certain distance from my sister, our DNA would start vibrating. We'd be like tuning forks, responding to each other.

Mr. Campbell chartered a big van, and we all piled in. My mother, brother, aunt, and a bunch of kids from school, including Redmond. Lucy and Pell couldn't come; they both wanted to, but their grandmother presided over some annual December tea and expected them to be there. That's okay. Although I'm not sure Travis felt the same way; I think he wished Pell were coming.

Redmond and I sat in the back seat. Up front my mother and aunt sat together. I liked watching their heads close together, whispering. I stared, and tried to make sense of something. I'd gotten a strange tuning-fork feeling about them just as we'd all boarded the van—and it seemed to have something to do with that guy in the wheelchair, on the sidewalk in front of Blackstone Hall.

Maybe it was a sister thing, the quivery vibration I picked up from my mother and aunt. They were both looking at the guy, as if they knew him from a long time ago. Something about him made them both sad. I stared at the backs of their heads, just waiting for the troubled feeling to go away. And it did—once the van drove out the gates and headed for the bridge.

I'd brought a few pictures of my sister, and I showed them to Redmond as the van sped north. He stared at them, not asking what he was looking at. Finally he raised his big brown eyes, gave me a quizzical gaze.

"That's your sister," he said.

"How can you tell?" Most people don't think we look that much alike.

"I'd know your sister anywhere," he said.

"I told you about her, that she ran away."

"I remember."

"And that we think she's in Providence," I said.

Redmond nodded and I turned to the window.

As we drove along, I watched intently. I wasn't sure how long it took to get to Providence, and I wanted to be ready to spot Carrie the minute we got within territory.

"Why would she be there?" he asked after a while.

I'd been wondering that myself. I knew Carrie better than anyone. If she'd come to Rhode Island to see Aunt Katharine, I could understand. But my aunt's farm was in Portsmouth, closer to Newport than Providence. So Carrie must have had some other reason. It hurt and confused me, to tell you the truth. To think of my sister having that big a secret.

"I don't know," I said. "But I swear, I think I'm going to see her today."

"Then I think that too," he said.

"Do you really?" I asked. I appreciated his support, but what I really wanted was to know if he had a real sense of it or not. Redmond, for as much as I tease him, is full of intuition and insight about people and situations. I see him watching me, and this is going to sound strange, but I know he gets me. After such a short time, he really does. He would be a good psychologist or psychic.

"I want it because you do," he said. "Because I know how much you want to see her."

"Will you help me?" I asked.

"Yeah," he said, eyes gleaming as if I'd just made him a Knight of the Round Table.

He took the photos from me, bending to look at them with such rapt attention he didn't even notice the big blue bug, a huge royal blue cockroach on top of a building and a favorite Rhode Island landmark, when we passed by.

The van drove us to Brown University, parked in front of the Rockefeller Library. "That's called 'the Rock,' " Redmond told me, pointing at the library. Then as we crossed the street, "Those are the Van Wickle Gates." Massive wrought-iron gates guarding the campus; we walked through, across the tree-shaded green toward a row of graceful buildings. Redmond grabbed my arm, pointed off to the right. I spotted a bell tower rising from the north-west corner of the green.

"That's Carrie Tower," he said.

I thought he was kidding me, and wasn't sure how to take it. But he was looking so serious.

"Really?"

He nodded, and we pulled away from the New-port Academy pack to go closer. Made of red brick, decorated with stonework, classically adorned with carved fruit, urns, and shields, the tower looked about ninety feet tall. At the top was a clock.

"It was built for Carrie Brown," Redmond said. "She was the granddaughter of Nicholas Brown, namesake of the university."

"What happened to her?" I asked.

"She died," he said, pointing. And then I saw the words inscribed on the base: **Love Is Strong as Death.**

I touched them with my fingertips. I thought of my father, and I felt Carrie, my sister, with me. Closing my eyes, I felt the warm mud of the lake bank, the sun on my face, the happiness of being beside her. We were about to get in that canoe. This clock tower would turn back time, and my father would be alive, and Carrie would be with us now.

She was with me now. I felt it, so surely, when I opened my eyes I was sure I'd see her standing right there. Students walked past, on their way to classes.

Redmond gazed at me with huge brown eyes. My mother called my name. I left my hand on the letters as long as I could. I wanted Carrie to see the words, know that they were true. Love is strong as death. If Carrie knew that, if she really felt it, wouldn't she come home? Wouldn't she know that we grieved our father's drowning, but that our love for her, for them both, was giving us life, keeping us going?

"I need you, Carrie," I whispered.

My mother walked over, put her arm around me. I pointed at the words written in stone. I felt her gaze at them, take them in. Then she led me toward Mr. Campbell and the rest of the group. Redmond walked alongside. We hurried through the campus, down the hill. I heard Mr. Campbell say the driver should have dropped us off closer, but I was glad he hadn't. I'd gotten to see Carrie Tower.

We found Kassar House, where the Department of Mathematics was located, at the corner of Thayer and George streets. By this time, all I could think about was Carrie. I heard Mr. Campbell giving me a pep talk, felt my mother's arm around my shoulders, saw Travis give me a thumbs-up, but my heart and mind were occupied by my sister. I glanced at Redmond, saw him looking around. Good. He'd memorized her face and was on the plan.

I went inside. The event was held in the Foxboro Auditorium in the Gould Laboratory, and the seats were filled with teachers and supporters, students from other schools. The competition organizer escorted us to our places and introduced us to the crowd. He gave the rules. Ten questions, one hour.

Here's what I did: I raced through and got everything right. Trigonometry and simple linear algebra is nothing compared with ideas of love being stronger than death. I'd already proved that, so why mess around with the easy stuff? I won that competition just so I could get the hell out of that auditorium, back on the streets of Providence, to feel close to Carrie again. I wanted to run to the tower. While everyone in my group had lunch at the place Mr. Campbell had found, I wanted to return with Redmond to the tower. I wanted Carrie to be hiding behind it, about to step out into my arms.

Of course, I knew what was happening.

The magic Lucy and I had started, calling for our fathers, was working overtime. Now, with the help of the right angle created by the height of Carrie Tower, and the calculus of longing, and the geometry of love, I had conjured my sister. She might not really be there, I mean in a physical manifestation, but she was there in spirit.

Just like Mary and Beatrice, just like my father and Lucy's, the essence of my sister was always with me. Love, baby—stronger than death or running away. With me, in my heart, of me always. My sister. She helped me win the competition.

I did it for her.

■

On Carrie's days off, she sometimes took Gracie walking around the campus of Brown University. Her parents had both been teachers, and she'd grown up near Ohio State, and she found comfort in academic surroundings. On one of her walks she'd discovered Carrie Tower. The inscription had hit her so powerfully, it sometimes felt engraved on her heart. She'd walk around the tower and think of her dad. Think of how she'd let him down, how she wished she could have saved him.

This early December day she bundled up Gracie, pushed her in the stroller Dell had given her up Waterman Street, straight toward the campus. The air was cold, wind blowing off the water, and people had started to decorate the colonial houses for Christmas. Evergreen wreaths and garlands filled the air with pine scent.

Carrie's heart felt heavy. She thought of her family, how they had always celebrated the holidays. Their decorations hadn't been fancy or extravagant, just special little touches to fill the house with cheer and light. Her mother had a box of ornaments, passed down from her grandmother, that her aunt had sent long ago. Early each December, her mother would pull them out, let the girls and Travis decorate the house. Carrie remembered placing two china carol singers on the mantel, seeing her mother start to cry. They reminded her of Aunt Katharine, of when they were young.

Carrie pushed Gracie along, wondering whether her mother had found Aunt Katharine again. They were both here in Rhode Island, so wouldn't they have done that? But proximity wasn't the same as closeness. Families got destroyed by simple hurts, broken hearts, things too terrible to understand or talk about. It was times like this that Carrie took a cynical view of the words **Love Is Strong as Death.** No. Sometimes love wasn't strong enough at all.

Gracie was asleep. This often happened on their long walks. Lulled by the movement, she drifted off. Carrie pushed the stroller gently, trying not to hit any bumps. She got to the tower, stood in its lee, let it block the wind. She looked up toward the clock. Time was passing so fast. She wanted her family.

Moving along, she headed toward Thayer Street. The college kids were getting ready for exams, finishing their papers before heading home for the holidays. She felt excitement in the air, a sense of hurry and purpose. Glancing down at her sleeping baby, she felt as far from a college kid as she could get.

But she did feel pressure in her chest, almost as if she had a big test hanging over her head. She felt as if she needed to cram, study all night, finish her work so she could get home. It reminded her of high school, when her biggest worry had been to pass exams and write good term papers, make her parents proud. Her parents would never be proud of her again. Her father was dead, and what would her mother think of the part Carrie had played in that?

The shops were decorated with red and green ornaments, strands of white lights. Speakers piped Christmas carols. Gracie suddenly woke up, squawked happily. Carrie felt so glad for her daughter's company. She crouched by the stroller, reaching into the pouch for a bottle.

Carrie's stomach rumbled. She felt so hungry, wished she had money to buy a sandwich. People jostled past, and she overheard them talking about a math competition, celebrating the winner. She glanced up, just in time to see them enter Andrea's, the restaurant on the corner. The sight was such a shock, she dropped Gracie's bottle in the street as she stood by the plate glass window and stared in.

Her mother, Beck, and Travis, along with a group of other people, were filling booths inside. There was Aunt Katharine, right there with them. Gracie fussed, wanting her bottle. Maybe the sound of her crying carried, because at that moment, Carrie's mother looked up, met her eyes.

Carrie stepped out of sight. She felt too raw, too unsure of what to say, what to do. Clusters of students swept along, hurrying to get warm somewhere—the library, their dorm room, a café. Carrie felt herself folded into them, moving with the tide of young people, crying harder than her infant daughter as she felt the distance growing between herself and her mother.

■

Maura tore out of the restaurant, into the midst of college students, yelling Carrie's name. Her family and the entire Newport Academy contingent stared through the window, watching her lose it in the middle of Thayer Street. Beck and Travis flew to her side, arms on her elbows, trying to support her. Katharine was right behind them.

"Did you see?" Maura cried to her kids. "Your sister? She was right here!"

"Mom, calm down," Travis said. "All these Brown students—you must have thought one of them . . ."

"I couldn't confuse Carrie with anyone," Maura said, running into the crowd as Katharine took the other side of the street. Maura glanced around, saw college students everywhere. Some were laden with packages—they'd gone Christmas shopping, or been to the post office and received boxes from home. Maura's heart felt crushed; when she'd dreamed of Carrie heading off to college, she'd always imagined making her care packages, filling them with brownies, power bars, protein shakes, bright socks, warm mittens, lip gloss—just little things to let her know she wasn't alone.

The thought of that, of Carrie being alone—by choice, staying away, not giving Maura the chance to love her, hold her—made Maura's knees go out. She sank down right onto the curb and cried.

"Mom," Beck said, putting her arm around her.

"Honey, I want your sister to come home," Maura wept.

"I do too," Beck said.

Maura always tried to hold the worst in. She didn't like to let the kids see her this upset. It was Beck's big day, and Maura was ruining it. But Beck stroked her head, pressed her face into Maura's shoulder.

"I thought I felt her with me," Beck said.

"You did? When?" Maura asked.

"Before the competition," Beck said. "She helped me win."

"Carrie did?" Maura asked, grabbing Beck. "You saw her?"

"I felt her," Beck said. "She was with me."

Katharine returned, shaking her head. Together they all went back inside the restaurant. The party had been so festive, but now it had a somber tone.

Stephen made a toast to Beck, congratulated her,

said that the next stop would be the Boston nationals. Everyone cheered, and Maura saw Travis clink his glass with his little sister. Maura tried to eat, but all she could do was stare out the big windows, watch all the kids pass by on Thayer Street.

She had seen her oldest daughter, made eye contact with Carrie. She heard Beck talking to Redmond about Mary and Beatrice, about the ghosts of departed quantities helping her to win, but Maura knew it had been real. Katharine watched Maura carefully, and Maura knew her sister understood exactly how she felt right now, as if the world was really coming to an end.

That night, back at the academy, she waited for Beck and Travis to go to sleep. Then she bundled up and went outside. The December air was pure and cold; the wind blew her hair and scarf straight back as she walked down the path.

Walking out toward the seawall, she hesitated, eyes drawn up toward the school's top floor. There were the lights again, the first time she'd seen them in weeks. It was freezing cold, her breath a cloud in the crystal-clear air. The stars burned above as only winter stars can do.

Maura felt herself pulled toward Blackstone Hall. Just as she'd done that night a month ago, she climbed the graceful, curving marble staircase. When she got to the fourth floor, the heavy lock was unlatched. She pushed the door open and stepped through.

The pool glowed blue-green, illuminated by lamps below the surface. Steam rose from the water, fogging the tall seaward-facing windows. The rest of the room was dark.

J.D. was swimming, strong hard strokes, the length of the pool and back. Maura stood still, watching. His body looked as leanly muscled as she remembered. His back rippled with every stroke. She listened to the force of each breath, rhythmic and steady.

After a while, she saw him slowing down. He'd been swimming the crawl, and now he switched to the breaststroke, his head above water; he stopped, looking at her.

"I saw Carrie," Maura said, her voice echoing in the marble room.

"Where?" he asked, swimming to the pool's side.

"In Providence," she said.

He nodded. He didn't ask if she was sure, didn't say maybe she was mistaken, maybe it was another girl her age. He started toward the lift.

"We'll call Angus," he said. "He'll drive us up there right now. We won't leave Providence until we find her. We'll bring her home, Maura."

Maura's eyes filled, and she shook her head.

"No," she said.

"What are you talking about?"

"She doesn't want to come home," she said.

"She's lost, Maura," he said. "She's all by herself, and . . ."

Maura shook her head harder. "You don't get it, J.D.," she said. "Our eyes met—she looked right at me, and saw me looking at her. And she ran away!"

She sobbed, feeling more pain than she'd ever felt in her life, and crouched down by the pool, curled into herself. Losing Andy, even having Carrie run away, was nothing compared to having Carrie appear, look straight into Maura's eyes, and then turn away. Time had passed, but nothing had healed. She bowed her head, crying.

J.D. was in the pool beside her. He stayed right there, saying nothing. After a moment, she felt him reach for her hand. He held it while she cried. His hand felt so warm.

"Maura," he said, after a few minutes.

They'd always been about water, Maura and J.D. Climbing the Jamestown Bridge, making love on the catwalk, the tide and currents of Narragansett Bay rushing below. She'd lain awake so many nights, seeing the island lights reflected in that black water, hearing the sound of the waves striking the shore down below the bridge, feeling his arms around her as she tried to push the thoughts away and fall asleep.

"Come here," he said now.

She looked at him, her eyes bleary with tears. He slid his fingers around her wrist. Holding on tight, he looked into her eyes. She needed his comfort, needed her daughter's father. Her breath was ragged as she undressed, aware of his eyes on her body.

Things had changed over the years. She'd had three children. Sorrow had weighed her down. Her posture wasn't that of the wild, exuberant young college graduate who'd spent that summer with him. But when she slid into the water, she still fit perfectly into his arms.

He held her close, their bodies pressing against each other. He kissed her, and she was so hungry for his mouth. The heat made her see stars, filled her with more passion than she'd felt that summer. They had had a baby, lived separate lives. Her body quivered, pushing against his, wanting every inch of her to be touching every inch of him.

His mouth covered hers; his touch was both gentle and rough. She ran her hands up and down his sides. His belly was flat, concave. Scars on his back and legs felt like thin braids, hard and upraised. She kissed his lips, then his neck, making her way down his body.

The glimmering green light surrounded them as she tugged on his bathing trunks. He helped them off, holding her afloat and pulling her onto him. His legs moved rhythmically; she noticed that, he was getting better. The warm water buoyed them as he entered her, she felt slippery and hot, and they held each other tight, balancing at the edge of the pool.

Maura's insides melted all around him. Their faces were touching, eyes, mouths, everything. They didn't want any space between them. They might as well have been back on the bridge, nothing but air below them, swaying with danger. But one arm slung around J.D.'s neck, feeling him support her with his arm and legs, with all that warm water embracing them, Maura knew she was safe.

The pool sloshed, the water making small waves that broke the surface, spilling out over the marble apron. Maura listened, remembering the waves at the foot of the bridge, how afraid she'd been to look down. If only she'd done then what she was doing now—gazing into J.D.'s clear blue eyes, feeling his love, knowing he'd hold her forever. Together they shuddered and released, all the years of being apart, all the fear and sadness.

Maura buried her face in his neck, wanting to hold on to this feeling. She was together with her daughter's father. He'd loved her. He'd built a light-house for her, for Carrie.

Thoughts poured in. Andy. Travis and Beck. Carrie on the lake. Carrie that afternoon in Providence. An echo sounded—voices coming up the pipes, perhaps from the library or students' rooms downstairs. The noise brought Maura out of something like a trance. J.D. held her loosely; he was watching.

"Do you hear those voices?" she asked.

"I only hear yours," he said.

"I hear them. Kids talking somewhere . . ."

"This room echoes," he said.

"The ghosts," she said. "Do you believe in them?"

"I believe in you," he said.

"Your great-grandfather," she said. "And his enemy. And the sisters—Mary and Beatrice."

"There's the past," he said. "And the present. I'm done with the past."

"Is that possible?" she whispered. "It's so much a part of who we are. . . ."

"Let's be right here," he said, holding her. "Right now. No more ghosts."

"You were swimming," she said, easing back from him, gently pushing his arms away. "Your legs . . ."

"I use my arms," he said. "The doctors in Providence did their best. But it didn't work."

"They said it would take time, didn't they?" she said. Blinking, she brushed water from her eyes.

He'd let her back up, put a foot of water between them. But at that, he reached out, hooked her with his hand, pulled her hard against him again. His breath was short, more intense than it had been when he stopped swimming.

"They said it, but I know what I know." He held her, staring into her eyes.

"I want you to get better," she said. "I can't stand what I did to you."

"You didn't do anything to me. I fell all on my own."

Maura knew he was trying to reassure her, and part of her wanted to be let off the hook. She'd been young, she'd been trying to protect Andy. Those are the things she'd told herself over the years. Now she shook her head, holding on tight. "You wouldn't have if I had done the right thing."

"What would that have been?"

And Maura didn't know.

" 'Right' is one of those pointless words," he said, pushing the wet hair out of her eyes, kissing her.

"I don't know about that," she said.

"We have a history, Maura. But we also have the present. We could have each other, the way I've wanted it all along. . . ."

"J.D.," she whispered.

"Don't give up hope," he said.

"She doesn't want to be found," Maura said.

"I don't believe that," he said. "And neither do you."

"I have to get home," she said, kissing J.D.'s lips. "My other kids might wake up and wonder where I am."

She pulled away, swam across the pool to the ladder. She dried herself off, got dressed, listening the whole time for him to tell her to stop.

But he didn't, so she just kept going, and didn't look back.

◼

He stayed by the edge of the pool, watching her go, a trail of water left behind on the marble floor. The room echoed, and he heard her footsteps. He heard his own breath. He felt her on his skin, in his bones. He'd held Maura in his arms; he could have called her back, and he knew she'd have come. They'd belonged to each other all this time. He'd stayed alive for this.

He would do anything for her, he would do the thing she needed and wanted more than anything in the world. People needed air, water, food. Maura needed love, she needed her children. Everyone meant well, and was trying so hard—Katharine, even Stephen and Ted. Angus.

But J.D. was Carrie's father. She had traveled all the way to Rhode Island from the lake, just to stand by his bedside and make sure he survived. She'd taken that risk for him, and he was going to do whatever it took to help his daughter find her way home. He'd do it for Maura.

Dell Harwood was the key. He was sure of that, and wheelchair or not, he was going to do what it took. Treading water, he listened for the elevator. It creaked upward, and the doors opened. He heard them close behind Maura. He didn't want to leave the water, where he'd been with her, but he hauled himself out of the pool. He had to move now, and fast. Maura was hanging on, but he saw what this was doing to her.

And J.D. couldn't live with that. Not one minute more than necessary.

Sisters

PART THREE

21 SEEING MY MOTHER FALL apart after the competition threw me for the biggest loop ever. My mother is so strong. Even at my father's funeral, she held me and Travis together, helped us know we could go on. I've never seen her the way she was on Thayer Street, wild and crying, so pale I thought she might dissolve. It scared me.

For comfort I sat in the reading room by the fire. Outside a storm was building, snow and wind—a blizzard. I had homework to do, plenty of it. Plus, having made it through the regional maths, I now had nationals coming up before Christmas break. Redmond was excited. He'd shown me Providence, and now we were going to Boston. I felt as if he was on a tour-guide roll—but how could he best Carrie Tower? That is the best landmark I've ever seen.

In spite of all that schoolwork, I couldn't concentrate. Maybe it was seeing my mother so devastated, perhaps it was the fact I'd been in Providence and, although I did feel close to Carrie, I didn't honestly see her. Not the way I'd hoped or even expected. I swear, I thought she'd be standing right there; but she wasn't.

My hand goes to the shelf, pulls down a book. I hold it, feeling the history flow into my skin. Sisters who lost each other pull me like a magnet. I've had it in my family for so long: my mother and Aunt Katharine, now me and Carrie. I guess that's why I feel such a connection with Mary and Beatrice, why the only thing I can imagine reading right now was written by Mary.

Mary's journal is written with blue ink, in beautiful penmanship, with flourishes. The book is bound in faded and tattered red leather; the word **Diary** was once embossed in gold, but the letters have faded. Mary's handwriting—and later, Beatrice's—outlasted the gold leaf.

Mary started this diary, and Beatrice finished it. That's how it is with sisters. They'd probably have fought like mad, during life, if one caught the other even touching it. But after Mary's death, Beatrice must have come upon her book—just as I have. She must have read Mary's words—just as I have. And then added some of her own thoughts . . .

It's cold outside. The wind is circling down the chimney, making sparks fly. The fire feels cozy, but outside the storm is picking up. I don't like storms; they remind me of the people taken from me.

My heart is beating fast. I try to calm down, tell

myself I'm with the Langley sisters. This is my favorite place in the school. Blackstone Hall has
thick walls to keep the storm out, and Redmond is
beside me. And reading this diary, now I know why
it's on the shelf right beside the book about Rose
Hawthorne. I've solved one mystery. . . .

Turns out Rose Hawthorne ran a cancer hospital
in New York, back in the days when people
thought the disease was contagious. She was a nun,
and Beatrice went to work with her, to honor her
and Mary's mother, who died of cancer. Beatrice
sounds so kind, caring, and good.

When I read her entries in Mary's diary, written
after the accident, I love her so much I can't stand
it. As an older sister, she reminds me of Carrie.
But as someone who's lost a sister, she reminds me
of me.

Here's Beatrice right after Mary died:

December 15
Mary.

January 10
I only want to write her name: Mary.
I have returned to Newport, because this
is where I last saw her. Her birthday, the
last days we would spend together. It is
impossible to believe. Uncle Percival drove
her away from this place, and his carriage

went off the cliff. Father cannot speak of it.
Mr. Blackstone had to tell me. Even he
wished not to divulge the details, but I
pressed him. If Mary had to suffer them, I
had to hear.

There was snow and ice on the ground.
A storm had blown off the Atlantic, bringing thick, wet snow, then air from Canada
had dropped the temperatures and frozen
everything. But the night of the accident,
the air had warmed. The worst ice had
melted, and fog rolled in.

People talk about Uncle Perce's judgment.
I expect Father feels the same way. Why did
he drive along the cliff edge during such
dangerous conditions? Sitting here, holding
my sister's diary, writing these thoughts,
I know that blame will do nothing but
destroy us. Uncle Perce wished to bring
Mary home for dinner with his family; she
wanted to be with them, and bring all of
us together. I know her. Christmas was
coming, and that was her Christmas wish.

My beautiful sister . . .

I walk along the cliff hoping to see her,
hear her. I pray to hear her voice in the
wind. If I listen hard enough . . . Mary,
speak to me.

Sitting here in the reading room, holding this diary, I feel what Lucy and I have felt all along: it's the small things that count. Things you might barely notice. Rose Hawthorne; was Hawthorne House named for her? Maybe those young girls wouldn't talk to Aunt Katharine or my mother. But I bet they'd talk to me. I think I have to go there. I turn to Mary's diary again, to the words of Beatrice—another sister listening, hoping.

Knowing she would see her sister again—because she had to.

And so would I.

■

Stephen sat in his small office, fresh from the triumph of Providence, looking over the schedule for Boston's math competition later that month. He had arranged for another large van, made room reservations at the Back Bay Inn, and found a place to take everyone for dinner. Redmond and Lucy were going along to support Beck. Maura too. Stephen thought of how traumatized she'd been in Providence, thinking she'd spotted Carrie.

Stephen stared at the inn's website. He'd never been there, but it looked warm and inviting: a townhouse on Newbury Street, fireplaces in the rooms. When he and Patricia had gone to Boston, she'd always wanted to stay at the Ritz. She'd liked the grand old elegant brick hotel overlooking the Public Garden; they'd have drinks at the dark Ritz bar, then dinner in the sweeping dining room with chandeliers and blue glasses. He'd wanted the opposite of that for this trip. As he thought about it, he realized he wanted the opposite of it for Maura.

"Hey," came the low voice.

Looking up, Stephen saw J.D. in his wheelchair just outside the office door.

"Hey!" Stephen said. "Are you here for the board meeting?"

"I'm skipping it," J.D. said.

"Really?" As great-grandson of James Desmond Blackstone, J.D. was a trustee of the Blackstone Foundation, which administered many charitable works. The academy was a beneficiary, and J.D. sat on the school's board.

"Yeah. This is it," J.D. said. "Angus is taking me to Providence."

Stephen stared at him. He pictured Maura falling apart the other day, and shook his head. "Can you ease up?" he asked.

"What do you mean?"

"You're getting Maura's hopes up for nothing. Jesus, J.D. Do you have any idea what she's going through? All of them, actually. Beck, Travis. Beck has another huge competition coming up."

"I know," J.D. said.

"Maura told you?"

"Yes."

"Well, when her mother's all stirred up, that can't be good for Beck. She needs this, J.D. Let Maura get through the holidays, will you? Let them all settle in here to Newport without you upsetting everyone. Maura thought she saw Carrie in the crowd—she practically lost it."

"Wouldn't you?" J.D. asked. "If your daughter ran away from you?"

"Look," Stephen said. "Maybe you mean well, but you're not helping."

"I'm Carrie's father," J.D. said, his voice rising. "And I'm going to find her!"

Stephen heard shuffling in the hall. He went to the door, saw Beck turning around, heading back the way she'd come. His heart nearly stopped, and he reached for her, touching her shoulder.

"Beck," he said.

She followed him into his office, as if pulled by a magnet. She stared at J.D., all the color drained from her face. Had she heard?

"Sorry to disturb you, Mr. Campbell. I'll come back later," she said.

"No, Beck," he said. "It's okay. We were just talking about you. This is J. D. Blackstone. J.D., meet Beck Shaw."

"Hi, Beck," J.D. said, nearly as pale as she was.

"I saw you," Beck said, staring at the wheelchair.

"Outside Blackstone Hall, the day we went to Providence for the competition."

"I saw you too. Congratulations . . ."

"Are you the man who swims in Mary's pool?"

"That's me," J.D. said.

"My mom . . ." Beck began, a small frown on her face. "She always looks up there. And I think she swam there the other day. She came home with wet hair. . . . Was she swimming with you?"

J.D. nodded. The look in his eyes was pure love; he looked uplifted, transformed from the lonely, ruined person who'd barely left Ted's guesthouse a few months ago. Stephen was one of his best friends, and he'd wanted him to get better, but right now he felt like grabbing Beck and leaving the room.

"Are you getting ready for Boston?" Stephen asked, to change the subject.

"Huh?" Beck asked, still frowning, distracted.

"The national competition," Stephen said, tilting his computer screen toward her. "This is where we're all staying." She barely glanced at the image of the brick townhouse.

"You're going to win," J.D. said.

"Thanks," she said, staring at him. Stephen saw her eyes boring in, felt her agitation start to shimmer. Had she heard what J.D. had said, or was this something else?

Stephen put his hand on her shoulder.

"I'm very proud of Beck. She has a talent for the abstract," he said. "She sees beyond, and always chooses the most direct route. To arrive at something we take for granted, volumes of work have to be done first. Like a poem: a few lines of terse verse but the poet has already filtered out the extraneous. Beck knows that math helps us describe nature in a precise, universal language. Right, Beck?"

She must have felt him pulling her back into the room, almost as if she were a wildly veering kite and he held the string, down from whatever emotions were rattling her into the stratosphere.

"Forces of gravity, speed of light, you mean?" she asked.

"Yes," Stephen said. "Architectural angles . . ."

She nodded, her breathing shallow and skin even paler than before.

"Exactly," J.D. said. "I used formulas to build the lighthouse." The words came out of his mouth, and Stephen wanted to punch him.

"I knew a lighthouse," Beck said, sounding like a sleepwalker. "On the lake where my sister disappeared. It hadn't been there until the summer before. But I stood on the banks with my mother and brother, and while the searchers looked for Carrie and my father, I stared at that tower. I thought of angles. Geometry, lines from the top of the tower down to the lake. I imagined them as lifelines, things for my sister and father to grab onto."

"That's what I wanted," J.D. said, his voice gravelly and his eyes suddenly brimming with tears.

"I heard what you said," Beck said. "When I was out in the hall."

J.D. nodded. "I built that lighthouse for your sister. I wanted to save them."

"Enough," Stephen said, standing between his old friend and Beck. "Stop it."

"Stop the truth?" Beck asked. "That's a mathematical impossibility."

Stephen tightened his arm around Beck's shoulder, but she tore away. He heard her pounding down the corridor as he looked after her.

He turned to J.D., fury in his eyes.

"Why did you do that?" he asked.

"Christ, I'm so sorry," J.D. said, putting his head in his hands.

"You know, I've had it," Stephen said, his voice rising. "Your goddamn stupid obsession. You call it love, but that's not what you felt for Maura. She was married, she had a family. . . ."

"She loved me," J.D. said.

"You wanted to believe that. You tracked her down, you wasted years of your own life thinking about what you couldn't have. You built that stupid goddamn lighthouse."

"It was for Carrie, it was all I could do."

"And what about Beck? Did you think about her? Or was it 'all you could do' to spill what

Maura's kept hidden all this time? Wasn't it up to Maura to tell her?"

"Stephen, Jesus! She overheard me. . . . I never meant for that."

"I don't care what you 'meant.' She's a kid, J.D. She's been through hell. How do you think she's going to take knowing you're Carrie's father?"

Stephen glared at his old friend, saw him a million miles away. Was he thinking of Carrie? Or Maura? Was he imagining the impact of what Beck had just overheard?

"Beck's a sensitive, fragile girl whose family has been devastated. Think of what Lucy and Pell were like after Taylor died, and you have a tiny fraction of what Beck's going through."

"I didn't mean to tell her," J.D. said.

"It doesn't matter what you meant to do," Stephen said. "It's what you **did** do, J.D. How's Maura going to feel?"

"I know, I **know**!"

Stephen tried to calm himself down; he and J.D. had gone to this school together, seen each other through a million scrapes and adventures.

Beck was Maura's daughter, and J.D. had just hurt her. That's all Stephen could think about. Leaving J.D. there in his chair, he left his office and strode down the hall to look for Beck and find Maura.

■

It was a shock and it wasn't a shock.

I didn't know, but I did know.

Mr. Campbell talked about the poetry of proofs, slicing away the extra material, cutting through what you don't need anymore. Denial is like padding, protecting you from the worst tumbles. It's like you've been pushed out of a plane, and you need all those pillows, cushions, aluminum panels, Kevlar shields to keep you from breaking apart when you hit the ground at a million miles an hour.

So that guy, J.D., yanked off all my protective gear with those words: **I'm Carrie's father.**

Okay, I get it. Now everything I've been wondering about, working around, makes sense. All the fights, the way my parents stopped getting along after Carrie's accident. Blood types had obviously come into play. You don't need a math whiz to realize that my dad's blood and Carrie's blood didn't match, that he added things up and $1 + 1$ didn't $= 2$.

And my mother staring up at the fourth floor, and her wet hair. And going back in time, Aunt Katharine not speaking to her. Because she knew. Betrayals and hurt and lying.

And the lighthouse. Built for my sister by her father . . . That little island had been covered with trees, rocks, scrub, and brush, home to deer and beavers. That next year, there were still trees, but on the very shore stood that beautiful, perfect tower. It was something out of a fairy tale. I just hadn't realized how much of a fairy tale there really was, full of bewitchment.

I was under a spell.

Leaving Mr. Campbell's office, I thought I'd go find Travis. I didn't want to see my mother. Not just then—ever again. Then I realized I couldn't bear to see my brother either. I'd have to tell him the truth. This was a secret no family should keep from each other. But how could I tell him? Look him in the eyes, say the words? So I went home and wrote him a note. I put the truth right down in black and white, left it under his pillow.

I felt pretty sick. Almost as if I was coming down with a fever. Clammy, crazy. I wanted my mother, but not the way she really was—the way I **thought** she'd been. My ideas were jumbled, and that's not like me. Usually I am able to hack through the poison ivy of emotion and get to the point. But right at that moment, I was all feelings, no logic. I forced myself to start thinking, and what came to mind were Redmond and Lucy. My only true friends. If only I could hold it together until Boston. Boston was the goal I had set for myself. To really turn the corner and start fresh. Put all the bad stuff out of my head for good. I **had** to go.

I imagined it like this: I'd go to the math competition, ace it, win a scholarship to the college of my choice, let Redmond show me around Boston.

But then I would leave Newport Academy, get away from all this. Get away **now.** Carrie had had the right idea. We would be the runaway family. Sisters who'd had enough. I got what she'd done, why she'd left. I was with her now, with her in spirit. That's all I could think about.

I'd been so good lately. I'd given back all my stolen objects, or almost all. The other day I'd gone down to Bannister's Wharf, put that small ceramic pineapple back in the glass jar I'd taken it from. Had my newly discovered goodness, my desire to go straight, amounted to nothing? Was I too late, and was this punishment for being so wicked and stealing? I didn't believe in hell and damnation, but I did believe in a sort of karma: it's pure math, if you think about it. When you do bad, you bring badness your way. It's like the law of percentages.

I remembered the ride my mother had taken us on, me and Travis, one of our first days here at the academy. Through the Point section of Newport. She'd stopped in front of Hunter House, shown us the carved pineapple above the door, told us it was a symbol of welcome.

I'd loved that ride, thought my mother, in her poetic and geometric way, had been wanting me to connect the dots, realize that she was introducing us to our new life. That ride had been a sort of cosmic pineapple, a sign of greeting and fresh beginnings to me and Travis: welcome to our new world.

But when I thought back now, I remembered that she'd shown us where old James Desmond Blackstone had come from.

The founder of our school, the man with the same name as this guy J.D. Had my mother been in love with J.D. all these years, all the time she spent with my dad? Had she just been waiting for the moment to arrive when she could be with him again? She reminded me of girls with crushes, who secretly walk past the houses of the boys they like, who arrange fake reasons to stand near their lockers at school. My mother, my wonderful mother, was that what she'd done?

The thoughts felt like nettles stinging my skin. No more padding, remember? As I left my house and went out onto the campus, I felt lucky about one thing.

I hadn't yet returned Angus's keys. I had been waiting for the moment to arrive, when he was away from his desk and the security office, when I could just slip in unseen and put them somewhere he'd think he hadn't looked yet. I had them with me at all times—in my backpack, wrapped in a woolen scarf to keep them from clinking and rattling.

So I pulled them out now. I knew just where I was going: to Blackstone Hall, to the fourth floor. Mary's rooms. I knew she had a bedroom, and that she'd studied up there. That's where I needed to be, to think about all this, figure out my next move. Maybe I could stay there in secret for a while so I wouldn't have to see my mother.

I couldn't look her in the eye. And that reality was so terrible—not wanting to see her, the first time in my life I'd ever felt any such thing, almost as if I'd lost her already, lost my mother forever. It was like needles in my heart.

I started to run. Keys in my hand, I flew across campus. I guess I was crying. The more I ran, the thicker my tears got. The day was cold, and snow was in the air.

Mary. She had crashed off this horrible cliff, into the sea below. What a terrible way to die, and Beatrice had suffered along with her. The Langley sisters had had lies and pain in their family, and they had loved each other through all of it. They would understand.

The anniversary of Mary's death was coming up. The whole school commemorated the occasion. Deep down, I know Lucy and I had hoped to break through with our proofs of infinity by then. Mary had guided us; all those days we'd heard her, thought of her, felt her presence. In a way I felt we were doing our math for her too.

Mathematicians are logical, but I found myself praying to that lost sister as I ran toward the building, not knowing where else to go. She had helped me and Lucy before, given us strength and let us know we weren't alone. But it really is a sign of how crazy I was that I talked to her out loud just then.

"Help me, Mary," I cried. "Help me, help me . . ."

And when I took one single key off Angus's key ring and slipped it into my pocket, I felt Mary's hand guiding me.

Everything happened so fast after that. The class bell rang, and kids started streaming out of the building, a little air between periods. My hands shook, holding the key ring. As I climbed the wide steps, I saw Redmond coming out, a big huge smile on his freckled face as he saw me. Then he noticed my tears and stopped short.

"Beck, what's wrong?"

"Everything," I wept. "The whole world is ending."

"Come on," he said, grabbing my hand, the one without the keys. "We'll go up to the reading room. We can talk there. . . ."

I was just about to relent. He knew the reading room was my favorite place. There'd probably be a fire blazing. My favorite little book would be there, the one about the Hawthorne girl, right beside Mary's diary. We could sit on the loveseat, and maybe I could tell him a little of what was wrong.

"Okay," I said. But the keys were the fruits of my last bad act. I had to return them right away. All but the one to Mary's pool.

LUANNE RICE

We entered Blackstone Hall, stood in the huge marble entry hall. It was dark outside, the weather bringing clouds across the sea from the east, so the enormous crystal chandelier glowed overhead. Just then a group of fancily dressed people came down the curved staircase. The men wore dark business suits, the women wore dresses and pearls. One wore a mink: Mrs. Nicholson. Angus walked behind them, laden down with a stack of reports.

"It's the academy board," Redmond said. **Bawd.** "The trustees are here for the annual meeting." **Heah.** His accent made me smile, reminded me that some of life was good; maybe things would turn out okay. He held my arm to ease me back so they could pass. And just then I lost my grip on the keys. They fell to the marble floor with a metallic, musical **clinkety-clink,** and Angus turned around.

"My keys," he said.

"I know," I said, meeting his eyes as the board members stopped to wait for him. He stared at me, perplexed.

"Where did you get them?" he asked.

I don't know why I didn't lie. Well, yeah; I do. I guess when my padding went away, so did my ability to squirm out of a jam. And I was so sick of lies, and what they did to people, what they'd done to my family. The longer I stood there, feeling his disappointed and accusing glare on me, the more I actually wanted to confess.

"I took them," I said.

Angus's face fell. Oh, he looked so stricken, as if I'd hurt him on purpose. I stepped toward him, wanting to take back what I'd done. "I'm so sorry, Angus," I said. "I was going to give them back." At that I crouched down and picked them up, handed them to him.

"Took them?" asked Mrs. Nicholson, stepping out of the crowd. She stood above me, her white hair coiffed and gleaming, her cherry red wool dress setting off the luminous pearls around her throat.

"Yes," I said.

"Do you mean," she asked, looking at me intently, as if she was honestly trying to understand, "that you borrowed them?"

A conundrum. I was quivering, knowing that I could lie and get out of it. Or I could be honest, come clean, continue on with my fresh start in life. I have to admit, the despair over my mother was clouding my mind slightly. "No," I said. "I **took** them."

To my shock, she looked hurt—as if this was a personal affront.

"Is that . . ." she asked, her mouth a straight line. "Is that another way of saying you **stole** them?"

"Grandmother!" Lucy said. I looked up, saw her standing on the landing above. She seemed frozen in place.

"It's okay, Luce," I said. "She's right."

"Goodness, this is a shock," Mrs. Nicholson said. "A girl right here at Newport Academy admitting to such—"

"Edie," Mr. Campbell said, striding up. He seemed out of breath, and I knew he'd been trying to find me after I'd left his office. I couldn't bear to look at him. Even worse, my mother was with him.

"Stephen," Mrs. Nicholson said. "What can be done about such behavior? Do you realize this scholarship student has just admitted stealing?"

"Mrs. Nicholson, try to understand, my daughter has . . ." my mother said, and Mrs. Nicholson gazed at her with sympathy.

"I am so sorry, Mrs. Shaw. This must cause you such heartache."

"Please, Mrs. Nicholson—" my mother said, but this time it was Mr. Campbell who cut her off.

"Edie," he said, "Mrs. Shaw is right—there are extenuating circumstances, which I'll explain to you and the board in private. I know Beck will apologize, and I'm sure an appropriate detention can be imposed. But let me tell you something that will make the board very proud. Beck will be representing Newport Academy at the Mathematical Society's national competition, one of only—"

"She will **not,**" Mrs. Nicholson said sadly.

"Grandmother!" Lucy exclaimed, running down the stairs to stand with me.

"If only it were possible. But you know we cannot sanction stealing at this school. What kind of message would we send to the other students? It is a crime, and Rebecca should feel fortunate that we don't call the police—we shall do our best to protect her in that sense."

Even Angus tried to defend me. "Edie," he said in his New England growl, "no harm's been done. She said she's sorry. I've got the keys back now, we can move on."

"We cannot move on," she said, sounding almost brokenhearted.

And suddenly I knew—someone had stolen from her. I didn't know who it was, or what they had taken. But I'd seen that same hurt in the eyes of my friends back in Columbus, hurt and bewildered that I could take their lip gloss, their gum, their fine-point pens.

"Rebecca will not be going to Boston," Mrs. Nicholson continued.

"Beck **is** going," Lucy said, arms folded tight across her chest.

"That is impossible," Mrs. Nicholson said, her voice cracking. "Because as of this moment, she is expelled."

I heard the words, and this is going to sound very strange, but they set me free. They told me what I had to do, where I had to go.

Where I should have gone all along.

I heard my mother cry out with protest, heard my friends telling me it would be okay, heard the high heels of Mrs. Nicholson and the other women board members clicking away down the marble hall. I felt my mother coming toward me, but I couldn't face her. My heart clenched as she drew closer. I wanted to scream at her.

I kissed Redmond on the cheek, shocking both of us. I hugged Lucy as hard as I could, the way I wished I'd hugged Carrie before I saw her that last time. And then I flew out the door to get the money I still had stashed at home. I didn't even glance at my mother. I hoped I'd miss seeing Travis. Goodbyes were impossible, unless you didn't realize you were saying them.

22 SNOW BEGAN TO FALL, GUSTS blowing in off the sea.

When Beck didn't come home for dinner, Travis really began to worry—not just about her, but about their mother. She was a whole new kind of frantic he'd never seen before—even worse than the way she'd been in Providence, even more upset than at the lake. The day they waited on the shore of Lake Michigan, there'd been some hope. Everyone said his father and Carrie might have swum to safety. So it was tense, but there wasn't dread, at least not in the first few hours.

Now it was as if his mother assumed the worst. She'd lived through the hell of his father dying and Carrie disappearing, and now Beck had run away. Because of the special circumstances—the fact Beck had gotten caught stealing again, after having a history of that, and especially because she'd received psychological counseling for it back in Ohio—the police took this seriously.

They considered Beck a troubled teenager who might try something desperate. Travis stood in the kitchen staring at his mother. She sat at the table like a zombie, clutching the smelly, sweaty hoodie Beck had left on the floor of her room, as if she were a psychic or bloodhound and could pick up a nearly lost scent.

"Mom, what can I do?" he asked.

She just closed her eyes, squeezed them tight, as if she wished he would go away too. He moved closer, stood right beside her.

"Where would she go, honey?"

"Maybe to Aunt Katharine's?" Travis said, although he didn't believe it.

"No, Katharine says she hasn't shown up. She's waiting there, just in case."

Travis stood there, fidgeting, afraid to ask what he wanted to know. "Mom, what upset Beck so much? I know how much the Boston trip meant to her; I didn't see her, but it seems like more than that."

His mother started to speak. He steeled himself, knowing that she had a lot to tell him. He couldn't bear to put her through it.

"Carrie wasn't Dad's daughter, was she?" he asked.

"No," she said. "Who told you?"

"Beck," he said, showing her the note his sister had left under his pillow. It had been scrawled, her neat mathematician handwriting reverting back to her little girl's scribble.

"I'm sorry I didn't tell you," his mother said.

And he saw a horrible shiver go through her, and she put her head down on the table and started to weep. Travis wanted to hug her, or at least say something, but he couldn't. She wanted to shut him out, be alone. He felt terrible, but he couldn't watch her like this, and he knew there was nothing he could do.

She didn't look up, and he couldn't speak, so he grabbed his jacket and ran outside. The cold, damp air filled his lungs as he started to jog across campus. Halfway to Blackstone Hall, he saw the slim figure coming toward him. His heart jumped at the sight of Pell, even as he changed course to avoid her. He felt too churned up and confused.

"Travis!" she called. He was running toward the field, and she called him again. "Travis, please wait!"

He slowed down in spite of himself, turned to walk slowly in her direction. The snow had stopped for the moment, and a layer of thin cloud drifted across the dark sky, shading the stars. He shivered, feeling chilled. The bare branches of the oaks and maples scraped the sky, and he heard the wind rustle through the pines.

"I had to find you," she said. "Is there any word from Beck?"

"No," he said, standing still and stiff.

She touched his arm, worry in her blue eyes. He

tried to look away. He'd been in the library, but had heard about what happened.

"I'm so sorry," she said. "I'm always apologizing to you for her."

"Your grandmother?" he asked.

"Yes," she said.

"Beck brought it on herself," he said. "She'd be the first to say so."

"What my grandmother did was terrible, to humiliate Beck that way."

Travis didn't speak. He didn't want to defend his sister for stealing, but Pell was right: to have that old lady cut her down in front of the whole school . . . It reminded him of Columbus, when people had started whispering about Beck, then openly talking about her, then laughing at her, making fun of her. When she was obviously so troubled, when her stealing was such a shameful symptom of everything else that had gone wrong with their family.

"I know what it's like," Pell said in a low voice.

"What?"

"To love someone so much, to worry about them so much it makes you sick, and to see them sabotaging themselves every step of the way."

"Who?"

"My mother," Pell said.

"What did she do?"

"She left," Pell said.

Travis was silent, waiting.

"She left us," Pell said. "Left my sister and me with our father while she moved to Italy. She lives there now, on Capri."

"Why should you worry about her?" he asked. "It sounds as if she's not worthy of your feelings."

"She's our mother," Pell said quietly. "We love her."

"Even though she basically abandoned you?"

Pell nodded. "She suffers for it. We almost can't bear to see how hurt she is. It comes through in her letters. The birthday cards she sends us."

"But she's the one hurting you!"

"I know," Pell said, taking his hand. "That's what I'm saying. Hurt is such a big circle. You can't tell where it begins or ends, who started it, who caused it. It's just there."

"And Beck . . ."

Pell nodded. "It doesn't matter if she stole—I mean, it does. But what counts right now is that she's suffering. She may have brought some of it on herself, but I know she didn't mean to hurt anyone. Lucy said she was trying to give back the keys."

Travis had been upset over what Pell's grandmother had done, but suddenly the blame melted away, and he slipped his arms around her. He started to kiss her, but she pulled back—very gently, but leaving no doubt.

Travis blinked, the cold wind blowing off the open water, stinging his eyes with salt.

"She'll come back," Pell whispered. "She loves you too much not to."

"How do you know?" he asked.

"That she'll come back, or that she loves you?"

"Both," he said.

"Because how could she not?" Pell asked, staring up into his eyes. "Because you're you."

"But you just pushed me away."

She gazed at him for a long moment, still and grave. He wanted her to smile, at least slightly, to let him know he hadn't made a fool of himself.

"There's been so much," she said. "For you to handle."

"Me?"

She nodded, her blue eyes wide open. "Losing your father, moving here . . . I went through similar things. My mother left when I was six, my father died when I was thirteen. I know that you're reeling."

He felt his shoulders relax. Until she'd said it, he hadn't realized he was.

"Even Ally," she said. "Breaking up with her . . . I know it's hard. It's a big change."

"It is," he said.

"Right now you need to find Beck," she said.

"But . . ."

She shook her head, her eyes clear and sad.

"That's all that matters. Bringing your family back together. I know . . . from my own."

"Is that the way you see life?" he asked. "People who love each other that much have to be together?"

A troubled look crossed her eyes.

"What's the matter?" he asked.

"It's almost as if you read my mind," she said. "I'm thinking about my mother. I miss her. And so does Lucy."

"You wish she was here?" he asked.

"More than anything," Pell said.

He nodded, understanding. "I have something to tell you." When she didn't reply, he swallowed hard. He'd been coming up with this plan for a while, starting at that game when her grandmother had made her points about the scholarships. "I'm starting a job," he said. "As soon as vacation begins. And I'll keep it up spring semester too. I told you I was going to pay back that scholarship."

"Travis, you don't need to," she said.

"But I do," he said fiercely. Pell's strength inspired his own. She was exceptional, unlike any girl he'd ever met. They stood still in the middle of the green, darkness all around, a storm blowing in. His sisters were gone, and his mother despaired, and Pell had pushed him away. But he stood beside her, feeling closer than he'd ever felt to anyone, and watched the snow start to fall again, harder than before.

■

The visit had not exactly been unexpected. From the moment the aunt had shown up looking for Carrie, Dell knew it was just a matter of time before someone would come looking and refuse to be turned back, refuse to hear the word "confidentiality."

So she'd been waiting for the phone to ring, expecting a private investigator, or the aunt, or even Carrie's mother. What she hadn't expected was for the man in the wheelchair to come at the start of what they were saying was going to be the worst snowstorm in the last ten years. Dell had shut down the diner. She'd packed coolers with food for Hawthorne House, and was just about to lock up and head over when she saw him there, snow falling all around, right in the middle of the sidewalk.

"Dell," he said.

"How do you know my name?" she asked.

"I looked into everything about you and this place," he said. "I know the work you've done to help young women. And I want to thank you."

"Thank me?" she asked suspiciously, snow blowing sideways off the bay. "What for?"

"For taking care of my daughter."

She turned back to the door, made sure it was double-locked, started carrying the last cooler toward the parking lot.

"I'll help you with that," he said.

She gave him a pitying look. Was he kidding? She was strong, able-bodied, and he was in a wheelchair. But he reached out, took the heavy cooler from her arms, held it on his lap. But he didn't move. Just stared up at her, snow falling in those hot blue eyes.

"Where is she?" he asked.

"Look," she said. "You have no idea how many people have come here trying to get information out of me. I don't know you. I have no idea what kind of father you are. I trust the girls. They know who loves them, who they can turn to. If it's you, she'll return to you. If not, that's her choice."

"Her mother loves her," he said.

"Same goes for her mother," Dell said. "If your daughter wants to talk to her, that's up to her."

The man balanced the cooler on his knees, started to dig into his pockets. Was he going to pull out money? If so, it wouldn't be the first time someone had tried a bribe. Dell was ready to yank the big Styrofoam box away from him, hurry to her car. She didn't need this, especially since the storm was getting worse and her feet were frozen.

He didn't hand her money. He handed her what looked like a medical form. Folded up, creased almost to the point of tearing, a pink carbon copy. He gestured for her to open it, and even though it was the last thing she wanted to do, her curiosity got the better of her.

"Line thirty," he said.

She found it, read the words, saw that the patient had died.

"That's me," he said.

"You died?" she asked. Was this a joke?

"Yes," he said. "I was in the hospital, got a staph infection. The kind that comes on fast, attacks every organ, kills people within twenty-four hours of getting it. That happened to me."

"But you're here."

"I know," he said. "Because she brought me back to life."

"She?"

"My daughter," he said. "Carrie Shaw. She came all the way to Rhode Island from Lake Michigan, after going through the worst trauma you can think of. . . ." He trailed off, then continued. "She stood by my bedside, and I saw her. I did. I was clinically dead—in a coma, my heart stopped."

"But it started again," Dell said, still holding the paper.

"Yeah," he said. "Because she was there."

"She saved you. That's what you believe."

"That's what I know."

Dell stared at him, holding the big container of

food for the girls. She saw his eyes glittering in the streetlight. She'd left the Christmas lights on in the diner, even though it was closed, and they flashed red and green in the snow.

It was getting close to that time of year where Dell couldn't stand all the families being apart. She knew that people did awful things to each other. She'd heard about almost unimaginable cruelty done to her girls. She knew about betrayals, the most hurtful things you could think of. But she'd look at the young women, at the loneliness in their eyes, at the way they'd cradle their babies, as if wishing someone could hold them with such warmth and love, and she'd wish they all had homes to go to. And she'd seen something else in Carrie: a real and serious love for her family.

"Once a girl leaves Hawthorne House . . ." she said finally, "confidentiality doesn't really mean the same thing."

"No," he said.

"So I'm thinking," she said. "That what you're saying here is that your daughter saved your life. And you want to help her get on with hers."

"Yes," he said. "That's exactly what I'm saying."

Dell wrote down the address of the pink rooming house. She handed him the paper, along with his hospital record, and tried to take the cooler from him. He wouldn't let her. He insisted on carrying it to her car. That might have been absurd, but he had help—his driver came out of the van, the same husky guy she'd seen with him on Thanksgiving, when they'd shown up at the diner.

Carrie had hidden from them. That might have given Dell pause, to realize that the girl didn't want to be found. But Dell remembered the way Carrie had cried after they'd left, as if her heart was breaking all over again.

"Thanks," Dell said, when the men had helped her load the groceries into her car.

"Thank you," Carrie's father said.

"Take good care of her," Dell said.

"We will," he said. "Her mother and I."

Dell nodded, and then she got into the car and started driving slowly through the storm across town to Hawthorne House, back to all the girls missing their families for Christmas.

■

Carrie sat in the rocking chair, holding Gracie. The heat clanked in the radiators, but wasn't making its way into her room. She felt freezing cold, tried to warm Gracie against her body. She held her daughter, smelling her hair, kissing the top of her head. She closed her eyes, thinking of those times by his hospital bed, when she'd thought he might die. But he hadn't.

Things turned around. She'd found her way to

Rhode Island, to be near him, to figure out that piece of her life's puzzle. Logic had escaped her; she'd been steered by her heart. Once she'd learned of his existence, she'd had to find him. It was like a salmon making its way back to the river where it was born.

She came from Rhode Island. Her mother and father had been in love here. Now her family was here again; she shook, thinking of her mother, the way their eyes had locked. Carrie had seen wild love there—the kind that overcame anything, forgave everything. In that moment, she realized that she was wrong to stay away a minute longer. She had to go home.

She held Gracie tighter, closed her eyes. She'd been trying to push these thoughts away for so long. But it was as if she was stuck. The terrible snowstorm outside was nothing compared to the turmoil she felt. She needed her family, but she couldn't move. It was as if the gale outside was spinning her back to another storm. The one on the lake, the day she'd destroyed everything.

Her family vacation. Usually it was her favorite part of the year, but that summer she'd dreaded it with everything she had. Going to the lake, being with her family, doing childhood things—those belonged to a different Carrie. The innocent girl she used to be, the one who had loved school, her

family, nature. Her family thought she was perfect.
She'd known that was silly, but deep down, it had
made her proud, given her a lot to live up to.

That year it all fell apart. The week before vacation, she'd started throwing up. She'd already suspected. She'd missed her period; her breasts felt so
tender. And her stomach kept flipping, lightly and
constantly, in a way she'd never felt before. She
went to the drugstore, bought a pregnancy test.
She knew before she saw the blue line.

She and Justin had been on the verge of breaking
up for months. Ever since the car accident, she had
changed. He said she'd gotten too serious—not
about him, but about life. And he was right: they
could have been killed. She was in the hospital for
weeks with internal injuries, and needed blood
transfusions. Her parents had visited her every day,
and she'd seen something shift between them. Her
mother always looked so worried, and her father always looked so angry. For the longest time, Carrie
had thought it was because of her—because of the
accident. Well, it was because of her, but not in the
way she'd imagined.

The day Carrie decided to tell Justin she was
pregnant, he broke up with her. She had watched
him after the accident—instead of getting more serious about life, he'd gone the other way. He got
wilder, drove faster, stopped working hard in

school. It was as if he wanted to dare death to come get him again.

They were behind the school, out by the athletic fields. Carrie's voice shook, telling him she had news. He'd stepped back, almost as if he could read her mind. He told her to stop, he had something to tell her first. He couldn't do it anymore; he needed to figure things out; he thought they should see other people. What killed her was the sight of his eyes filling with tears as he said he hated himself for hurting her. She was struck silent, couldn't move as she watched him walk away.

So she brought all of that with her to the lake. Arriving at their cabin, her favorite place in the world, she gazed across the water. She saw the lighthouse, the one that had appeared as if by magic, and she let it soothe her. Both she and Beck had loved that lighthouse from the moment they had first seen it the previous summer. All winter they had looked forward to seeing it again, and had vowed they would visit it the next time they were at the lake. Made of brick, so tall and true, with a strong iron balustrade, it gave her strength.

She needed to clear her conscience, tell her parents about the secret she was keeping. She hadn't told her family any of it—not about the pregnancy, not about Justin. She'd thought she might, if she found the right chance, talk to her mother. But it was so hard, and her parents weren't getting along, and she couldn't make herself do it.

She and Beck were about to go out in the canoe, take a paddle around the lake. Carrie had thought it might relax her, help her put things into perspective. But then her father had come along, asked Beck if she'd let him go instead. Carrie hadn't wanted that, but he'd insisted.

They'd climbed into the canoe. Glancing over her shoulder, she'd waved goodbye to Beck. Blue sky, sparkling lake, every stroke propelling the canoe along. Her father sat behind her, breathing heavily as he paddled hard. She looked back at him and the look on his face shocked her. His cheeks were red, and she saw anger in his eyes. Did he know that she'd heard the tail end of the fight with her mother? The part about her accident and the blood.

"What's the matter?" she asked, willing him to break the tension.

"Are you having a good vacation?" he asked.

"Yes," she said. But her heart was breaking.

"I'm glad," he said. "I try to make everything good for our family."

"You do, Dad," she said.

He let out a strange sound, a kind of snort, as if he didn't believe her.

"You do!" she said again.

"Thank you, Carrie," he said. "I'm glad you

think so." A beat. Then: "This might be our last summer here."

"Why?" she asked, nearly dropping her paddle. She turned all the way around to face him, and they stopped right there, way out on the lake.

"Things change," he said. "So do people."

Such a mysterious thing to say, and suddenly she knew—he was talking about **her.** Her chest ached as if he'd punched it. He **knew.** Somehow he had figured out that she was having a baby. First the accident, now this.

"I'm sorry," she said, barely able to speak.

"Don't be," he said.

"I didn't mean to hurt everyone."

"Hurt everyone? Not you, Carrie. You never could. . . ."

His voice was tender, and his words so loving; suddenly she felt everything well up, and she knew she couldn't hold it in any longer. She couldn't have her father go on thinking she was so good.

"Dad, I'm pregnant," she said.

"You're what?" he asked, his voice sharp.

"I'm pregnant."

"You're kidding." And then, when she just stared at him without saying anything, his face flushed dark red.

"God, Carrie," he finally ground out. "How could you be so stupid? What does Justin have to say about it?"

"He doesn't know."

"He's the father, and you haven't told him?"

"No," she said. "I can't. He . . ."

And for some reason, her father lost it.

"Jesus Christ, you are just like your mother. Exactly. She did the same thing you're doing."

"What do you mean?" she asked, afraid of him for the first time in her life.

"She got pregnant, Carrie, with you, and she didn't tell your father."

"But you knew!" she said nervously. Why was he saying this?

"I knew nothing!" he snapped.

"What are you talking about?"

He let out a low sound that was half sigh, half moan. "You might as well know," he said. "You're going to find out anyway. Like mother, like daughter."

She stared at him, terror rising in her throat, thinking she was going crazy. The canoe was drifting, and suddenly the wind picked up. It rocked them, but her father did nothing to steady the boat. She couldn't move. The sky began to darken fast, clouds billowing over the distant shore. She heard thunder.

"The summer your mother spent in Newport," he said. "She got pregnant, just like you. And she didn't tell the father . . . Blackstone. A man named J. D. Blackstone."

"You're my father!" Carrie screamed.

"No, I'm not," he said, shaking his head hard. "I thought I was, all these years. I've loved you since before you were born. I'll love you till I die. But he's your father, Carrie."

"I don't believe you!" she shrieked.

"That's why this is the last vacation," he said, his eyes turning hard again, his voice as loud as the wind. "I told your mother this morning. I'm moving out. Do you know how much I've loved you? You were my baby!"

"I still am!" she cried. "You're just saying this because you're mad at me. I made a mistake, I'm not perfect. . . . Dad, I'm sorry! Please don't say these things, please don't go!" She jumped up, lunged at him. All she wanted was to throw her arms around him, to make him know that she was **his** daughter, that she'd love him forever.

"Carrie!" he shouted as the canoe tipped.

And suddenly everything changed back—she was in his strong arms, his eyes softened, full of love, and he was her dad again. But the sky came down, black all around them, wind and rain and waves crashing into the rocking canoe, and they went over.

They were in the water. The lake was warm, and the rain felt cold. Carrie came up first, grabbed the overturned canoe, and held on, trying to keep her head above the churning waves. She looked around, shouting for her father. He was the only one, her only father, anything else was a mistake.

"Dad!" she screamed over and over.

He never came up. Lightning sliced the sky, and the thunder was so loud she thought it was pounding inside her head. She dove again and again, down through the black water, flailing wildly with her hands, searching for him. The waves whipped up harder, tossing the canoe, and the hardwood frame struck her temple. The impact made her dizzy, and she swallowed water.

And then she turned away. Above her, she saw a light sweeping through the inky clouds, and she half floated, half swam to shore. But not the mainland: the island where the lighthouse stood.

Crawling up the bank, she was in shock. Blood trickled from a cut in her head. Her thoughts were crazy. Her father was fine—he'd simply swum the other way, to her mother, to safety. He had been angry, but now he loved her again. That name, seared into her mind: J. D. Blackstone. He was no one, he meant nothing.

But lying on the wet ground, feeling needles of rain in her face, things began to fall into place: her blue eyes. The other women in her family had hazel eyes, but hers were blue, and not the same blue as her dad's or Travis's. Theirs were dark with a golden ring around the iris. And hers were light, clear, a different blue entirely.

And her blood. Why had neither of her parents been able to give blood for her transfusions after the accident? They had fought over it, and she'd assumed it was because they were so worried. She'd never suspected it was because she had a different father.

Her mother had slept with someone else.

You're just like your mother, he had said.

Her mother got pregnant and didn't tell the father. **Her** father. It was because of **her** her parents had been fighting for months. Even in those first moments, alone on the island at the foot of the lighthouse, she was beginning to know the truth.

They rescued her. A boat, lights flashing, blankets. Took her to shore, to the arms of her mother. But Carrie was numb, and she didn't know her mother anymore. She heard people talking, saying they were searching the lake for her father. But he had drowned, and it was because of her, and he wasn't her father anyway. She was frozen solid, half dead. She wished she had drowned.

An ambulance came. She and her mother got in, Beck and Travis staying behind with the rescue people. Carrie couldn't think. She was a block of ice, wrapped in blankets. She heard someone say she was going into shock. She didn't care.

At the hospital, in the ER. Her mother stroking her head. Whispering that she loved her, that everything would be okay. A technician came in, said he had to take her vital signs. And that's when Carrie's mind began to work again. They were going to do tests on her. They'd figure out she was pregnant, but Carrie didn't care about that. She cared about her mother, how hard and fast her world was about to fall apart.

The picture of her father's face, disappearing under the waves. He was dead, and Carrie had done nothing to stop it. She was selfish, pregnant, "just like her mother." Her chest nearly exploded, wanting to sob into her arms, tell her everything, repeat what her father had said to her. But if she told her mother that, that he'd said those words with such hatred for both of them, Carrie thought her mother would die too.

Someone called her mother, said she had to fill out paperwork. Carrie felt her mother's lips on her forehead, heard her say she would be right back. The curtain closed behind her. And Carrie sat up. Put on her wet things. Walked out.

Never stopped walking. Here she was, so many months later, with Gracie. She'd found her real father, walked into a new hospital, stuck around until he got better. Her family was all in Rhode Island now, living in Newport. All she had to do was get there. She didn't have a lot of money, but she worked hard and could afford a bus ticket.

Carrie dressed Gracie as warmly as she could. She

pulled on her own coat and boots, stuck the picture of her mother into Gracie's diaper bag. She had left home right after a storm, and she would return in this one. Suddenly she knew she couldn't wait another day, another minute. She lifted Gracie into her arms, ran down the hall, down the stairway, toward the pay phone on the first floor.

But she stopped on the landing. There, right in the hallway, in front of the phone, were two men. One big and burly, the other in a wheelchair. Her eyes lasered in on him, the man in the chair. The last time she'd been this close to him, he'd been lying in a hospital bed.

"You're all better?" she asked.

"I am," he said. "Because of you."

"No," she said. "It was the doctors. I just wanted . . ."

"It was because of you," he said gently.

"I've done so much to hurt people," she said, clutching Gracie.

"Everyone loves you, Carrie," he said, holding out his hand. "They just want you home."

"Are you sure?" she asked.

"More than anything," he said. She reached for his hand. He held hers, and she felt tears overflowing. "Come on," he said. "Let me take you home to your mother."

■

Stephen knew the cops were on the case, but their fourteen-year-old quarry had given them the slip. They had checked bus terminals in Newport and Providence, train stations in Kingston, Mystic, and New London, even the T. F. Green Airport. Maura was despairing. The police were perplexed and frustrated. The administration of Newport Academy was vexed. But Stephen understood. Never underestimate a young math genius.

Redmond and Lucy had helped him out. Lucy gave him a list of friends on Beck's Facebook page, kids who lived in Columbus. Stephen had Lucy email them all, tell them to contact Beck's mother if they heard from her. Redmond told Stephen she'd always looked at two certain books up in the Blackstone Hall reading room, the biography of Rose Hawthorne, and a battered-looking old diary.

Redmond led Stephen upstairs to look at the books and seized the diary as if he was positive Beck had left a clue inside. All they found was a torn scrap of paper marking her place. There was her handwriting, but it seemed to be just a fragment of a proof she'd been working on. Nothing to reveal her plans.

"She's out there all alone," Redmond said.

"I know," Stephen said.

"She misses her sister so much."

"You think she went to find her?" Stephen asked.

"I don't know," Redmond said, sounding desolate. "My family never split up. Except for me and my brother going away to school. I don't know what she might be thinking."

"Happy families are lucky," Stephen said.

"I wish Beck were happy," Redmond said. "And that she'd come back. I wanted to show her around Boston. I could still do that, whether she goes to the math competition or not."

"You could," Stephen said, putting his hand on the young man's arm, feeling his own heart split as he considered how it felt to be faced with a woman whose feelings he wished he could change.

He stared at the book in his hand, at the notation Beck had made on the bookmark in it, and suddenly he knew exactly where she was.

"I have to go, Redmond," Stephen said, edging toward the door. "But try not to worry about her. Everything's going to work out."

"Thanks, Mr. Campbell," Redmond said, sitting down heavily on the loveseat and staring into the fire, looking not at all convinced that anything in the world was going to be okay.

And then Stephen ran.

23 WHO KNOWS WHAT I WAS thinking? That's the crazy thing about me. Half the time I do things I don't want to do, for reasons I don't understand, just because I have to. Taking one single key off Angus's ring, just before I got caught trying to give it back, is the perfect example. Part of me knew I had to make my way up here, to Mary's room, before the rest of me had any clue.

I know the whole school was talking about me, what a thief I am, and I didn't feel very good about that. But is that the reason I came running upstairs, three flights, to let myself into Mary's quarters? Not really. Yes, it's a good place to hide out; I doubt anyone will look for me here. But there are stronger reasons.

Unlocking the door, closing it behind me, I found myself staring at the pool. There were fluted columns, big windows facing the sea, cream-and-honey-colored marble steps, but mostly there was water. Aquamarine water. Clear, still, with three curved steps leading into the shallow end.

My chest was thumping, my heart aching so hard I wanted to make it stop. I really just wished it would stop beating, stop hurting. I want to say I had thoughts, but I didn't—not any. All I had were feelings, and they didn't come with any words at all. They had to do with my poor father, drowned in that lake, and my mother, and the secret she'd kept so long, and my sister so far from all of us. And they had to do with J.D., and the fact that he swam here, and the look in his eyes when I faced him—sorrow, regret, even something like love.

Those were the feelings rushing around in my body, and the only word I could think of came babbling out of my lips . . . "Mary." I kept saying her name as if she was really there, in the room with me, as if she could hear me somehow.

Off came my winter boots and heavy socks, and I guess that's good. Because if I really wanted to go into that pool and never come out, I probably would have left them on my feet to weigh me down. Up, up, I rolled the legs of my pants. I put one foot onto the top step, into the water, then the other.

Mary had swum here. She and her sister had stood in this room, talking and laughing. I sat on the edge of the pool, feeling the warm water bathe my ankles, and I tried to surround myself with their sister love. Why go on? I was young, only fourteen, and already I'd lost so much of what I loved. Wouldn't life just keep taking things away?

Beautiful things that seemed so easily given, and so quickly and just as easily taken back? We'd been so happy, our whole family. We'd had those summers on the lake. The sunrises and starlit nights. The laughs and stories around the fire. My father's strong arm around my shoulders.

I no longer believed that Carrie was coming home. I stared down at my feet in the clear water of Mary's pool, and could almost see myself walking into the lake, my bare feet on the pebbly shore, water lapping against my legs. That water had taken my father; no matter where she might be that moment, it had taken my sister.

My eyes burned with tears so hot they hurt. J.D. was Carrie's father, not my father. My mother had lied and lied. Our family story dissolved like bubbles in the pool. What we thought had been real was false, what we hoped would last forever had never even existed.

How would it feel to drown? Would it hurt? Would it be like going to sleep? I wanted Mary to hold my hand, help me stop the pain. I know it's crazy, but I reached out for her. I closed my eyes, waiting for her to come for me. I must have sat there a few minutes like that. Then I heard the latch click, footsteps on the marble.

"Beck."

The voice didn't belong to a girl, to a ghost. It was a man's. Mr. Campbell.

I looked up with what must have been a pretty funny expression on my face.

"How did you know I was here?"

"Redmond showed me Mary's diary," he said. "And I looked inside and saw what you'd written."

I remembered the scrap of paper I'd left there, notations from the work Lucy and I had done, trying to bring our dead back to life. We'd always imagined it happening right here, at the pool. I opened my eyes and looked at my feet, magnified by the water.

"What are you doing?" he asked.

"Nothing," I said.

I looked up at him, saw him standing very close, as if about to grab me.

"I'm not going to jump in," I said.

"That's good," he said. Great timing: his cell phone rang. I watched him start to smile as he looked at the number on the screen. "Uh, I have to take this call," he said. "Awkward timing."

I shrugged in a very be-my-guest way. He talked in a low, excited voice. It did pique my curiosity, but I tried not to show it.

"Come on," he said, pocketing the phone.

"Let me stay here awhile," I said.

"I think you'd rather come with me. Don't you want to see your sister?"

I stared at him, feeling sad for him. I know he was concerned about me, hearing what J.D. said. He was such a teacher. He wanted to get me all involved with solving the problem. Equations, axioms of proof. I just shook my head.

"You're giving up?" he asked.

"Giving up on what?" I asked. "There's nothing to do. We don't even know that she's alive for sure. Not for sure."

"Maybe we do," he said. Just three words, but they made the hair stand up on the back of my neck.

"What are you talking about?"

"Get your boots on, Beck," Mr. Campbell said.

"But . . ."

"Hurry up," he said. "We have to go **now.**"

So I grabbed my boots, tugged them on over my socks, and rode Mary's ornate brass elevator with Mr. Campbell down to the school's first floor. The cables creaked. Wind whistled down the elevator shaft and I swear I heard it, or Mary, or Carrie, saying my name. And the elevator doors opened, and we ran through the marble hall and out the building as if someone's life depended on it.

And I'm pretty sure that someone's did.

24 STEPHEN AND BECK HURRIED down the steps of Blackstone Hall, through the falling snow. He opened the passenger door of his rusty red Panda, eased her inside. He locked the door behind her, just in case she had any notions of escape. Then he got behind the wheel, started the car, and turned the heat on full-blast. The salt air seemed to hold the cold, conduct it straight through his skin and into his bones. Glancing over, he saw Beck shivering wildly.

"Here," he said, slipping off his down jacket. "Put this on."

"No," she said.

"Come on, Beck. You're freezing."

Darkness had fallen fast, the storm had moved in. The wipers were working hard. Ribbons of head- and taillights streaked up and down Memorial Boulevard. He headed downtown, inching along the slippery pavement. If he hurried, J.D. would have a welcoming committee.

Stephen took his eyes off the road for a second, glancing over at Beck. She stared straight ahead, seeming almost calm. Snow mixed with sleet; a sand truck went by in the opposite direction, spraying a burst of grit against the car doors. Beck didn't react.

"Are you okay?" he asked.

"Where are we going?" she asked, ignoring his question.

The car skidded; he held the wheel, wondering how much to tell her. He'd been afraid for her ever since seeing her react to J.D.'s news. The wild look in her eyes, the way she'd run off. Then the incident with Mrs. Nicholson, and finding Beck sitting by the pool, coiled as if she was about to jump in.

"You scared me up there," he said.

"I wasn't going to kill myself," she said.

"I know you're upset about what happened," he said.

She shrugged. "I'll probably get expelled, but I don't really care."

"First of all, I won't let anyone expel you. But that's not what I'm talking about," he said after a moment.

"J.D.?" she asked.

"Yes. He's sorry for what you heard," he said.

"Grownups keep too many secrets," she said after a moment. "They think we can't handle what's real. But guess what? We can't handle what's not."

"I'll try to remember that," he said as he angled through the Newport streets, down past the White

Horse Tavern. They drove slowly along Farewell Street, between the two graveyards. His gaze flickered, and he turned the wheel hard to avoid hitting a girl running across the street. "Did you see that?" he asked Beck.

"I think so," she said, peering through the snow into the Common Ground Cemetery. "Look, there she is!"

Stephen slowed the car. They pulled over to the curb, staring past the black iron gates. He felt a shiver go down his spine, gazing through the falling snow at the tall white marble mausoleum.

"Who is it?"

"I think it was just a gust of wind," he said. "Blowing snow across the road . . ."

She kept staring through the iron fence, and so did he. The snow fell heavily, obscuring the Langley family crypt. Had that been Mary? Stephen's scalp tingled, the way it always did when he thought he'd seen her at Blackstone Hall. The spirits were out tonight.

"What are we doing here?" she asked after a moment.

"Waiting," he said, checking his watch. J.D. had said they'd be there in forty minutes, and they were right on time.

"For what?" she asked.

He looked up, and saw Angus's van moving down the ramp of the Newport Bridge, merging onto Farewell Street, heading straight for them. Beck leaned forward, the palms of her hands on the dashboard, staring into the van windows, right into her sister's face.

"Oh my God," she said.

25 TRAVIS NEEDED TO BE OUT searching in the storm. He had put on his warmest clothes, the boots his father had given him before they went ice fishing two winters ago, and looked everywhere he could think of. Beck had always loved secret hiding places. Back home in Ohio he'd known all her spots. But here, in Newport, he'd been so busy settling in, he realized he barely knew anything of how it had been for Beck.

He checked around Angus's guardhouse, the maintenance sheds, the athletic center. Snow and sleet blew into his eyes, making them water. He skirted the cliff, knowing she wouldn't go anywhere near it: she hated the water, that hadn't changed. The snow was piling up fast, covering everything in a thick white blanket.

"Beck!" he yelled, again and again.

No response, just the silence of the school. The lights burned brightly in the dorms; everyone was studying, getting ready for end of term. He had work of his own to do—History, English,

Calculus—but none of that mattered unless he found Beck.

He made his way to the long-abandoned root cellar. He'd been there only once, early in October, with two guys he never hung out with—Loring Donay and Nick Williams, after a History test.

Most of his friends were athletes, and these guys weren't. They were both rich, from New York, kind of intellectual and artsy, in a different crowd than the football team. But Travis had gone along.

Despite all their success and outward friendliness, he hadn't really felt accepted by the guys, not the way he had been with his teammates in Columbus. Maybe the heroics were even part of it, although he always put the team first. Chris and Ty hung around together, included him as an afterthought. So when Loring invited him to hang out after the test, Travis had said sure, even though the blond hair and black turtleneck seemed a little lame, and heading down to a root cellar seemed completely stage-set.

They'd brought weed and beer, sat around talking in almost total darkness. According to them, fifty years ago, a select group of Newport Academy students had started a secret society called **Quo Vadis,** Latin for "Where are you going?" and held their meetings in the cellar. Travis had listened, trying to ignore the smell of mold and old carrots and potatoes.

He had gotten the strange sense Loring and Nick were feeling him out, to see how he felt about such things—as if maybe the secret society still existed and they were testing to see if he was the right material, if he'd want to join. There was no light down there—they'd used a lantern. It had thrown spooky light on the stone walls, and he'd seen a skull and candle on a table. It had seemed so dumb and childish to him. He'd finished his beer, thanked them, and left—feeling lonelier than before.

Standing there now, he cleared away the snow that had drifted against the battered wooden door. He pounded hard with his fists, calling his sister's name. The padlock was new, but the rusty iron fittings attached to the door were old; the screws that held them in place were loose. He knew he could break them in a second if he had to. But Beck wasn't here.

As he turned away from the old cellar door, he knew he was looking in the wrong place. His sister wasn't hiding. She was doing something. That was Beck all over—even when she seemed to be still, her mind was working.

She'd been thinking about Carrie—they all were. But Beck would have been calculating ways to rearrange the molecules so that Carrie would come home, or Beck would go to her. Sister magnets.

The paths hadn't been cleared yet, so he trudged through the snow, wondering where to go next.

His legs were so tired, and his spirit felt weighted down. Walking in front of Blackstone Hall, he considered going inside to warm up for a minute, maybe check through the big building again, when he heard his name.

Turning, he saw Pell coming around the corner with Chris and Tyler.

"Hey," Chris said as they walked over to him. "Where do we look?"

"Look?" Travis asked.

"For Beck," Ty said. "We want to help you find her."

"Where do we go next?" Chris asked.

"I've pretty much checked campus," he said.

"And the wharf area is covered. . . ." Ty said.

"What do you mean?" Travis asked.

Chris glanced over at him, eyes puzzled. "Didn't you know? Ty and I went down there as soon as we heard. Pretty much the whole football team has been searching for her."

"We'll find her," Ty said.

Travis couldn't speak. He met Pell's eyes as he felt the universe tilting. He was losing his family, one person at a time. His father, Carrie, now Beck. But Pell was here, and so were his friends.

"Come on," Chris said, with a light pat on his shoulder. "Let's get out there."

Pell didn't speak, but she touched Travis's arm.

And they started the search all over again, together.

■

Maura and Katharine sat together at the kitchen table. Katharine had brought food, but no one had felt like eating. Maura wanted to be in the car, out looking for Beck. But the roads were terrible, and J.D. had called, told her to stay close to home, that she needed to be there, but wouldn't tell her why.

"I can't stand this," Maura said, jumping up yet again to look out the window over the sink. "Look at it out there. . . . The storm's getting worse, and Beck's all alone in it. We have to go find her."

"Travis is out searching the campus," Katharine said. "Everyone is. And you know the police, Stephen, Angus, and—"

"It's not enough," Maura said, going to the closet and pulling out her winter coat. She wriggled into it, pulled on her boots, and jammed a hat onto her head.

Katharine was right behind her. There was no way she would let her sister go out alone in the storm. They walked outside, making sure to leave the door unlocked in case Beck came home on her own. The school grounds were pure white. Heavy snow blew off the sea, covering the lawns and flowerbeds, coating the east side of every tree, branch, and building, drifting along the roads.

Maura had no idea where to look. She headed along the main drive, out toward the stone pillars and school entrance. Could Beck be holed up somewhere on campus? Would any of her friends help her hide, not grasping what it was doing to her mother, her family? She glanced over at Blackstone Hall. The fourth floor was dark.

"What have I done?" Maura asked. "I feel as if I've destroyed everything."

"I know that's not true," Katharine said, putting her arm around Maura as they trudged through the deep snow. Maura leaned into her sister, holding on to her support and warmth like lifelines.

In the distance, they saw headlights. A car and a van were coming along Cliff Avenue, moving slowly. The car fishtailed, then swerved.

Maura held her breath. For a minute she thought it was going to crash, and she thought suddenly of Mary Langley, of how it must have been a storm like this that had sent her carriage over the cliff, into the sea. How could people be out on a night like this? Didn't they know the dangers? The suffering that an accident would bring to the people who loved them? If they had any idea of that, they would all go home to their families.

As Maura stared, the car went into a snowbank just before the school entrance, barely missing the granite pillars. She let out a long sigh of relief. The driver tried to get out of the drift, spinning the car's wheels.

"Should we help them?" Katharine asked.

Maura nodded, and they started toward the car. Just then the passenger door opened. Maura saw two people piling out; she wondered if they were students. Friends of Beck and Travis's, children in Maura's classes at school. Wordlessly she and Katharine made their way through the curtain of white to help. She thought of their mothers, wherever they might be.

"Mom!"

For a second she thought it was Beck, and her heart stopped.

"Sweetheart!" she called out. But she saw her daughter tearing toward her, holding a baby in her arms, calling "Mom, Mom," over and over again—it was another familiar, beloved voice, and she hadn't heard it for over a year.

Maura cried out, started to run.

"Carrie!" Maura's arms were around her oldest daughter in a second. They held on to each other, rocking, sleet stinging their faces and mixing with their tears. They shielded the baby between them, Maura embracing them both.

"This is Gracie," Carrie said.

"You have a daughter," Maura said.

"Mom . . ." Carrie began. Maura heard apology,

confusion, despair in Carrie's voice. They had so much to talk about and understand, but none of it mattered then—Carrie was home, and they were together.

"We have to get her, both of you, inside," Maura said.

"Stephen's car . . ." Carrie began, and Maura turned to see.

Yes, it was Stephen's little red Panda, and Katharine had climbed behind the wheel as Stephen and someone else stood in front of the car, pushing it out of the snowbank. Maura would know the back of that head anywhere.

"Beck!" Maura called, feeling a surge of joy.

"Hang on, Mom," Beck said, heaving her shoulder against the hood as Katharine eased the car backward, out of the drift. Arms around her oldest daughter and granddaughter, Maura helped them walk through the snow, back to the car.

Stephen flashed a grin, opening the car door to let them inside.

"I don't know how to thank you," Maura said, catching his hand.

"I'd give anything to take credit," he said.

"J.D. found me, Mom," Carrie said. "He brought me home to you."

Maura saw the van, idling behind the red car. She saw the window roll down, J.D. sitting inside. She stared at him.

"You did this," she said.

"Carrie was on her way," he said.

"But you . . ."

J.D. glanced behind her. Maura turned, saw Beck staring at him with stony eyes. Maura knew she felt he'd ruined her family even before she was born.

"Go home, be with your kids," he said, meeting Maura's eyes. "Gracie needs to get warm."

But Beck walked straight to the open window, stuck her hand inside. "Thank you," she said, and Maura watched as the cold look in Beck's eyes turned to warmth.

J.D. shook Beck's hand. "You don't have to thank me," he said.

"But I do," she said. "We were apart, and now we're together."

And Maura stood beside her sister, her arm around Carrie and Gracie, hearing Beck's words so strong and clear, and she knew that she had never heard anything so true.

EPILOGUE

IT'S MARY LANGLEY DAY, A school holiday, the anniversary of Mary's death. Feels so strange, a whole school commemorating a death when it feels as if our family has just come back to life. Carrie and Gracie have been with us a week now. Having them come home was the best Christmas present anyone could ever dream of.

The snow is beautiful. White, thick, filled with these ridiculously lovely ice crystals that make everything sparkle like a Christmas card. The sun gleams behind dark clouds, throwing molten silver on the surface of the rough, gray sea. I can't stop staring at the water right now. It started the night my sister came home, when I put my feet in the pool. Later, driving home from the bridge, when Mr. Campbell's car slid into the snowbank, we met my mother on the road. I saw my mother hugging Carrie, and I heard the waves crashing, and I shook J.D.'s hand. And I stopped being afraid.

Redmond says he'll take me out whale watching next summer. There are boats that leave right from Boston Harbor. I laugh, because I can't wait. A week ago, I would have preferred life imprisonment to having to go anywhere on a boat. Life takes some peculiar twists and turns, I think you'll agree.

Everything's going my way. It's pretty remarkable. Here's what's happening this afternoon. The whole school is gathered on the cliff—snow boots, ski parkas, knitted hats, mittens, and all—to remember Mary Langley. Angus has brought a huge wreath—it's a tradition he follows every year—to throw into the sea at the exact spot where Mary's carriage tumbled in.

Mr. Shannon, the teachers, the whole school board, people from Newport join the ceremony. It's rather solemn. A bagpipe plays. I am standing with Lucy and Redmond, looking across the crowd at my mother, Aunt Katharine, Carrie, and Gracie. Dell Harwood, a woman who helped Carrie, is here, along with some of the girls from Hawthorne House.

J.D. is beside my mother. He's part of this, part of our lives. I'll say it, even though I have mixed emotions: he is part of our family. The truth is the truth, no matter how you feel about it.

I keep thinking about that great night—when Carrie came home, and the snow was still falling, and J.D.'s garage apartment had lost power and so did our carriage house, and we all wound up staying in Blackstone Hall. I don't think any of us, except Gracie, slept for even a minute that night.

Angus built a roaring fire in the massive marble fireplace, and we pulled the sofas close, and put sleeping bags on the big red Oriental rug, and felt how amazing it was to have Carrie and Gracie with us. J.D. waited for the right moment, when he saw me looking over at him, to gesture me over. I could have turned my back, pretended not to see. But something made me cross the floor to him. I think it had to do with how peaceful Carrie seemed—as if something in her life had just been solved.

"Hi, Beck," he said.

"Hi, J.D."

"Are you okay?"

"I'm better than that. I'm good," I told him. "When I shake hands, I mean it. Ask anyone. You found Carrie for us."

I saw his gaze slide to my mother. She was watching from across the room, sitting quietly beside Carrie and Gracie. It hurt to see my mother look at another man that way, and I thought of my father. It still tears me apart, the truth of what happened in our family, and probably always will. For a long time, anyway. I briefly considered stealing J.D.'s gloves after he fell asleep.

But those days are over, and I decided to let it be.

As I told J.D., I'm good. Lucy and I have made major strides in our quest for infinity. Soon we'll find our fathers. Our breakthrough involves a proof I worked on. I won't bore you with the details, but we are **well** on our way.

So much so, Mr. Campbell took my case to the board. He met with them in secret. I'll never know what he said, but I have the feeling it had to do with my sorry background. I do know I had to give permission for my psychologist in Columbus to fax a letter. I guess she explained to them the stuff I went through that made me steal. Whatever she said, they voted to not expel me.

And to let me go to the nationals in Boston this coming week.

The biggest surprise: guess who spoke up for me? Mrs. Nicholson! I have no idea why she had the change of heart, but Mr. Campbell said she was adamant. She said, "People deserve second chances. I've missed opportunities to give them before, and I don't want to miss this one. Let Rebecca go to Boston."

There she is now, standing in a knot with her fellow board members. Mrs. Nicholson's mink is ruffled by the sea wind; you can see the little dead creatures on her back, their fur zinging in the breeze. Her pearls match the snow. I want to go over and thank her, but she is staring with strange, shimmering hope, and I'm not exaggerating, at my brother.

Travis. He's the one member of my family who's not totally happy right now. He's standing with Pell. She is going away. Either for Christmas, or for the summer. Lucy told me the whole story. Pell is going to Italy. She's traveling over to see their mother—the first time they'll have spent a holiday together since Pell was six. It's also the first time Lucy will be without Pell in her whole life, and she's dreading it. Her sleeplessness is worse than ever.

It's not as if Pell is running away, and I'll help Lucy. There are algebraic ways of bringing the lost back home. Then there are the more straightforward methods: Pell's going straight to her mother, to get to know her and tell her that she and Lucy need her.

She told Lucy she's not coming back without their mother. I think, although I'm not sure, that that explains the weird, shimmering hope in Mrs. Nicholson's eyes. I think she's giving Travis silent kudos for setting the ball in motion.

I get that, I do. Lucy says that Pell was so inspired by Travis and our family, by the way we pulled together after such a big break, the way we couldn't stay apart. Lucy said it hit Pell hard the night Carrie came home. Apparently she and Travis had quite a talk. He asked why she wouldn't go to Italy to see their mother.

I guess he was thinking of how Aunt Katharine

came back into our lives—how hard she tried to heal the rift, to give my mother what she wanted more than anything: her daughter back. Travis told Pell the whole story then, as they looked for me in the snow, about Aunt Katharine and my mother.

I think Pell began to develop her own notion of seeking . . . of leaving a comfortable life to go in search of the person you need more than anyone else, the one you believe will make you whole; Travis's story of our family, of what it took to get us all back together—even, in a strange way, J.D.'s lighthouse on the island—took hold of her soul, shook her out of accepting something that was so wrong.

See, the Davises have been split up a long time. It was one thing for us to miss knowing our aunt. Imagine how Pell and Lucy feel, missing their mother. Mrs. Nicholson is the matriarch of a family suffering with demons—I have the feeling many of them are her own. She's not easy, but she's smart. And I think she somehow understands that Travis and our family's story may help hers.

I gaze at my brother. He is right beside Pell, staring down at her. Her attention is focused on the sea, all the way across the water, as if she is looking over to Italy, trying to imagine what her mother was doing, what awaits her there.

I've seen Pell talking to Travis, watching him at every game. I know she saw me steal that emerald

earring, and I know she was the one who returned
it to Lucy. I know Pell has helped my brother
through the breakup with Ally, and I realize that
she's been holding back her own feelings for him,
waiting until they are both ready. She is wise, and
has a certain stillness I've never seen in a girl about
our age. I look up to her and I feel proud to think
that she learned something from us—from Travis.
And I know, from the bottom of my heart, why she
has to make this journey. It makes me respect her
all the more.

The sun dips down behind Blackstone Hall, and
the sky darkens. Mr. Shannon gives a signal and
the academy lights up, illuminated by thousands of
tiny white Christmas lights. I've never seen anything like it before. I must have gasped, because
Redmond squeezed my hand.

Now Angus bends down and picks up the huge
evergreen wreath. One lucky student will get to
throw it into the sea for Mary. I've heard students
whispering, that usually Mary and Beatrice let their
presence at the ceremony be known by some sort of
mischief: one year the lights didn't go on, another
year Mr. Shannon's scarf twirled off his neck and
blew into the waves, and once a gust of wind
caught the wreath and nearly pulled the student
throwing it over into the sea.

But this year, things seem quiet. I catch my sister's eye. She is beaming, as if she knows some-

thing. Maybe she is thinking of next semester, when she'll be enrolled as a student. Or perhaps she is dreaming of the future, when Gracie can go to school here.

Mr. Campbell walks over.

"Beck," he says, "will you and Lucy please come with me?"

I freeze. "Did I do something wrong?" What if Mrs. Nicholson changed her mind again? I'm set on going to the competition, proving myself, making my school proud. Seeing the town with Redmond, and kicking Boston math butt.

"No," he says, smiling. "You've done something good."

Lucy beams, and together we walk through the snow. The crowd parts for us. I hear Gracie laughing, and I swear she is saying "Beck!" It makes me laugh too, or maybe this is just how it feels to be really, really happy.

When we get to the cliff's edge, I look down. The waves are dark and swirling, topped with frothy white edges as they advance, break, and split apart. One wave after another, eternally. I think of Mary. She died in the water, just like my dad. I hope that they are at peace; I want them to know that I will never stop trying to make a connection.

Mr. Campbell puts his arm around my shoulders, and Angus comes stomping over with the wreath.

"Here," Angus says, giving me a big smile under his walrus mustache.

"What?" I ask.

He pushes the wreath into my and Lucy's arms.

"Give it a good throw," he says. "You'll be sending it into the wind, so make sure you put all your strength into it."

"But . . ." I begin. **I'm a disgrace, I was nearly expelled, I stole your keys.**

Angus pats me on the head. "Mary's sleeping," he says. "For the first time since I've worked at this school, she and Beatrice are at rest. I don't know how to explain that, but I have the feeling it has to do with all of you being together here. All you sisters."

I look around, and my mother, Aunt Katharine, Carrie, and Gracie have come to stand with us. So has Pell. Lucy and I hold the wreath between us. Pell and Carrie flank us on either side. Four sisters paying our respects to Mary while two more—my mother and aunt—stand behind us with the baby.

"To Mary," Lucy says.

"And don't forget Beatrice," I say.

The wind blows into our faces, straight across the sea from Italy. It is cold and full of salt. We taste the sea. The bagpipe plays "Adeste Fideles." It sounds so sweet. Angus and Mr. Campbell count to three. We wind up, and with all our might send the wreath spinning into the air. It twirls once, twice.

For a second it seems to rise, as if it has sprouted wings, as if it is about to fly away all on its own.

"Mary," I whisper.

I know mischief when I see it. She might as well have materialized, shown herself, sung the carol along with our school. Because I know she is here with us.

The evergreen wreath lifted a little more, then swooped down the rocky cliff into the sea. We stand there, all us sisters, staring down and watching it disappear into the cold, cold waves. But I am not sad.

Because, you see, I know: some things are forever. It's pure math.

And then we turn back, our faces to the crowd, who come to greet us and embrace us and remind us where we belong: at school, on earth, in life, with the people who loved us then and love us now and will always love us forevermore.

ACKNOWLEDGMENTS

For his valuable help with mathematics, I thank Injae Choe. All errors in this book are my own.

With gratitude to Teresa Lonergan for introducing me to Rose Hawthorne.

I am enormously grateful to everyone at Bantam Books, especially Irwyn Applebaum, Nita Taublib, Tracy Devine, Kerri Buckley, Betsy Hulsebosch, Carolyn Schwartz, Melissa Lord, Cynthia Lasky, Barb Burg, Susan Corcoran, Gina Wachtel, Paolo Pepe, and Virginia Norey.

Thank you to Andrea Cirillo for everything.

ABOUT THE AUTHOR

LUANNE RICE is the author of twenty-six novels, most recently **Last Kiss, Light of the Moon, What Matters Most, The Edge of Winter, Sandcastles, Summer of Roses, Summer's Child, Silver Bells,** and **Beach Girls.** She lives in New York City and Old Lyme, Connecticut.